# Foreign & Domestic

## *Part III*

## *By the Dawn's Early Light*

Published in the United States by
DJK Publishing House

ISBN 978-0-692-57182-8

Printed by Create Space, an Amazon Company.
Electronic Distribution by Kindle Direct Publishing.

For my Mother, who rightfully claimed that,

'I never met a word I didn't like…'


You will be missed

# Foreign & Domestic

## Part III

## *By the Dawn's Early Light*

*By: David J. Kershner*

# Character List – Part III
(alphabetical by last name/maiden name)

*Alysin Baker* – Pathologist, member of the Tin Foil Hat Club

*Mimi Bessum* – Proprietor of Mama Renie's Restaurant

*Bryan Billson* – former neighbor to Josh and Amanda Simmons, friend of the Simmons family

*Carlton Bloom* – USN Corpsman (retired)

*Jacques Boules* – Culinary Chef

*Emmitt Calhoun* – Lawyer, husband to Sonja Calhoun, father to Emily Calhoun Chastain, grandfather to Declan Edward Wrigley Chastain

*Sonja Calhoun* – Collegiate Biology Professor, wife to Emmitt Calhoun, mother to Emily Calhoun Chastain, grandmother to Declan Edward Wrigley Chastain

*Tyler Chaffee* – Gang member

*Declan Edward Wrigley Chastain* – Orphaned child, adopted by Gregg and Emily Chastain

*Emily Calhoun Chastain* – Doctor, researcher, wife to Gregg Chastain, adoptive mother to Declan Edward Wrigley Chastain

*Gregg 'Longbow' Chastain* – Weapons Specialist/Linguist U.S. Army (retired), husband to Emily Chastain, adoptive father to Declan Edward Wrigley Chastain

*Chester Daniels* – Nuclear Engineer, member of the Tin Foil Hat Club

*Kristen Delgado* – Sister of Amanda Simmons (deceased), former sister-in law to Josh Simmons, aunt to Layla and Katherine Simmons

*Josselyn Dell* – Refugee, mother to Eve and Nick Dell

*Eve Dell* – Refugee, daughter to Josselyn Dell, sister to Nick Dell

*Nick Dell* – Refugee, son to Josselyn Dell, brother to Eve Dell

*Sophie Desjardins* – Colonel in the French Foreign Legion, mother to Philip Marceau

*Javy Dolbrow* – Drug dealer, rapist

*Abbas Esfahani* – Iranian terrorist, brother to Suhrab Esfahani

*Suhrab Esfahani* – Iranian terrorist, leader of jihadi cell, brother to Abbas Esfahani

*Lawrence (Larry) Fielding* – Secretary of Defense

*Harold Goodspeed* – Prime Minister of United Kingdom

*Victor Henry* – Portland (Oregon) Police Officer

*Brent Howard* – Chairman of Joint Chiefs, General in USMC (retired), Josh Simmons' former CO, father to Jessica Howard (deceased), grandfather to Heather Howard

*Heather Howard* – Actress, stage name Heather White, daughter to Jessica Howard (deceased) and Josh Simmons, grand-daughter to Brent Howard

*Wilson James* – Colonel in the U.S. Army, Doctor of Psychology

*Samantha (Sam) Jameson* – USAF Colonel (retired), Hyloset CEO (a GMO corporation)

*Tim Knightsbridge* – Gang Leader, former neighbor of Josh Simmons and Bryan Billson

*Philip Marceau* – Capitaine in French Foreign Legion, son to Sophie Desjardins

*Abelardo Martinez* – Assistant Farm Manager, son of Juan and Basilia Martinez, brother to Jesus Martinez, friend to Simmons family

*Basilia Martinez* – Doctor, wife to Juan Martinez, mother to Jesus and Abelardo Martinez

*Jesus Martinez* – Tracker, son of Juan and Basilia Martinez, brother to Abelardo Martinez, friend of Simmons family

*Juan Martinez* – Manager of Josh's farm, husband to Basilia Martinez, father to Jesus and Abelardo Martinez

*Elias McInerney* – USDA Secretary, granduncle to Mara McInerney

*Mara McInerney* – Exec assistant to USDA Secretary, grandniece to Elias McInerney

*Dallas McKutcheon* – Childhood friend of Josh Simmons, friend to Simmons family

*Edward Monahan* – Secret Service Agent, currently assigned to former President James Sarkes

*Evan Noosman* – Unofficial protection detail to Layla and Katherine Simmons, friend to the Simmons family

*James (Jim) Rayburn* – President of the United States (current)

*Carlos 'Hoplite' Rayna* – Captain in the U.S. Army, former CO to Gregg Chastain

*James Rooney* – USMC Sergeant (retired), former NCO to Josh Simmons, friend to Simmons family

*Maria Sanchez* – Long-haul truck driver

*Thomas Sarkes* –President of the United States (former)

*Amanda Simmons (deceased)* – VA nurse, ex-wife to Josh Simmons, mother to Layla Simmons and Katherine Simmons

*Josiah (Josh) Grant Simmons* – Farmer, USMC Lt. Colonel (retired), former POW, ex-husband to Amanda Simmons (deceased), father to Layla Simmons, Katherine Simmons, and Heather Howard

*Layla Simmons* – College student, former kidnapping victim, daughter of Josh and Amanda Simmons (deceased), sister to Katherine Simmons and Heather Howard

*Katherine Simmons* – College student, former kidnapping victim, daughter of Josh and Amanda Simmons (deceased), sister to Layla Simmons and Heather Howard

*Eustace Stokes* – Lieutenant in the U.S. Army, Combat Engineer platoon CO

*Cecil Sullivan* – Airmen in USAF, brother to Anna Sullivan

*Lily Summers* – Biochemist, member of the Tin Foil Hat Club

*James (Jim) Watson* – Sheriff of McArthur, Ohio, friend to Josh Simmons

# Chapter 1

As soon as President Rayburn reviewed the satellite imagery of the English ships making their way toward Cleveland via the Saint Lawrence Seaway, he immediately ordered the platoon of combat engineers and the handful of members from Gregg's former unit to hold in their current location. If Josh weren't such a patriot, he could have raised a third amendment issue. However, given the bounty in the hills, Josh rather preferred having Hoplite and his men being run covertly from the farm to guard the horde in the abandoned railroad line.

The day after the Moonville Tunnel was collapsed on top of over eight billion dollars' worth of gold bullion, the remains of the Wrigley's were interred in the family plot with little fanfare. Grave markers for the deceased would be prepared in time. It wasn't until Josh and several others had dug the graves in preparation for the subdued service that they understood the late man's eternal pain. The existing Wrigley family headstones told the tragic tale.

Junius and Martha Wrigley had produced five children in their sixty plus years of marriage. Circumstance, time, and history had cursed them to outlive all of them. Given the dates on the grave markers, it was clear that their daughter had passed away a few days after her birth, in 1959. Two of the four boys lost their lives before they were even twenty-one in the jungles of Vietnam. The third met his end in the late 80's. The rumor around McArthur was that he had contracted AIDS.

The lone surviving son perished with two thousand six hundred other souls when the towers came down on 9/11. Now there was this. Not only were Junius and Martha gone, but their grandson and his wife were situated in plots nearby as well. It was a tragic tale that the newborn baby, Declan Edward Wrigley, would have to be told one day.

To this end, Gregg and some of his men secured every piece of family history from the house. Whatever they found, wedding and photo albums, yearbooks, wartime correspondence; everything was packed in a box for when Declan came of age or became curious. Until that time, Emily swore that he'd never to be put in harm's way.

Unfortunately, her overly protective decree was already being overridden as a new war had already started. Now that legitimate news agencies were putting stories and incidents together, most of America was waking up to this reality.

With regard to Declan, or baby Deeks as he was no being referred to, Josh and the group conferred with Sheriff Watson and decided to leave children services out it. With no known living relatives, baby Deeks would merely wind up in some state run facility or a foster home if and when the balloon went up. With Abbas running around and the English with their scheming, no one was confident in the long term viability of those options. If Declan were lucky, he could be adopted quickly by a family that was barren. The paperwork and background checks alone would delay any placements for weeks, maybe months.

Being raised on the farm by Gregg and Emily Chastain was by far the best possible outcome available. Jim Watson was skeptical of the Abbas story, but gave the Chastain's a week for it to come to fruition. If it didn't, the child would be placed into 'the system' and they would have to navigate the bureaucracy like everyone else.

It took some doing, but old man Wrigley was buried with full military honors. Most of the residents that knew the recluse and his wife were long since deceased. The rest had moved away years ago. As a result, the service was sparsely attended.

Lt. Eustace Stokes, from the Combat Engineering platoon, and Sheriff Watson managed to find a bugler from the local Vinton County High School while the engineers provided the three volley salute. Josh and Brent, donned their dress blues and observed while Dallas and Alysin led a brief memorial service. Carlos, Gregg, Eustace, and three of Carlos' unit lowered the four bodies into the graves. The grandson, his wife, and their newborn baby boy represented the only progeny the elderly couple had left. Now it was just Declan.

Junius Wrigley was the last to be lowered.

As they were interred, an American flag, donated from the front porch of the cabin, was neatly folded by James, Dallas, Josh, and Brent. General Howard then presented it to the Chastain's and the infant child.

For Gregg, it seemed only fitting that the home the old man had built with his own two was turned into Suhrab's own personal hell box.

\* \* \*

No sooner had the transport touched down in Minot as Cecil Sullivan and Colonel James were hit with a barrage of information and updates. Cecil's methodical and detailed description, coupled with an artist's rendering, allowed base personnel to positively identify Abbas Esfahani as the Airman Hector Ortiz doppelganger.

While the pair was in flight, a security detachment had stealthily surrounded the dwelling shared by the imposter and his unknowing roommates. Thermal imaging proved useless as the ambient temperature inside the structure was approaching ninety degrees. It was apparent to the team leader that Abbas had turned up the thermostat in an effort to obfuscate whatever lay inside.

The Base Commander met the transport on the flight line with a waiting Humvee. With Col. James' blessing, he had received a rather useful phone call from the F.E. Warren installation. Greasing the wheels of the bureaucracy was deemed to be an added plus by the travelling pair. Cecil and his doctor were quickly spirited into the vehicle and driven to the rally point.

The armed detail held at the outer perimeter until the VIP's arrived. No one was going to be given permission to breach until they had a confab. When they arrived, the force that had been sitting on the house for several hours was squawked by their commander. Once they were on the horn, they were ordered to pull back and debrief the new arrivals. A lone forward observer was left to monitor the structure. He was aided by the presence of an ultra-quiet drone from far above while the assault team regrouped and deliberated.

As the group arrived, the General, Cecil, and Col. James were brought up to speed. When they finished, the Colonel stated, "This Abbas character is one crafty SOB. He seems a touch smarter than his lunatic brother. Can you see anything in there… at all? Do you have another way to view the interior?"

"We've scanned it and viewed it with every imager we've got. There's 'no joy' there. Our regular scopes are useless as well. All we do know is that there appears to be no movement. From the looks of it, two are in bed and one is watching TV. What we can't see is if any of the three are alive," the team leader replied.

"I think it's safe to say they aren't," Cecil provided impassively.

Shaking off Cecil's comments, the Base Commander inquired, "Based on what you *have* seen, what's your best estimate?"

Before the man could respond, the former airmen asked, "Has anyone bothered to try and call?"

"The house received one call from an Arizona number," Lt. Carrigan answered. He continued to provide details by adding, "We traced it back to Hector's mother. There was no movement toward the ringing phone observed… not that we could see a whole hell of a lot to begin with. It went to voicemail. What do you want us to do?" the Lieutenant asked the General, disregarding the Colonel and his patient.

"Breach it!" the fatigued Cecil blurted out startling the group. "I want this man dead!"

"Whoa! Hold on there, buddy," the leader replied. "If this guy turned up the heat, he obviously knows we're coming. At a minimum, he knew that we *would* come. That means he was most likely tipped off. Assuming he killed his three roommates, there's no guaranteeing that the house isn't rigged. What we need is an EOD unit."

"Do you have a telescopic scope? Slide that under the door and take a peek. See if there are any wires, pressure plates, or whatever. Look at the doorjambs and knobs. From where I stand, all you have are three corpses. I'm telling you, he's not in there. Abbas turned up the heat to slow us down so we'd waste time on this conversation. He could have executed those guys a couple of days ago. The heat is merely a mask to disguise the body temperature variations. How long are we going to stand here before we realize he's in a launch facility (LF)? Check the duty logs if you don't believe me."

"We *are* checking. Answer this though, why would he be in one? He can't fire anything without the keys and they're held by flight officers in the launch control center (LCC)," the young team leader remarked.

Cecil slapped a stupid looking grin on his face while Colonel James just shook his head.

"Ahh, crap. Are you friggin' serious?" Lt. Carrigan replied and then radioed the man he'd left behind to observe.

"Sioux 1 here," came the immediate reply.

"Any movement from inside?"

"Negative."

"Hold one, we're on our way back."

"Roger that."

The Lieutenant then turned to Cecil and Col. James. "All right gentlemen, let's go and see if you're hunch is correct."

The Base Commander and the other three men climbed into the General's Humvee and returned to Abbas' former home. The remaining members followed closely behind. Within minutes, the advanced team was reassembled and geared up.

The Lt. and his twelve-man group quickly dispersed to their assigned positions. Two four-person teams rapidly worked their way to the front and rear doors while covering fire was provided by an overwatch for each to their six o'clock. Individual members were positioned to the remaining sides of the structure in case anyone opened up with small arms or jumped from a window. Cecil, Col. James, and the General sat patiently in their armored vehicle.

While they waited, the former POW remarked to the Base Commander, "Wow. Where did you get the pearl handled .45?"

"Oh, that," he replied as he leaned and removed it from its holster. "My dad gave me that to me when I graduated from the Air Force

Academy." He held it for the pair to see. "My grandfather wore it in WWII while he was dropping ordnance all over Germany."

"Do you mind," the former Airman asked.

"Not at all," the General replied and handed it back to Cecil.

As he felt the weight of the pistol in his grip, the three watched as Lt. Carrigan retracted the small whip like camera and nodded. They could see his lips moving with the countdown as he spoke into his mini mic. When he closed his fist, one of the four team members stood from his crouched position and slammed the battering device into the wooden obstacle next to the locking mechanism and handle. A similar scene unfolded at the back door. As both ingress points were thrust open, nothing happened. The building didn't explode and erupt into a mountain of flames. Cecil had been correct.

The eight men entered the structure and cleared each room efficiently. Several tense seconds went by before they saw movement from the four members that remained outside. Eventually they too were called into to aid in the search. One man immediately came back out and puked over the front porch railing. The stench of death was too overwhelming.

* * *

After spending a fair amount of time returning the 'favors' Suhrab had bestowed upon him, Gregg was exhausted. The terrorist's comment in the caves of Iran regarding his knowledge of torture and coercion resistance had proved true. However, Suhrab quickly discovered that understanding and practice were not always synonymous. Gregg's beatings and strategically placed electric shocks were yielding information, albeit slowly. Both men knew it wouldn't be long before Suhrab was strapped to an inclined door or table and experiencing the very real sensation of drowning.

As Gregg was about to resume a new round of data collection, Emily burst through the door with Josh's Beretta in hand.

"You've had your chance, dear," she stated with enough inflection to almost be condescending. "Now it's my turn!"

Before Gregg could get to her, she began to level the weapon at Suhrab. The man immediately started pleading. When she quickly pulled the trigger several times in rapid succession, he urinated on himself and the floor.

All three of them were shocked, none more so than Emily, when the weapon failed to fire.

Fortunately for Suhrab, Emily was inexperienced with firearms and, while she'd managed to turn off the safety, she didn't know a round needed to be chambered.

As if flipping a switch from a psychotic bent on revenge to demur housewife, she said, "Honey, can you help me make this thing work please?"

Her husband stood there dumbfounded.

"Uh… I'm gonna go ahead and deny that request, sweetie. You're far too emotionally compromised to make decisions."

"What did you say to me?"

Gregg had no reply.

"This *man* single handedly took everything away from me! I would have carried our child to term, I know it! How dare you say that!"

Before the 'discussion' went any further, Josh came through the door out of breathe.

"Sorry, bud. I was playing with Declan and she must have taken it when I wasn't looking."

"It's okay. We were just discussing why, as of right now, her decision making process is a bit –," he started to reply but stopped when she glared at him. "Correction, might be ever so slightly, I mean it's hardly perceptible, barely a skosh even, ah… disjointed?"

"I don't know why you're upset at me, Mrs. Chastain," Suhrab interjected in a hardly audible horse-like whisper. "I saved your life."

"Oh shit," Josh mumbled.

She quickly whipped her head in his direction. Her hair defied gravity as it wrapped around her neck only to eventually settle into its natural position. "Give the man some water," Emily ordered. "I want to hear what he has to say."

"No, no you don't," Gregg stated. He then turned toward his host and said, "Do me a favor, please take her back to Three Sisters so she can cool off."

"Don't either of you sons a bitches touch me!" she growled as she step away from both. "I swear to Heaven Almighty I'll start messin' with this thing until I get the bullet thingies to go off! And don't correct me! I know it's not a thingy!"

"Okay," he replied calmly, "Okay." Then, in an extremely compassionate tone, her husband asked, "What do you think he's going to tell you? No matter what he says, or does, it won't bring our child back."

Emily shifted on her feet contemplating a response. In the end she decided not to reply. Gregg watched as his wife dejectedly placed the gun on the table. She then poured the water and assisted a bound and nude Suhrab to take a drink. When her back was turned, Josh slowly reached out and retrieved his handgun.

"All right," she began as she put the empty cup down. "Let's start at the beginning. Hold on a sec," she said and went to the corner, picked up a bloody rag Gregg had discarded on a car battery, and placed it over the man's exposed groin.

"There, that's better," she started. "Now, I'd like some answers," she continued as she shimmied backwards up onto the table. "I know you have them. Everyone else around here seems to think I'm too 'emotionally comprised' to hear the whole truth, and you seem willing to talk, so let's have it."

"Thank you," he said in a stronger voice.

"For what?"

"The drink and the modesty."

"Oh," she answered and glanced at the empty cup and thought to pour another. "You're welcome," she continued when she noticed the gun missing. "You better put my gun back, right now!"

"Ah, first off, this is my weapon," Josh interjected. "You took it without permission. Secondly, when you have some training and understand how to respect a firearm, and stop referring to its internal parts as a 'thingy', I'll give one to you. Not a second sooner than that."

"Fine!" she stated emphatically. "Gregg, tomorrow morning I want to be trained. That evening, I expect you to present me with my own gun."

The two started chuckling until they realized she wasn't joking and stopped.

"There, now that that's settled, Suhrab, why did you shoot down my husband's plane?"

"We were test firing the portable EMP weapon to see if the technology worked," he responded with a grin in Gregg's direction. "I'm happy to report… it did."

"When did you start having people follow me? How did you know I was pregnant? When did you bug my house and hospital room?"

"There are sympathizers everywhere. We put out a request through the mosques as soon as we knew Gregg's identity and skillset."

"Were there any other survivors on the plane?"

"Seven."

"And where are they?"

The prisoner looked up as if he were searching for the answer. "You must understand, we didn't have the best medical –,"

"Suhrab, where are they?" she asked, cutting him off.

"He pitched them over the cliff. I saw the bodies when he was showing me that there was no possible means of escape," her husband offered as he crossed his arms and stared at the floor.

"Three died on the operating table, two didn't survive interrogation, and one got blood poisoning. That left only you, Mr. Chastain. Survival of the fittest, no?"

Gregg started toward him with his fists clenched and forearms bulging. *This guy is in dire need of another beating*, he thought.

"As you were, honey," she ordered and then turned to Josh. "I think I said it right. It is, 'as you were,' correct?"

Her husband stopped his progression and Josh nodded.

"I'm gettin' good at this military stuff," she said with pride to the room.

"Their names were –," Suhrab began when Emily raised a hand.

"I don't want those. You can give them to Gregg after I've left," she interrupted. "Where's your brother? I mean, that's what sent my husband on a wild goose chase across the country instead of coming home to me as soon as he landed back in the States."

"No idea."

Emily was taken aback. "I find that hard to believe."

"That's what he and I have been discussing, dear," Gregg inserted. "So far, he's been less than forthcoming."

"Hmm, all right. Change of subject, what did you mean when you said you saved my life?"

"It's simple, really," Suhrab replied thoroughly enjoying the exchange. "If I hadn't shot your husband's plane down, the good Chaplain wouldn't have come to your house. You wouldn't have fainted and lost your child, thus requiring a hospital stay. Without that, they wouldn't have found the cancer. Maybe you carry the baby to term maybe you don't. If you had, though, you most likely would have been dead shortly thereafter."

Emily looked back at Josh. "May I hold that for a sec?" she asked and gestured toward the Beretta tucked into the front of his jeans. Before he could answer, she added, "Oh, you can take the clippy thing out."

He glanced over at Gregg who shrugged. Hesitantly, he removed the weapon, dropped the fully loaded magazine into his other hand, and slid the pistol across the table toward her.

Emily picked it up, immediately noticing the difference in balance and weight. Then, suddenly, she lunged forward at Suhrab.

"That wasn't your choice to make!" she screamed at him as she grabbed him by the throat and cracked him in the side of the head. "That was my decision and you took that from me!" she wailed as she hit him again and again and again.

After a number of successive blows, the blood was flowing freely from Suhrab's wounds. The two men quickly came around the table and forcibly pulled her off of the man before she pistol whipped him to death right in front of them.

"Get off of me!" she spat. "That was my decision!" she continued to wail through her tears.

Josh rested the gun from her hand once Gregg immobilized her arm.

"I think you can take her back now," Gregg said over his wife's protestations.

"No! I need to be here! I need to see him suffer!"

Her resistance toward her removal was so fierce and strong that Josh had to pick her up and carry her out of the house. To her credit, Emily grabbed every door jam on their way through the rooms and held on for dear life until Josh overpowered her. All the while, Emily wailed and protested.

Gregg watched from the front window of the house as Josh marched his wife back to the farm. Satisfied that Emily wouldn't be returning, Gregg quit the subtle tactics and started the waterboarding. Suhrab resisted mightily, but like all prisoners enduring interrogation, he contradicted himself, offered tiny fragments of truth, until eventually… he cracked. When he did, he was practically laughing for being allowed to stall for that long.

Attempting to use the Wrigley's wall mounted phone, Gregg hastily called the farm. He cursed repeatedly when no one answered… as usual.

* * *

Col. James' cell started chirping in his pocket. No one had come out of the house to tell them what had been found so he figured he'd take the call. He assumed the assault team was still investigating and clearing the structure. The Colonel opened the Humvee's door and began exiting the vehicle to answer it when he glanced at the caller ID. It wasn't a number he was familiar with, but he knew that Gregg had returned to Ohio to find his wife. The '740' area code didn't give him a confirmation either way. Aside from his staff back in Germany, nobody had the number.

He depressed that 'Accept' button and answered, "This is Col. James."

"Colonel! Where are you?" came the frantic reply.

"Gregg? Is that you?"

"Yes! It's me! Where are you?" he repeated. "Is Cecil with you?"

"Yeah. He's with me. We finished up at Warren and now were outside Abbas' house at Minot. Why? What's wrong? What's going on?"

"That little bastard Suhrab finally broke! Cecil's a Taliban sympathizer! Abbas and his brother didn't murder his bunkmate and abduct him at Bagram! He did it himself and walked off the base to find *them*!" Gregg practically screamed into the phone. "It was a setup! That's what he meant when he said Cecil 'had been placed'. He helped plan it! Kill him! Kill Cecil now!"

Colonel James instinctively started to reach for his Beretta. Before he could draw it from its holster, he heard the distinctive sound of a hammer being cocked behind him. A second later he felt the building pressure from the muzzle of the General's pearl laden 1911 being pressed against the back of his head.

Very calmly, Cecil started counting down, "Three, two, one."

Without warning, the house that Abbas had shared with his roommates exploded into a mass of flying debris and carnage. Timber, glass, and body parts spewed from the erupting fireball like Vesuvius. The concussive blast from the detonation knocked the Colonel and his brainwashed, psychotic patient to the ground. In the midst of all that chaos and confusion, Col. James had the wherewithal to pull his Beretta.

While the two men tumbled and wrestled in the dirt, the psychiatrist started squeezing the trigger every time the muzzle passed in front of Cecil's frame. He managed to get six shots off before the seventh finally ended the man's flailing. Once his grip was lessened, he extricated himself from the dying man's deathly embrace and observed his shallow breathing.

Out of breath himself, the Colonel asked, "Why? Why would you aid these people?"

Through his labored pains, Cecil picked up his arm and began trying to point the General's pistol at his head to commit suicide. When he pulled the trigger, it didn't fire. He chuckled and then smiled. "Figures, friggin' General's. Damn thing's not loaded."

Before he could say any more, he rolled slightly and coughed out a mouthful of blood. As he spat the last of it out, he answered the Colonel.

"Life is too short and precious to be spent on lies. I refused to spend any more time helping fools with ideas that were wrong. Islam is the light to which we all should aspire. I followed my conscience and it has led me to this glorious revolution."

Col. James stood and stared at him. The man's shirt slowly began changing colors due to the leaking fluid. Before all of the pools merged, the Colonel counted three entry wounds. He had no desire to provide medical assistance, but he *did* want to know what he could tell him.

"Where's Abbas? Which LF is he hiding in?" he pleaded.

"No idea," the Airman replied as he winced in pain. "I only provided the information needed to gain access to the missiles. It's your precious golden boy, Gregg, that told him how to circumvent the security protocols. If the Air Force and the government are anything, they're predictable." Cecil grimaced his way through a chuckle and added, "All of the LF's were designed and configured the same. He could be in any of them."

# Chapter 2

"Josh!" Dallas yelled across the cabin. "It's starting!"

His friend quickly exited the kitchen and ran to his office. "What have you got?"

"I just got off the horn with a buddy down in Beaufort. He said that he'd been in contact with his buddies up and down the east coast. Apparently, there are three flotillas with at least two-hundred ships each steaming towards Hampton Roads and the Chesapeake, as well as the Hudson River and the Port of Miami."

"How far out are they? Are they separating into smaller packs? What about the Gulf or out west? Any news on those fronts?"

"Nah. Nothing else other than the three groups... not so far at any rate. All they could tell me was that all three battle groups are inside the twelve nautical mile territorial water boundary and all hell is breaking loose. Missile batteries aren't firing, the military is flailing. It's a mess!"

"See if he –," Josh started to say when Gregg burst into the room.

"You need to get that thing in the barn if you plan on ever using it again!" he said out of breath.

"What the –," Dallas replied. "Did you run all the way here from Wrigley's place?"

"Had to! None of you people ever answer the damn phone! Come on! Help me break this down!" Gregg answered frantically as he leaned in, started powering off the device, and disconnecting wires.

Josh and his old friend immediately began working with their new compatriot to get the transceiver disconnected. One grabbed the headset and the mic while the other hauled the radio.

As the three sprinted to the barn, Josh asked, "What the hell is going on?"

"Suhrab broke! Cecil, that lying little dirt bag! He walked off the base and went looking for those ass clowns! He played us! Colonel James just put him down with a couple rounds in the chest," the former POW answered as he wrenched open the massive door to allow the others to enter unencumbered.

The group made their way past the machinery and Josh's Hi-line railroad truck to the back of the structure. Josh handed off the transceiver and dug in his pocket for the keys. He fumbled for a few seconds to find the right key.

"Come on, man! Hurry up!" Gregg said in a distressed tone. He hadn't realized it, but he was dancing around like a toddler in need of the bathroom.

After several tense laden moments, Josh proclaimed, "Got it!"

With the lock removed, the broken seal on the door allowed a rush of air to enter the eight-foot square Faraday room. Chester and Reginald had constructed the contraption for him years ago. It was also through their tutelage that he was able to build the protective shrouds for the generators as well.

Dallas and Gregg quickly entered, stowed the mechanism and its assorted parts on an open shelf and dove back through the opening. Before they were barely out, Josh was closing the door behind them. He hurriedly bolted it shut, replaced the lock, and smoothed the seal. With the excitement waning, he put his back to the wall and slid down to a seated position.

"Now, would you please tell us what that was all about?" Josh asked calmly. "How much time have we got?"

"Couple hours at most. Cecil didn't say which site Abbas was hiding in. All he does know is that the shifty bastard led them into a trap. A twelve-man assault team was eviscerated when the house blew. He damn near killed the Base Commander too."

"So what are they doing now?" Dallas asked.

"They're moving through the silo's one at a time, it'll be slow going. I don't think they'll find him in time. It seems that Abbas took out his roommates several days ago if the duty logs are any indication."

"What do you mean?"

"None of them reported for duty in over four days. He's got at least that much of a head start to watch and observe and get into position. If it were me, I'd have been scouting with every shift I was assigned. I would have staged pieces of equipment so I wouldn't have to carry it all in at once." As an afterthought, Gregg added, "Oh, and compounding this misery, he's been on base for several months."

"How long does it take? Start to finish, how much time does he need to bypass all of the security and launch?" Josh questioned.

"With the information I provided coupled with the amount of time he's had to prepare, conceivably he could spin one up in a couple hours and fire several on a timer all at once. He's had more than enough of an opportunity to write a script or a program of some sort to open the blast doors without it being detected in the LCC."

"But what's the target? A single missile is plenty to handle the bulk of the lower forty-eight," Dallas wondered and stated aloud.

"I didn't get the impression that Suhrab and his faction of lunatics are looking for surface detonations. Their little portable EMP's tell me they are…" Gregg started to say before a thought occurred to him. "Son of a bitch! That's what he meant!"

"What?" Josh asked.

"When I was being held, he said he wanted to 'level the playing field'. I assumed that he was trying to physically flatten something. I think that cheeky little shit was referring to humanity, to our civilization. Put us *all* back at square one."

\* \* \*

"Hey, Chester... Scott," Lily called into the basement. "Josh wants you guys to come up for a second."

"Huh? Why? What for?" he replied without taking his eyes off of the task of breaking down the portable EMP device.

"I get the impression that he'd like to talk about that thing you're working on, but on a grander scale," she answered and walked away.

A few minutes later the pair exited the stairwell. When they reached the top of the stairs they saw that the dining room table had been placed perpendicular to its original position. In the corner, in front of the large wooden obstacle was an easel Josh had squirreled away from his project management days after the Corps. It had a few pieces of paper still attached and an assortment of colored markers in the tray.

Chester looked over the faces of the people assembled. Captain Rayna and Gregg looked bored. Basilia was nervously chewing on her fingernails and Emily was quietly feeding the baby a bottle. The rest looked on in eager anticipation. Then a thought struck him and he chuckled.

"Something funny? Josh asked.

"Nah," the scientist replied casually. "It's just you all kinda look like the last supper sitting behind that table."

His friend leaned forward and surveyed the assembled mass gathered around and smiled. "Well, it wasn't by 'design'," he answered and flashed air quotes.

Heather groaned audibly and added, "Papaw, was he always this corny?"

Her grandfather held up is hands in surrender.

"Lemme guess," Chester started. "I'm your dancin' monkey for the next hour?" When no one responded, he shrugged and said, "Okay, what would you like me to teach?"

Josh leaned back and offered simply, "Most of us understand what a high altitude nuclear explosion is, but what some do not know are the effects. So, instead of everyone guessing or running for cover for fear of fallout," he continued as he motioned toward Basilia. "I thought it would be good to have it explained in lay terms by an expert in the field."

"That's it?"

"That's it," he answered.

Chester turned to Scott and said, "Would you like to do the honors?"

The young man unlocked his longing stare at Katherine and glanced over at his new mentor. "Really? Sure!" he replied excitedly.

Scott proceeded to walk over to the easel and pick up a marker. He drew multiple columns and labeled each 'E1', 'E2', and 'E3' respectively. Chester nodded his agreement.

"Okay. Regardless of altitude at detonation or magnitude contained within the warhead, an EMP from an atmospheric blast is basically comprised of three components," he began and pointed to the labels.

"The E1 phase is very fast and extremely intense. This is the part that causes electrical surges and begins to fry everything. The gamma radiation travels at almost 90% the speed of light and it does this by using something called the 'Compton Effect'. That gets kind of technical so we'll just write 'electrical surge' for E1.

"E2 is like lightning," he continued and paused to write the term under the 'E2' heading. "Most everything is shrouded against common weather related power surges and electrical storms through USB's and surge protectors, but E2 adds insult to injury because it immediately follows E1. The E1 phase provides a gateway through the protection because, as I said, it fries everything. To be clear, by 'fries everything' I mean the amount of energy coursing through the lines amps up so quickly and intensely that the blast of electricity pushes the insulators and diodes beyond their maximum thresholds. Once the E1 component takes out the initial defenses for the protected system, E2 comes along and hits everything as if it were never protected to begin with.

"E3 is the big brother sucker punch that keeps on giving. The first two components only take seconds or milliseconds, but this piece, on the other hand, can last a few minutes. Once E1 and E2 are done, part three shows up like a solar flare, or geomagnetic storm. This is commonly referred to as the Carrington Event."

Scott paused and turned to the board once more. He wrote 'solar flare' under the appropriate heading and then chose a different color and jotted down 'milliseconds' under 'E1', 'seconds' under 'E2', and 'minutes' under 'E3'.

"The EMP aspect of this phase takes out the high voltage lines and low orbiting satellites. You'll know it when you see it because it will appear similar to an aurora borealis." The student then paused and turned to Chester and asked, "How'd I do?"

The mentor smiled and began clapping. "Bravo, Scott. Bravo! I do have one correction though. The blast needs to occur above thirty thousand feet in order to induce ionization, but that takes us well in to the realm of the technical."

"Dang!" Scott replied. "I'm sorry. I knew that."

"Don't beat yourself up. I've met juniors in college that couldn't have done what you just did."

With that, Scott and Katherine smiled at each other.

She elbowed her sister Heather and whispered, "That's my guy."

"So no fallout?" Basilia said, still deeply troubled.

"No, my dear," Chester answered. "You can leave your cuticles intact."

"What kind of area are we talking about? What I mean is, how far will the effects be felt?" Evan asked.

"Well that depends on a lot of factors," the teacher replied and casually walked over to the easel and flipped the page. He then drew a rough outline of the continental United States. "The Earth's magnetic fields tilt downward at high altitude in the northern hemisphere. Because of this, the blast effects are shaped like a horseshoe. Do we know what weaponry is being utilized?"

The assembled mass turned and looked at Gregg. He hung his head out of shame or pity and softly replied, "Minuteman III's out of Minot."

Chester whistled at the response and asked, "Are they MIRV's?"

"I'm sorry. MIRV's?" Basilia said nervously.

"It stands for 'multiple independently targetable re-entry vehicle', Chester began in reply. "Originally, when this variant was first developed, each missile carried three warheads, not one. As a result, each nuclear tip could have a different set of targeting instructions. Now, assuming that the ones at Minot AFB have all been refitted with the single W87 warhead from the Peacekeeper missiles, the blast radius would look something like this," he offered and then drew a large 'U' covering the bulk of the lower forty-eight states.

"This first line indicates the maximum effect of the atmospheric detonation at three hundred kilometers over North Dakota. If it detonates at a higher altitude over say, Kansas or Nebraska, the entirety of the United States would be affected to some degree. However, an EMP can only be felt by line of sight. The curvature of the Earth will protect Central and South America, as well as the southern hemisphere."

"Great!" Hoplite exclaimed. "We get sent back to the Stone Age while the Mexican cartels get to keep the lights on. Nice!"

"Well, yes and no," President Sarkes replied. "In some ways they'll be worse off."

"You can't be serious," Captain Rayna responded incredulously.

"Absolutely. The United States imports billions of dollars of goods from overseas. A lot of U.S. based companies relocated their manufacturing down to Central America. Their customer base is still here in the U.S. We are the primary recipient of their exports."

As the side conversations continued, Chester continued to doodle on the large pad of paper. Inside the original maximum effect line, he drew a bubble letter shaped 'U'. Within that was a much smaller 'smile' outlined area. Above both was an egg shape with two concentric ovals inside. Every state from the Mississippi to the Rockies north of Texas was contained inside at least one of his overlays.

"What's all of that," Evan's wife asked.

"That, my dear, is where the full effect will be felt the most," he replied as he pointed to the 'U' and the smile. "Because of the curvature of the Earth, coupled with the downward tilt of the magnetic field, anything south of the blast is going to get the worst of it. Conversely, this region to the north sees the least damage."

Something clicked in Gregg's mind and he popped his head up suddenly.

"Have something to add to our little training session?" Josh asked inquisitively.

"Actually, yes. A minute ago you said you were assuming that all of the missiles at Minot had been swapped from the triple tipped W78 to the single re-entry vehicle W87." Gregg quickly turned to address President Sarkes. "Sir, can you confirm that all of those warheads were swapped out? We had to comply with the SERV program, right?"

Tom Sarkes knew exactly where the man was headed and reached in his pocket for his phone. "No, but I know someone who does," he answered and dialed the SecDef.

Emily leaned into her husband and asked, "What's that?"

While Sarkes waited to be connected, her husband provided the answer to the group. "It was an initiative to introduce 'Safety Enhanced Reentry Vehicle' protocols. The older W78 warhead package didn't contain enough safeguard features to prevent something like this. As a result, we started putting safer warheads in our missiles."

"So if we knew which ones are still MIRV's," Hoplite interjected, "We might know which launch facility, or facilities, Abbas is headed to on Minot."

Gregg nodded his agreement. "Suhrab never asked me about the W87's, only the W78's."

* * *

*One last connection... and... done*, Abbas thought as he sat back on his haunches. *Four nights, four missiles rewired.*

Over the course of the last several days, since he had murdered his roommates, Abbas spent his daylight hours sleeping and or dodging whatever maintenance crews showed up. Military protocols being what they are, the LF's were typically devoid of personnel unless there was an issue detected in the LCC's or regularly scheduled checks dictated a physical visit. His nights were spent carefully working his way through the terrain between LF's, avoiding motion detection and cameras, and rewiring four of the ten Minuteman III missiles controlled by the L-01 LCC.

Every time he cracked one open, he was grateful for the scopolamine and Gregg's intel regarding the numerous booster sensors that, had he not known, he most certainly would have tripped and alerted personnel within the control center.

Several minutes after he replaced the protective panel on the last missile, he was standing under the star laden night sky stretching. The darkened landscape had not yet given way to the morning sun as he set the timer to start the sequence and get moving. As soon as his birds were airborne, all hell was going to break lose.

Cecil had been quite forthcoming with his detailed descriptions of the LF's. What the wayward Airman neglected to mention was the fact that each silo facility was miles away from its counterparts. That had been a bit of a shock when the man reported for duty as the late Hector Ortiz. However, his intel regarding the ten missiles under the direction of the L-01 LCC was a stroke of genius. Emboldened by the knowledge that these were the last to be integrated into the SERV program allowed his brother, Suhrab, to better direct his scopolamine derived line of questioning on Gregg.

Given the pre-programmed coordinates, the three warheads would jettison the launch vehicle and spread out like a trident. Hyper accuracy was achieved by spinning each similarly to a bullet exiting a barrel. However, accuracy was a relative term. Generally speaking, being within a football field was usually accepted as being considered 'close enough'.

With an apogee of a thousand kilometers, the warheads would eject, separate, and arc out toward their intended blast altitude. By the time they were triggered, each projectile would be spaced almost eight hundred miles apart. He was practically giddy that he was assured that the entirety of United States, Western Europe, and the bulk of the Asian continent would go dark instantly as each detonated. Even if a country managed to launch an interceptor missile, the chaff would, hopefully, confuse the radar. One or two of the jettisoned MIRV's were sure to get through. From there it was a waiting game.

Suhrab and Abbas were convinced that once the die off was complete, the religious right and the fanatical left would further reduce a nations population through infighting. After that, the world would be fully prepared for the spread of Islam. For them, chaos and panic would descend like a comforting blanket and rid the planet of the last empire. It didn't matter to the brothers if roving gangs of cannibals, rapists, and thieves did the majority of the bloodletting. The ends justified the means and it would still suffice. If someone retaliated with nuclear strikes of their own due to an itchy trigger finger, then so be it.

Abbas glanced at his glowing iridescent watch face; it was just after 4:00 AM CST. If his programming worked as designed, at 4:09 his first missile would begin the minute long pre-launch procedure. At 4:10, it would exit its silo and scream into the night's sky unchecked. Each of the hi-jacked weapons would blast off at specific intervals, none more than five minutes from the previous. If he had the flight times and trajectories correct, all would detonate within seconds of each other. The whole of the Christian dominated northern hemisphere would soon be reduced into lawless chaos.

* * *

"Got it!" Col. James responded abruptly as he disconnected the call.

He quickly turned and reentered the Base Commander's room at the infirmary. "General! We've got a location! How long does it take to get to the L-01 launch control center for the 742d Missile Squadron?"

The man groggily sat up in his bed and replied, "About an hour and half by road. Why?"

"Abbas is going after the ones that haven't had their warheads swapped out! All of those are under 'L' facility command, right?"

"Yeah, but if there's an issue there are redundant systems in place that will allow another LCC to handle them," the weary man answered.

"Can we fly there?"

"Sure," he replied and then looked at the Colonel quizzically. "Do you really want to be up in a helo if were expecting an EMP though?"

"Damn it!"

"What?" the General asked.

Colonel James pulled back the curtain, "Look."

The two watched for the next fifteen minutes while the night's sky was repeatedly illuminated by rocket boosters as they exited the silo.

# Chapter 3

"We didn't do it! Don't return fire! They are set to detonate in the atmosphere! These are NOT, I repeat, NOT surface detonations!" President Rayburn screamed into the camera.

On the wide screen panel in front of him were the grim and haggard faces of Presidents and Heads of State from seven of the eight nuclear nations. Only the English Prime Minister had the gall to refuse the call.

"What assurances do we have that this unprovoked attack is set to detonate in the atmosphere?" the Russian President asked. "We would be well within our rights to erect our launchers and return fire."

"Yes, you would," he answered solemnly. "But I'm asking you not to!" he said more forcefully and directly. "We are currently tracking the man responsible. An Iranian terrorist named Abbas Esfahani."

"You have not addressed President Tarlakov's question, Rayburn," the Indian Prime Minister inserted as a rebuke. "How do we know these are going to be high altitude detonations?"

The POTUS sighed and decided to let the chips fall where they may.

"About a year ago, one of our special operations teams was shot down in southeastern Syria. We believed that all souls were lost. That is until the lone survivor walked into a FOB in northern Iraq. He had been held by a militant Islamic faction bent on starting a holy war. It is their belief that if everyone were on equal footing then the world would seek out and willingly convert to Islam."

"How could you possibly know this? Do you have a communique from this Abbas character? Did he leave behind some sort of manifesto? And you still haven't answered the question," the Chinese leader stated in halting English.

"Damn it! Stop interrupting me! I'm saying that these lunatics shot our guy up with scopolamine. I don't have to tell you what happened after that... I think you know because our birds are inbound. We also have his brother, Suhrab Esfahani, in custody. He was the mastermind behind all of this. He previously stated, and I quote, 'we need to level the playing field'. After he was interrogated he divulged his brother's intentions to put us *all* back at square one.

"We don't have a lot of time. Our techs tell me that the first missile will detonate in just a few minutes."

"Again," the Chinese leader said as he interrupted once more. "How can you possible know that?"

"We have a laptop used by Abbas, damn it!" President Rayburn replied forcefully. "According to the programming we analyzed, once the missiles reach apogee, they'll jettison their warhead, and detonate at three hundred and seventy-five kilometers! That's how I know!" he concluded as he growled the last.

Once he finished, the 'Leader of the Free World' sat back in his chair and closed his eyes. *I can't tell them these things are MIRV's or they'll shoot back for sure*, he thought.

Resigned, Rayburn said, "We shot a Patriot Missile at the one above the continental United States, but it was out of range. We hit the thing with one of our ship-based missile defense rockets, but the warhead had already jettisoned. We're screwed any way you cut it," the POTUS declared dejectedly. "I don't know what else to say. If I'm wrong, these two lunatic brothers started World War III and whether we knew or not, we fired first. If I'm wrong... then I guess you need to do what you have to."

Rayburn slumped in his chair. In a resigned tone he said, "Fire away... I don't know. All I do know is that I'm imploring you to not turn my country into a nuclear wasteland. This was an act of terrorism pure and simple and it wasn't initiated by us."

His comments were greeted with muted conversation as the various Heads of State conferred with off screen advisors and aides. Aside from retaliating, the only other option would be to try and shoot them down from the leeward side.

"Mr. Rayburn," Russian President Tarlakov began, "I hope for your sake that you are telling the truth." He then turned his head to someone off camera and said, "Fire!"

\* \* \*

Josh awoke and rolled toward his clock in an effort to not wake Samantha. Sharing a bed again after so many years alone was going to take some getting used to. The clock read 5:17 AM. *Still have power*, he thought. *Guess they caught Abbas.* Then it dawned on him that he had overslept by more than thirty minutes.

He slowly turned his head and found his future bride still sleeping, cuddled up next to him. As he started to extricate himself from her comforting embrace, she awoke.

"Good morning," she said sleepily. "Where are you sneaking off to at this hour?"

He reached over and checked the on/off slide on the clock radio. It was in the off position. Either Sam did it as they were preparing for bed or himself when it started going off at the customary 4:45.

As he rolled out of bed, he replied, "I overslept. Did you turn off the alarm?

"Yeah. I got up in the middle of the night to pee and switched it off. You have been so busy, I thought you could use the rest."

"You looking out for me already?"

"Somebody's got to," she answered as she yawned. "You sure won't admit it. Come back to bed."

Josh smiled a little before saying, "Sorry, kid. The chores won't get done by themselves. Go back to sleep. I'll be here for breakfast around eight."

Shortly after the pair had become engaged, they agreed to wait until they were married to consummate their relationship. Between the two of them, and the issues surrounding their first marriages, they figured that they didn't need *any* of the bad karma that might come by violating one of God's laws. They had violated enough of them over the years.

Their agreement to wait was followed by the 'suggestive' conversation where Samantha, half joking, tried to ascertain whether or not he would be *able* to consummate their marriage. When she had slighted his manhood by referring to its 'dusty coating' from 'lack of use', Josh had crudely replied, 'Ah hell, damn thing greets me nearly every morning!'

With an eye barely cracked open, Samantha surveyed the man that was about to be her husband. She took in his scar adorned torso and physique, but paused when she visually made it to his waist. She half giggled and said, "I guess you weren't lying."

Josh followed her eyes and realized what she was referencing. "Yeah well, a cold shower will fix that. Besides, I'm too old to go diving into closets," he replied and adjusted himself before throwing a pillow at her and putting on his bathrobe.

Samantha smiled and deflected the flying object. With a yawn and smile, she quickly fell back asleep.

Following his usual morning routine, Josh shuffled off to the kitchen to start the coffee brewing before heading to the shower. Before he even entered the barely lit room, he could smell the black liquid gold. As he turned the corner, he saw the illuminated red indicator declaring that the machine was already on and stopped walking. Then, movement on the porch caught his eye.

Instinctively, he quietly backed up and went to the recess where he kept his Beretta. He wanted to activate the CCTV monitors, but the ambient light would give away everything. Instead, in one fluid motion, he grabbed the weapon and yanked the front door open. As he peered down the sight, he was startled to see Gregg sipping a cup of coffee holding his new son.

"What are you doing?" Josh whispered so as to not wake the sleeping child. "I almost shot you!"

"I've got Brent's cell. Colonel James called. Said he just watched four birds take flight out of Minot. So I grabbed Declan, a bottle of milk, and a cup o' Joe. Thought I'd come out here to see the show," Gregg replied casually.

"Crap. I'll be right back," Josh stated as he retreated back into the cabin.

He quickly stowed his weapon and bolted back to his bedroom.

"Sam!" he whispered forcefully as he shook her while trying to get dressed. "Sam! Wake up!"

Samantha slowly began to stir. "What? Let me sleep."

"Okay, but you're gonna miss the light show. They didn't catch Abbas in time," he replied and left the room.

She threw the covers off and practically leapt out of the bed and followed Josh to the kitchen.

"What are you doing?" she asked as he navigated the cabin in near darkness.

"I thought I'd enjoy some coffee while I watched. You want one?"

"Seriously? How can you be so cavalier?"

As he opened a cupboard and retrieved two mugs, he said, "What's the sense in freaking out and panicking. We can't control it. We didn't have anything to do with it. Life will go on, albeit more slowly. Don't get me wrong, parts of it are most definitively going to suck, but I have my entire family here. You, all three of my daughters, my friends... even a father-in-law of sorts."

Josh walked over to the window, pulled back the curtain, and gestured. "There are combat engineers and a Special Operations team sleeping in my barn. Hell, there's an ex-President sleeping upstairs. As far as safest places to be right now, it's either this farm or a weather station in Alaska."

By the muted light of the under cabinet lighting, Josh noticed Sam was only wearing a thin pair of pajamas. "Come on. How many times do you get to see something like the Northern Lights in rural Ohio? Grab a blanket out of the closet, it's kind of chilly. I'll have your coffee on the porch waiting for you." Then, with a smirk on his face, he added, "Oh, and find a bra. Those things are flying all over the place."

Sam quickly covered her chest under her crossed arms.

"I suppose that's for the crack I made earlier," she replied rhetorically.

"Yup," Josh answered all the same.

Samantha sighed and resigned herself to the inevitable. She noticed him smiling as he continued to monitor the night sky through the window.

"What the hell are you grinning at?" she proclaimed.

"Oh, nothing," he declared casually. "It's just that I followed Reggie's and Chester's advice and stock piled some stuff. I budgeted a monthly allowance and procured what I could as insurance. I'll show you once the sun is up and the group stops freaking out. You'd be surprised what you can sock away with only a couple hundred dollars a month for a decade."

Far off in the distance, the 5:30 train could be heard making its way through the rural Ohio backwoods. The horn blast, coupled with the rumble of the engine and the steel wheels mating with track, was unmistakable. Josh glanced down at his watch and smiled his crooked little smile.

"Manna from Heaven and right on time too," he said to himself.

Sam just shook her head and went off to retrieve the blanket.

As she exited the room, she whispered, "I suppose the solar panels marked on your railroad maps were inspired by those two as well?"

"Yup. Today's gonna be a real interesting day," Josh replied as he filled their mugs.

Before heading out to join Gregg, he struck upon an idea. *Worth a shot*, he thought.

"How much time we have?" he asked as he poked his head out of the front door.

"No idea, probably five minutes or so," the new father answered in a hushed tone.

Josh walked with purpose back to the kitchen, opened their junk drawer, and retrieved a screwdriver. He entered the closet door in the foyer and accessed the breaker box. Once the main breaker was in the 'off' position, he worked quickly to remove all of the breakers from the electrical panel.

Sam cursed the pile of plastic when she stepped on them.

* * *

At 5:31 PM Moscow Time, Russian made ABM-4 Gorgon anti-ballistic missiles intercepted the three inbound MIRV tipped Minuteman III's headed for the European and Asian continents. From 5:28 AM to 5:32 AM EST, the continental United States was awash in the aurora borealis. Green, red, purple, blue, and yellow waves of light danced across the sky from the outer banks of North Carolina to the shores of the Pacific.

While the bulk of America and her citizens slept, all of the mass transit systems, long haul truckers, and cars of various make and models slowly came to a stop. If it didn't have a carburetor, plugs, and wires the vehicle became a glorified, and more often than not, a very expensive paperweight.

Hydro-electric dams, nuclear reactors, as well as water and sewer pumping and treatment stations across the U.S. ground to a halt. Some did so gracefully, but a hand full did not. Reliable electrical and water sources blinked out of existence. The Internet, smart phones, and advanced computer systems were a thing of the past.

The two million residents of Manhattan were stranded on an island. Fortunately, they had the capability to walk to the outer boroughs on a half dozen bridges.

After meeting heavy resistance on their initial assault, the Prime Minister received a 'tip' from his Iranian counterpart. Their forces quickly moved their flotillas as far out to sea as possible in the allotted time. There they sat and waited, completely unaffected by the atmospheric detonations. When word came from Downing Street, the group was prepared to occupy the now defenseless cities and ports of New York, Baltimore, Virginia Beach, Charleston, and Miami. Unseen by Dallas' band of HAM radio brothers, the PM's second wave were assembled and lay in wait near the Yucatan Peninsula, as well as off the southern end of Baja, and the northern edge of Graham Island on the west coast of Canada.

The Gulf of Mexico contingent was assigned to handle Mobile, New Orleans, and Houston. The western most forces would begin their pacification operations in San Diego, the port of Los Angeles, San Francisco and Seattle. All major means of waterborne escape were soon to be closed. The only aspect of the invasion force that could have potentially been affected was already safely anchored in the Cleveland-Cuyahoga County Port southwest of Hopkins International Airport. At 6:00 AM, the Royal Marines would mount their hardened armored assault vehicles and helicopters. Then they would drive less than a mile down East 9th Street to the Federal Reserve Bank, and make a hefty withdrawal. The citizens were about to wake up to the reality of an occupying army in their streets.

Abbas' timing spared hundreds of thousands of airborne travelers in the U.S. as many flights had not taken off yet due to the early morning hour of the attack. Had the detonation occurred during peak flight operations, the death toll from the passengers and the people on the ground quickly and easily would have reached six digits in a matter of minutes.

Lifesaving operations currently underway ended in darkness as backup generators failed to initiate their start-up protocols. Patient's dependent on machines to live almost immediately coded and died. Anyone with an older style pacemaker simply didn't wake up. Several million people in the care of hospitals and convalescent homes never had a chance to see the dawn of a new day. Those that were hospitalized, but required round the clock monitoring, would only last as long as their medications held out. After that, millions would meet their end, painfully. The Prozac nation would descend into chaos and mayhem as soon as the anti-depressant and anti-psychotic meds were exhausted.

As far as Suhrab knew, the great die-off was beginning. The man was grinning wildly as the blaring screen of static displayed on the old tube style television blinked off. Through the window he saw the pre-dawn sky lit up with waving strands of light.

*Allah be praised*, he thought as he shut his eyes and finally got some sleep for the first time in days.

* * *

The three adults sat sipping coffee as the night's sky was illuminated for as far as the eye could see. The infant child slept as he was passed from one adult to the other. The colors and the patterns were awe inspiring. It's was nothing short of a Fourth of July fireworks show.

When it seemed as if the light show overhead ended, but two continued further off to the east and west, Gregg muttered, "Damn," under his breath.

"What?" Josh asked.

"Stupid scopolamine."

"What does that mean?" Sam wondered aloud.

"I was hoping that this was it. That it was just the lone aurora. Can you see how there isn't anything really in the middle anymore?"

"Yeah, so?" Josh answered.

"That means that Abbas figured out how to program all three warheads. He must have jettisoned them separately so there'd be a spread of a couple hundred miles. If he followed the generally accepted apogee altitude for ballistic missiles, they could have conceivably been released then. No one really knows for sure because it hasn't been tested, as far as I know. Those things, in theory, could have been a thousand kilometers apart by the time they detonated.

"In any event, it looks as if he blanketed the entire lower forty-eight." He paused for a few moments and then added. "I hope they find that little bastard and put one in his head."

Josh, his fiancée, and their new compatriot watched the sky by the dawn's early light as the horizon was lit up by the various phases of the high altitude explosions.

As the aurora's neared their end, Josh said, "Well, I guess there's no going back now."

"You're telling me," Sam stated incredulously.

The two men cocked their heads at her with questioning looks.

"This little show just cost me a personal family fortune over four hundred and fifty million dollars!"

Gregg spat his mouthful of coffee across the porch.

"Whoa!" Josh exclaimed.

Choking of what remained of his coffee, Gregg added, "Ding, ding, ding! We have a winner!" He managed a hard swallow and added, "Holy shit! Where did *that* come from?"

"My dad started Hyloset almost forty years ago. It was nearly a two billion dollar a year company when I went to bed last night. I didn't even get laid for my trouble!"

A deep ruckus belly laugh emanated from the two men.

As Josh wiped tears from his eyes he glanced over at Sam. She was dead serious and visibly pissed.

He quickly straightened up and compassionately said, "You never told me it was that large, but we talked about this, hun. Were you able to get some of it out and converted into something more tangible?"

"Not as much as I would have liked, that's for sure. Most of it was medical gear for Basilia. I added some antibiotics and over the counter stuff, as well as a formula and diapers for Declan. I was just getting started. I didn't see the need for good and silver, not with that cache under all that rock. If push came to shove and we do ever need some gold for barter, I guess we could dip into the piggy bank in the tunnel. Take out a couple bars and break 'em up or melt them down or something and distribute it to the townsfolk so everyone has some form of currency for bartering. People are gonna need something more than chickens, bullets, and canning supplies to trade after a while."

Josh slowly brought his head back and his face took on that far off look Sam had seen when Dallas would plant barely the thought of an idea.

"I did it!" she proclaimed. "I finally planted something in that wired mess. What is it? What did you think of?"

Her future husband only glanced at her with his crooked little mischievous grin at her.

"Señor? Do you see this?" Juan announced from a distance as he approached on foot and motioned skyward.

Josh quickly looked down at his watch, which was still functioning because it needed to be wound.

"Dang. Sorry, Juan. I got caught up watching the light show."

"Si, no hay problema," he relied casually in Spanish. "How soon can we try and start machinery to see what survived?"

"Chester and Scott said the final phase only lasted a few minutes. Unless there aren't any objections, I'd rather play it safe and not try for a few hours. Everything living out here can go on just fine with a minor delay. The greenhouses might be the exception. We should probably check on the pumps and batteries to see if the shrouds actually worked."

"Do we know, ballpark, what made it?" Sam asked. "They didn't really get into all of that when they briefed us."

"According to the Tin Hatters, and what I've read, no one's sure what will or will not survive an EMP. It's all educated guesses and circumspect based on decades old atmospheric test fires. Chester messed around with it for them for a few years and what he found scared the daylights out of him.

"The last major high altitude blast was almost sixty years ago. According to those results, low altitude satellites are definitely toast, we know that much. If it was 'on' and plugged in to the grid, then yes, it's probably fried too. The rest of it could very well be a crap shoot.

"Was it 'off', but plugged in? Then it's probably gone. Was it 'off' and NOT plugged in or was it 'on' and running on batteries? Maybe it survived and is okay. It's really going to come down to how well the device was engineered. How hardened were the components designed to be? What were the thresholds?"

The three just sat there and stared at him with blank looks on their faces.

Seeing this, he sheepishly concluded, "Ya know. Stuff like that. We'll find out more in a few hours."

When no one spoke, he said, "What?"

Gregg blinked first and said, "Where do you come up with this stuff? You're like a freaky little savant or something."

"Most of it is online, or was. That and I got people," Josh replied with a smile.

"So what's with the pile of circuit breakers on the floor in there?" Sam asked.

"Oh, that? That's a hunch. I'm curious if the E1 or E2 phases will jump the line and fry the stuff that's still plugged in. I don't think it will. If I'm right, once the borealis is done, I'll put the breakers back in, throw the transfer switch, and see what the generator turns on… and yes, the genny had a cover as well… Tin Hatters to the rescue."

# Chapter 4

*The First Days…*

"Yes, Prime Minister. It appears as if the event is over," the Royal Marine Major said in response to the question on his hardened SAT phone. "We monitored President Rayburn's communication to the other nuclear nations and we believe we shut everything down on the ship's bridge and in the engine room in time. The Captain is following protocol. The systems are set to be tested according to those timetables."

"When will you know what was affected, Major?"

"The ships were hardened by design and most of our vehicles have been as well over the years. However, but to what extent is still uncertain. If we do manage to get anything to start, we'll have to either try to repair the damage on the ones that didn't or tow the pieces off of the ship and leave them at port.

"Sir, having said all of that, I would like to request a delay until 08:00 local time before attempting to execute our assault on the city and the Reserve facility. We have the element of surprise and we are detaining all of the dock workers as they enter the port. No one knows we are here. I'd prefer to not risk the men and machinery if it's not absolutely necessary."

There was a pause on the other end of the line while PM Goodspeed contemplated the request.

"How many vehicles do you have onboard, Major? Find something that is expendable and try and crank it up. I'll hold," the PM responded through gritted teeth.

The career Marine pulled the phone away from his ear and stared at it. Not realizing he was doing it, the man started shaking his head at the device in disbelief. *Since when does the Prime Minister direct military operations?*

On the far side of the Atlantic, Goodspeed heard, "Sergeant, climb in that 'Husky' in the back and see if she starts."

Thirty seven hundred miles away, the throaty roar of the engine made the PM smile.

"Right, very good," the Major said and the engine was shut down. The man put the phone against his head to speak and concluded, "Given this development, I'd like to retract my request, and offer a new timetable, sir."

"I thought you might. You have fifteen minutes, Major."

\* \* \*

"Well, the cows still seem to work," Gregg sarcastically observed as one lifted its tail and began crapping in the pasture.

"It's a good thing to," Josh replied ignoring the sarcasm. "We'll need the fertilizer. Same with the chickens."

From behind the pair, Josh's daughters approached.

"You couldn't come over and wake us up so we could see it too?" Layla whined somewhat annoyed.

Their father glanced at his watch and turned toward them.

"Uh, Gregg, what time was the first detonation again?" he asked the man nonchalantly.

"If I'm not mistaken, I believe it was on or about zero 5:30… that's in the AM in case you were wondering," he answered as he crossed and arms and leaned back against the fence railing.

"And what's the time now?" their father said as he held his wrist up for him to see the face.

The newest resident let out a long slow whistled. "I believe that watch there says it's quarter 'til eleven."

"Yeah, yeah, yeah," Heather interjected. "Smart ass."

"I sure am glad that our efforts here today have allowed you girls all that extra shut eye, aren't you Gregg?"

Katherine cut through all of the ribbing, walked into her father's embrace while yawning, and gave him a hug. "Morning, Daddy. Thanks for letting us sleep in."

"Good morning, girls. So, what works over at Three Sisters?"

"We have heat and hot water, but the electricity is out," Layla replied as she took her father's coffee cup and sipped at the contents.

"So it appears that all of the well pump shrouds worked perfectly. Everyone has running water. The underground fuel oil and propane tanks are still working as well. We'll check the diesel and unleaded when we fill up some of the tractors and trucks later today. We can deal with the lack of electricity in a little bit, maybe tomorrow. Until then though, you girls will need to get the lanterns out of the barn."

"Dad, I've been thinking about the greenhouses," Layla said without preamble as she gave her dad's coffee cup to Heather to finish off.

"Oh, what about them?" her father asked as he returned his focus on the structures.

"It seems to me that with all of the power out, the timer settings on the lighting will act like a beacon in the morning and evening hours. Since there isn't any other ambient light from the nearby towns to wash out their glow, it might attract people. I don't think we want that."

In a bit of play-acting he said, "Damn," under his breathe. "I hadn't thought of that. Anything else?"

"Actually, yeah. We don't need to run all of these bays anymore either. Nobody's going to magically show up in a delivery truck. Since we are only providing for ourselves by and large, I think we could grow enough with some extra for the root cellar in only one, or maybe, two of the bays. That'll keep the strain off of the deep cycle batteries. Those need to last as long as possible."

Gregg started slowly shaking his head.

"What," Josh said.

"It's nothing. I'm sure you've already thought about it," he replied.

"So far, I'm a big fat 'oh-fer' this morning. Spill it," he ordered continuing the charade.

"It's just that these things aren't that defensible from the cabin or from Three Sisters. There's too much ground to cover in an emergency. The Martinez family is the closest and when people see the glowing on the horizon they're going to head to their house first," Gregg answered. "Can we move the one or two bays that we need closer to the cabin, further away from the road. They should be tucked behind a couple of thick hedgerows."

Heather instinctively raised her hand.

Josh sighed as he exhaled.

"Yes, Heather?"

"Shouldn't we sell or barter the other bays instead of leaving them here to go unused? We are bound to need something sooner or later," Heather stated. "Maybe somebody wants them. The controls and pumps and stuff that the hydroponics required are pretty useless. It's essentially a hot house or an over grown cold frame after all. At a minimum it'll allow someone to extend their growing season."

"What the hell," Josh exclaimed incredulously. "The power's been out for less than a day and you four are just full of ideas."

His daughters and Gregg looked at him somewhat sheepishly.

"Tell you what. I am assigning you guys with the task of solving each and every one of these questions. Heather, I'll give you some names so you can try and line up a couple of buyers. Negotiate a fair trade, no paper money. Also consider that we may need to hold on to a few of them disassembled for a couple of weeks until people realize the power's not coming back. So don't be too eager to advertise their availability or the quantity just yet.

"Gregg and Katherine, you guys work on location and defensibility. Layla, grab Juan and his sons and you three handle the movement of two bays to a spot designated by them.

"Before any of that can be done though, every single piece of ripe fruit and vegetable in there has to be picked and stored in the root cellars. Take all of the plants that aren't ready and consolidate them into one bay and we'll continue to let them grow until there isn't any more to pick. Save me the last five or ten percent of each variety for seed harvesting. Those will be extremely valuable for bartering as well."

The three girls started walking up to the greenhouses to begin picking the produce and start the planning process for the move, but Gregg lingered behind. *That was far too easy*, he thought.

As if he was suddenly remembering, Josh yelled from behind them, "Grab some of the engineers and have them help out. It'll give them something to do."

The girls adjusted course and began working their way to the haylofts to collect any 'volunteers'.

"Wow. Four little questions generated all of that? I don't believe for one second that you hadn't thought of any of that."

His new friend smiled and then answered, "That's what they get for sleeping in. Come with me. I'll show you where I want the two bays put and then we'll go check on that train."

"Train? What train."

"You'll see," he replied. "Today is gonna be fun."

Before turning to follow, Gregg motioned toward the root cellars. "What do you have the Tin Hatters doing out there?"

Josh glanced over his shoulder, "Oh, them? Alysin is a carb junky. They are collecting some fruit to start making yeast water."

"This day keeps getting stranger by the minute," he muttered as he fell in line and started walking. "Okay, I'll bite. What's that?"

"Uh, yeast in water… just like it sounds," he answered.

Gregg stopped and stared at him with a look on his face that said, 'really'?

"Fine. Everybody is so serious today, geez. Take some pieces of fruit, apples in this instance, don't wash them, then cut them up and leave the skin on. Fill a jar about half way with that. Then pour a couple cups of spring or filtered water over top until it's about three quarters full. Just don't use alkaline water. Put the lid on loosely, or some cheesecloth with a rubberband, and then let it sit somewhere warm for a few days. The yeast and the carbohydrates that are already in the fruit will start to react to one another. After a couple of days there should be bubbles, that's how you'll know if it worked. If you have some sugar you can add some to force a faster reaction. When you want to make

48

some leavened bread, replace the individual yeast and water ingredients from the recipe with the yeast water, maybe a little more for good luck, and voilà, you'll get a nice fluffy loaf... with a hint of apple, or pear, or peach, or raisin, or whatever you used."

Off in the distance, their attention was beckoned by a fingered whistle from the cabin. The two turned to see Sam and Emily standing on the front porch waving them in.

"Any idea what that's about?" Josh asked.

"Actually, I think I do. Betcha all my swear jar donations that it's something you *didn't* think of."

The Simmons family patriarch replied with a, "Hmm."

The pair progressed toward the house while Gregg started playing twenty questions regarding the train. To Josh's credit, he gave non-committal answers in order to preserve the surprise. Just for fun, and to distract him, he mentioned an out of the way metal barn tucked in the corner of the property. By all appearances, it looked dilapidated and unused. The height of the weeds had the desired effect of it being empty or possibly abandoned.

To take Gregg's over active mind off of the train, which he was now regretting the mention of, Josh made a request for him to assemble the engineers and the remaining members of his old squad to meet at the barn after lunch.

"What's up?" Josh asked casually as they neared the porch.

"We need to talk to you and Gregg about some things," Sam replied. "Have a seat."

"This ought to be good," Emily's husband stated from under his breath.

"I heard that," retorted his wife.

The pair ascended the front steps, but the farmer in him paused to take in Gregg's handiwork at repairing the damage from his .50 cal fueled rampaged.

As he surveyed the repair and put pressure on various parts of the step, he turned and said, "Not bad, Sergeant. We'll make a carpenter out of you yet." With this he shifted his focus to his fiancé, "So what's going on?"

"Family," she stated bluntly. "Specifically, ours," she concluded while motioning to herself and Emily.

Josh arched his eyebrows, but didn't say anything.

"If everything is about to go to hell in a hand basket in the next few days like you say, now is the best time to head over to Springfield and retrieve Aunt Jenny along with Emily's parents. Coincidentally, they live about fifteen minutes from each other. Now's the best time to go if you're right and the people are still confused as to what happened and nothing's organized... it's only been five hours.

"Plus, it was so early in the morning that the roads should be practically empty. There shouldn't be any logjams out there. We've done the math and we think that this is a six hour round trip deal, a day at most, assuming they can pack with any degree of urgency."

Josh was starting to form his reply, but was cut off before speaking. He did manage to retrieve his wallet and remove a ten dollar bill and hand it to Gregg.

Sam waved off the anomaly and continued. "I know this is going to put an extra burden on us, but they are all the two of us have left in terms of family outside of the people already here. And that brings me to my next point, which is, what are we out here? What I mean is, are we a military compound or is this more of a communal type of living? Are we all civilians adhering to the Constitution and existing state law or is the UCMJ in effect? Or is it both?"

Josh smiled and said, "All of the above… for now. Anything else?"

Sam placed her hands on her hips.

Josh sighed.

"Fine. All active duty personnel are bound by the UCMJ. Everyone is armed at all times and the buddy system is in place. The Constitution is in full effect. Happy?"

Surprised at the lack of debate, Sam stammered, but managed to eke out, "Well, yes, actually. We've completed our task of going through your lists and comparing it to of all of the crap you squirreled away in the barns and in the basement and there were some minor deviations. However, it seems to me that they were accurate as of a month ago. We couldn't make heads or tails from the cryptic reference of "MB" though. What's that, where is it, and what's in it? It wasn't broken out in list form."

"That's part of the surprise. Have I ever told you about government liquidation auctions?" Josh replied.

"Nooo," she answered in a hesitant tone.

"You'd be amazed at what the fed is willing to sell to civilians. Are Dallas and James in there?"

"Yeah, they're fixing some lunch, Why?" Emily asked.

"Would you do me a favor and go in and tell them to bring it with them. I'll give the five of you a quick preview before you head out on your little road trip."

\* \* \*

Josh spent the next several hours answering questions, taking advise, and generally being inundated by various requests. His brain could hold no more data. To that end, he assembled all of the family's, Tin Hatters, Sarkes and his lone remaining Secret Service Agent, as well as Lt. Stokes from the Combat Engineering platoon and Captain Rayna. The group went point by point through each item presented throughout the course of the morning.

Once everything had been hammered out, Josh looked over at Samantha, who had been taking notes, and said, "Okay, I think that's it. Sam can you please read back the decisions we've made so far."

Sam stood with her notepad in hand and started ticking off the items, personnel, destinations, and time tables.

"Basically, we are going to fan out for the next twenty four to ninety six hours while the window of opportunity is open," she declared to the assembled group. "In Juan's truck, Emily, Gregg, and I are headed to Springfield for our remaining family members. Greg's concession to Josh will be to utilize back roads for the return leg. We are planning on being in and out and return here by noon tomorrow, dinner at the latest.

"James, Dallas, and Brent are in the Hi-Line railroad truck along with ten jerry cans of fuel. They will head to their school in Virginia. Anything of use in terms of gear, food, weapons, reloading supplies, etc. is to be loaded up and brought back or cached. The structures there will be prepped for our relocation should the need arise. They are due to return in two to four days' time depending on the state of the rail lines."

Samantha paused for a moment to review her notes to see if she missed anything, then flipped the page.

"Okay, given the fact that we have two squads of combat engineers, we've decided to divide and conquer with those assets too. Lt. Stokes," she stated as she turned to address him directly. "The final assignments are yours, but in a nut shell, the units will be broken into four separate five man teams.

"Team One will take the equipment out of the metal barn and start assessing its viability and make any repairs, if possible and if needed."

"I still can't believe you had a 10kW diesel generator and a field kitchen in there. That stuff must have cost a fortune!" Hoplite interjected emphatically.

"Nope, government liquidation auction," Josh answered. "All told, I only spent three fifty apiece on those. I had a monthly budget of five hundred for various 'necessities' and those were too good to pass up."

Ignoring the blip in her synopsis, Sam continued. "Team Two will recon Lake Hope while Team Three heads to the old Hotel McArthur downtown.

"Lt. Stokes?" Sam asked as she flipped a page and tore out a separate sheet of notes.

"Yes, ma'am," he replied.

"Here's the list," she said as she handed the slip of paper to Dallas so it could be passed down the line of attendees.

Before it reached him at the far end of the table, Sam began detailing the contents of the note for the others.

"Team's Two and Three will need to verify Josh's intel. There should be over sixty cabins available for use by the engineers and any refugees. The hotel should be in good shape as it was repurposed for office space. We believe there are at least fifteen to twenty rooms there as well. Talk to the Mayor in a few days and find out who owns the building. Whoever they are, they should be notified that they now own and operate a boarding house.

"Oh, and at the park, above the lake, there is a lodge and there should be two or three laundry facilities. Don't forget to look for those and assess their viability. Should the need arise, the portable chainsaw mills are at your disposal too."

"Okay, that about covers it," Josh started to say before Sam cut him off.

"I wasn't done with my debrief… honey," she said curtly.

"Oh," he replied sheepishly. "My apologies. I thought you were. Please continue."

Sam glared at him.

"For the benefit of transparency, Lt. Stokes has agreed to move the engineers over to Lake Hope State Park once it is prepped for their relocation. As an added bonus, once refugees arrive, it will allow the squads, with Gregg and Captain Rayna, to move discreetly among the people and quickly identify new personnel for training and it will allow them to comply with Rayburn's request to monitor the collapsed tunnel passively.

"The folks here at the farm should be able to make weekly deliveries of produce so no one gets scurvy until the greenhouse and cold frames can be assembled and crops can be grown in earnest out there.

"Once the full platoon arrives at the lake, they will begin assisting any campers that are currently stranded. Given the fact that it's a Monday and late winter, the park should be empty. From there they'll start making preparations for the refugees once they begin their mass exodus from the cities and larger towns."

"We are still gonna need fuel for all this stuff," Captain Rayna offered.

"Fear not Captain, I have that covered… in spades," Josh answered cryptically. "But that reminds me. All three houses are now on heat oil rations, no exceptions. I'm talking Navy showers, and supplemental heat from wood. If we're lucky, we might be able to locate a wood burning stove."

"Uh, what's a Navy shower?" Heather asked.

Hoplite offered a response, "There are two types of showers. You, I'm sure, are quite used to the Hollywood variety. That's where you lollygag and leave the water on while you lather. A combat shower, or a Navy shower, is where you have enough water to get wet and rinse. They're about two minutes max and they're cold as hell." Carlos then turned toward Josh and stated, "In light of this new directive, I'd like to suggest shoulder length haircuts for the women, sir."

"You didn't date much, did you?" Heather asked rhetorically as she playfully and seductively ran her fingers through her new non-regulation hair. Seductively she added, "Maybe you just weren't showering with the right people, Captain Rayna."

The man sat and stared transfixed.

"Heather!" Brent boomed. "That's enough! These men are here on orders from the President. They have a job to do! They don't need you enticing them with –,"

"I'm sorry," she replied as she interrupted her grandfather. "I must have missed the part where you lied to me for twenty-seven years… and I'm sure I've *completely* forgotten that I'm a grown-ass women capable of making her own damn decisions!"

Her grandfather grumbled and muttered under his breathe for a moment, but relented.

Dallas leaned over to Hoplite and quietly said, "Better to keep your eyes, and your thoughts, on your work, son. The 'Old Grunt' is liable to rip off your head and shit down your neck."

"If you two are done with your verbal grab-ass…" Sam directed at Heather and Carlos. "I thought I'd continue."

The pair immediately straightened up.

"Good. Now, as for the farm, the Tin Hatters along with Heather, Layla, and Katherine, they will remain here and continue their various tasks and canning operations. Basilia is set to join them once she's inventoried all of the medical supplies from her office and the three houses. Juan and his sons, along with any volunteers, will take down the designated greenhouse bays and reassemble two of them at Josh's assigned location near the cabin. The remaining bays are to stay in place and functioning until the last of the crops are harvested.

"Chester," she continued as she turned.

"Yes?" he replied as he started listening in earnest.

"You'll oversee the movement, placement, and disbursement of the battery banks currently housed in the greenhouses. All deep cycle batteries are to be divvied up and placed, along with an appropriate amount of solar panels, at each of the three houses. Once the greenhouses are moved, you, along with Juan, Jesus, and Abelardo get on horseback and begin removing all of the previously identified remote DOT panels as well as those noted on the railroad maps. These collectors will be used for barter or for distribution to locals for communication and recharging purposes."

"Umm, I have a suggestion," Lily said as she raised her hand slightly. "Alysin and I could go on horseback and handle the solar panels on the railroad lines while they handle the greenhouse tear down."

Sam looked at Josh who merely nodded his approval. His fiancé turned back at Lily and an expectant Alysin and smiled warmly.

"Alright, you two handle the rail line panels."

Addressing the group as a whole once more, Sam continued.

"Lastly, Josh, President Sarkes, Special Agent Monahan, Hoplite, Lieutenant Stokes, and Engineering Team Four are taking the three deuce and half's, once they are emptied of their existing contents, and heading back to Columbus and procure as much as humanly possible from the Defense Supply Center (DSCC). Sarkes has already called SecDef Fielding and made him aware of our various needs. They are expected back here shortly after nightfall."

Josh looked at Sam expectantly.

"Now I'm done," she offered.

"All right people, let's get to it," he said as he pushed off from the table.

"Not so fast," Hoplite started to say.

"Walk with me, Captain," the former Officer replied cutting him off and dismissing the others with a wave. He and Samantha met in the doorway as they both headed toward the kitchen.

"Are you okay?" he asked her. "I'm sorry for cutting you off. I thought everyone knew their responsibilities. It seems you desired a more thorough briefing."

"Sorry. Old habit from the Air Force. I think I'm just nervous about Aunt Jenny. What if she doesn't want to come? On top of that, I'm crampy."

"Phew!" Josh said emphatically. "I was worried you might be pregnant!"

Sam playfully punched him in the gut. "Once we are home, we should go and get the Reverend to perform our wedding ceremony. There's no school schedule to conflict with anymore. Then maybe I can show you where babies come from."

Josh smiled. "Works for me!" he declared. Wrapping her in a tender embrace, he softly kissed her forehead and said quietly, "Be careful."

"You too," she replied and then grabbed the back of his head and made a show of kissing him. Once she broke the embrace and felt he was thoroughly embarrassed, she said, "See you tomorrow."

In an effort to show it didn't have the desired effect, he slapped her loudly on the butt as she turned and headed toward the door.

"Dad!" Layla admonished him.

"What? She started it," he replied playfully as he shrugged.

* * *

Josh reached into the kitchen and grabbed the two pocket sized notepads he had placed there prior to the impromptu meeting. Hoplite followed him out of the cabin and continued as they headed off into the woods. After several hundred feet, they made the turn onto a game trail and began working their way down the hill toward the creek and the railroad tracks. The pair spent ten silent minutes just walking through and climbing over downed trees and limbs until they abruptly exited on to the gravel bed of the Norfolk Southern railroad line.

"Here's your diesel, Captain," Josh said as he gestured up and down the line.

"What the hell," Hoplite replied in amazement. "How did you know this was here?"

"This train comes through here every twenty four hours. It passes my farm around 5:30 in the morning," he answered.

"What's on it?"

"Usually kiln dried lumber, fuel, and coal. On occasion there will be a handful of cars that are full of live ribeye and bacon."

"As in, on the hoof?" Hoplite asked as he smiled. "How many boxcars are on this thing?"

"Typically there are around a hundred or so. Generally there is an equal mix among the three primary loads. Wanna take a look?"

"Absolutely!" Capt. Rayna responded as Josh handed him one of the two little notepads he swiped on his way out of the cabin.

"You go north, count up what you see, and take notes. I'll head south and do the same while I try and find the engineer or conductor. If there are any hogs or beef cattle on here, let me know. We can get the ramps and trailers and move them up to the fields. We'll save a few of the pigs, but we'll probably set most of 'em free."

"Why would we do that? What good would come from that?"

"Well for one thing, assuming there are any, we don't have the feed for all of them. The cows I can turn out into the pasture or barter a side of beef. If we turn most of the ham out, they'll find mates and cross bred with the boar in these parts. After a couple of generations, depending on a how many are harvested by hungry travelers and locals deeming them a nuisance, we will have increased the wild population two or three fold."

"Did you just sit in that cabin of yours thinking up this stuff over the years or what? Gregg might be right, maybe you are a savant."

Josh laughed. "Farmers, by nature, are the original survivalists. If it doesn't serve a purpose, you don't need it. Overly expensive material possessions are generally out of reach for most of us. You just have to make do with what you've got and what you can afford."

"How much did you earn as a farmer, if you don't mind my asking."

"Before the greenhouses, we were just making do with the sale of wheat. We aren't a large operation with thousands of acres so the profit margin was infinitesimally small.

"Ballpark it," Hoplite said.

"Figure an average of fifty bushels per acre. Multiple that by a hundred acres, and then multiple that again by an average of eight bucks a bushel."

"Forty grand," Hoplite replied.

"Now take away the cost of fuel, seed, organic fertilizers and pesticides, and labor. That'll run ya an average of fifteen. So now you're down to twenty five grand. Thankfully, that only lasted about two years before the produce company approached me. After the greenhouses were built, we were able to remain steady at a shade over six figures, but that was only because we diversified. We still had to subtract all of that other stuff for the wheat operation plus now we had the hourly rates of any workers we employed in the greenhouses. In the end, it worked out to about sixty."

"Technically, you're down to fifty four after if you deduct six grand a year on preps. That's assuming you spent the full five hundred dollar allowance you set aside each month."

"Captain Rayna was paying attention *and* is apparently a math major! Well done, Cap'n," Josh replied jokingly. "There were some pretty lean years in there too. Hard winters followed by horrible springs. It's a tough living, but you do your level best and pray you don't need a government subsidy or have to take out a loan against your land. We maintain all of our machinery meticulously and carry spares of what we can. We survive by being *prepared to survive* is the best way to put it."

"What about the solar panels, windmill, and battery banks? The EMP protection for the pumps?"

"Why do I feel like I'm being interrogated, Captain Rayna?"

"Oh, I'm not. I'm just curious is all," Hoplite quickly replied. "I've never told anyone, but I was looking into getting out of the Army before all of this. I've seen and done my fair share of nasty shit on several continents over the years. I've been in and out of the sandbox so many times I think I lost count. I'm jealous actually. Just looking at what might have been... that's all."

Josh was surprised by the candor, but didn't feel the need to question the man's assertions or credentials. Anything Hoplite said was already verified through conversations with Gregg, his former subordinate.

"Do you have any family you want to try reach? I mean, after we get back from DSCC," Josh asked and then clarified.

"Nah, my dad split shortly after I born and my mom died a few years ago. It was just me and her. I don't have anywhere else to be," the man answered reflectively.

"Well, you're welcome to stay as long as you like. Now let's count these cars. I'll tell you about the other stuff on the hike up the hill."

# Chapter 5

Juan walked Gregg, Samantha, and Emily around the exterior of the truck and pointed out its various attributes and deficiencies. When the two men went all 'gear head' on the woman by checking fluid levels and yammering about the engine underneath the open hood, Em pulled Sam aside.

"Hey, Sam, as one of your bridesmaids, I think it's my duty to ask you something."

She cocked a weary eyebrow in response.

"First off, do you have a dress? If not, it might be a little late."

Sam smiled, "Actually we picked one up a few weeks ago when we went to visit. We're picking it up along with Aunt Jenny."

"Look at you, you little planner," Emily replied. "And the shoes?"

"Those too."

"How about the wedding bands?"

"We got all of it, Em. Unfortunately, everything except for the rings is in Springfield." Sam could see that the questions were just a pretense for something else that was bothering her. "What's really on your mind?"

Then her friend delicately asked what she really wanted to know. "Josh sure has been at this a long time."

"At what?" Sam answered casually in an effort to get to what she really wanted to know.

"I mean, he had us validate all of those lists and all of that stuff. It's almost like he knew this was going to happen. Maybe not this exactly, but –," she started to continue before Sam raised a hand and she stopped.

"I know, I know," she said sounding exhausted by the topic of Josh and his preps. "I asked him about it when it was just he and I out here, this was before the Congressional Hearings and Javy Dolbrow. That's when he took me in to his office and for the first time in my life I finally got it. He showed me all of the research he had done and told me that when he bought the farm and moved the girls out here, it was for their safety. But, there was more to it than that.

"He explained how everything was interconnected. Trade, money, technology, all of it. Global commerce is both a blessing and a curse. I'd spent so many years in the Air Force that I'd become insulated, to an extent, from the wild throes of the world around me. Suffice it to say that, in actuality, he was wrong. He thought it would be a financial crisis that would be our undoing. He could never have dreamed of this scenario. Regardless though, the man is a certifiable pack rat!"

"Well, he's damn giddy about it," Emily countered. "I think he's the only one out here that seems to be enjoying himself."

"Yeah, I've noticed that too," she replied casually trying to keep the conversation light. "Don't let his exuberance fool you though. He knows what's coming in terms of the toll on American lives. He's just happy knowing that he has his family and friends around and knowing they are safe and out of harm's way."

"And the fact that he's getting remarried," Emily stated with a smirk.

"Well, there's that too," Samantha answered as she reached out and the pair hugged.

As the two separated, Em added, "Oh, you can give my Diva Cup's to someone else. I don't have the internal parts anymore after the cancer scare."

\* \* \*

As Josh and his group headed toward Columbus and the DSCC, he stopped the convoy in McArthur to speak with Sheriff Watson. The man was sitting at his desk reviewing files by the filtered sunlight of the window.

"Hey, Jim," he said as he entered the man's office. "Do you have a minute?"

"Close the door," he answered without looking up. He finished reading through the stack of papers, shuffled them back into a neat pile, and pushed them aside. "What's up?"

"I'm guessing you noticed the light show this morning. The power won't be returning any time soon. I thought you should at least know that much for certain."

"I figured, what with all your subtle clues of late. Care to provide an estimate on its return?"

"Ballpark? Couple of years," he answered matter of factly.

The small town lawman sighed heavily. "Can't do anything about it now, but you came to see me. What's up?"

"It's simple, really. I would 'suggest' that you post deputies at the banks, gas station, and grocery store."

His friend furrowed his brow and Josh reminded him that the residents had made a half-hearted run at some of the banks and credit unions in town after Rayburn's radio broadcast. He explained that with no power, and with the town still gripped by winter, people would panic. They *would* test the system just to see what they could get away with.

"Plus, the presence of uniformed officers has an added incentive of discouraging price gouging by unscrupulous managers and cashiers looking to make a quick buck."

The Sheriff chuckled. "But we have such fine, upstanding, and law abiding citizens, Josh... folks like yourself. I shouldn't need to worry about that," Jim said sarcastically. "Actually, I was just going through the rap sheets of my usual suspects to try and get a gauge on what kind of depravity these idiots have."

"Well, with no power and very little transpo available, I think you can safely assume that the drug traffic from Meigs County will cease and the meth houses in the area will be closed for business."

"Honestly, that's what troubles me. When these folks start going through withdrawal, it's gonna be hard on all of us if they decide to do anything stupid to try and satisfy their urges. The ones with meth-mouth are easy enough to spot and keep an eye on."

"I'm sorry?"

"Yeah, they look like they have a mouth full of rotted teeth, if they have any left. Plus they're skinny as a rail, not a lick of fat on 'em, and they can't seem to stand still for very long. Always shifting around and looking over their shoulder."

It was Josh's turn to sigh.

In the end, the Sheriff heeded Josh's warning. In so doing, he prevented the town from consuming itself in the panic that might have erupted.

\* \* \*

By 3:00 PM, the three deuce and half's had lumbered up Route 33 and made it to the outskirts of Columbus. The engineering platoon was as surprised as everyone else when the engines cranked right up earlier in the day. For all of the shortcomings of the diesel hulks, the power plant was still just as basic as ever. The onboard radios and upgraded dashboard electronics were toast, but the Detroit motors purred all the same.

As they approached the I-270 outer loop for the city, the unofficial convoy began seeing the first of the abandoned cars. They had seen maybe three or four on the rural roads, but now pockets of vehicles, five, six, seven deep, were grouped together where they had stalled. The drivers at least had the wherewithal to put them on the shoulder of the road.

"What do you make of that," Sarkes asked from the cab of the lead vehicle.

"Nothing for now. Just some unlucky souls caught on the road when it went off." Josh squawked his radio and said, "Changing lanes. Abandoned vehicles on the right."

The driver whistled as he drove by, "Brand spanking new Mercedes S-Class. Bet that guy's pissed beyond all get out. As for your previous comment, everyone is still dazed and confused. That's why we're doin' what we're doin' when we're doin' it. The people driving those probably walked to a gas station asking about a tow. In about a week, I would have crossed the median and floored it thinking it was possibly an ambush."

"You really think society will turn on itself like that? That quickly?" Sarkes asked.

"Our society is inherently broken, sir," Josh replied. "You saw New Orleans after Katrina. You've seen the violence from the far left when they don't get their way. This country has been one lit match away from a second Civil War for some time."

"Yeah well, Katrina was shocking to say the least... and only four years removed from 9/11 too. We're Americans. Americans aren't supposed to don't do that. We rally together when times are tough," the former President responded plaintively. "The America I know at least."

His driver didn't reply with words, but the snorted sigh of a chuckle told Sarkes all he wanted to hear.

Unable to let it go and wanting an explanation, Sarkes said, "You and you band of merry misfits don't seem willing to see society fall apart."

"That's because, for better or worse, we are all of similar mind when it comes to certain things. Don't get me wrong; you and your eight years in office did a great deal of good. Hell, I voted for you... twice."

"I'm sensing a 'but' in there somewhere, Josh," the President replied.

The driver smiled and nodded. "There is still a whole lotta distrust and resentment towards Congress, the Executive Branch, and for the policies and civil liberty redactions Washington tried cramming down our throats for years. Why do think we bought, sold, and traded guns without the involvement of FFL dealers? Because none of us believes that it's the governments business to know what we have in our gun safe. Have you considered why so many people started living off-grid and took to the homesteader lifestyle? Because the common man got tired of their paychecks being eaten away by higher taxes to pay for government programs we didn't want in the first place.

"That's not to mention the federal regulatory crap for the utilities that they so graciously passed on to us, the consumer. They still made their millions and billions, but we got stuck with the bill... twice. Those people on 'The Hill' stopped listening to their constituents a long time ago. Even with your Amendments, we saw from the Congressional Hearings that the people supposedly governing our country were just as corrupt as ever."

"I swear, nobody ever seems to vet this crap through before you propose it or sign it into law. Shall I go on?"

"No, son. I think you made your point."

"Dang," Josh replied somewhat jovially. "I had a whole spiel about the trampling of states right and the lack of border security. You sure you don't want to hear about that?"

Sarkes shook his head 'no'. "I would be interested in hearing your ideas for fixing it though. Assuming there's even still a functioning government."

"Oh, that's short and sweet. Try enforcing the Constitution. That would solve about ninety-five percent of the citizenry's discord. We can delve into the meaning of that a little deeper later tonight. Right now we need to concentrate on getting in and out before everything goes haywire."

Josh paused to take in the man's demeanor after his last comment. He detected a hint of smile. If he didn't know better, Sarkes looked as if he was looking forward to the possibility of a policy discussion.

To change the subject, Josh added, "Look on the bright side, sir. We were able to at least reach the POTUS. Beyond that, no one fired back at us and the Russians spared the European and Asian continents from a similar fate."

"Yeah well, after you guys finished your 'kid in candy store' routine with the SecDef, Rayburn told me that the Russian's salvation of Europe might devolve into a full blown curse."

*  *  *

"Turn right at the next corner," Sam directed as she provided the navigation to her aunt's house. Gregg did as instructed.

"It's the fourth one on the left," she added.

"Got it," he replied.

"How far are your parents from here, Em?" Sam asked.

"About ten or fifteen minutes. They live close to the university. Mom's been teaching in the Science Department there for years. Dad's law office is downtown though."

"You don't think he's down there do you?"

"I doubt it. He doesn't even walk the golf course anymore so he definitely didn't hoof it down there."

"Uh, Sam?" Gregg asked interrupting the two. "Do you know this guy coming out the front door?"

Samantha quickly glanced up to see her aunt's caregiver exiting the home. The African American man was dressed in a freshly pressed Navy enlisted service uniform.

The uniform took her aback, but she replied, "Yeah, that's Mr. Bloom. He's supposed to be here, but I have no idea why he's wearing that outfit though."

Gregg pulled the beat up farm truck into the drive and shut off the engine. Sam was the first one out of the vehicle.

"I had no idea you were in the service. Neatly pressed, boards in the right place, and Chief Petty Officer to boot too," she said as she approached.

He didn't return her gaze. He looked ashen and slowly sat down on the front step.

"Carlton?! What is it? Where's Aunt Jenny?" Samantha asked mortified.

He didn't answer.

After receiving no response from her aunt's caregiver, Sam bypassed him on the porch and flew into the house calling her name.

"Aunt Jenny!" she screamed as she searched room after room.

"She didn't make it," he said in an almost imperceptible whisper.

"Oh no!" Emily gasped as she covered her mouth.

Gregg and his wife took in the man's demoralized state for a few moments before Em asked compassionately, "What happened?"

"I had just finished pressing my uniform and the house went dark. Then… then I saw the lights in the sky. Damn it!" he exclaimed. "I knew what it was, but I didn't want to believe it. I promised Miss Jenny I'd let her see me in my uniform on the anniversary of her late husband's passing. He was Navy too. I do it every year. I finished getting dressed with a flashlight and got in the car, but it didn't start, nobody's would. All of the porch lights, street lights... everything was out. The whole town was pitch-black in the blink of an eye. Ain't never seen it that dark in Springfield before."

"So how did you get here?" Gregg asked.

"Had to walk. Wasn't anything else I could do," the man replied. "By the time I made it halfway I remembered Miss Jenny's medical file.

She had a pacemaker put in a few years back. Her heart wasn't strong enough, ya know."

Samantha exited the house with tears streaming down her face.

Emily ascended the front steps and wrapped her in a comforting embrace. "I'm so sorry, Sam."

Gregg gave the three a few minutes to at least try and reconcile themselves with their new reality before attempting to coerce his wife back in the truck. *We need to move this show along*, he thought. He didn't know what else to do or say, so he just waited patiently.

"Miss Jenny was the sweetest lady I ever knew," Carlton stated without prompting. Then he stood up and replaced Emily in the consoling. "Sam, I'm so sorry. There's wasn't anything that could be done."

"She went peacefully, right?" she replied. "I mean, this was because of her heart wasn't it?"

"Yes, ma'am. I doubt she even woke up. If she did, it was quick."

Sam released herself from Carlton's hug and wiped her tears. "You guys should go. It'll take me a few minutes to collect myself. If Carlton doesn't have any place to be, he can help me."

"Chief?" Gregg asked trying to seek confirmation.

"It's alright. I don't have a wife and kids waiting at home. I'll give her a hand," he responded. "Where are ya'll going, if you don't mind my asking."

"We're getting the hell out of Dodge is where we are headed," Emily's husband answered flatly.

Carlton looked longingly at the three as if desperate to tag along. He knew what was coming, whether he wanted to admit the full breadth of it right then and there or not.

Gregg surveyed the women's faces. There didn't appear to be any dissent. "Do you have a skillset we can use?"

"I was a Corpsman for a little over a decade. Will that help?"

"Hell yeah it will!" he answered enthusiastically.

His wife immediately shot him the look of temperance. The one she often flashed when he was being inconsiderate.

Recognizing her disapproving glare, he changed his tact to a more subdued, "I mean, yes, we could probably use that experience. Emily and I will go get her parents. We should be back by sundown. While we're gone, and Sam I'm sorry for having to say it like this, but go through the whole place top to bottom, out buildings too. Find any boxes, bins, and containers to put the food and anything else in. When we leave tomorrow morning, I don't think we'll be headed this way again. Once we return, I'll unload those three then take Carlton to his place for whatever he needs. Come on, Em."

As Gregg made his way toward Juan's truck, he added as an afterthought, "Oh, and make sure there is room to park this thing in the garage. Once we load and pack it, I don't want to leave it in the driveway with all of their belongings in it if we don't have to."

Gregg then turned to address Carlton specifically, "How far do you live from here?"

"Couple miles," he responded.

"Do you have much in the way of gear you need to bring?"

"Nah, maybe a few bags of what not."

"Okay, good. Once I drop of those three, be ready to go. Come on Em, Let's go get your parents."

\* \* \*

Emily's mother, Sonja, could barely believe her eyes when she glanced through the kitchen window. Before her she saw her daughter *and* her daughter's husband coming up the front walk hand in hand.

"My Lord! Emmitt, wake up! Emily and Gregg are here!"

Without the use of his car, electricity, or his phone, Emmitt Calhoun's original intent was to start reading one of the hundreds of books he had bought and set aside, swearing he was going to read it when he purchased it. But, as usual, he'd only made in through the first couple of chapters before he slid gracefully into his second favorite hobby, napping.

"How did they get here?" he managed to ask groggily, but still sound somewhat enthusiastic.

Emmitt exited the darkened family room to see his wife wrapped in the loving embrace of their daughter.

As he approached, his son-in-law stepped forward and offered a handshake, "How are you, Mr. Calhoun?"

"Cut the crap, son," the man thundered angrily. "What the hell do you think you're doing stepping foot in my house!"

Gregg slowly retracted his hand and took a step back not knowing if his father-in-law was joking or if he was truly angry enough to try and take a swing at him.

Emily quickly left her mother's arms and stepped in front of her father. "He came of his own accord to get you two out of here before all of these people start coming unhinged!" his daughter retorted. "Gregg has apologized to me for his repeated lies and I'm the only one he needed to apologize to."

"Em, I –," Emmitt started to say before she cut him off.

"Daddy, momma, I love you, and I'm telling you this with all of the love in my heart. We have exactly two hours to pack up anything you feel is of value and get it in that truck. There are sixty thousand people in this city and as soon as they figure out that the power isn't coming back on and that there's no rule of law, quiet college professors and pacifist lawyers are going to wind up dead in the street."

"How could you possibly know that, sweetie," her mother asked resolutely while smiling nervously.

"Because I told the terrorists how to do it, Mrs. Calhoun," Gregg answered. Then he turned to his father-in-law. "Sir, I understand that she told you I don't owe you an apology, but if it's all the same, I am sorry for not having trusted your daughter about my job description in the Army. Believe me when I say that she is telling you the truth now. We need to get the two of you loaded and back to a safe house on the outskirts of town by sundown."

"This is absurd!" her father thundered. "I've known these people forty years! Why wouldn't Springfield be as good as any other place?"

"Sir, if I may. You're a defense lawyer. I imagine you got some clients off of some pretty serious charges over the years. Murder, rape, burglary, attempted this or that, right?"

Emmitt contemplated the comment, but eventually nodded his agreement to the statement.

"None of those people are in jail because of your efforts. Now look at those same defendants in a world where there is no law, courts, judges, or police. What do you think they'd do in that scenario?"

He was dumbfounded. It took him more than several seconds to even process.

"I... I just... It's –,"

Gregg had had enough and wasn't going to debate the matter. He cut the man to the quick and said, "Sir, let me put it another way. If the two of you don't move your collective asses with some real purpose, I'm going to leave you here. And let me be even more clear. If I do leave you here, in a couple of days, after you've been bludgeoned half to death and watched your wife get gang raped right in front of you by one of your former clients, your last thought will be that you should have listened to your daughter and son-in-law."

"We've spent over forty years in this house. We can't possibly fit it all in that truck," Sonja said a little agitated after hearing Gregg's prediction.

"We're gonna pack five outfits for each season. Gardening clothes only for you, Momma. Daddy, while we're upstairs packing, you need to grab all of your hunting gear," Emily answered. She turned back to her mother and continued, "You get two suitcases a piece, that's it. Forget about things like your hairdryer and curling iron. Anything you have to plug in isn't coming."

Em was really on a roll now and quickly switched to her husband. "Gregg, after his hunting closet is emptied, you boys need to go and empty the wall safe of any documents, jewelry, and hard currency. And don't let him lie to you either. I know he has little silver bars stashed all over this house, not just in the study. Daddy, in the meantime give him the combination to the gun safe down in the basement. Anything of value needs to be loaded. We'll meet in the kitchen in one hour to review."

Her father was standing there blankly staring at the wall. He couldn't move. This was all just too much for him to try and process all at once.

"Emmitt!" Emily barked at him.

"Huh? What?" he answered snapping out of his catatonic state.

"The faster you come to grips with the fact that the electricity isn't coming back, the sooner we're outta here."

When he still didn't seem to be fully with it, she went to his go-to weakness. "All of your bank accounts have a zero balance. I'm sorry, but that's the way of it. Grab the stuff that can be used, easily repaired, or traded in order to survive without power. Now move it! We don't have a lot of time!"

"Heirlooms… picture albums," he stammered.

Emily sighed deeply and made a show of hanging her head. To her surprise, Gregg offered a compromise.

"How about we empty that old steamer trunk in the guest bedroom? Keep only the warmest blankets in there and use them as packing material. Wrap some of your more precious memories in those. Fair?"

After a moment of contemplation, Sonja replied, "I guess that'll have to do. Emmitt, get to work, dear."

# Chapter 6

The three vehicle convoy went through the concrete chicane without difficulty and approached the manned guardhouse. Josh and Sarkes quickly changes seats while the man casually began to visually inspect the undercarriage and the truck.

The Defense Supply Center of Columbus (DSCC) was one of three inventory control points for the United States Defense Logistics Agency. In short, if service men and women were being deployed, the Center was the place that was going to ship equipment. It didn't matter if it was as large as the Armored Brigade Combat Teams or a unit as small as Gregg's former Special Operation team, if someone needed gear; it was being funneled through an Agency operation. During WWII, DSCC became the largest military installation in the world. By the end of the war, it was housing munitions and making considerable contributions to the war effort due to its proximity to three major rail lines. It wasn't advertised, but it also eventually housed German POW's.

Without looking up at the driver, the guard raised his hand and said, "Manifest, please."

Sarkes looked down at the man and handed him his phone.

The former President had been blissfully unaware until that morning that his personal cell had been swapped out by Secret Service. The one he handed out the window was a replica with some distinct advantages. Least of which was the fact that it was hardened and connected to a secure high altitude orbit military communications satellite.

The guard stared at it and then looked up at Sarkes.

"What the hell is –," the Corporal started to say and then stopped himself when he recognized the driver smiling back at him. The man immediately went to attention, shifted the cell to his left hand, and saluted. "Sorry, Mr. President. We weren't notified to expect VIP's."

Having some fun with the role, Sarkes replied, "I'm on 'black op'. This never happened and I was never here."

"Sir?" he asked questioningly.

Unseen by the man's distracted gaze at the President, Capt. Rayna and Lieutenant Stokes approached quickly from the right.

"Stand at ease, Corporal," Hoplite barked as he neared. "We don't have a manifest," he said in a normal voice after he shocked him with the command. "However, what we do have is a direct line to the SecDef and 'Gardener'," the Captain continued and referenced the sitting President by his Secret Service codename. "As you can see, we have 'Ironside' with us. So, either take that at face value or call the current POTUS. You decide, but make it quick 'cause we are in a bit of a hurry."

The guard looked at the Captain and Lieutenant bars on their covers and then up at Sarkes. His decision was made for him when an ancient Willy's Jeep approached at speed. Two civilians hopped out and walked directly toward the security structure.

"That'll be all. Thank you, Corporal. You must be Stokes and Rayna. We've been expecting you."

The man entered the guardhouse and quietly shut the door. Still not believing what he was seeing, he decided to sneak a peek out from behind the closed miniblinds. The guard quickly stopped his prying when Lieutenant Stokes withdrew his sidearm and casually pointed it at the window.

Josh moved back into the driver seat and the three vehicles followed the Jeep to a remote warehouse not associated with the rest of the main buildings. The passenger got out, unlocked, and raised a large roll-up door. Once open, he motioned for the lead vehicle to drive inside.

Over the whine of the diesel, as he neared the civilian at the entrance, the man said, "Pull up to the red line."

Once the third vehicle was beyond the opening, the Willy's entered and the two pulled the overhead down. By the time the men made their way down to the trucks, all of the passengers from the deuces were standing there waiting for them.

Underneath the filtered light working its way in from the skylights above, the driver of the Jeep addressed them collectively.

"Okay, gentlemen. What are we into? I received a very frantic phone call from the SecDef telling me to give you whatever you need. And if I'm not mistaken, I'm sure I heard the President screaming at people in the background."

"What have you got that works?" Lt. Stokes asked. "Oh, and thanks for the trucks you guys sent to Rickenbacker. I really appreciated it."

"I'm still waiting for those to be returned, Lieutenant."

"Well, one of 'em is a burned out twenty ton paperweight and the others won't start. The bridging equipment works though."

"Seriously, you blew up my truck? Whadidcha do, use it for target practice?" the man said incredulously.

"Actually, a terrorist detonated himself with a suicide vest underneath it. Damn near killed a half dozen men," Rayna quickly answered. "They're in a burn unit right now and probably won't make it because of this morning's festivities."

"Oh, I'm sorry to hear that," the man stated and paused. "What can we do for you?"

"Well, that depends on what the SecDef had to say?" Josh asked.

The DSCC administrator gave a wry smile and answered, "I believe I am quoting him accurately, 'If it starts and they have a driver and need it, they take it. If it fires and you've got ammo for it, it's theirs. Anything else they need, give it to them'."

"Excellent. These guys each have their own wish lists, but I'm curious as to whether or not you have some eight inch howitzer shells? High explosive (HE), rocket assist, or anti-personnel, whatever's laying around" Josh stated.

"Where'd you get a Howitzer!" Hoplite interjected surprised at the request.

Smiling, he answered. "Motts Military Museum in south Columbus has an 203mm M110A2 self-propelled howitzer. That's a Vietnam era weapon so it'll probably still work after this morning. Our Sheriff trained on it before they decommissioned the hardware. If they have some shells, we can set that thing up twenty miles away and fire at will. Whoever we're shootin' at will never know what hit them."

"Who are we gonna be shootin' at?" Hoplite questioned.

Josh smirked.

"I don't think you boys have a full appreciation for just how sideways this country is about to get given the EMP blast this morning," Josh answered. "Just as soon as the bad actors in these major cities figure out that the rule of law blinked out of existence at 5:30 this morning, you can bet your bars that the proverbial shit is most certainly gonna hit the fan."

"So that's what it was? An EMP?" the DSCC official inquired.

Josh nodded.

"Sounds like you boys are about to step in it pretty good, but you have a problem," the man stated. "The young Lieutenant here just said that the M1070 HET's (Heavy Equipment Transporters) we sent to Rickenbacker were toast. You'll have to either swap out all of the electronics to get one running or you'll have to drive the M110 wherever you need it under its own power. We don't have anything here that works that can pull it. It's a twenty eight ton piece of hardware, son, and that deuce has a rated towing capacity of about five tons."

"We've got the fuel and we can move it at will if necessary. The question is, do you have the shells? Oh, and we'll take replacement electronics for the HET's, just in case," Josh replied with a smile.

* * *

Darkness was starting to creep its way into the mountains of West Virginia when Dallas came around the bend and saw the eighteen-wheeler on the side of the road.

"Might as well see if he needs a lift too," Brent said.

The trio had attempted to 'ride the rails' to Wytheville, Virginia on the patchwork of railroad lines Josh had laboriously mapped out over the years. Everywhere they turned, no matter what line or alternate rail system they tried to navigate, they were seemingly thwarted at every turn. Given the detonation time of 5:30 am, no one would have guessed that the EMP had stopped as many of the diesel locomotives as it did. Up and down the eastern seaboard, long haul freight blocked nearly every attempt to stay off of the roads. Needless to say, the narrow rail network cutting its way over, around, and through the Appalachian Mountains wasn't an enviable place to make a U-turn.

Having had their fill of hairier than expected travel, the three opted to get off of the rails and use the much faster I-77 corridor. Here, the detonation time seemed to work in their favor. Aside from making excellent time given the un-enforceable speed limit, only a handful of stranded truckers and hard charging sales reps were encountered. Upon picking up their first lost soul, James moved to the bed of the Hi-Line vehicle with the trucker in case anyone got any bright ideas.

When the stranded trucker removed his concealed pistol in an effort to get more comfortable atop the luggage, the former Marine quickly drew down on him. From then on, all would-be passengers were asked to turn over any side arms. The weapons would sit in the cab of the truck until they disembarked. Surprisingly, many of their passengers asked to be dropped at the closest exit where there was some form of civilization. Only a few were willing to take the humanitarian gesture as far as it went south.

As Dallas approached the disabled semi, the driver door swung open too rapidly for his liking. He abruptly slammed on the brakes and squealed the tires on the pavement. When he saw the double barrel shotgun being aimed in their general direction, he threw it into park, exited the vehicle, and took cover behind his own open door.

James jumped down from the bed of the truck with his weapon leveled. He quickly pressed his back against the sidewall of the trailer and waited for the hand signal from Dallas.

His friend observed the cab for several long moments. When there was no movement or change in direction from the business end of the double barrel, he motioned James onward.

The large man began inching his way forward. "We mean you no harm," he said commandingly. "We can offer you safe passage as far as Wytheville, Virginia if you are so inclined. If you are not, please close the door to your rig and we will be on our way. If you would like to come with us, aim your weapon skyward, exit slowly, and keep your hands visible at all times."

"How do I know you're not here to try and take my load?"

James and Dallas stole a glance at one another. Female truckers weren't unheard of; they'd just never met one. The pair shrugged at each another in an effort to reply, 'what now?'

This was unchartered territory for them. No traveler had pulled a gun on them throughout the course of the day. The husband and wife driving team they had picked up earlier wanted no part of a shootout on I-77, but they damn sure didn't want to walk to Wytheville. Instead of jumping out and making a run for it, they pancaked themselves as low as they could into the bed of the truck and started piling luggage on top of themselves. The other passenger sat huddled up against the front of the bed, praying that the third man in the cab, and the body of the vehicle, would be enough to stop the slug or buckshot from the shotgun.

Without warning, their remaining passenger exited.

"Ma'am, my name is General Brent Howard. You have my word as a Marine, and a Christian, that these men and I are honorable people. No harm will come to you or your load as long as we are standing here."

The scared driver slowly poked her head out.

"How do I know you won't get me in the back of that truck and try and deflower me once we're on the road?" she asked somewhat authoritatively.

"I guess you're gonna have to take a leap of faith. We can drive you as far as Wytheville if you want or you close the door and we'll be on our way. The choice is yours."

"How do I know you're really a General?"

"More faith, I guess," Brent replied.

After several quiet tense seconds, the feminine voice said, "My brother was a Marine."

"Well then I like him already," the retired Four Star answered noticing that his compatriot was continuing to inch his was toward the cab.

"He died over there."

"Oh, I'm sorry to hear that. What was his name?"

"Sergeant Ernesto Mattone."

Dallas' eyes got as big as saucers.

James' filled with rage.

His best friend in the Marines had been Ernesto 'Ernie' Mattone and he didn't have any sisters! At the mere invocation of Ernie's name, the hulking man lunged forward, grabbed the barrel of the shotgun from the cab of the truck, and wrenched it from her hands.

He threw the weapon down, spun into full view of the open driver side door, and leveled his Sig at the young woman who was lying prone across the two front seats. She stared back at him in shock and disbelief. With tears starting to well in his eyes at the mere mention of his fallen friend, James grabbed her by the hair and pulled her out of the truck.

"Get your ass down here! Ernie didn't have any sisters!" he screamed at her. "Where do you get off using his name like that!" he continued as he pressed the barrel hard against her forehead.

"He was my step-brother!" she pleaded. "My father married his mother while he was deployed. He knew all about it. I was twelve. We were waiting for him to rotate home to have the reception with him! I swear it's the truth!"

"Bullshit!" he spat at her in his deep commanding voice.

"I swear," she said as she continued to beg for her life. "I have all of his letters to his mother in the lockbox in my sleeping quarters! Please!"

"I oughta maim you and leave you out here for these cracker *Deliverance* hillbillies for making that shit up! We were brothers!"

"James!" Dallas yelled as he approached.

"Sergeant Rooney!" Brent barked from behind him. "Stand down, Sergeant! Don't make me shoot you!"

The pronouncement of his name and rank in the practiced commanding tone of a General forced him to quickly turn. He rotated his head the other direction toward the sound of the original declaration. Two men, his friends, were directing their gaze and their as of yet unfired weapons at him.

Slowly, he retracted the Sig. For the first time, he saw the look of sheer terror on the woman in front of him. As he released his vise like grip on the clump of hair he had in his hand, she curled up into the fetal position right there on I-77, buried her face in her hands, and began sobbing uncontrollably.

No words were exchanged as he holstered his weapon. He abruptly turned, walked passed Brent, entered the cab of railroad truck, and slammed the door shut.

"What in the world was that!" the General asked Dallas as they approached the weeping young lady.

"James was the sniper providing overwatch for Ernesto's platoon as they worked their way through Falluja. He watched his friend take one in the gut. The insurgents left him there, alive, in the middle of the street. They used Ernie and his wound as frickin' bait.

"Every time someone in his squad came out to try and get him, they were hit too. After three hours and four dead, he was ordered to put his best friend down."

"Who was the idiot in charge that gave that order?"

"No idea, but he beat the holy hell out of him when he got back to the base," Dallas answered.

"Did he comply?"

"No, he refused the order."

"What happened? Did they get his friend out?"

"Not that day. Some FNG had the bright idea to launch a Javelin at the building the insurgents were hiding in. It brought the whole damn thing down on top of Ernesto. They found him under the rubble about a week later. After James cooled off and got out of the brig, he was offered a choice. Face court martial or retire. He already had his twenty so he retired."

Not realizing that the young female trucker was listening, she broke up their conversation when she asked, "Ernesto was going to bring that lunatic to the wedding reception to meet his new family?"

"For your sake, you better be telling the truth, young lady," Brent offered politely.

She wiped tears from her eyes and concluded, "It's in the letters. They were supposed to come home together on leave once their deployment was done."

"Can you show us this letter?" Brent asked as he helped her up.

The girl nodded as she opened a small door near the rear of the tractor and reached inside. She felt around aimlessly for a few seconds until she pulled out a biometrically locked pistol gun safe.

"I can't open it."

"Why not?

"Whatever disabled my truck fried the electronics on the reader," she explained.

The three stood there staring at the useless piece of electronic protection not really sure what to do with it.

"What your name," Brent asked reassuringly as Josh's oldest friend continued to inspect the box.

"Maria, Maria Sanchez," she offered.

"Hey," Dallas said as turned the small safe over in his hands. "When the lid is open, where does it latch, in the center, or off center, above this keyhole? I don't suppose you have the key?"

"Nah, I lost that some time ago, but it springs open once it reads my fingerprint. I believe it latches in the middle. My dad bought this for me."

"No disrespect, but you seem a bit young to be out here driving cross country," Dallas said as he walked back to the truck to retrieve some tools.

Brent and Maria followed suit as she answered him. "I'm twenty eight, but you could say it's in the genes I guess. I rode with my dad for years after mom died. It was just me and him on the open road until he met Anita, Ernesto's mother."

Curious, the three passengers had started to poke their heads over and around the side rail and cab of the truck. As they approached, the wife from the drive team asked, "What's your handle, honey."

Maria smiled at the sound of another female voice. "Sweet Miss Georgia, and you?"

"Really? We know you! We're the Shag Dancers!" she replied. Then she turned toward Brent and said, "General, we've been on the road with her for years. We've never met, but she's 'Okay' in our book."

Dallas started pounding the screw driver into the seam of the lockbox and distracted everyone from their conversation. The noise startled James and he thrust the door open. In a calmer, but still commanding voice he asked, "What are you doing?"

"I'm trying to," he said as he grunted between swings of the hammer, "Get this," another swing, "Thing open," another swing, "So we can prove," another swing, "You're a douche!"

His friend sighed. "You'll never get it like that."

Dallas stopped his pounding and looked at him. Without seeking an explanation, he removed the screwdriver he had managed to insert half an inch into the device and handed it over.

James took it, walked to the end of the truck, and placed it in the dirt on the side of the road. "Ya'll stand back."

Their large emotionally comprised man unholstered his Sig and put a round through the locking mechanism in the center. He then fired successive rounds through the lid at specific points. When the fourth round discharged, the cover bounced free and rested on the safe. Without saying a word, James picked it up and gave the two pieces to Maria.

The travelers just stared at him as he climbed in the back of the pick-up and sat down, slamming the door once more.

"Do you have anything in the rig you want to bring? Clothing? Bedding? Any food or water?" Brent asked

"Yeah, gimme a minute," she answered as she handed him a stack of letters and started heading to her open driver door. Dallas went with her.

The General turned and glared at the sulking hulk.

"Here," the General said as he offered the pile of letters to James.

The man couldn't take his eyes off of his bootlaces. Without looking up, James removed the envelopes from the General's hand and began reading.

"What the hell was that?" Maria asked quietly under her breath.

"That was his apology. Eventually, he'll form it into words. He and Ernie were close. They went through boot down at Parris Island together. Hell, it took him four years to tell me the whole story," Dallas answered.

"Let me guess, I'll really like him once I get to know him, right?"

"Something like that."

"So how did he do that?" she asked. "Pop open the box I mean."

"Oh, he made a lot of friends in the military over the years. He occasionally gets calls from a few of them. They usually want him to test gear and equipment for their companies. I would venture a guess that yours was a model he was familiar with."

Marie shrugged her acceptance of the explanation.

"Well, I won't hold you guys up too long, I don't have that much in my rig," she said and started handing Dallas bundles from the sleeping compartment.

# Chapter 7

Samantha heard Juan's old truck before it even turned onto the street. Without the ever present white noise from the surrounding world, the sound of a solitary vehicle on pavement traveled a good distance.

While the pair waited for the Chastain's and the Calhoun's to arrive, she and Carlton had efficiently packed all of Aunt Jenny's food into laundry baskets and cardboard boxes found throughout the house. Aunt Jenny was eighty-four years old and ate like a bird so there wasn't much to box up. It was apparent she loved her Ramen Noodles, mac and cheese, and spaghetti with pasta sauce though. In addition to that, the basement held a trove of vegetables the woman had canned herself. Once discovered, this caused Samantha to go on a hunt for the pressure cooker.

As they waited for the others to return, Sam was struck by what she saw around the house and surrounding area. Nothing in her memory aligned with the environment. She hadn't really noticed the changes when she and Josh had visited. With no children of their own, Samantha's aunt and uncle had been selling off the family farm for years as the pair aged. The national interest in farming, 4H, and FFA Clubs was replaced with materialism, urban living, and technology as the 'Big Ag' companies managed the unseen food industry for the American people.

What was telling to Samantha was what *wasn't* there. Gone were the endless fields of corn and soy, chickens, goats, and horses. The only thing Sam was able to reconcile to her childhood memories was the large oak tree in the back yard that held the tire swing.

As she and Carlton worked to get everything ready for the evac, they discovered Uncle Jerome's truck in the garage. The man had bought the old Ford F-150 in 1977 when it was top of the line and brand new. The odometer hadn't cleared sixty thousand miles yet. The family caregiver didn't even know it was there, but Sam had vague recollections of it. The pair had smiled at each other like mischievous kids as they climbed in and turned the key. Unfortunately, their exuberance was tempered by the amount of dust and cobwebs. When he tried to turn it over, nothing happened. It was apparent that no one had maintained it since the day Sam's uncle had died. A more direct secondary review revealed, in addition to the dead battery, cracking belts and hoses coupled with deflated tires. The former Navy Corpsman set himself to the singular task of finding spares and getting it running. The man spent the remainder of the afternoon attempting to complete that. Fortunately, farmers plan for the rainy day they hope doesn't come.

Emily swung Juan's truck into the drive and continued on toward the outbuilding. When the headlights illuminated the tailgate of the Ford, Carlton came out from behind the raised hood covered in grease. She put it in 'Park', shut off the engine, but left the lights on assuming they would turn off by themselves, just like her BMW. Em and her parents exited the bench seat as Gregg jumped down from the back.

Her husband had been relegated to the bed of the vehicle out of deference and respect towards his wife and the aging couple. He couldn't in good conscience put his seventy something year old in-laws under blankets while he and Em rode in the heated cab. Plus, he *wanted* to ride in back. As a result, he willingly accepted his wife's suggestion. Besides, from there, he was afforded a three hundred and sixty degree field of view and all of his Emmitt's long guns were packed. It only made sense for him to provide the covering fire if it were needed.

"Mr. and Mrs. Calhoun? I'm Samantha Jameson," Sam said as she introduced herself to the pair and brushed dirt off of her clothing. "Come on inside."

Gregg came up the side of the truck shaking his head. He opened the door, reached in, and pushed the headlight knob in. *Old habits die hard*, he thought.

"What have we got here?" he asked as he approached Carlton and the open garage.

"Sam and I found her uncle's Ford out here when we were looking for stuff to stage. The battery is dead, and I already replaced some belts and hoses, but I figured I'd have a look at the rest of it. If you could give it a jump, maybe we can use it too. That is, assuming the tires hold air. We might be able to get some spares at the salvage yard on the way out tomorrow morning."

"Where did you find the light?" Gregg asked.

"There's a good sized toolbox over there in the corner," he answered as he nodded in its general direction. "He had this battery powered deal in there. The old guy never did have electricity run to this building."

"We definitely want to get that rolling toolbox loaded and take it with us if we can get this old Ford running," he replied as he began snooping through the garage using the headlamp he had scrounged out of Emmitt's hunting gear. As he came to the other side of the vehicle, he saw that Carlton had left the hand pump leaning against the truck.

"How long ago did you put air in the tires?"

The Corpsman raised his dirty wrist and looked at the time. "'Bout three hours, why? How are they doing?"

"They seem to be holding, for now. We'll probably have to refill 'em in the morning... given the night time air temps." As Gregg came around the vehicle, he finally got a good look at the man. "What the hell happened to you?"

"Grave duty. You didn't think we were gonna leave Miss Jenny in there… in her bed, did you?" Carlton answered and asked.

"No. I guess you're right. Buried her out back did you?"

"Yeah, we did that before we went through the house though. Afterword, Sam headed on out there. She was just sitting with her 'til you folks pulled in."

Gregg nodded his understanding. "Sorry you guys had to do that."

"Wasn't the first grave I ever dug and I know it won't be the last, not after today."

"I hear ya," he responded and then paused. "That's too damn depressing to talk about right now. How's the engine and carb look?"

"The oil, power steering, and tranny fluids all looked good. No metal in the transmission. The carb was a little gummed up so I cleaned that out. Hey," Carlton said as if he were remembering something. "Did you guys bring any gas cans back with you?"

"Yeah, why?"

"Miss Jenny's husband died seven years ago. Had to drain the tank. The tires are only our second highest concern. We ain't going anywhere without some fuel. How much you got?"

"About twenty gallons," he answered.

"That'll fill this beast up," Carlton replied as he pulled the hood halfway down. "Gimme a hand pushing this thing out of here. Let's try and give'r a jump."

With air in the tires, it only took minimal effort to push it far enough out. While Emily's husband was putting the F-150 into 'Park', the corpsman went back into the garage and retrieved the ether and cables. Juan's truck was pulled alongside.

As he attached and grounded the jumper cable, Gregg busied himself by pouring a gallon of gas in the tank. He wasn't about to dump a full can into something that might not even start. While he did that, he asked, "Did you guys find anything else useful?"

"Sam found his old double barrel ten gauge shotgun in the back of a closet along with a big ass muzzleloader."

Gregg whistled at the proclamation. ".50 cal?"

The man nodded.

"There's a man's gun for ya," he declared. "Were there any shells for the shotgun? Primers, powder, pellets, and rounds?"

"Yeah, all of that stuff was sitting on the shelf. Miss Jenny might rest a little easier knowing it didn't wind up in some strung out gangbangers hands," Carlton answered. "Hop in and try and start it. Let's see if all of this oil and grease on my dress uniform was worth it. I'll hit the carburetor with the ether just to be sure."

Gregg climbed in and the old shocks creaked under his weight. Out of habit, he put his foot on the brake so he could attempt to turn the key. *Idiot*, he thought and shifted over to the accelerator so he could give it gas if it happened to spin.

When he turned the key, Carlton gave the carb a quick shot of ether. Beneath him in the cavernous engine cavity he could see the starter belt jump into action and begin the herculean effort of turning the crankshaft. It didn't start, but all least they had juice flowing through the system. He tried a few more times. Each time he rotated the key, he could tell that it wanted to turn over. He could hear the engine become more and more powerful with each revolution.

After several unsuccessful attempts, Carlton came around to the open passenger window and asked, "What do you want to do? I'm not a mechanic so I'm out of ideas."

"Let's leave the cables on for a few minutes, put a charge on the battery, then we'll give it another shot. This bitch wants to run… I know it does," Gregg replied earnestly.

"Wait, lemme try something," he said as he turned and took a seat in Juan's truck and revved its engine a few times. After a couple throaty roars, he let it come back down to idle. He repeated the procedure two more times. Once he was finished, he returned to the F-150.

"What was that all about?"

"Beats me. I always see the old timers do it so I figured I'd give it a try. Hit it again."

The man shrugged and turned the key. The 351 modified big block engine coughed once then rumbled to life. Gregg slowly began depressing the accelerator as black acrid smoke began billowing out of the dual tailpipes. Every time he mashed on the pedal, the frame rocked side to side from the torque.

"What's going on out here," came an elderly voice from out in the darkness.

He quickly shut it down, exited the truck, and pulled his Glock. "Who goes there?" the Corpsman asked in a commanding tone.

"Carlton? Are you in there?"

"Mr. Barrington?" he answered.

"Thank Heavens! I thought it was a home invasion," the neighbor said in relief. "You finally got that thing working?"

"Oh yeah, she's just purring like a kitten," he replied calmingly. "Everything alright over there with you two?"

"We're doing just fine. She's madder than a hornet that she couldn't watch her game shows, but we're doing good. How's Miss Jenny doing? Is she okay? I didn't see her out and about today."

Gregg heard their new medic say 'damn' under his breath. *This guy's with the program. He knows we can't take everyone with us.*

"Oh, you know her, already turned in for the evening. She said me and my mechanic friend could tinker on Mr. Jerome's old truck. I was thinking about buying it from her. Sorry if we woke you."

"It's no bother. I'm just glad it was you and not some of those damn hoodlums. Have a good night."

"You too, Mr. Barrington."

The pair watched as the elderly neighbor shuffled down the street and entered his house. The soft glow of the moonlight glinted across the long barrel of his .44 Magnum as he swung the storm door open. They both swallowed hard. Neither had realized the man was armed with the hand cannon.

"Damn, that was close. Let's put these things in there and lock it up. I'll take the first watch. Get yourself cleaned up and grab something to eat. We'll swing by your place and grab your stuff at sunup."

The pair split up, started both trucks, and slowly pulled them into the out building. Gregg let the Ford run for a few minutes to try and put a charge on the battery. If push came to shove, they could jump it again in the morning. Thankfully though, the structure was more akin to a small barn than a garage, so there was plenty of room for both to be pulled in one behind the other.

Once the door was closed and relocked, he asked Carlton, "Why didn't you say anything to the old man?"

"Wasn't much point. Both of them are Type I diabetics and she's practically home bound. If they're lucky, they might make it a month or so depending on the amount of insulin they have."

\* \* \*

Josh backed the deuce and a half into his friend Bryan Billson's driveway. When the rear end was next to the gate for the backyard, he killed the whine of the diesel behemoth's engine. Before he doused the lights, he took in the sight of the empty lot where he and Amanda had shared a home and shook his head. It was nothing but a bare patch of dirt now.

"Thirty minutes and we're out of here," Josh decreed to Sarkes and Agent Monahan as he exited the cab and stepped down onto the asphalt driveway.

Before he even had a chance to knock on the door, Bryan was standing on the stoop holding it open. "I figured I'd be seeing you again. Come on in. Kristin and I are just about packed."

"What? Are you guys playing house now?" his old friend asked jokingly as he entered the dimly lit family room.

All of the blinds were closed, but the battery powered Coleman lantern was on low. It managed to illuminate a space that didn't look all that dissimilar from the last time he'd been in the home when the plane crashed. The chief difference in the layout was extremely noticeable though. The love seat had been pushed to the other side of the room up against the massive seventy-inch flat screen and accompanying built-in's. In its place, a building pile of toolboxes and electrician gear now stood guard.

"What the hell is all of this?"

"Hi, Josh," Kristin said cheerfully as she came down the stairs with a suitcase in each hand. "We knew you wouldn't leave us to rot in this affluent target of a suburb. When the alarm didn't go off this morning and the cars didn't start, we started packing instead of panicking."

"Uh huh," he responded as he crouched down and began picking mother boards, circuits, and testers off of the well-formed debris pile by the back door.

"Well, get a move on. Ya'll have thirty minutes and the clocks ticking. I've got a Secret Service Agent that thinks this was a bad idea and a nervous ex-President waiting in the cab."

"Really?" Bryan asked. "*The* President is in the truck? Wait. Sarkes or Rayburn or that socialist excuse for a Commander in Chief that preceded them?"

"Sarkes. Now quit yapping and start packing this crap up. We gotta go before the gangbangers get bored downtown."

"Oh, we've got more to worry about than those idiots. According to the chatter I heard on my HAM, the British have seized the Federal Reserve building up in Cleveland. They been emptying the vaults all day and loading it on their ship. I tried reaching you, but you weren't on."

"Mine's still locked up and protected. How'd you manage to keep yours up and running?"

"Please, I'm an electrical engineer. After your last little visit, you didn't have to tell me twice. I started swapping out parts and building a

Faraday cage the minute you pulled out of the driveway," Bryan answered.

"Pretty smart guy. I knew I always liked you," he provided sarcastically. "As for Cleveland, we already knew all about it."

Kristin and Bryan's eyebrows shot up curiously.

"Sarkes has been in contact with Rayburn so there isn't much we don't know about the Treasury building. That area is a burning wreck. The troops they had in place held for a couple hours, but then the British offloaded their heavy machinery and it was a slaughter." Josh then shifted the conversation to something they could control. "What about your boys? Were you able to warn them and get them out of Houston and New York?"

"I contacted them via email and told them to start getting someplace safe. Peter landed back in the U.S. a few weeks ago. He's with his mother in Sedona. George is with friends at a ranch in north Texas, and Callen's with his girlfriend and her family in western Pennsylvania."

Josh nodded and pointed at the pile. "So what's all of this?"

"That," he replied as he approached the hardware, "Is all of the stuff from my trunk and basement. I figured we might need to build some communication devices in order to distribute them to friends and neighbors... like the French during WWII. If I know anything, there's going to be a resistance and I'm guessing you'll be right in the middle of it."

His friend sheepishly shrugged. "Yeah well, I've kind of grown accustomed to my freedom."

"Josh!" Agent Monahan yelled from outside. "You better come out here!"

The three quickly exited the house to see the driveway filling up with former neighbors.

"Uh oh," Bryan said as he cleared the end of the parked behemoth and saw the phalanx of flashlights dancing on his driveway.

"Who's truck is this? Where are you headed?" a man asked in a cordial, but distressed tone.

From behind him, Josh stepped out and replied, "It's mine."

"Simmons? Where did you come from? Where'd you get this?" the neighbor wondered as he directed his beam.

"You don't need to concern yourself with that right now, Tim," Josh answered bluntly. As the crowd grew deeper, he knew these curious onlookers weren't going to just up and disappear without a satisfactory bit of information.

As a result, he hopped up on the front bumper of the deuce and addressed the gathering mass. "Listen folks, I know you're confused and seeing a running vehicle is just adding to it. I'm will tell you what happened and then I want you to disperse and decide what is best for you and your family."

Josh quickly leaned down and grabbed Bryan's shoulder. Quietly he whispered, "You and Kristin head into the house. I'll keep their attention on me. Load as much of your stuff into the back in the next five minutes. Go!"

Bryan grabbed Kristin's hand. "Let's move," he said and the pair discreetly disappeared behind the deuce.

"First, I see a lot faces that I know, but there are some new ones as well. For those of you that don't know me, my name is Josh Simmons and I used to live right there," he began and pointed to the barren patch of dirt across the street. "What I am about to tell you is likely to produce several reactions. Some of you won't believe me. That's natural. Some might be upset while others will become incredibly angry. Regardless, I'm not going to lie to you. However, I'm a rip the Band-Aid off kind of guy so it won't be sugar coated either.

"On December twenty fourth, the plane that crashed through your suburb was brought down by Iranian terrorists using something called a portable EMP device." Josh said this even though it had no real bearing on their current predicament. This statement wasn't for anything more than shock value, an attention getter. It was merely a piece of information that each of the assembled could quickly relate too.

"At 5:30 this morning, these same terrorists detonated a nuclear missile above the continental United States. The resulting electromagnetic pulse destroyed most, if not all, of our electrical and communication infrastructure. That means water, phone, power, gas, sewer, heat... air conditioning... everything... all of it... everything you knew, or that you thought defined your reality, has changed. We are going to have to reinvent this country from the ground up starting at a Pre-Industrial Revolution point in time. On the plus side, any debt you may have incurred has now been wiped clean. Sadly, any savings you squirreled away in retirement accounts has also been taken out. Those of you with precious metals, along with excess supplies of stored food and water, are ahead of the game. What you do from here on out, is entirely on you... and up to you."

There were several muted conversations starting, but the grumbling could be heard.

"Listen folks, let me finish. Given the wide scale nature of the EMP, I would not expect that any of the services you have grown accustomed to will be returned in the next nine to twelve months. That's a best case scenario. Now, knowing this, each of you is faced with a decision."

"What choice could we possibly have?" a man shouted from the back of the crowd.

"I'm getting to that. Please be patient. As I see it, this neighborhood has two choices. You can stay here in the relative comfort of your homes. However, spring isn't going to be here for a few more months so heat and food will be scarce."

Josh didn't want to 'out' anyone that may have stockpiled anything so he left his previous comment where it stood.

"Given that, I would recommend that families start doubling and tripling up in order to share resources.

"Also, at some point, you may be forced to defend what you have from roving gangs and marauders. If you opt for this, if you intend to stay, you need to begin planning your defenses, blocking access to the neighborhood, figuring out who owns what, and who *needs* what."

"What's the alternative, Josh," Tim demanded angrily from the front of the crowd.

"The other option is to flee. If you have an older car, it might still run. If you have bikes, pull behinds carriers, wagons, a jog stroller even, I recommend that you utilize these –,"

"Why can't we just ride with you?" a panicked mother asked with a toddler on her hip.

"Ma'am, we are unable to provide this type of assistance at this time. Believe me when I tell you that you do not want your children in this vehicle. All I am able to offer you now is information," Josh replied.

"Why not? What's in the truck?" came from the back of the crowd. "You said you weren't going to lie to us, but you won't answer a simple question?"

He sighed and mumbled, 'You're an idiot', under his breath. "You're right, I did. Currently, this vehicle is loaded with extra ordnance. These munitions are live and I cannot, and I will not allow any of you or your children to ride in the back until it is unloaded."

"What do you want us to do, Josh?"

*I know that voice.* "Bob, is that you?" he asked.

"Yeah, it's me. We'll catch up later. Why the bikes? What do you have in mind?" the man replied.

"Those of you that decide to flee, I am recommending that you utilize any and all forms of transportation that are available and strap on enough food, water, clothing, and any weapons that you might have. Use these means of transport to lessen your load. You'll make it further faster if you reduce the physical burden of having to carry some, or all of it."

"Where do we go? What are we fleeing from? I mean, *really*? This all just sounds like a bunch of Fox News scare tactics," a woman's voice he didn't recognize offered.

There were nods and laughs emanating from the audience.

"Oh, shut up you liberal hack!" someone barked at her. "You and your left wing Democratic Peoples Party of socialist Nazi's flushed this country right down the crapper! If the idiots in Washington had protected the grid when they had the chance we wouldn't be in this mess. Instead, they created a hand-out dependent nanny state while the Islamists were re-arming and re-grouping! It's the fucking VC and Tet all over again!"

"Whoa! Whoa! Everyone just calm down," Josh proclaimed as he raised his hands. "The people that did this want us to behave in exactly this manner. They need you turn on one another to succeed," he stated then paused. He audibly sighed at the fact that he was actually going to have to spell it out for them.

"Ma'am, I don't know you, but some of your neighbors here do. They can attest to what I am about to say. A number of years ago, both of my daughters were abducted during a home invasion. They were held prisoner for several days, drugged, and then one of them was raped. This event took place when we *had* a functioning judicial system and the rule of law.

"What do you think is going to happen to you and yours when the public servants don't report for work because they have to protect *their* family? What do you think life will be like when there's no police force, no fire, or EMS to call in an emergency? Now, imagine, on top of that, what do you think is going to happen when the medications for the psychotic, depressed, schizophrenic, and bi-polar run out? How do you imagine that's gonna go?"

The color drained out of her face as well as a number of others.

Josh paused and surveyed the crowd. Their stance coupled with the demoralized gazing at their feet said they were starting to understand. "How many of you are Buckeye fans?"

Just about every hand went up.

"Okay. Less than a mile from here are over fifty five thousand college students. In about three days, those that weren't smart enough to get as far away from campus and the downtown area as possible, are going to come looking for food. Where do you think they'll head first?

I don't know about you, but I can't hold off their offensive line on my best day."

Many of the residents had season tickets to the OSU football, basketball, hockey, and baseball games or graduated from the school and were avid supporters. Hitting them where they lived only served to drive his point home regarding just how vulnerable they truly were.

For any last minute doubters, Josh added, "The suburb of Upper Arlington was a target long before the power went out. When the gangbangers get bored tearing up high rises or run low on supplies, they'll head this way make no mistake. Towns like Bexley, Victorian Village, Grandview, and German Village too. All of these suburbs are perceived to be affluent and they *will* be targets."

"Listen folks, all that being said, I'm not here to scare you into doing one thing or another. I am presenting the facts as I see them. I'm leaving any and all decisions up to you. However, to answer your question, ma'am, to answer you more directly, Lake Hope State Park is currently being prepared to receive refugees. Those of you that choose to flee should head there. If you have an alternate location with family or friends outside of the cities and suburbs, then you might consider heading there. Does anyone need to know how to get to the park?"

Several hands were raised coupled with a few nods.

"Okay. I'll see you in a minute," Josh stated as he nodded in their general direction.

Before he could continue, Tim interjected, "That's over seventy five miles from here! How do you propose we make it there? On foot?

"That's specifically why I suggested that you load up your bikes and what not. You'll need at least three days of food and water for the trip. In addition to that, the group that decides to head that way should position men and women in the front and rear that are armed and prepared for whatever you may encounter. If you leave at first light, you could conceivably be well beyond the airport ten miles away and headed out on 33 South by lunchtime. The sooner you get outside the outer belt, the better."

He then addressed the neighborhood as a whole one more time. "I've given you all of the information I have. At this point I'd like to ask everyone to head home and begin preparing for the consequences of your decision. Either start packing or start defending. Pick one and get busy."

Josh jumped down from the front of the deuce as several people approached. Behind him he heard the driver side door shut.

"Nice speech," Sarkes said. "You sure you don't want to think about politics when this is all over?" he continued with a wry smile.

"Nah," he replied. "I'd like to keep my soul intact."

The former POTUS chuckled and then headed into the house to see about using the restroom. Josh busied himself by giving those who had already made their decision the directions to Lake Hope State Park. Many stated that they would head out immediately.

As they dispersed, Tim approached with several other men. "Hey, we heard what ya said, but I find it interesting that you never answered my question. The one I asked you before you set yourself up on high and started giving orders."

"I don't have time for this. Stay or go, I don't care," Josh replied as he began to turn away from them.

"Now hold on a minute," Tim continued as he pressed the issue and grabbed him by the arm. "You told everyone what *they* needed to do, but you didn't tell anyone what *you* were doing."

"I'm gonna ask you once, let it be," he intoned calmly, but inched his hand toward his Beretta all the same. "What *I* am doing and *why* is not your concern. Just leave it at that."

"Screw you, buddy! I'm not gonna drop it and I'll be damned if I trust a word you say! How about we thump you and *take* your truck. What do you think about that, asshole?" Tim responded as he tried to make himself look tough by cracking his knuckles.

*Here we go*, he thought.

From the shadows behind the men and the gathering storm, Josh saw a hand holding a weapon rise up and quickly come down on the back of Tim's head. The man crumbled to the ground in front of him. His friend's stood there staring at the huddled mass on the driveway wondering what had just happened. Before they could turn and see the assailant, a high intensity beam of light was directed at their faces.

"Gentlemen, my name is Special Agent Edward Monahan and you people are interfering with a national security matter. I'd love nothing more than to stomp a mud hole in your collective asses right now, but I've been hanging out with Mr. Simmons for too long."

Josh smirked at the remark, but the context and tone of the message had the desired effect. All bravado was sucked out of them.

"I'll be monitoring the comm chatter for this area. If I even hear a sniff, an inkling, that some dumbass has tried something like this, I will personally drive up here and shoot every last one of you sons a bitches! Do I make myself clear?"

The men swallowed hard and quickly nodded.

"Good. Now pick up this piece of shit. He's blocking my rig."

The three hurriedly struggled to grab Tim. After a few clumsy seconds, they managed to get a grip on their unconscious friend and started heading up the street.

When they finally turned and headed up the man's driveway a few doors down, Josh began laughing.

"Where did you come from?"

"I went around the other side of the house. Was standing across the street in case anyone got stupid. Good thing too," he replied as he handed him some folded dollar bills.

"What's this?"

"It's for the swear jar," Monahan stated as he turned back to him. "I think that Tim character might have actually taken a swing at you," he concluded.

Josh nodded his agreement, but started chuckling again.

"What?" the Secret Serviceman wondered.

"I've always wanted to do that to that guy. Where'd national security and comm chatter come from? Sounded like a movie. You went all Liam Neeson on them."

Agent Monahan shrugged and said, "Eh, I improvised."

Chuckling, Josh turned back toward the backdoor of Bryan's house and mumbled, "I have a specific set of skills…"

# Chapter 8

"That's it! I quit! If I have to can one more stinking tomato, green bean, or cucumber, I think I might just keel over!" Heather declared as she flopped into her father's easy chair. "I've got more burns and scalding marks on my arms than I care to count!"

"Oh, stop your whining, you big baby. You only had to do the water bath. The pressure canner is where the real fun is," Layla playfully jabbed at her sister from the kitchen as she continued to make tomato sauce.

While Juan and his sons were busy with the cows and pigs from the train, Josh's daughters, along with Basilia and the Tin Hatters, had been tasked with the canning of anything not already allocated to the root cellar. While the Martinez matriarch handled the kitchen in the cabin, Katherine was handling the Tin Foil Hat Club members at Three Sisters.

"Don't get too comfortable," Basilia called out. "Your jars will be done in a few minutes. After that, then you can rest. We need to be out of this kitchen before your father gets home. He needs to do whatever he does to make jerky and pemmican with the freezer meat."

Heather groaned at the pronouncement. "I know. I just needed to sit down for a sec," she groused. "I should have gone with Juan and your sons to bring the cows up from the train."

As if on cue, the Martinez men came through the front door. They were dirty and smelled like a stall that hadn't been cleaned in weeks.

When Juan and his sons began entering, Heather proclaimed, "Hey, guys, you're back! Did you –," she started to say before being suddenly overcome with their stench, she declared, "Good grief you guys! You're not supposed to roll in it?!"

"Cows are just another one of God's creatures, Señorita. They go whenever and wherever... sometimes it's on you," Juan replied."

"Oh, the poor little Hollywood star can't tolerate the fragrance of nature?" her sister continued jabbing from the kitchen.

Holding her mouth and nose under her shirt collar, Heather managed a, "Yeah, yeah," back at her. Returning to Juan and his sons, she asked, "Are all of those things up into the fields?"

"Si, finally," he replied. "I think we might have to distribute them around though. Either that or Patrón will need to lose some of his wheat acreage. The paddocks are only big enough to handle what we've got and maybe a few extra, but not eighty head. We'll talk about it when they get back, or in the morning. I'm actually looking for Katherine. Have you seen her? We had to borrow some of the other farmers and we owe them a side of beef in return."

"Our first bartered trade... a couple hours of labor for meat. Is it fair?" Heather asked.

Juan shrugged and replied, "Señor Simmons usually negotiates these things, but I think it is. Those cows were muy luca after being on that train car. A couple of their men got stepped on and kicked at a few times."

"Gimme a few minutes," she said as she went back to the kitchen. "Do you guys want something to eat?"

"Si, that's would be great," he responded.

"I'll be out in a few minutes with the food and then we'll go get Katherine together, she's over at Three Sisters. I want to see her breakdown a whole cow."

"Are you sure that's a good idea? You were not feeling so well on the mountain," Juan offered compassionately.

"That was my first time," Heather said with a wink. "Katherine's had me working on squirrels and rabbits after that. I think I'll be okay with the mess now."

"There's going to be a lot more blood and internal stuff with this, twice as much as a deer," the old farm manager suggested.

A chill went up Heather's spine; her confidence was waning at the thought of double the goo.

"I'll make do. I need to learn this stuff. In the meantime, you guys have to go back out on to the porch! You stink!"

\* \* \*

"Okay," Katherine said as she finished tying on her apron. "A cow is a pretty big beast so two people can easily work on it at the same time. I'll take one side and tell you what I'm doing while you handle the other. Are you sure you want to do this? You think you're ready?" she asked as she pulled her hair back in to a high pony tail.

Heather was dressed top to bottom like she was about to perform an operation with a machete. She was wearing a clear plastic face protector that practically went to her sternum, a black vinyl coated butcher's apron that went from her neck to her calves, and cut resistant gloves. She nodded her agreement as the cover rattled on her head.

Katherine, utilizing only her own apron as protection, had broken down numerous animals over the years. She had never really tried to teach anyone how to butcher anything larger than a deer, but the concept was the same. Apparently though, she now had an audience in the farm hands and a somewhat willing pupil in her older sister. Layla, she determined, was a lost cause when it came to this skillset. The pair didn't speak about it, but she suspected it was because she had witnessed her father's retribution in the warehouse.

"What is all of this stuff?" Heather said as she gestured toward the assembled implements lying between the two.

Katherine turned and started ticking off the supplies she'd thrown into the front-end loader. "Okay, so what we've got here is a gambrel. We'll need that to run through their back legs in order to hang it up, that's why I brought the tractor. Once we've cut most of the hide free, I'll install that, lift it with the tractor, and then we'll attach the skinning clamps to pull the rest of it off. Once we split her open, I'll try and get everything into the gutbuckets. The handsaw is needed for the head, chest, and sometimes the back legs."

"You're gonna cut off its head!" her sister exclaimed.

"Seriously? How many cow heads have you ever seen in the grocery store?" she replied as she put her hands on her hips. "Oh, that's right," she remembered. "You were tossing your cookies in the bushes when I did that to the deer."

Heather already looked like she was going puke.

"You gonna make it?" Katherine asked compassionately.

Heather nodded again and rattled her plastic visor.

"Okay, as I was saying, the handsaw is needed for several things. Mostly it's for the head and chest, but sometimes I need it for the legs. Occasionally, I can just break their back leg, but not every time. It comes in handy."

"So what's the chainsaw for?"

"That's my gas powered meat saw," she answered enthusiastically. When Heather looked as if she might turn another shade of green at the prospect, Katherine clarified. "Butchers have a band saw to process the carcass into sides and quarters, but we've never had one. I use this to cut through the spine and split it into halves."

"I hope you don't have regular bar oil in that thing," an older man stated.

"Oh, no sir," she immediately answered. "That would taint the meat something fierce. I've always added rice bran oil instead. It gives the chain the lubrication that it needs, but it's natural, not a petroleum based product at all."

Katherine picked up a piece of firewood she intended to use as a chock and asked, "Okay, which one did you guys pick?" to the assembled makeshift farmhands.

"Any of 'em's fine," their spokesmen answered. The man pointed a craggy gnarled finger and said, "They all look healthy and about the same size. Hell, they were headed to slaughter anyway so they ought to be good."

"You wanna 'knock' it?" she asked in return. "Or do you want me to do it?"

"Junior," he called out as he turned to others. "You got your .22 pistol on ya?"

"Yes, sir," his son answered.

"Go on out there and put down that one over there," his father instructed as he pointed off toward a straggler. "Remember, two inches above the eyes and a little off center."

"Yes, sir," the boy replied.

The stillness of the night afforded the crack of the weapon to travel unobstructed. Katherine didn't seem overly concerned with the unchecked noise pollution given the extreme remoteness of the farm, but the thought did occur to her.

"Alright, Heather. Grab the other chock and let's get to work."

\* \* \*

Shortly after 10:00 that night, the last of the military workhorse deuce and half trucks passed through the gate to the secluded property. The group had originally departed with just the three vehicles, but arrived home with eight. The only one that wasn't towing a trailer of some kind when it returned was being driven by Josh. The girls suspected something was afoot when he all too casually put the truck in the now emptied metal barn. The structure was the furthest from the cabin and Three Sisters as possible. As usual though, their father wasn't forthcoming with any details.

The first of the returning convoy had appeared hours earlier and by all accounts, had navigated the route unmolested. Captain Rayna and Lieutenant Stokes immediately had the men start staging the gear and equipment. The scout team had confirmed Josh's suspicions that the park was empty and the officers were as equally pleased to hear that the state of the cabins had been maintained throughout the winter. Come morning, the combat engineers would begin preparing for the influx of refugees from the larger cities and towns.

In their report, the advanced team had produced several ODNR generated maps of the park. There were a total of sixty-five cabins. Forty of which contained a wood burning fireplace. The lodge itself could house fifty residents easily. If those structures ever filled up, there were almost two hundred additional campsites scattered throughout the east side of the area. The laundry would need to be relocated with the possibility of a second to be constructed from scratch. There were negatives noted though. The terrain was extremely rugged and the sizeable water obstacle essentially split the park in half with a nearly equal amount of cabins on each side. This would make responding to a situation problematic.

The recommendation from Team Two was that all travelers be placed on one side until it was full. They also suggested that they forego the laundry and concentrate solely on the showers and latrines.

However, the strategic importance of the park's location could not be underscored enough. From the southern entrance of the park, the Moonville Tunnel and its buried cache of billions stood a scant five 'klicks' southeast. If they utilized the overgrown and barely perceptible hiking trail that following the old rail line, the soldiers could knock almost two kilometers off of the distance.

Once Josh and the President were back however, the pair had relayed the happenings in the neighborhood.

"Are there any other areas where we can relocate people?" Hoplite asked as the discussed their collective synopsis. "Are there any other parks nearby?"

Their host went to his hutch and retrieved a map of the Hocking Hills region. He, along with Lt. Stokes and Capt. Rayna began reviewing the paper once it was spread on the table.

"The first thing I see is one huge headache," Carlos said. "How many residents are in the towns of Chillicothe and Athens? We could possibly become the center of this Shinola sandwich."

"Twenty thousand in each, give or take. Athens is a college town and effectively doubles in size when the university is in session though," Josh explained.

"What about these, Fox Lake and Lake Snowden? They are between us and Athens," Hoplite stated.

"I don't think so," he replied. "Those are wildlife areas only, no facilities. There aren't any structures on those lakes. If we head there we'd need to build everything from the ground up."

"Okay, what's this off to the east? Strouds Run State Park? Can we use that?" Stokes asked.

"Maybe," Josh said. "But again, no cabins. There are campsites, latrines, and a couple shelter houses though. I haven't been there in years, but it might work in a pinch."

"That doesn't leave us many options, but who's to say we need to offer this stuff anyway?" the Lt. offered to the group. "I'm just playing 'devil's advocate' here. I mean, we aren't the National Guard. We are a combat engineering platoon with orders to observe and defend a stash of gold so the British don't get it."

Josh sat back in his chair and contemplated the comments. The man wasn't wrong. Why were they wasting all of this energy and expending what limited resources they did have on people that didn't have the forethought to plan ahead and think for themselves. Were they just providing this so that the transition from the technological present to the steam engine past would be less traumatic?

"The best answer I can think of right now, Lieutenant, is the Sermon on the Mount. Do unto others as you would have them done unto you, but your point is well taken nonetheless. However, I am also a strong believer in teaching a man to fish. We aren't going to be doing this for them. We are going to have them do this for themselves. Maybe we give them a push and a head start, help them to expand a previously dormant knowledge base, but they *will* learn a new set of skills."

He paused to let the rebuttal sink then offered a compromise.

"How about this, let's say we stick to 'Plan A' with Lake Hope. If it becomes too much, we'll circle back to plans 'B', 'C', and 'D' in Fox, Snowden, and Strouds later if the need arises."

\* \* \*

Dallas, Brent, and James dropped the stranded truckers off in Wytheville as promised. When Marie hopped out of the vehicle, James would have none of it. His scrawny friend took her aside and essentially translated for him. The man was still seemingly unable to form enough words to make a coherent sentence.

"Maria," he explained. "I think what the big lug is trying to tell you, is that he would like you to continue on with us."

"Why would I do that? He dragged me out of my truck by my hair!" she retorted. "He put a gun to my head! Brother's best friend or not, people just don't do that. That man needs help."

"They all do, Maria. Every single one of those guys who went over there came back changed in some way or another," Dallas replied compassionately. "To be honest, James still hasn't made his peace with what happened to your step-brother. Being ordered to commit fratricide stays with a guy."

Maria struck a less defiant pose at being reminded of the issue foremost in James' mind.

"As to your other points, yes, he did do those things to you. We almost had to put him down because of it. Regardless of his actions, I know in my heart that he's extremely repentant for that. I'm not quite sure you know just how much those two grew to depend on each other over there. When he gets control of his emotions, I can guarantee you that he will very eloquently state that because he was unable to protect Ernesto he feels honor bound to keep you out of harm's way."

Maria sighed and crossed her arms over her chest. "Where are you headed?"

"We own a Wilderness and Survival school out past Elk Creek, down along the New River. We'll be picking up some cached supplies and heading to southeastern Ohio in just a few short days," Dallas answered.

She continued to stand steadfast, but she didn't rebuke his offer.

"How about this," he pressed. "Why don't you stay with us until we are ready to leave? You'll be fed, sheltered, and protected. Decide then if you want to come back with us."

Maria contemplated the request and then eventually nodded her agreement.

The four said their goodbyes to the Shag Dancers and the other hitchhikers they had accumulated along the way. When the truck rolled through Independence, Virginia, they were taken aback to see that the large plate glass windows for the bank were boarded up and black soot streaks were visible above each. Grocery stores were being guarded, as were the pharmacies. The burned out building was evidence that the townsfolk did not receive President Rayburn's interrupted radio broadcast with open arms and a gracious heart.

Within twenty minutes of arriving at their property, the generator was humming along and Dallas' stilted river front home was awash in lights as he began packing. Most of his hunting clothes were already in a go-bag, but he couldn't just leave his fishing gear. His staging and continuous conversation with Maria was interrupted an hour later.

In a moment born out of habit, James had walked out onto his back deck and rang the cast iron bell signaling that dinner was ready. No sooner had he started the ringing, as he abruptly stopped and silenced the clapper. *Idiot*, he thought. *This thing can be heard for miles.*

For security, it was decided that the group would all stay in James' home halfway between the valley floor and the ridgeline. Throughout the evening, the normally affable and gregarious man was unable to look at the other three. He had threatened to kill one while the other two were almost forced to do the same to him.

After dinner, the generator was shut down and the lanterns were extinguished to conserve fuel. With the exception of some slow burning nine hour candles, darkness blanketed the region. The lack of ambient light from the distant towns afforded the group with the ability to observe stars and planets that had previously only been seen in books and planetariums. Maria excused herself from the star gazing and headed to her room after only a few minutes.

"Listen, James," Brent said. "I'm not going to sit here and pretend to know what's it's like to have to deal with Ernesto's death. However, in spite of that, what I am going to tell you is that you need to get your head out of your ass, get in there, and make amends."

The man shifted his gaze to his boots. "I don't even know where to begin," was all he replied.

"How about you start by saying you're sorry and see where it goes from there," Dallas offered.

James just nodded and turned to go inside. Eventually, he found himself standing in the darkened doorway of his guest room watching her read an old field manual by headlamp. After a few moments, he startled her when he quietly knocked on the partially closed door.

"Ma'am?" he asked.

Maria gasped at the sound and reflexively clapped the book shut.

"I'm sorry," he offered. "I didn't mean to scare you."

She reopened it and proclaimed, "We need to put a bell on you or something." Eventually, her heart rate began decreasing.

"Occupational hazard, I guess. I'm used to trying to *not* be heard," he replied as he pushed the door open and entered.

He slowly stepped forward and placed Ernesto's letters on the bed. "Here," he said. "You can have these back. I've finished reading them."

"And?" Maria asked.

"And it seems that Ernesto cared very much for you and your father. I am truly and unequivocally sorry for my actions today. I have no excuse. It would seem that I have not moved on from the events surrounding his death."

"Have a seat, James. Let's talk about the man we both called our friend," she answered as she accepted the olive branch.

The pair spent several hours crying, laughing, and recalling the life of Ernesto Mattone, their brother. At five the next morning, Dallas found the man sleeping on the floor under a blanket. Maria was on the edge of the bed under her own comforter. The two had fallen asleep holding each other's hand.

# Chapter 9

The day after the HANE, Samantha and the Springfield contingent returned with an extra truck and one added soul, Carlton Bloom. The giddiness with which Josh was approaching the creation of the communication centers was tempered by word of Aunt Jenny's death. Upon their arrival and hearing the news, a brief service was held and led by Alysin. From that day forward, the oddest of the Tin Hatters was tasked with handling all religious matters at the farm.

When a 'polar vortex', formerly referred to as an 'Alberta Clipper', barreled its way into the Midwest from Canada that night, the group was unable to sit idly by when they knew scores of Josh's former neighbors were trekking towards them. All eight of the deuce's were fired up and screamed up Route 33 looking for the refugee's encampment.

Once located, the trucks hauled as many people and possessions as possible with each trip until all were squared away in the cabins of Lake Hope State Park. Food, water, and firewood were waiting for them when they arrived. Josh was informed that Tim and a handful of others had opted to stay and fight, or wait it out.

Several days later, the group from Elk Creek, Virginia showed up with two spare vehicles loaded to the gunnels and an old friend's sister, Maria Sanchez, in tow. The Wilderness and Survival School was abandoned and staged as a secondary retreat should the need ever arise to relocate in a hurry. The belief was that if any form of a resistance movement against the occupiers came to fruition, it would definitely be needed.

Given Carlton's medical background, and Maria's Spanish speaking abilities, the pair was housed with the Martinez family. Jesus and

Abelardo had grown accustomed to shifting bedrooms with all of the visitors of late, so to finally have a fairly permanent living arrangement where they would share a room was a welcome development.

All beds and rooms were accounted for in Josh's cabin as well. President Sarkes and Agent Monahan were in one with James and Dallas in another while Josh and Amanda enjoyed the spacious confines of the master bedroom. The basement was inhabited by Chester and Bryan. Given their night owl nature and similar skillsets, the two could prattle on down there until all hours undisturbed.

The Three Sisters farm house held the rest. Josh's daughters took to racking together and wouldn't have it any other way. That left Gregg, Emily, and baby Declan in one room, while Alysin, Lily, and Kristin took the other. Brent, along with Emily's parents, was relegated to the basement. The arrangement couldn't have made them happier. The old defense attorney and the retired General found kindred spirits with regard to Josh's communication center. The pair could monitor the comings and goings around the country with Josh's HAM radio setup and converse with Bryan and Chester when they got bored.

Gregg had taken to the habit of bringing Declan to the basement while he offered the infant his midnight feeding. Brent actually enjoyed the intrusions. He wasn't home much when Jessica or Heather were that age so he became overly fascinated with the entire production. The new grandparents were all too happy to assist as well. With the baby in hand, the former operator and the Marine Corp General swapped stories throughout the nighttime hours. His in-laws were astounded at the lengths to which our soldiers went for love of country. To say that Emmitt and Sonja Calhoun had a new found respect for Gregg and his military career would be an understatement.

As the twenty-four to seventy-two hour window for egress closed, chaos filled the vacuum. Angry gangs of looters descended and began their rummaging for easy scores of food that made the ration riots look pale in comparison. Anyone with any sense got out of Dodge before the opportunity slammed shut. Those that remained quickly found themselves on the wrong end of hungry mobs looking for resources. The full effect of winter's unrelenting wrath killed hundreds of thousands from exposure as the unprepared attempted to flee the cities. Those that had become dependent on the government for assistance stayed in place and waited for FEMA. That aid never came. Those that didn't freeze when their wood ran out simply starved to death.

The battle plan for the UN forces was practically accomplished for them by the rampaging hordes. Affluent suburbs were pillaged, resistant and protective fathers, brothers, and uncles were shot. The women didn't fare much better. Those that weren't raped were beaten to within an inch of life and left to die in the gutter. The willing and foolhardy quickly re-established the oldest profession as brothels were up and running inside of a few weeks. As the first month of post-EMP life came to a close, there were just as many dead as there were orphans.

Old scores were settled at the end of a barrel.

\* \* \*

During that first month, barely a week had gone by when Josh was awoken by Gregg. He had opened his eyes with a start, but his mouth was immediately covered.

In a low whisper, he said, "Get dressed and come with me," and then left the room as silently as he had entered it.

He quickly did as asked and met him on the porch.

While he gently closed the front door behind him, the part time interrogator stood and offered a steaming cup of coffee as he instructed, "Take a seat."

"You better have one heck of a good reason for waking me up like that, brother," Josh declared.

Before he was even fully seated, Gregg stated unemotionally, "Suhrab's dead."

"Oh," he replied as he sat. "How'd that happen? You guys finally put him out of his misery? Frankly, I'm surprised it took this long. Rayburn authorized his execution days ago."

"Nope. He didn't die at our hands. I went to take him his breakfast and someone snuck up there during the night and shot him. Stuck one in his head, two in the heart. There are powder burns on his chest."

Josh didn't have a response. The two sat in silence sipping at their black coffee and enjoying the coolness of the early winter morning. When the sun crested the ridgeline to the east twenty minutes later, he cleared his throat.

"How many people knew he was there?"

"I count nine. Only four had a legitimate ax to grind though."

The former Marine arched his eyebrows at the last remark.

"Me, Em, Hoplite, and I hate to say it, but Sam as well.

"And the others?"

"You, Dallas, James, the Sheriff, and Brent," he answered bluntly.

"Explain Hoplite."

"He was the commanding officer for half the men killed on my transport. If rumors contain a kernel of truth, he didn't take their deaths especially well. That was why he was looking at getting out and resigning his commission."

"He told me. And Sam?"

"Aunt Jenny. The woman was old and frail and maybe she wouldn't have lasted very long, but that wound is still fresh. You should have seen how distraught she was in Springfield."

He contemplated the man's responses and reasoning and could find no flaw. "What do you suggest?"

"Bury the body and let it fester in whoever did it. They'll own up to it in time."

"Just like that?"

"Yes, sir. Just like that," Gregg replied and paused. "Oh, we could go on a witch hunt and start accusing people for sure. In my experience though, that's counterproductive. They'll fess up."

"What then?"

"Then nothing. Give 'em a friggin' medal, I don't care. The man was a terrorist and sociopath, pure and simple. You can call him an enemy combatant or whatever political buzzword fits these days if it makes you feel any better. He had an execution order on his head from the POTUS and that's only because we couldn't get to a black site. We damn sure weren't gonna let him go."

Gregg paused a few moments and then concluded, "He told us everything he knew anyway. As far as I'm concerned, this is a completed Op and I'm not losing anymore sleep over this guy."

"True enough."

When Josh offered no other response, he felt compelled to ask, "But?"

"I'm not inclined to let it fester, Gregg. We can't have people running around executing prisoners."

The new father sipped at his coffee and sighed.

"You can do whatever you want. I'm not going to try and stop you. I don't care a single iota who did it, or why. I've put enough folks out of their misery. This is one that most definitely earned it, but it's not on my conscience."

* * *

"Do you have any idea what Josh wants to discuss, honey?"

"I do," Gregg replied to his wife.

"That man sure does love his meetings," Emily's mother, Sonja, declared as she finished changing Declan's diaper.

"Well there are a lot of things that need to be organized. Power's not coming back for a couple years and people require direction," her son-in-law rebutted.

Without skipping a beat, she turned her attention to her husband of four decades, "Emmitt, don't you dare light that cigar in this house."

"Does it really matter?" he asked as he gave his wife a 'look'. Emily saw it, but said nothing.

"No, I guess it's too late for you," she answered with a sigh. "The rest of us would appreciate it if you didn't stink up the house though. Go outside," she ordered.

"Come on, son," Emmitt decreed as he exercised his shoulder.

"You alright, Mr. Calhoun?" Gregg asked.

"My arm has a weird pain. Mustuv slept on it wrong," he replied. "Hey, I've got an extra one for you if you want it," Emily's father concluded as he headed toward the porch.

His daughter watched as the pair exited the front door. When she heard it click shut, she turned to her mother. "I saw that," she declared as she placed another log on the fire.

"What's that, dear," Sonja replied as she swaddled Declan in the hospital blanket.

"The look daddy gave you when he said it didn't matter. What's going on?" she asked as she poked the embers.

"Oh, sweetie. When you've been married as long as we have, sometimes that's all you need," her mother answered undeterred from that task at hand.

Something was up. Emily could feel it.

"So what was with the comment, 'too late for you'? That mean nothing too?" she continued the interrogation as she placed the fireplace tool back in its cradle.

Thinking quickly, realizing she had slipped up, Sonja offered a casual, "I just meant that he's been chomping on those nasty cigars for so long there was no hope for him ever changing his habits. What's with the twenty questions?" Redirecting her daughter, she asked, "Everything alright with you and Gregg?"

With a doubtful look on her face, Emily answered her mother. "Everything's fine. Better than fine, actually. We talk a lot more than we ever used to."

"That's good. Communication is probably more important in a marriage than sex."

"Mom!"

"What?" Sonja replied and realized she had embarrassed her daughter. "Oh, don't be like that. What I mean is, intimacy is a key ingredient too, but do you really feel any kind of connection when you're, you know, if the two of you aren't in the same place mentally? That's where the communication comes in." As if a wave of nostalgia washed over her, she added an emphatic, "The stories I could tell you about me and your father!"

"No! Ewe! Gross! I don't need to hear those, Mom! Like ever!"

Having successfully diverted her daughters questions, Sonja replied with a shrug. "Suit yourself. We better get going though. We don't want to be the last ones to arrive."

Twenty minutes later, the Calhoun's and Chastain's walked onto the front porch of Josh's cabin. The Martinez's were right behind them

"Emmitt, are you okay?" Basilia wondered as he ascended the steps. "You look pale."

He waved her off, "Just tired is all. The little one has us working a lot of late nights."

"Please have a seat," Josh stated to the assembled group. "I've asked everyone here because we have an issue." Now that he had everyone's attention, he added, "It seems that someone has taken matters in to their own hands, Suhrab is dead."

He paused to let that sink in. No one offered any comments.

"Ah, Señor," Juan interjected. "Isn't that a good thing?"

"Well, yes and no. He had an execution order from the POTUS, so that's been fulfilled. Unfortunately, he didn't meet his fate by any of those authorized to carry out the task."

"Who was supposed to do it?" Sheriff Watson asked.

"Gregg, Carlos, or Agent Monahan. Hoplite and Ed have confirmed that they were unaware of Suhrab's untimely demise as Gregg was the man assigned to chow duty this morning. He found the body. I was made aware of it shortly thereafter. So," he stated and paused, "That leaves this group."

Silence permeated the group.

"Why wasn't it carried out when the order was given?" Evan offered the group.

"We wanted to give it a few days to see if he'd offer up anymore intel," Gregg explained.

"So, now what?" Samantha asked.

"Now's the time for the person that did it to fess up is what," her fiancé rebutted. "We can't have people running around executing prisoners."

"But he had an execution order, what's it matter who did it?" she offered.

"Because, Sam, we just can't. Many of us have had to do unthinkable things. It's a tough thing to live with."

"Which is exactly why I did it," Emmitt stated catching Josh and the group off guard.

"Daddy!?" Emily exclaimed.

"He damn near killed my daughter!" he growled in response.

He immediately began to feel weak, feeble. Something was building in his chest. He grabbed the front rail to balance himself.

"He was responsible for the death of hundreds of thousands of people," he continued. "Probably millions before this is all said and done. Most of all though, I did it because he killed my grandchild," he concluded solemnly.

Gregg placed a hand on the man's shoulder and squeezed. "Thank you," he whispered.

Emily turned to her mother who hadn't uttered a word. She observed her as Sonja cooed at Declan and rocked him gently in her arms.

"Mom? You knew, didn't you?"

"Emmitt," she replied.

"I told her this morning… after. She didn't know anything until it was all said and done."

"No!" Em demanded on the verge of tears. "Lifelong pacifist lawyers don't just turn a switch and start murdering people! Something else is going on here and I want to know what it is… right now!" she concluded sternly.

Emmitt pulled his daughter into his arms and half whispered, "I'm dying, sweetie," he offered with a faint smile. "I've got cancer and it's advanced. I don't have long according to the doctors… couple weeks at most."

"No! No! No! It's not true!" Emily pleaded as she pushed away. "Mom?" she asked looking for her tell her it was a lie.

Sonja couldn't do anything but nod and confirm the truth.

"We found out a couple days before you and Gregg showed up in Springfield. Your father didn't want there to be a death watch so I swore not to tell. I'm sorry, sweetie."

The pain in Emmitt's chest was building again. He reached out to grab Gregg's arm.

"Sir?" his son-in-law asked.

His legs had no strength to support his weight. He slowly began to wilt. The aging attorney released his grip on the steadfast arm of his son-in-law and clutched at his chest.

"Shit!" Gregg exclaimed. "Basilia! Get over here! I think he's having a heart attack!"

"Emmitt!" his wife shrieked as she hurriedly dashed in the direction of her husband. Chaos consumed the porch as people began rushing toward the fallen man.

The country doctor was by his side within seconds.

"Stay with me, Emmitt," she commanded. "Sonja, get down here! Talk to him and keep him talking!" She attempted to check his pulse. "Abelardo, go to the house and get my bag!"

Her youngest son leapt off of the porch in an effort to avoid the chaos at the other end. Like a shot, he was in his father's truck screaming up the rutted tractor road.

"It's okay, Emmitt," Sonja said softly. "I'm safe here."

Her husband nodded, his scared eyes betraying his truer mental state.

"I'm losing him," Basilia decreed as she ripped open his jacket to begin chest compressions. The second she put her hands on his chest she knew there was something seriously wrong. It was far too malleable, squishy even. She almost recoiled, but began attempting the lifesaving maneuver all the same.

Sonja reached out and placed a hand on top of Basilia's. "He has a DNR. Please don't. Just let him go. It's what he wants." Calmly, his wife of four decades turned toward their only child and compassionately stated, "Em, come say goodbye to your father."

Emily dropped to her knees with the fear and panic written across her face, comingling with her tears.

"Daddy, no! Please!" she wailed. "Stay with me," she begged.

"It's going... to be okay," he said through shortened breaths. "You're... a momma now."

"No, Daddy, no," she passively protested while her mother smoothed his hair.

"Declan?" he asked.

"Right here sweetie," his wife replied.

"Let me... hold him... one last time."

Sonja carefully placed the baby in the crook of her husband's arm. Emmitt softly kissed the top of his head.

"New baby... smell. Going... to miss... that," he offered. Then he turned toward to his adoring family. "Miss you... too. Love... you both."

The group cried as they watched helplessly while Emmitt Calhoun slowly slipped away. He was laid to rest under a shade tree near Three Sisters so Sonja and Emily could visit often. Eventually, years later, he was moved to the McArthur Cemetery, just a few rows away from the Wrigley family.

* * *

Through Dallas' efforts prior to the HANE, and subsequent introductions thereafter, the group was able to keep track of the various movements of the UN forces as they fanned out across the country. They had decent coverage of the Eastern and Mississippi flyways, but anything west of Mississippi River was unknown. Anything from Maine to Louisiana was now their primary concern. The socialist left coast would have to fend for itself against the foreign troops. Fortunately for them, citizens residing in Idaho, Montana, Wyoming, and the surrounding area weren't much for being ruled.

Through the HAM network, Dallas and the others learned that the Royal Marines departed Cleveland soon after they emptied the building of all its resources. Unfortunately, once the vaults were empty, they turned their attention to the surrounding buildings. The exhibits within the Rock and Roll Hall of Fame and Museum were pilfered of Mick Jagger's cape, Keith Moon's velvet outfit, and Jimi Hendrix's guitar along with scores of other items. The cages, coolers, and refrigerators at the Horseshoe Casino, which was located only a thousand yards from the Treasury, were relieved of their contents as well.

As the ship backed away from its mooring, deck guns fired a dozen incendiary rounds and bathed the lake front and city center in flames. The structure that formerly held the national cache and twenty square blocks burned to the ground before the rains arrived to slake the fire's appetite.

While the English continued their conquest of the northeastern United States, the Spanish handled the southeast, and the French took over the Gulf Coast. The Russian Northern Fleet was divided among the three and served as follow on forces. Their Pacific Fleet performed a similar purpose on the western shores as it complemented the Asian berthed vessels. The Japanese military thoroughly enjoyed the retribution for the treatment and sequestration of their citizens on American soil during WWII. They greedily created internment camps for 'undesirables' and those with a propensity for inciting rebellious thoughts throughout the population. Many of them were not heard from again.

The United States land based forces were overwhelmed after the HANE. None of the hi-tech gear they had grown so reliant on worked as it should. If a piece of equipment managed to survive the original EMP, it was rendered ineffective and useless when massive experimental ship mounted RF devices blasted the coastline with targeted electromagnetic pulses. Any resistance the U.S. coastal defenses could have offered once the UN troops came ashore was wiped away after three solid weeks of shelling from the offshore Naval forces.

The ports of Charleston, Virginia Beach, and Miami fell in relatively short order, as did New Orleans, Long Beach, Seattle, and Los Angeles. Within a week of relieving Cleveland of its assets, the Royal Marines from that assault were forced to get creative. Since they were effectively cut off from their supply chain on the coast, they used the cloak of darkness to transfer personnel and gear to barges and made use of the New York State Canal System.

West Point never stood a chance.

While the cadets and auxiliary reinforcement units were busy defending against the brigade attacking from the south, the lack of any satellite imagery of the battlefield left them exposed. They were eventually flanked and crushed by the Royal Marine battalion floating down the Hudson River from the north.

\* \* \*

*'Declan, this is Mac! Where the hell are you?'* the voice inside Dallas' noise cancelling headset said harshly.

*'I got pinned down at the Wendy's by a sniper on the Route 50 off ramp,'* the man shot back tersely.

"Whoa!" Dallas exclaimed

*'What are you doing on the east side of town? Get your ass over here!'*

*'They were taking more fire than we were plus I was out of ammo! These little bastards seem to be coming from everywhere! How's the north side holding up?'*

"Oh crap!" Dallas blurted to no one.

The basement comm room was empty except for him and the equipment. He couldn't believe what he was hearing. Some town nearby was being raided. Given the frequency he was on, the signal strength, and the terrain, he figured it was about twenty to thirty miles away.

"No! No! No!" he said aloud as he adjusted the tuning knob to reduce the static. Eventually the channel was re-tuned.

"Josh!" he bellowed from underneath the cabin. His tone left no doubt that this wasn't something innocuous.

*'The south and west are clear. We seem to be holding up here in the north end. You guys over on the east side are taking the bulk of the assault!'*

"Damn it! Where are they?" he asked himself. "I need a friggin' map down here!"

"What!" Josh yelled back as he yanked open the door.

"Get down here!"

His friend took the steps two at a time not knowing what was wrong. He was closely followed by Sam and James.

The man pulled off the headset and flipped a switch. The running battle was able to be heard throughout the basement on the speaker.

"What is it," Samantha said excitedly.

*'Mac, we need some reinforcements over here! Send what you've got now!'*

"That one is a guy named Declan. He and 'Mac' are trying to coordinate forces and defend a town somewhere near here," Dallas added quickly.

*'As soon as we knock off a few more of these assholes we'll be right over. Can you tell what they have left?'*

*'It's hard to tell! Every time I pop my head up some of those Gangster Disciple mother f –,'* the man started to answer before static permeated the signal.

"Damn it!" he mumbled as he set himself back to the task of returning the conversation.

*'Where did they come from, Declan? I didn't think that many got out of the prison!'*

Josh flashed boiling hot. *Prisoners? Escape?*

"How far away are they? Could we get a signal from Chillicothe out here?" he asked his friend.

*'Hell, Mac. You know as well as I do that as soon they were released from their cells, they climbed the fence, and hauled ass straight up Route 23!'*

*'You ain't lying! Looks like they brought the whole damn gang down here from Columbus?'*

"It's possible," Dallas replied.

Josh quickly picked up the handset. "This is Mother Goose transmitting on two-zero-seven-point-one-eight-five megahertz. Declan? Mac? What's your twenty, over?"

"Mother Goose? I don't know that handle, identify yourself," the man ordered.

"Not on an open channel. That'll have to suffice. Do you need assistance over?"

"Fine, have it your way! This is Declan Bennett. The town of Chillicothe is currently under assault from an unknown number of hostiles and hell yes we could use some help!"

"ETA forty five minutes! Hold on! Help's coming!" Josh responded.

# **Chapter 10**

Shortly after Dallas and James had returned from Virginia, they briefed the group on the state of the roads and the towns they blew through trying to get back to Ohio. What they saw and encountered was merely a mild precursor to what was to come, and Josh knew it. Therefore, he insisted on prepping one of the deuce and half's for when the inevitable call for help rang out and the need arose. By planning ahead, no matter what, a vehicle would always be loaded, fueled, and in the barn ready to roll. When the transmissions from Chillicothe were intercepted by Dallas, all Josh had to do was assemble his team.

In theory, all they would need was there body armor, helmets, and weapons. Since getting the engineers out of the park in a moment's notice was next to impossible, they agreed to stage their kits along with some useful 'counter measures' in the back of the specified deuce. In addition to their personal protection gear, the truck also contained a crate with three bazooka rounds, its requisite launcher, a half dozen claymores complete with two clackers and wiring, and last but not least, Josh's .50 cal BMG.

Once all of the pre-positioned gear was decided, his oldest friend, Dallas, had quipped, 'If we need more than that, well, we shouldn't have left the damn house!'

At Hoplite's insistence though, the deuce was also loaded with ten extra 5-gallon jerry cans of diesel from the abandoned train, enough food from Josh's stash for six guys to eat well for three days, plus several two man tents, and sleeping bags. After the setback on the mountain, Dallas even managed to swipe Layla and Katherine's night vision headsets.

Josh was actually surprised by the fact that the first call for substantive aid had taken nearly a month to be received after the EMP.

"The girls don't know where we're going do they?" Josh asked Sam from the driver's seat of the cab.

"Nah, they're over at the park helping Basilia with her medical team. I'll put you down on the log as a half day barter trip. I figured you could tell them once you're home," his fiancé answered.

He smiled back warmly. "Thanks. We'll radio as soon as we can. Couple of hours at most."

Sam climbed up on the foot hold, leaned in the window, and gave him a kiss. "Please be careful."

"I will," he replied as he turned the key and started the massive diesel motor.

Once they were clear of the barn, Sam closed the doors behind them.

"How long do you think it'll take before she remembers that Javy is in the Chillicothe prison hospital?" Dallas asked.

His friend glanced is the driver's side mirror in time to see Samantha raise her hands up in protest then start rubbing her brow and temples.

"Right about now," he replied as he watched her kicking at the frozen sand and gravel in the driveway in frustration.

\* \* \*

When Route 50 merged with Route 35 three miles south of Chillicothe, Josh reached out and hit the roof of the deuce. Thick black smoke could be seen rising up off in the distance. James, Gregg, and Hoplite had busied themselves the entire trip by checking weapons and gear. Everything was loaded and ready to go by the time he gave his signal. The only thing left to do was load a round in the bazooka.

As they neared, tracer fire could be seen emanating from the Route 50 bridge. Whoever was doing the firing was raining holy hell down on the buildings below. The entire span across the Scioto River was littered with haphazardly parked vehicles. It didn't take long to realize that the acrid smoke was coming from both the nearby structures and the cars on the road.

Without warning, Gregg launched the rocket over the roof of the deuce. Josh and Dallas watched in amazement as the track went straight into a cluster of automobiles where the tracers had originated. A massive explosion and accompanying fireball obliterated whoever was in there.

Hoplite quickly reloaded the tube and armed the second shot as they progressed closer to the vehicular logjam. On the backend of the pile up, several men scattered and tried to advance toward other operable vehicles at the far end of the bridge. They didn't get very far before a cacophony of three-round bursts exited the buildings below.

Once the truck's approach was spotted, small weapons fire began sporadically heading their direction. The two men in the cab crouched down and ducked as low as they could and placed as much of the engine block between them and the hail of lead outside. All the while, Josh still managed to navigate their way through the chicane of smoldering cars. Rounds pinged off the fenders, hood, and bumper.

"Holy crap!" Dallas exclaimed as James awoke the .50 over his head and blew a man's leg off. In less than a minute, while Josh kept his steering movements smooth and his low speed constant, his friend efficiently worked the bolt, acquired the targets called out by Hoplite, and emptied the massive five round magazine. None of the targeted got back up.

No sooner did the long range rifle go silent as a second rocket exited the tube. Another large explosion closed the end of the bridge from escape.

The fireball had barely exhausted the available oxygen as an armed contingent of residents began pouring out of the buildings and advancing up the hill of the exit ramp. When the deuce reached the first of several dozen concrete bridge spans crossing the meandering Scioto River, the massive truck abruptly halted and the five men from McArthur emptied from the cab and bed.

"Shoot and scoot, two by two. I'll cover the rear," Josh commanded. "Dallas, you and Hoplite are up."

As one pair sprang up to provide covering fire, the other quickly relocated. Josh, covering their six, moved with the first team in a staggered pattern.

After leap frogging from obstacle to obstacle, Dallas peered around a vehicle that had leaked its oil and antifreeze all over the road. Three assailants were hiding behind the broken down hulk arguing over whether they should run or fight. He immediately relayed the information to Hoplite, who in turn, provided the appropriate hand signals to the trailing teams.

When Gregg and James unleashed their latest round of covering fire, Dallas went right and Carlos left. Their shots rang off of the vehicles and drew the attention of the gang members. Having had their decision made for them, the gang bangers immediately returned several rounds in Josh, Gregg, and James' direction.

*Guess they decided to fight,* Dallas thought as he and Hoplite closed in.

With the attacker's focused elsewhere, the diverging pair exposed themselves from the relative safety of cover and cut the three down.

There was no time to relax as additional shots were heard at the far end of the bridge. The five men from McArthur immediately continued their advance toward it. The group was slowed by the gaping hole in the concrete bridge left by the exploding bazooka round. As they gave it a wide birth, chunks broke off and splashed into the river below.

Just as they cleared the impediment, the world around them went eerily silent. Hoplite held up the 'halt' hand signal and the five men paused their progression to listen.

When an occasional moan or pleading wail was heard, it was immediately followed by a gunshot. Josh counted four single shots aloud as they cracked through the afternoon air and reverberated down the slow moving river channel.

"Guess they aren't taking prisoners in Chillicothe today," he said, stating the obvious.

After a final coup de grâce was fired, he and the rest of the men slowly exited from behind cover. Each declared, 'Clear,' as they showed themselves to the townsmen now occupying the bridge.

"You the folks from McArthur?" was called out as they approached.

"We are. Dallas McKutcheon, and you are?"

"I'm Mac. I'm the unofficial-official Sheriff," the man answered as they shook hands.

"Sorry to hear that," Dallas replied. "What happened to your predecessor?" he asked.

"He got caught up in a gunfight with some looters. They had some armor piercing stuff, blew right through his vest. Didn't even make it a week after the lights went out," Mac stated. "I can't thank you enough for the assist though. We really appreciate it."

"You had it well in hand. Just a few stranglers for the relief pitcher is all," Josh responded. "By the looks of things, you could use some help setting up some defenses… Maybe reduce the number of these ingress points."

"We'll take whatever assistance you can offer at this point," Mac replied. "What did you have in mind?"

"For starters, I'd drop those two bridges in the river for damn sure," Hoplite interjected.

"After today's festivities I was thinking the same thing," the new Sheriff responded.

"We've got some guys that specialize in that type of stuff. I could send 'em over in a couple of days, if that'd be all right," Josh offered.

"Really? Hell yeah!" the man answered excitedly.

"What happened here, anyway? From what we heard of your conversation before we cut in, this was the result of some former prisoners that got out?"

"That's about the long and the short of it," a bystander said as he approached. "Declan Bennett," he stated as he extended his hand. "Are you Mother Goose?"

"That's just the handle for our comm room. Call me Josh. What can you tell me about the prison?"

"Ah hell. When the power blew, most of the gennies never cranked up. Those that did fire up ran out of fuel after a day or two. I imagine it was the same all over the country. After a few days, most of the guards didn't come back. Those guys still reporting for duty got pretty desperate when the food was gone. We heard that they expedited death row sentences over in Lucasville... same thing for lifers. I hate to say it, but it wasn't all that different here."

"Why? What happened here?" James asked.

"Prison staff was fairly fortunate that all of the prisoners were still in their night-time lockdown stance. However, that didn't stop the inmates from causing floods by stopping up their sinks and toilets and lighting their bedding on fire. The sympathetic ones were foolish enough to open the doors for lesser offenders.

"Once out, they quickly overran the rest of the staffers. Most were beaten, some were executed. All told, I'd say millions of felons have been released back into the population across the country. I'm talking the worst of the frickin' worst. Can you imagine the depravity coming out of Rikers, San Quentin, or Joliet?

"If you don't mind my askin'," the unofficial-official Sheriff said. "Why so curious about the prison?"

"I have a keen interested in one of its residents. I'd like to verify that he was put down by the guards, assuming he was," Josh stated bluntly.

"You came all this way in a world gone to hell... for that? We coulda just looked for ya and then radioed back," Mac offered.

Dallas stepped in and explained, "My friend is of the type that needs to see it with his own eyes before he'll rest easy."

"Why so much attention in an inmate?" Declan chimed in.

"Not to put too fine a point on it, but that little cretin sexually abused my daughters and physically assaulted another," Josh answered candidly. "If possible, I'd like you to have a man lead me to the final resting place of Javier 'Javy' Dolbrow."

Declan's eyes grew large.

"What's your name, mister? If you don't mind my askin'," the former guard asked as he gestured toward Mac.

"Josh Simmons."

Chillicothe's unofficial Sheriff flashed a knowing smile. "That'd be short for Josiah, I'd imagine."

"It would."

"Well, Mr. Simmons, today's your lucky day. Declan here was a guard over there. He'll be your guide, take you to see what you need. You'll get the closure you're looking for."

"Sounds good," he replied as the two shook hands.

"You and me are up front," Josh stated with a nod to Declan. "The rest of you, in the back. Safeties off,' he ordered.

* * *

The cab of the deuce was silent except for the occasional direction while they drove from the bridge to the northeast side of town. As the armed contingent rammed their way through the closed gate of the prison, the passenger directed Josh to the infirmary wing of the structure.

"Why are we headed there?" he asked.

"Your man was still awaiting trial and recuperating from surgery. Apparently his last attempted victims didn't appreciate his advances and shot him. I'm guessing that'd be your daughter's handiwork... if the rumors are true."

He just nodded.

"Good to know," Declan replied. "Well, he was slated to be moved to Columbus, but the lights went about out a week before that date. Go ahead and park here."

Once the truck was shut off, the prison was eerily silent. There were no noisy prisoners in the yard lifting weights, jogging, or playing basketball. The PA system was dormant and the slamming of heavy metal doors couldn't be heard either.

"Your man's in there," the former guard said as he pointed toward a door marked 'Infirmary' above its berth.

"Lead the way," Josh replied as he motioned to the man and withdrew his Beretta.

Declan reached around for his satchel and pulled several fairly clean bandanas. He threw one to each of them.

"Here, put these on. The stench in there is pretty noxious."

Each of the McArthur men unfurled the folded cloth, formed it into a triangular mask, and securely tied it behind their heads.

Inside the building, the smell of death and decay was pungent and overpowering. Almost a month had passed since the HANE and the bodies hadn't been moved. As they worked their way through the dozen or so beds headed to the isolation room, most were empty and appeared to be freshly made, but some were not. Those still holding their handcuffed occupants were blackened and swollen; others had leaked their internal juices on the floor. Rats scampered off of the corpses as they approached.

"Javy's in there. One door in or out and you need a key card access to unlock it."

"That explains the broken frame," Dallas observed.

"He better be in there," Josh warned.

The man sniffed. "He is."

"You seem to have an awful lot of info about this prisoner."

The former guard just stared at the floor in contemplation.

"Something we should know, Declan?" he asked as he slid the slide partially back to check that a round was chambered.

In an almost whisper, he replied, "I never killed a man before that day. The prisoners were starting to get each other out of their cells 'cause some idiot decided to take pity on a few of the level one felons. It was chaos. I was assigned to the infirmary."

"What happened? Tell me now or so help me."

"Javy fuckin' Dolbrow happened, that's what!" he snapped. "As soon as that son-of-a-bitch got here he was inciting the other prisoners. If he wasn't singin' up a storm he was regaling the female staff with his conquests. They finally had enough and drugged his ass just to shut 'em up! Once he was out cold, they handcuffed his butt to the bed and stuffed him in the isolation room," he answered as he motioned toward the back. "One of the more hard core residents was a fan and attempted to get him out," he added.

"I didn't know what else to do. I'd had my ass whipped pretty good by that lunatic over there," Declan continued, but paused to point at the bed next to James. "So I ran to my truck and retrieved my Sig. By the time I returned, your man was free and they were almost out of the room. That guy," he said as he motioned toward to decaying body again, "He had exited, saw me, and then bull rushed me. I put one in his head."

"What happened to Javy," Josh demanded.

"He was coming through the cracked up opening right behind him. I hit 'em three times in the chest. Me and another guard dragged that dude out of the way, but it wasn't easy…" As an afterthought, he added,

147

"I never knew dead people were so heavy." Then he paused again. Once his moment of remembrance and reflection wore off, he concluded. "Anyway, we waited for him to just bleed out."

"How long did that take?" Hoplite asked.

"It was the longest half hour of my life. Damn," he sighed at the recollection. "It seemed like it took a hell of a lot longer."

"Did he suffer?"

The man chortled, "You could say that."

"Good!" Josh stated emphatically then dropped his pack on the empty bed.

He retrieved his flashlight and slowly worked his way through the opening into the isolation room. The last thing he needed was an infected wound or tetanus, so he took his time with the splintered wood, bent metal, and broken glass. Once he was finally inside, he saw a blackish trail on the floor. Josh cautiously approached the bed and shone his light. The hand and leg shackles were dangling from the rails. Javy wasn't in them.

*Damn it*, he thought. *So much for the easy answer.*

As he looked further, he noticed that the sheets were a crumbled mess. There was definitely blood residue all over them. He checked the corners of the room only to find medical equipment gathering dust. Turning back to the bed, he peered on either side, nothing.

Josh backed up and followed the path of dried goo with his beam. It led under the heavy hospital frame. When he directed the stream of light underneath, the bare soles of two feet pointing skyward greeted him.

He jumped.

The father bent on revenge heaved the single bed over against the wall with a crash. In front of him lay the decaying corpse of Javier

Dolbrow. Sprawled out on the floor, the man looked like an animal that had been put out of its misery. The surgical bandages covering the bullet wounds from his daughters well placed shots were still affixed to this shoulders. His hands were firmly clasped on what he imagined were the gut shots Declan had mentioned.

*That explains the trail on the floor.*

Josh had been robbed of the opportunity to see the little bastard squirm on the table on his execution day. In fact, aside from his upcoming nuptials, there was nothing he was looking forward to more. However, he received extreme satisfaction when he emptied the magazine from his Beretta into the man for good measure.

* * *

It took some doing, but after three days and nights of discreetly moving materials and reassigning men, Lt. Stokes and his platoon of Combat Engineers arrived in Chillicothe. Sheriff Mac and his deputies were surprised when the convoy came rolling up to the horribly configured roadblock.

"Can I help you gentlemen?" the guard asked as he approached.

The engineering commander exited the lead vehicle and advanced steadfastly. The man truly did not like being exposed out in the open especially when there were gangs running around in the hills with high powered automatic and semi-automatic weapons.

"I'm looking for either Mac or Declan. A mutual acquaintance said they should be expecting us," Stokes replied.

"You found 'em," Mac answered as he withdrew from the shadows and holstered his sidearm. "What have you got in those?" he asked as he motioned toward the three trucks.

"Enough men and materials to get you folks squared away for the long haul. How'd that be?"

"I'd say you have a deal, sir," Mac declared as he extended his hand in gratitude.

As they shook hands, Lt. Stokes asked, "There a place where we can park and have my guys stretch? We need to review this aerial map and Josh's notes."

"Absolutely!"

In an effort to make good on his promise to the Chillicothe Sheriff, Josh sent the engineers on an organized 'midnight run' out of the park. He figured they could use the deployment to reacquire skills that lay dormant from lack of training time.

Mac, Declan, Lt. Stokes, and his Senior Sapper, Jake Carmichael, sat in a candle lit hole-in-the-wall bar sipping black coffee as they reviewed Josh's map. Unfortunately, it depicted the entire state and didn't provide the detail or scale needed to make the decisions for the problems they were looking to solve. As a result, the Sheriff asked one of his deputies to retrieve an enlarged diagram of the city from the Chamber of Commerce building.

With the new drawing laid out before them, the Lt. and his Sapper were in quick agreement with Josh's observations.

"Okay, here's what I see," Stokes began. "This town is damn near perfectly situated. You can't get in here without crossing either the Scioto River or Paint Creek. That's good."

"Why's that?" Declan asked.

"It means natural obstacles that can't be easily crossed," Jake replied. "I'm thinking that because of the route of the riverbed, we could blow these two main bridges to the north and leave the southern ones standing with increased defenses. If someone is hell bent on getting in here, we'll at least make them burn what precious fuel they *do* have to drive all the way around to the open side of town."

"What about these ingress points?" Mac asked as he pointed to three other points of entry.

"We'll place heavily fortified barricades at the Route 104 / 35 exchange, maybe some pill boxes with claymore backups. You guys have any Jersey barriers laying around?"

The two men from Chillicothe started laughing.

"If you could see this town in the daylight, you'd have seen the DOT building in all its glory. We've got concrete highway dividers coming out of our ears!"

"Perfect," Lt. Stokes replied. "That'll make this whole thing go a hell of a lot faster. I don't suppose you have any working machinery capable of lifting and transporting them around?"

"We might get a farmer to help us out. Someone's gotta have a working backhoe. We'll have to look around for one of those. If not, we can definitely drag them where you want 'em. How'd that be?"

"That'll work," the Sapper answered. "Maybe build some sort of lift and lever system to manhandle them up into place if we can't find a piece of machinery to lift it though. We'll need to find some strong backs by morning? Those things are two and half tons of concrete and re-bar."

"Shouldn't be a problem. Let's just hope we locate a working backhoe or something larger," Declan answered.

"Narrow your focus to people with older machines. As far as we can tell, the old stuff survived the EMP," the Lt. interjected.

"So that's what it was? An EMP?"

"Yup," Jake responded flatly.

Stokes half expected a million questions to start coming at him, but all either said was, "Well, that answers that."

When nothing else was mentioned, the Lieutenant continued.

"Okay, so we'll demo the two northern bridges and, unless you guys can think of a good reason, we should probably blow this other small bridge while we're at it. That'll close off the town to the north, east, and west. The only thing south of this place is Cincinnati and Huntington. What's that, an hour an half by car to either? I doubt they are coming this far on foot or horseback looking for resources."

"Sounds about right," Mac replied. "But we've got some residents that live out there though."

"Do you think they'd be willing to relocate to this side of Paint Creek?"

The pair looked at each other and furrowed their collective brows. Almost in unison, they said, "Can we have a minute?"

"Not a problem," Lt. Stokes answered as he began to stand. "It's your town guys. We're happy to do whatever you like. We're only pointing out what we would be doing in a combat zone given these circumstances. Unfortunately, that's exactly where you currently find yourselves. Come on, Jake. Let's let these guys discuss some things."

The two engineers exited the table and went to the counter where a disinterested bartender was reading a well-worn book. The men placed their empty cups on the bar and then leaned against it to observe. Declan and Mac weren't exactly having a heated or animated conversation, but they seemed at odds over something.

"Wonder what that's all about," Jake asked.

"How would you feel if some group of thugs just rolled into your hometown and shot the place up?" Stokes replied.

"Oh, hell boys, it ain't nothing like that. Declan's sister lives a few miles west of town. Husband ran off a decade ago. Son-of-a-bitch left her to fend for herself with three kids under the age of five. Youngest one must be goin' on thirteen or fourteen now. Ya'll blow that bridge and she and number of other families are exposed on our left flank."

The engineers turned in time to see the old bartender rolling up his sleeve to expose what was left of his tattoo. The shape and markings were still unmistakable though. It was a deeply aged Airborne tat. The two men whistled at the age of the ink and the fact that half was missing.

"You damn right, sonny," the barkeep said with pride. "This thing's probably older than both of you… combined."

"Where in the world did you get that?" Jake asked in amazement.

"Little Vietnamese girl did me in town called Saigon… you might have heard of it. The rest of it is in some rice patty on the other side of the Pacific. I was twenty years old when they airlifted me out of that shit hole."

The three men sat and swapped stories about the jungles of 'Nam and the deserts of the Middle East for what felt like a lifetime. Stokes and Jake were completely enamored with the man and his tales of Southeast Asia. Just as the bartender was finishing up the abridged version of his time in-country, the unofficial Sheriff, Mac, interrupted his reminiscing.

"You know what you boys could do," the barkeep called out as the pair headed back over to the table. "Ya'll could install a submerged crossing somewhere down stream. Saw the villagers under VC control do it all day and night when I was out there in the bush."

The pair looked at each other quickly before the Mac declared, "Charlie, you're a genius!"

Jake turned slightly to the bartender and sarcastically quipped, "Charlie? Really?"

"Yeah, yeah, smart ass. I see the irony in it."

Once it was decided, the men set themselves to the task of fortifying the town of Chillicothe from the Columbus raiders descending from the north. Declan was confident that it was the inmates from the 'Gangster Disciples' local chapter.

"They and their brethren must not have enjoyed their time in our fair city," he had quipped.

For the next several days, every piece of machinery that could be located, and was operable, was put to work. An old International tractor was given a singular task; drag one highway concrete Jersey barricade after another out of the DOT facility to each of the three specified locations. Twenty-six went to the 104 / 35 exchange as well as the two standing southern bridges. Each location would receive dual pillboxes. Both were positioned to provide a murderous crossfire.

The Sheriff, Declan, and the townies were amazed with what the engineers concocted.

Each pillbox was comprised of thirteen barricades. Four were used to form the square foundation while the remainder went up above. Before the massive highway dividers were placed on top, the inside of the structure was dug out either by hand or by using the one

154

temperamental backhoe, which seemed to only work half the time. It did manage to run long enough to construct the submerged crossing.

An old warehouse forklift was used to scoop up the immense dividers. As each was positioned, several six-by-six pieces of wood about a foot in length were situated length wise atop the exposed side of the foundation with space in between. As a result, the roof was slanted to shed water and the gun ports were already present. This meant that no drilling would be required.

Because the concrete pieces were almost two feet wide at the base and only a few inches at the top, every other one was placed upside down. When they were all installed, the fortification had a solid concrete roof several feet thick.

Before the exterior was backfilled, a tarp was laid on top to waterproof the ceiling. The entire structure was covered with several feet of dirt. Camouflaged next to each was a claymore. The clacker was placed in a secondary position some distance behind the primary fortification along with a wired box.

Once the structures were complete, the engineers unloaded the bang and staged each of the bridges destined for demolition. Since it wasn't their town, and there weren't exactly any strict Army regs to adhere to, Lt. Stokes and Jake let three residents trigger the detonations… much to their collective delight.

# Chapter 11

*Spring*

President Rayburn was beyond himself. He could no longer maintain any degree of composure in the face of the onslaught. Sarkes had made numerous attempts to draw the man back into the fray, but the POTUS's depression was all consuming. Every decision weighed on him. He was exhausted trying to keep the wolves at bay and the Union intact. Therefore, it was under doctors' orders that he retired for the evening. Before departing for his quarters, he instructed the SecDef to wake him in the event of any considerable progress in the west.

Several hours later, Larry Fielding finally received the report he was looking for. A band of fighters located near Coeur d'Alene, Idaho had stopped a Russian advanced party just west of Spokane. Another set of resistance cells out of Crestline, California had ambushed a resupply convoy on I-15 headed from Edwards Air Force Base to San Bernardino. Everywhere the UN forces turned, they were meeting heavy combat on both coasts. Slowly but surely, supply lines were being severed. The news was too good not to share with the slumbering POTUS.

"Sir? I've got an update on the –," he started to say when he noticed that the man had fallen asleep in a chair in front of the fire. His eyes were closed, a book was in his lap, and a half empty glass of bourbon was on the side table next to him.

He opted to wake him gingerly.

As he approached to gently shake him he sniffed something rank. If he didn't know any better, it smelled like the latrine.

"Sir," he said quietly as he shook the man's shoulder.

President Rayburn's head slumped forward from the slight movement.

SecDef Fielding quickly placed two fingers on his neck and tried to detect a pulse in the man's carotid artery. The man was cold. *There's that smell again.*

There was no pulse. Fielding surmised that the smell was the result of the man releasing his bowels after expiring. The Secretary of Defense realized that the POTUS was dead and had been for some time.

His friend, James Rayburn, the Commander in Chief… was gone.

Calmly, he picked up the phone on the desk. The Secret Service detail immediately responded to the call.

"Agent Crespin," said as he identified himself.

"This is SecDef Fielding. Fetch the medical team and Vice President Culpepper."

"Is there a problem, sir?

"You could say that, son," he countered with a sigh. "The POTUS is dead."

As he hung up the receiver, he turned to see if there was anything out of place. Nothing was. Everything was exactly where it should have been.

* * *

"This is Sarkes," he stated as he answered the ringing cell phone.

"Hey Tom, this is Larry Fielding," the SecDef replied in a melancholy tone.

"Long time no talk. How are things in Omaha?"

"Ah, they're not so good. I'm afraid I've got some bad news."

"Oh? What's up?" the former President asked sounding concerned as he stood up more straight.

"Jim's dead, had a massive heart attack… if the coroner's report can be believed."

For the first time in his life, the man was at a loss for words. An eerie silence permeated the call as the crestfallen leader slumped down in the nearest chair.

After a few seconds, the SecDef said, "Tom... you still there?"

The former President was in shock. His friend, and political rival, had passed away. His head began spinning with thoughts. *If the autopsy report could be believed? What does that even mean?*

Before he knew what he was saying, he blurted, "That's impossible! The man didn't smoke, rarely drank, and ran five miles a day since I don't know when."

"Exactly," was Fielding's reply, but there was a little too much of a hint of something distressing in his speech.

"Is this a safe line?"

"Sure is. I wouldn't call you if it wasn't."

"Who found him?" Sarkes asked quickly.

"I did."

"Was there something out of place or odd about the situation?"

"Nope, not a thing. He was just sitting in his chair by the fire with a half empty bourbon."

"Secure that glass!" Tom commanded. "The Jim Rayburn I know never would have had a drink of anything by himself!"

"That's what I thought too. I've already grabbed that and the bottle too. Both are being tested as we speak."

"Good… that's good," Sarkes said in a relieved tone. "Can you trust the person doing the testing though?"

"I hope so, he's my son-in-law."

Tom's mind was racing with questions. *When will the tests be done? What do we do if they come back positive with some sort of poison? What about toxins in the body?*

To Larry Fielding's credit, he already had a plan of action ready so he could to answer all of the man's inquiries.

"One last question and I'll let you go," Tom said.

"Fire away," the SecDef replied.

"Do me a favor and check the Secret Service logs. See who the last person was to use that room."

"Did that too."

"And? Who was in there?" he asked impatiently.

Fielding audibly sighed.

"What? Who was it man!"

"VP Culpepper and the Secretary of State. According to them, the meeting's purpose was to devise a plan to extricate our country from this fucking mess."

Eight hours later, the SecDef placed a second call to Sarkes.

James Rayburn, the forty-fifth President of the United States, had been assassinated.

* * *

With a heavy heart and anger permeating his soul, Tom reluctantly initiated his first debrief at the farm. The former POTUS cherry-picked a select few and divulged the breadth of the information he had received.

To say that some were just as angry would be an understatement. However, none were totally surprised. The nation was on its knees. A power grab seemed inevitable.

"Murdered? Are you sure you heard him right?" Josh intoned.

"The toxicologist didn't turn up anything in the man's drink so Fielding had them re-examine the body. There was a small red mark on the man's neck so the ME didn't pay any attention to it the first time around, assumed it was a bug bite I guess. Hours later that same dot showed deep reddish purple streaks. The man was poisoned," Sarkes answered bluntly.

"Now what?" Brent asked impatiently. "Do we have any idea who did this? Are there any suspects?"

"Not as of right now, but they are letting the heart attack story run awhile on base in Omaha as a handful of people observe to see who comes to the forefront to claim the throne, as it were."

"What else did he say?" Agent Monahan demanded.

Tom then proceeded to brief the collected leadership.

According to the SecDef, by all accounts, the union was in capable hands with Culpepper assuming the Presidency. On the plus side, even though Abbas may have sent the civilian population back to the 1800's, the military could still carry on secure communications due to their high altitude orbit satellites. VP Alan Culpepper, weary of taking the mantle of responsibility for the office of the President after an assassination, was actively planning and communicating with the remaining commanders on the ground and ships hiding behind islands. When the timing was right, Fielding stated that the man would willingly order a land based counter offensive coupled with a retaliatory strike at sea.

As a result of the available communication channels, President Culpepper was able to successfully contact base CO's in the sectors occupied by the Indian, French, Dutch, and Spanish. Each command was brought up to speed regarding the subversive allying between the United States and these nations. The ability to share sensitive intelligence and UN troop movements between foreign and American commanders allowed the U.S. military command structure to identify the key infrastructure necessary to rebuild. The prevailing thought was that, presumably, our allies would then be able to better direct their troops and leave that framework intact.

Before Sarkes' first debrief was over, the leadership team he had assembled agreed to begin planning area reconnaissance and patrols. Additional groups would train willing civilians to provide a force large enough to safeguard what was left of the enclave in and around McArthur. To them, the question was, if the political class was dealing with these types of issues, what was possibly headed their way?

\* \* \*

From a global perspective, the Monarchy was ecstatic with the international financial progress. The King had successfully cleaved the U.S. from the world economy in one fell swoop. Because most nations had already replaced the irrelevant American Dollar as the monetary standard, the economic hit felt by the other exchanges was minimal. Of course, national coffers would be diminished by the lack of export revenue, but that deficiency provided a surplus of raw materials and goods. The previously unattainable 'New World Order' that the EU had long sought and desired was quickly becoming a reality across Europe.

Nationally, survivors with the know-how to construct or repair radios were taking to the airwaves nationwide. Most relayed horror stories regarding their escape from some major city. However, there were several notable exceptions that, given their sensitive nature, they could not post.

Locally, as Dallas, Brent, and Bryan learned of developments through their continuous monitoring, a bulletin was posted the following day in downtown McArthur and at the park. News from across the country and the atrocities being committed graced the board whenever they were available.

At President Sarkes' request, items relating to the other cache of gold in Omaha, the Strategic Command structure at Offutt AFB, or the POTUS bunker located there were not announced.

Regardless of what was posted and when, Dallas could not in good conscience ignore the need for better communication between the towns.

"Hey, Bryan," Dallas declared as he entered the basement workshop and sleeping quarters.

Behind thick magnifying glasses and smoke from the soldering iron, he answered, "Gimme a sec. I have to finish this real quick."

He stood patiently as the man finished his work. After a few additional moments of absolute silence and concentration, Bryan gently blew on the circuitry and cleared the smoky remnants.

As he lay the tool down on the table, he took off the glasses and said, "What's up?"

"I was thinking," the walking interruption began.

"Every time one of you guys has a thought, I have to come up with some sort of device. It amazes me that Josh didn't think about the need to communicate," he interrupted. When he realized Dallas was staring at him with a blank look, he corrected, "Sorry, man. I guess I'm tired or hungry… or both."

"No problem. I'll see about having some food brought down if you can't pull yourself away to come upstairs. As for Josh, you know he hasn't owned a cell phone in decades. I think he figured any communication would be face-to-face. That being said, do you have anything in your bag of tricks that will allow us to talk to the other towns? Or at a minimum relay messages to them through weigh points?"

"You're a day late and a few dollars short my friend. That's what I'm working on now. Carlos and Gregg were standing right where you are now asking me the same question yesterday. So far, between Chester and myself, we've bastardized four truck stop CB's. I'm about to finish the fifth."

"Oh. Where are they going?"

The electrical magician stood as he motioned to the work bench behind him. Leaning against the cinderblock wall was a white board. Between the two, Bryan and Chester had divided it into three columns. The first column contained the list of parts needed to make a functioning two-way radio. The middle held needs, and the third was product destination.

"We got lucky with a couple of the radios. They were still in the box and on the shelf at some truck stop gas station that Hoplite and one of his patrols found. Those have already been delivered. After that, they pulled some from immobile trucks. Most of them needed to either have some circuit boards repaired or swapped out. If that didn't do it, we had to dive into what I brought with me. Those are running dangerously low though. I don't suppose you know where we could get our hands on some parts?"

"You might ask Hoplite and his patrols to check all of the office buildings they encounter. If you guys can repurpose any of the boards and circuitry from PC's, printers, and what not you could find some useful stuff there," Dallas replied casually as he reviewed the whiteboard. "Assuming the circuits aren't fried," he added as an afterthought while he admired their scribbled notes. "There are a dozen deliveries on this list and you've got eight working radios. If Carlos and his boys strike out you could try War God?"

"I'm sorry?"

"I've been tasked with generating code names. I'm trying that one out for Brent. Thoughts?"

"Hmm, could work. What else have you got?"

"Sheriff Watson is 'Opie', Katherine is 'Rodin', and that wrestler MMA dude we picked up last month is 'Grappler'. Evan's 'Shades'."

"Shades?"

"He's got his prescription in his sunglasses. Gregg and Carlos retained their SpecOps call signs of 'Longbow' and 'Hoplite'."

"This is kind of fun. What are Josh and Sam and Lt. Stokes?"

"They are 'El Jefe', 'Lady Stepford', and 'BB'."

"What's a 'BB'?"

"Short hand for 'Bang Brothers'."

"Nice, and Juan, Basilia, Chester, and Scott?"

"Uh, let's see. Juan is 'Machete' and Basilia is 'Shaman', but I haven't finished yet. I was thinking of code naming all of Basilia's medical team with medicinal herb names, but it might get too confusing. I'm open to suggestions."

Bryan sat there for a few seconds then started smiling.

"What?"

"We could call Scott 'Tinkerbell', or 'Tink' for short.

"That's just cruel and unusual punishment," Dallas surmised with conspiratorial smirk. "I love it," he added.

The two shared a hearty laugh for a couple moments at Scott's expense before Dallas started to excuse himself.

"Well, I'll let you get back to it. Sorry to intrude."

"No problem. Stop in anytime, but I'll take that lunch you offered."

"Sure thing. Hey, one last question. Where'd the whiteboard come from? I could use a few of those in my own comm room."

* * *

On the coasts, natural impediments in the form of thousand mile long mountain ranges, coupled with a brutal winter, worked to slow the UN advancement. On the east coast, Interstate 95 appeared to be the general line of demarcation for the invading troops in the Mid-Atlantic States. The I-5 corridor was the holding mark in the west. Seemingly overnight, the Bear Claw Saloon transformed from a local watering hole in to a trading post. A resistance movement was already well on its way to being firmly established.

The largest cities from coast to coast were still smoldering from the chaos of the first month. Weeks of anarchy and lawlessness increased the toll on the inhabitants exponentially. Even with the decreased population, the UN flagged troops recognized that house to house fighting would most likely be their welcoming committee. As a result, the formerly bustling metropolitans were simply bypassed until later if they weren't shelled outright from offshore just on principle. The Eisenhower Interstate Highway System worked according to its Cold War era design and the invading forces took full advantage.

When the UN forces reached Fayetteville, North Carolina, they were not surprised to find that most of the city had burned to the ground. The small military town was always considered a blight by the other neighboring communities anyway. The residents didn't shed a tear when rows of endless strip clubs, tattoo parlors, and cash advance businesses went up in flames.

However, as the foreign forces drove through the gates of Fort Bragg, they expected a furious resistance given the base occupants in the form of the 82$^{nd}$ Airborne and Delta Force, However, no resistance ever materialized. Not a single shot was fired at a foreign troop or vehicle. The base was deserted.

"Sir, we have a big problem," the Lieutenant began as he and his Sergeant approached his Commander's vehicle.

"Explain," his CO replied tersely.

"I've dispatched Recon teams throughout the base and every group not only returned unharmed, but they also reported the exact same thing."

"And what's that?"

"Abandonment. All vehicles, munitions, and hardware have vanished. Anything that wasn't taken was destroyed and burned beyond all recognition. An entire garrison just up and disappeared."

"Bloody hell! How long?"

The man turned to his Sergeant.

"Based on the amount of damage and ash present, this place cooked for at least a week. Also, if you'll recall, it rained for several days recently."

"Yes, I remember. It reminded me of home. What of it?"

"The rain wasn't needed to put the fires out, sir. I'd say they relocated almost a month ago, few weeks at a minimum."

"Thank you Sergeant. I have to radio this in. Find them!"

As they departed, the man yanked his comm device out of its cradle. He barely had the handle to his mouth before he said, "Urgent message for Brigadier Smythe."

"Understood. Patching you through," was the reply.

After a few seconds of dead silence, he heard, "Smythe here."

"Sir, this is Major Murphy. We've reached Fort Bragg and the post has been abandoned. Do we have any satellite imagery available?"

* * *

Through the clandestine movement of survivors outside of D.C., the informal resistance network was made aware of the English preoccupation with the FBI's J. Edgar Hoover Building. Chatter on all bands and channels were rife with speculation for the next several days. Josh was vindicated and angry after his conversation with Sarkes regarding this development.

"All this time… the feds were storing all of the requests for backgrounds checks in a database? I friggin' knew it!" he stated emphatically.

"It's the FBI's dirty little secret. They built it in house using only their people. No contractors, no congressional approval or oversight," the former POTUS replied candidly.

Dallas and the rest of the gun enthusiasts just sat there dumb founded.

"So what are they storing? It was only a request for a background check. There's nothing on those forms about *what* was purchased."

"Beats me, but you know those ATF guys… technology being what it is, or was. They could have easily made copies of the purchases during their inspections with concealed pocket scanners or even a smart phone with decent resolution."

"Well, we're screwed," Dallas declared as he stood up.

"Meaning?" his friend asked.

"Think about it. The British targeted that building on purpose. They had to have known the server was in there with all that data on it… and they have to be under the impression that the server was hardened against an EMP. So, if I had to make an extremely, yet highly, educated guess, I'd say those guys are about to go on a gun confiscation binge. Hell, I've got at least a dozen entries in there."

"Me too," James added.

"I guess I drew some sort of lucky straw. Em sold all my gear when she unloaded the house," Gregg stated. "All of my stuff is now registered in someone else's name now."

"Well, all I can say is that you aren't in Virginia, Dallas. Those guns, and then some, are here in Ohio or already cached down there. If they go looking for them, more them half are out of state," Josh offered in rebuttal.

"And when they show up at our doorstep and pull the ol' Gestapo 'name and address' show me your papers routine, they're gonna find 'McKutcheon, Dallas J.' in their rolodex of pain and haul my scrawny redneck ass out of here!"

"Oh, good Lord," Gregg interjected. "Theatrics aside, what are the options? What are you going to do if anything comes of this?"

Josh shrugged and answered.

"I'll open up my little Stack-On gun locker and give them a tour of the five I bought from FFL dealers. If they take 'em, then so be it. They'll need a metal detector and some informed intuition to find the cache under the barn."

"And when they roll into the park, what then?" Lt. Stokes asked. "We've got so much military ordnance in there it looks like a weapons depot in places."

Josh thought for a moment and then decided on a course of action.

"Alright 'BB', then we'll just have to hide them in plain sight. You said yourself that it's a Renaissance festival in there. Let's build that little band of merry minstrels a stage."

Stokes groaned. "That reminds me. I'd like to make an official request for a call sign change."

\* \* \*

As the communities and small towns around McArthur continued to assess their assets, an old barn yielded a long forgotten wood burning stove. After much discussion, it was decided that Mama Reni's would transition from a local pizzeria to an 1800's era tavern. As a result, the stove was ear-marked and installed at the restaurant. In an effort to keep the beast stocked, Josh gave a training class on how to make charcoal so the establishment would always be well supplied with fuel. Unfortunately, the current owner was beside herself. After spending several days muttering under her breath as she re-learned how to cook, her salvation arrived.

"Mimi? Are you in there?" Layla called out.

"I'm back here," she answered from the kitchen.

"I have a gift for you."

"Piece of junk! she exclaimed. "Burned another one!" she moaned as she dropped the heavy cast iron pan on top of the stove. "Be there in a minute."

Josh's daughter looked at the former restaurateur turned refugee and said, "Maybe we should come back later. She's been fighting that stove for weeks."

"No, no, no, mademoiselle. She shouldn't be fighting it," he answered as he peered through the cased opening that served as the order-up window. "There's no need for introductions. I'll just go and help her. You'll see," he responded.

"Okay, but it's your funeral," she replied.

The man swept his way through the worn double doors into the kitchen and proclaimed, "Ma chérie, you needn't fight with it." Then he caught sight of the old stove. "C'est magnifique! Where did ever find such a beautiful stove?"

"This piece of junk? Somebody found it in a barn and installed it in here. Now that," Mimi said, "Is magnificent," and pointed to her Garland eight burner thirty-three thousand BTU commercial stove. "With the power out," she continued as she sighed. "The natural gas won't make it to my baby without the pressure stations."

170

"Perhaps, if you showed the same kind of love and devotion to this old Pittston stove, she would perform for you just as admirably. You only need to listen to her speaking. She will tell you exactly what she needs."

Mimi had a befuddled look on her face. *Who is this crazy man with the wild accent?*

"Layla honey, can you come in here please."

She started laughing before Mimi could say anything more.

"You like your gift? We picked him up this morning."

Mimi was still confused.

"Meet your new chef, Jacques Boules. We used to supply his high-end French restaurant in Columbus."

"My what? Mama Reni's doesn't need a new chef. What it needs is a new stove! Preferably one that doesn't talk!"

"Oh no, ma chérie. I will teach you… show you techniques and have you taste things you never thought possible. Come," he said. "Come, come," the man cajoled as he turned her and led her back to her nemesis. "Let me give you your first lesson."

When the two approached the contraption, Jacques said, "At the outset, release yourself from your previous thinking. This isn't a pizzeria anymore. Try visualizing a family dinner on Sunday, hearty meals like soups and stews."

"Crock pot meals then?" Mimi asked.

"Exactement," he replied in French. "One-pot meals are the order of the day from here on out. Whatever you cook en masse is what everyone eats."

"What about bread? We need our carbs, Jacques," Mimi said warming to the Frenchman's presence.

"In time, ma chérie. I'm sure Mademoiselle Simmons can help us procure the materials needed to build a brick oven, but first, let's create a dish to make you swoon. It's called Pot-au-Feu."

"Pot a what?"

"It's a roast that will melt in your mouth and excite your senses in ways that you have never imagined. Now, every good kitchen needs a healthy herb garden," he continued as he began inventorying the kitchen.

Giggling, Layla backed away. As she was exiting the front door, she heard Jacques exclaim, "Sacrebleu! No fresh herbs. Okay, okay," he stammered as he calmed himself. "We can fix that. In the meantime, let me show how to make love to your stove."

*Crazy Frenchman.*

# Chapter 12

When winter started releasing its icy grip on the country, gang activity outside of the cities initiated in earnest. Having exhausted whatever resources they scavenged to survive February and the better part of March, the raiding parties began venturing further and further. The suburbs with their plush homes and gardens, which had managed to avoid the gaze of the downtown clans during the cold months, burned first. Anything that wasn't nailed down was hauled back to the inner-city. Smaller towns and rural enclaves within a sixty-mile radius of Columbus were deemed fair game. The orgasmic free-for-all was relentless and unabating.

In mid-April, Josh and the rest of the group screamed toward Chillicothe as the marauders attempted to sack it once again. With better defenses in places, by the time they got there the fighting had subsided and the invaders were easily repelled.

However, the second battle only proved to heighten Josh's state of alert for McArthur. The former state capital of Ohio was less than an hour from their little Hamlet's doorstep. Hell's bloodhounds would be knocking on their collective doors if the town and its neighbors weren't closed off soon, and he knew it. As a result, Josh and Mayor Cranston gave what amounted to a press conference where they announced the creation of patrols, training, and perimeter defenses. Before Josh was able to even ask for volunteers and finish his announcement, the crowd outside of Mama Reni's interrupted the message with the calls of 'where can I volunteer'? The scene reminded him of big budget Revolutionary War movies.

The Sheriff's office across the street had a line two dozen deep within minutes. When the new recruits entered, they were met with clipboards and paperwork. Sarkes' initial debrief, and the subsequent leadership planning meetings it spawned, produced questionnaire criteria. In short, those with police, military, or management experience would be grouped together and assigned to the 'Squad Leader' training regimen. The survey document completed by each volunteer was merely the first step in trying to assess their individual qualities and characteristics. The rest of the assessment for these volunteers would be observational.

Avid hunters and experienced trackers that had the capacity to quietly observe for hours on end, were placed into 'Forward Observer' (FO) training. Anyone completing this course would man and work with the engineers to construct the stations that they would occupy. Any existing or acquired concealment knowledge would be used to aid in this endeavor.

As a result, when plans were being discussed for FO's, extra scrutiny was being emphasized with the volunteers manning the OP's (Observation Posts). These sentries would need to observe and assess from a distance and make a judgment call on the fly. Throughout the training and construction of the OP structures, stragglers continued to arrive in pairs and whole family groups as word spread of the safe haven located in southeastern Ohio.

As each site location came online, it was inserted into the list of available placements. The posted sentries immediately began paying dividends. This was in no small part some due to the training received from the like of James, Hoplite, and Gregg, who were working wonders. As each group of refugees passed the concealed earthen structures, the headcount and description was radioed ahead. Welcoming committees intercepted the foot draggers before they ever came within sight of the park entrance. Before entry was permitted, questions were posed and answered and skillsets were reviewed. Any suspicious activity was reported and could result in the person or the entire group being turned away.

So far, no one needed to be.

By and large, if a potential resident had a tradable knowledge base, they were directed toward that endeavor. Useless abilities like computer programmer and software tester made up the bulk of the water and firewood committees until new skills could be acquired.

As the camp neared the end of the third month, they had accumulated an interesting cross-section of American industry. Iron and steel workers, coupled with carpenters, formed the 'Construction Battalion', while analysts of all persuasions, accountants, and the mathematically inclined were placed in 'Intelligence' and "Communication' groups. Bow hunters with their gear were in high demand as ammunition was relegated for defensive purposes only.

Commodities like water purification tablets and iodine tincture liquid were being reserved for patrols and a potential guerilla campaign. The raiding parties and small unit teams would need it more for cold camps as building fires while encamped was not a good idea. As a result, all of the lake water and the rain collected in barrels at the park had to be boiled. The entire point of the encampment wasn't to coddle and provide a safe haven. To Josh, and the rest of the people responsible for its use, the single overriding purpose was to simply give residents time to acquire or reacquire skills needed to survive on their own.

The state park eventually came under the control of an electorate known as the 'Board of Governors'. Each of the committee's had one representative and all had equal voice during discussions. The only expressed military presence in the park was represented by Gregg and Hoplite. At the insistence of President Sarkes, Lieutenant Stokes and his men were assimilated into the park population posing as civilians and dispersed throughout the camp's working groups. They were to function as the eyes and ears and alert the others if there were issues.

\* \* \*

"Okay, I think the wind speed is good, Katherine. The wiring looks right. Go ahead and release the break," Scott said from atop the windmill.

"Climb down a little bit first, sweetie. I don't want you to get hit if it rotates."

The young inventor looked around at his surroundings and realized he was standing on the upper platform.

*Dummy*, he thought. "Sorry," he called back down.

When he was a little over half way down the structure, the youngest of the Simmons daughters released the break holding the blades of the wind pump in place.

Once he was finally on terra firma, he explained to Josh and the rest of the Tin Hatters what he and Katherine had done.

"I know how you like to have back-ups for your back-ups, Mr. Simmons, so I installed a motor salvaged from an old treadmill behind the rotor. This way, if the solar powered well-pump you and the Tin

Hatters protected ever goes out, we'll still be able to use wind energy for water."

"So what's the upgrade for?" Josh asked confused.

Chester stepped in and explained, "What the lad here is trying to explain is that when the blades rotate, everything spins, including the wellhead. The newly installed part is being used to push an electrical current down the wiring apparatus to these batteries."

"He built you an 1800's version of a battery charger, Daddy," Katherine gushed.

"Right! What they said!" Scott exclaimed nervously.

Josh looked the agitated man up and down and shook his head.

"Son, come here," he stated reassuringly as he placed his hand on his shoulder and turned him away from the others.

"Oh, umm… okay?" he replied while flinching and hunching to the paternal gesture.

When they moved off a couple dozen feet, Josh said, "I'm not sure what you're so nervous about, Scott, but you're doing wonderful work out here. The things you've built and conjured from thin air have made a huge difference."

"Really?"

"Yes, really. You're inventive, driven, creative, intelligent, and a whole host of other descriptors. So what's the problem?"

The young man kicked at the dirt as he contemplated his response.

When none came, Josh sighed and stated somewhat forcefully, "Spill it, son."

Before he even knew what he was saying, Scott blurted, "Fear of God, sir."

The father of three actually chuckled his reply, "I'm sorry?"

"I went to school with Katherine and Layla for six years and every boy in that place lived in fear of you. You've always been so protective of them, and for good reason now that we know what happened in Columbus, but that's not what I'm saying," the boy began in a rambling response.

"When I'm in my workshop, I feel like a genius. I am the smartest, most clever person alive. Katherine will come in and tell me how proud of me she is. Then I leave that protective bubble and I see just how much I don't know when I speak with Chester, Bryan, even Dallas and James. It's just that – you're very intimidating to be around. I mean –, it's…" the boy stammered and then paused.

"Oh, don't stop, you're on a roll."

"I'm in love with your daughter, sir, and don't want to wake up hanging from a girder if things don't work out between Katherine and me. I can't believe I just said that." Dejectedly he added, "You can kill me now."

And there it was. The one thing every man in McArthur feared when it came to his daughters and Scott just blurted it out.

Josh was taken aback and stood stock still. After Javy had been captured near the farm, the story of his vengeance in the warehouse had spread throughout the town. Many of the residents had either attended the local schools or were parents who had children in school with his daughters. When they heard the information, their reaction wasn't shock and horror. Most simply said, 'Well, that explains it.'

Regardless, the budding scientist and inventor had just summed up the feeling of every man in the town in just three words, fear-of-God.

When Josh didn't say anything, Scott asked, "Sir?"

The highly over protective father raised his hand to silence him. "I'm processing this news," was all he replied.

While he weighed the pros and cons of the new information, he finally landed on the same conclusion Sam had provided weeks earlier. His daughters moving on, leaving the nest, and eventually finding love was inevitable. He just never imagined that it would be so soon. In a way he felt guilty for not pushing them sooner.

When he did speak again, Josh offered Scott some insight as only a father of daughters can provide.

"What happened to those men took place a long time ago for something far more serious than simply dating my daughter. You have nothing to worry about in that regard."

The love struck man-child let out the breath he didn't realize he had been holding for the last minute.

"I've known you and your family for a number of years and two things are abundantly clear. First, I know you were raised right and come from good stock. Second, I don't believe that the chemical make-up of those men in that warehouse exists anywhere within you. Now, as for your profession of love towards my youngest daughter; the only time you and I will only ever have an issue is if I hear about any form of disrespect or abuse."

"Oh, no sir! I would never. I couldn't even kill a spider," he blurted without thinking.

Josh chuckled at the comment.

"No, seriously! I had one crawl across my workbench and I had to call Katherine over to come do it for me!"

"Good to know," he replied smiling. "Don't get me wrong, couples occasionally disagree. It's natural. I get that. However, should that disagreement lead to something more physical, you and I will be having an entirely different and one-sided conversation. Are we clear about that?"

"Yes, sir, but I don't think that conversation would be needed or ever take place."

"And why's that?"

"Because… Katherine would kill me first, that's why!"

Josh laughed out loud at that proclamation. "She can be a handful. Of that I have no doubt, but here's the thing. You're a good kid, Scott," he began as he placed his meaty hand on the scruff of his neck and turned him back to the group. "Treat her with respect and you'll do fine." As they started walking, the fatherly figure continued, "Now about this," and gestured toward the windmill. "To be fair, I wasn't sure how this wind pump battery charger mechanism would turn out. By all accounts it seems to be –," he started to say.

"Uh, Scott. We've got a problem," Katherine called out and interrupted as they neared.

The two men glanced up to see her pointing towards to the upper platform. The gearing was starting to smoke and an occasional spark dribbled from the housing. After a few feet, it would burn out... at first.

"Throw the break lever!" he hollered to her as he started running toward her.

She held up a metal pipe that used to be attached to the apparatus and screamed, "I did throw the break!"

For the better part of an hour, the group watched on in disbelief as the structure burned. While Scott and Katherine sat off in the distance comforting each other over the mishap, Josh stood with Chester and observed as pieces fell to the ground.

As the last of the cross brace members collapsed, adding to the heap of smoldering debris, the pair approached.

"We're really sorry about your windmill, Daddy," his daughter began.

"Yeah, I didn't see a problem with the motor. I thought it was good. Don't you worry about a thing though, Mr. Simmons. We'll fix this and you'll have a new wind pump in no time."

"I know you will. I have faith in you. Get it fixed, son," he said with a little bit of warmth and walked away.

\* \* \*

At the end of April, an emergency broadcast was transmitted on the high frequency bands. It contained a message from the new POTUS. The message repeated for ten minutes and then went silent. Chester was on duty at the time and recorded it for the others. Once he had the full message, he played it for Josh, Sarkes, Brent, and the remaining leaders.

"Holy crap!" the retired General exclaimed when it completed its playback. "What are we supposed to do with that?" he posed to the assembled group.

"We type it up and post it with the other pertinent messages downtown and in the park, that's what," Dallas offered. "We're not the information police."

"Ah, that's not entirely true," Lt. Stokes rebutted. "We didn't advertise what was going on in Omaha, now did we."

"That was national security," Sarkes interjected. "This is an entirely different animal. This is a call to arms."

"That may be, but we're talking about a population that has no idea how to fight. To me," he explained, "It's analogous to any other third world hell hole we've been in. The civilians have pitchforks and rocks and the bad guys have modern weapons."

After a few minutes of discussion, the decision was made that the message was to be transcribed in its entirety and posted on the board the next morning.

Sheriff Watson delivered it aloud to the assembled residents before posting it. It read:

*My Fellow Americans,*

*This is President Alan Culpepper. It is with great sadness that I inform our nation of the following information. On March 25th at 10:15 PM EST, President Rayburn passed away as a result of a massive heart attack. His leadership in good times and bad was a model and an inspiration. He was my friend and he will be missed.*

*However, from that day forward, I have worked tirelessly toward a singular purpose. Our banks and vaults have been looted, our cities have been set ablaze, and our military has been decimated both on land and at sea. Regardless of that, my goal, and that of our remaining commanders, has been to strike a retaliatory blow against our illegal UN oppressors and their European masters.*

*I am here to tell you now that we are succeeding in that endeavor.*

*At 2:00 AM, just this very morning, I issued two orders. First, I ordered the sinking of all British ballistic and fast attack submarines. Once completed, my second order took effect. At sunrise today, a massive counter offensive was launched by elements comprising the bulk of the assets previously housed at Fort Bragg. Similar engagements* are taking place on both coasts with whatever forces we could muster. We will push these UN occupiers back into the sea!

Here and now, I am calling on all able bodied Americans to stand up and fight for your nation! Resist these invaders at every turn! Fate rarely appears at a time of our choosing, but there is a holy righteousness in this action and I have faith that we will be victorious! You have my solemn pledge that we will not stop resisting. We will continue the battle through the rockets' red glare and the dawn's early light until our flag is where it belongs! We won our freedom once, we can do it again.

To that end, I am calling on all current and former military members. Head into the forests and swamps and use the skills that this nation has provided you. Observe from the craggy mountain tops of the Rockies and Appalachians. Stand guard in the brackish waters of the Mississippi. Coordinate among other bands of Patriots. Resist them at all costs. You have my solemn word, that all freedom fighters will receive complete and unequivocal amnesty for actions committed in defense of THESE United States.

The following warning goes out to every foreign soldier on American soil:

Lay down your arms and you will be escorted back to the coast. Units not currently engaged in combat operations have fifteen days to reach the nearest coastal facility and board your ship. Any person found in-country after May 15th is to be detained as a foreign combatant and/or shot. Furthermore, all ships are subject to search.

To every foreign Navy at sea and in port, you have twenty-four hours, until midnight on May 16th, to clear the United States territorial

*waters and enter international water. Any ship that cannot make that*
*distance is to be sunk. Do not make the mistake of testing our resolve.*

*May God Bless you and may God Bless the American people.*
*This is President Alan Culpepper, signing off.*

The transmission did not have the full effect that the new POTUS desired. Only the Asian nations heeded the warning and departed. Japan had no desire to see any more of their cities leveled by an American bomb. India, while a nuclear 'power' in their own right, had no stomach for the game of chicken that was ensuing. Sarkes' covert allies were now down to three as a result.

In a move that would have shocked President Culpepper had he known, the French, Spanish, and the Dutch leadership spoke at length and considered following the lead of India and returning home. When they communicated that they would be staying to 'assist' though, the POTUS expressed his sincere gratitude at their willingness to stay the course. The remaining allies were asked to continue to maintain their subversive activities within the back channels until a time of their collective choosing.

Conversely, as a result of the President's ultimatum, the UN soldiers were told in no uncertain terms by their governments that they too would not be hampered by articles of war. Rapes and murders increased three-fold nearly overnight.

The British Prime Minister, after informing his men that they were to conduct a ground campaign as they saw fit, signed off by saying, "Gentlemen, God speed, happy hunting, and feel free to make a mess of the place." Then, in an effort to put the soldier's minds into the proper perspective, he quoted Milton's Paradise Lost, "Better to reign in Hell, than serve in Heaven."

\* \* \*

The handful of folks that were enrolled in the 'Forward Observer' course was subject to Hoplite's rigid standard operating procedures (SOPs). These were met with the typical groans and grumbles. However, they were giddy when it came to tactics training.

Josh took the OP construction to another level when he 'suggested' a Coastwatcher program. He was not ashamed to admit that he drew his inspiration from on an old Cary Grant movie, not his military history knowledge. At strategic locations ten to fifteen miles from downtown McArthur, he placed his version of the island Coastwatcher's from WWII. These volunteers would be left in place with enough provisions for three days and then relieved. For communication, Bryan and Chester repurposed and constructed several six-volt battery operated CB radios. The batteries were a 'gift' requisitioned from some looters that had cleaned out a sporting goods store shortly after the power outage.

The weeks following the second attempted Chillicothe ransacking saw smaller towns between Columbus and Athens hit one after another. It was like watching domino's fall in a perfect line of succession straight down Route 33.

# Chapter 13

"Nigel," Brigadier Smythe stated as he entered the Royal Marine communications tent.

"Good morning, Sir!" the young communications officer answered excitedly. "You're never going to believe the chatter we picked up overnight."

"Really? What have you got?"

"Remember that convoy that went missing?"

"You mean that disaster out of Denver where those jihadist idiots torched every city in between? How could I forget that mess, why?"

"I think we've been able to narrow it down to southeastern Ohio. It's kind of confusing though."

"Lay it out for me, Lieutenant," Smythe replied.

"Right. We've been hearing for months about a refugee camp called Lake Hope. This isn't that unusual as camps like that have sprung up all over the country. A few weeks back we picked up some bounced signals where we clearly heard about treasure in a tunnel. I had a friend do some searching and it turns out that it's roughly seventy-five kilometers from the firefight that saw the convoy escape."

"Indeed. Please continue, Nigel."

"Well, I think it went there, sir. Previously, the closest military presence was a National Guard outfit from Rickenbacker Airport and Wright Patterson Air Force Base."

"And the tunnel? What's the connection to that? You need to give me something more if I'm to order a reconnaissance mission to the area. How far is it from here?"

"I haven't been able to determine the correlation yet. The Internet isn't what it used to be since the Yanks servers went offline. However, the military presence and the proximity to the last known whereabouts of the convoy should be enough to warrant a look. Unfortunately, from our location in Charleston here on the coast, that would be seventeen hundred kilometers. For the most part, our eastern landing forces have been hampered by resistance efforts."

"I know, I know," the Brigadier Smythe lamented. "Whitehall greatly underestimated the American propensity to blow things up! Most mountain passes have been closed due to 'unexplained' rock slides or piles of trees that mysteriously sprouted in the roadway.

"So how do you expect me to get a recon team to southeastern Ohio, Lieutenant?" his CO asked.

"We could flank them with our West Point contingent?"

"I'd prefer to leave the dragoons where they are for the time being. Any other options?"

"There's always the French, sir. Last report had them camped outside Cape Girardeau, Missouri. They are already on the right side of the mountain range. No real impediments between them and Ohio."

The man contemplated the statement for a few moments then replied, "That is until they start dropping bridges into the rivers. Let's hope they don't do that. This is interesting though, go on."

"Yes, sir. That would be a serious setback. You are correct though. The French were able to make it up the Mississippi as far as this town here, Cape Girardeau. The commander there, a Capitaine Marceau, he's half the distance from the park compared to us here in Charleston," the Lt. answered as he placed a map on the old wooden table that was his workstation. "If they went around Louisville and Cincinnati, they could be there in a couple of weeks."

"Weeks? That's a two-day drive at most!"

"Therein lays the problem, sir," the comms man replied.

His CO sighed heavily as he exhaled. Dejectedly, he asked, "No petrol?"

"Ran out almost a month ago," the Lieutenant responded. "I'm afraid the Yanks have been quite efficient at sinking and disrupting our ocean going supply lines. Without electricity, the refineries in-country can't go online and refine what we need. On top of that, sir," he continued. "The tools required to withdraw the fuel from the underground tanks have been destroyed by their owners before we arrive. It's like they know we are coming. To say that the locals are being less than cooperative is an understatement. All the Legionnaires do have are confiscated horses and crude wagons."

"How very... French of them."

The Communications Officer smiled.

"What have we got left?" Smythe asked while striking a more serious tone.

The man turned and retrieved a ledger from a bookshelf. Inside were handwritten notes regarding UN troop locations, force strength, fuel and equipment status, as well as each unit's mobility capabilities.

"You'll have to forgive the manner in which we've resorted to logging our assets. Petrol rationing has affected our ability to keep our tech gear charged."

The Brigadier waved it off and started reading. As the man read the contents, he just shook his head. When he finished, Smythe quietly closed the book and laid it on the table.

As he stood, the Lieutenant asked, "Sir? Your orders?"

"Nigel, several things are coming into sharp focus. Without the necessary resources, we are the proverbial sitting duck. Unless we get some reinforcements, we are likely to be thrown out of this county… again. Send a message to the French in Cape Girardeau."

"Very good, and Omaha?"

"I don't believe one is warranted. She's next in Presidential succession since the mobs castrated Washington in the first weeks. They actually did us a huge favor when they started to hang Congressmen and Senators from the Capital Dome though."

"How's that, sir?" Nigel asked.

"Two of the men hanging were third and fourth in line for the Presidency after the Vice President. The rest of their precious Congressional body were either shot or scattered into the wind."

"How did you learn so much about their government? I'd wager one in ten don't even understand that we have a Parliament."

"Know thy enemy, Nigel. Our only salvation may reside in Omaha. Let's leave her be. She'll figure out a way to remove the new President in time."

"I'll see that the French are notified," the Lieutenant said as he saluted the Brigadier.

As he began to exit, Smythe stopped and turned. He paused a moment while he contemplated.

"Sir?" Nigel asked. "Anything else?"

"On second thought, do communicate a message to Omaha."

"Very good, sir. What would you like to say?"

"Remind her that this was a six month operation at best and that her window is closing."

"I'll transmit it myself," the Communications Officer stated. "If I may be so bold, but what happens when it closes?"

"That's when the supplies run out... and we are all dead."

\* \* \*

"Oui, Monsieur. Orders received and understood. Over and out," Capitaine Marceau answered and tossed the mic on the table. *Merde*, he thought as he pondered the latest request.

"And what do the English have for us now?" his mother asked as she entered the room.

"While they sit on the beach and enjoy the sun and surf, we've been tasked with traversing half the Midwest to a place called McArthur, Ohio. I was just about to consult the map to see what that journey might be like."

"You've got to be joking," she stated.

Her son looked at her quizzically.

"Mon cher fils (my dearest son), don't you remember the stories I told you? Don't you recall meeting the man?"

Then it dawned on her only child.

"The father with the two daughters?"

"Oui, one in the same. He lives in McArthur," she answered matter-of-factly. "His accommodations are bound to be better than Cape Girardeau, Missouri, no?"

"Ach," he decried incredulously. "Cet endroit est un trou de merde! (This place is a shit hole)!"

"How soon can we strike the camp and get moving?"

"What? Mother or not, you are not coming with us! I'm sending you back to New Orleans. This was only supposed to be an inspection visit –," her son started to say in dissent before she cut off his protestations.

"I may be your mother, Philip, but I am also your Mon Colonel! Like it or not, I'm going. Besides, wouldn't you like to thank the man whose sacrifice allowed your life to exist?"

Colonel Sophie Desjardins had been an Aspirant (Officer Candidate) in the French Foreign Legion when she and her squad, along with Josh and the offending soldier under his command, had been abducted from their base in Bosnia. Try as she might to miss or graze him, she was the one that had put the bullet holes in his torso. However, even after being shot, he still wouldn't comply with their demands.

Josh's screams of agony from the torture and then the eventual gunshot wounds almost broke them both. In the end, it was the man's protective instincts that had kept the woman's virtue intact. When several men within the abducting clan began eagerly undressing in preparation to gang rape Sophie, Josh capitulated.

She had watched on in horror as the bleeding, half-dead man castrated his soldier. When the deed was done, he was subjected to further abuse until unconsciousness came floating in like an angel. His wounds were eventually treated by their abductors and, as he was regaining his cognitive skills some days later, their rescuers arrived.

Over a decade and a half would pass before they would see each other again. Josh, needing to get as far away from Columbus as possible, had tracked her down through the French Foreign Legion in Paris. He truly didn't know what else to do or where to go. Getting out of the country seemed like a good idea at the time. With his daughters in tow, fresh from the nightmare that was Amanda and the trial, the weary travelers appeared on her doorstep in Avignon, France.

The remnants of the Simmons family spent several weeks with Sophie and her teenage son recuperating. Being out in the country and enjoying the peace resonated with Josh. While the children played, the pair would lazily stroll through the lavender fields of the Provence region and sample the available vintages. After a night of excessive 'sampling', the two made love. It was only after they departed that she told her son what happened in Bosnia.

Over time and circumstance, all of the other captives had passed on. Only they remained to tell the tale of their shared hell of Earth.

When they returned home, an invigorated Josh bought his farm and sent her a letter. It contained an open invitation to visit anytime as well as the address. It was the first and last time the man wrote that information down for anybody. As instructed, she had committed it to memory.

* * *

Dallas sat quietly and manned his post in the comms room of Josh's cabin basement. Most of his four hour shift was usually spent listening, recording, and transcribing broadcasts from around the country. If he heard anything pertaining to troop movement, resistance or other, he would make notes on the 'boards'.

In actuality, they were three medium sized white boards and easels that had been procured from the local middle school. On each was a map. The easel closest to his desk held the continental U.S. The center stand narrowed the scope of the country to cut outs of each coast, while the third was a blow-up of Ohio. The state of affairs nationwide was written in dry erase marker next to the national map, UN troops movements were marked on the coastal board, while local matters were documented with the state rendering.

"Briar Patch, this is 'Charlie Whiskey One'. Come in over," the radio crackled.

Calls from the remote outposts were few and far between. The SOP for the hidden structures dictated that radios were not to be used except for two express purposes: in the case of an emergency where the structure had been spotted or when the watcher had seen activity.

Dallas snatched the mic off of the table and immediately responded.

"Channel clear," he said in return.

This was a pre-programmed response. When heard by the others on the net, it indicated that there were to be no other transmissions on that frequency until the 'channel open' call came from the comm room.

"State of emergency or report, Charlie Whiskey One?" he asked.

"Report, twenty-three vehicles headed south on Route 33," the sentry replied.

"Disposition?" he asked.

"Fourteen trucks, eight sedans, estimate fifty to sixty passengers, heavily armed."

"Roger that. Channel open. Mother Goose out."

When the same call came from Charlie Whiskey Two ten minutes later, Dallas didn't wait for the report from the third Coastwatcher outpost. He quickly changed channels and queued the radio operator at Athens General (AG) Hospital.

"Mother Goose calling AG, come in AG."

Only a few seconds passed before they answered.

"This AG1. Go ahead," came the reply.

"Be advised, twenty-three hostile vehicles inbound. Say again, two-three hostiles inbound. Acknowledge, over."

"Acknowledged. Approximate strength?

"Charlie Whiskey One and Two independently estimate force strength of five-zero to six-zero, heavily armed, over."

"Roger that. We're on it! Thanks Mother Goose! AG1 out!"

The radio operator stationed in a shack atop the hospital tower bolted from the tiny tin roof structure and sprinted to the edge of the building. He grabbed the air horn stored at the base of the wall and blasted the device four times, one long followed by three short.

The town of Athens immediately went on high alert. Additional horns sounded across the quad of Ohio University and the small downtown area alerting everyone to man their posts at the north end of town.

By the time the hostile convoy made it to the concrete chicane on the bridge over the Hocking River, all able bodied residents and what remained of the university's student body were armed and waiting. The little Hamlet took a heavy toll and was left wanting, but they had managed to fend off the horde. Those that attempted to cross the water obstacle were gunned down and simply floated away.

A few days later, word reached McArthur that the handful of wounded survivors had been hung from a makeshift gallows on the north end of town leading into Athens. Their bodies were left to hang there as a warning for several weeks.

# Chapter 14

The arrival of spring in the foothills of the Appalachians brought tasks and chores. With Lake Hope State Park teeming, a little bit of extra land had been cleared for crops and several of the dismantled greenhouses from Josh's farm. That left two near the cabin and three more for bartering. Mayor Cranston talked Josh into donating one of the reserved barter structures to the town and they erected it on a vacant lot behind Mama Reni's. Jacques and Mimi were ecstatic, but refrained from telling anyone that they had constructed a private reserve herb garden on the roof of the restaurant.

Within the park, several sticks of dynamite donated by a farmer were used to enlarge an existing cave. The stone dwelling, coupled with the installation of a door, served as the sites root cellar. The construction battalion, affectionately known as the Sea Bees although it was considered an insult to the U.S. Army Combat Engineers, took Josh's suggestions to heart when it came to the building of the stage. Under the guise of excavating for posts, a recess was incorporated. They weren't told for what though. The engineers were giddy at the prospect of doing something secretive and clandestine nonetheless. It was then that Josh realized just how much sway he held throughout the community as a whole.

As each day passed however, a new issue would seem to arise. None of the homes at the farm were designed for prolonged periods of high occupancy. As a result, the septic systems were filling faster than the microbes could work. Therefore, slit trenches and latrines were constructed to ease the burden. Spring allergies combined with the last of the cold and flu season kept Basilia and Carlton, as well as Layla,

Lily, and Alysin busy at the cabins. A great number of the people being treated had mild forms of dehydration and exhaustion. Extensive physical labor was a foreign concept. So far, there had only been limited incidences of head lice. Bed bugs hadn't been detected, but according to Basilia, it was only a matter of time. Also, without the state of Ohio spraying for mosquitos, coupled with a hundred plus acres of standing water in the lake, she was predicting that the West Nile virus was bound to become a problem come summer.

"Are you guys out here?" Carlton called out.

"Yeah," came the chorused reply.

"Where?"

"In the greenhouse," one of the three replied.

As he approached he explained his issue. "We're almost out of borage. Can I use pleurisy root instead?"

"What are you treating?" Alysin answered from inside the small glass laden structure.

Juan and his sons had built the out-building expressly for the cultivation of medicinal herbs. It measured twelve by fifteen and was constructed almost entirely from vinyl replacement windows. Jesus and Abelardo had removed them from a building supply warehouse on the outskirts of Nelsonville during one the group's reconnaissance missions. The floor was gravel with two courses of cinderblock forming the base. A three foot wide sliding glass door served as the entrance. Bryan and Chester aided the medical effort by installing a small space heater wired into two deep cycle batteries. Solar panels kept enough of a charge on them so the hut remained warm during the night hours.

"I've got a little girl with a cold and an infant with colic," he replied from the Martinez back porch.

"Does she have a fever yet?" Basilia asked.

"No, but I can hear something in her lungs."

"Use lemon balm for both," Lily answered. "Pleurisy is for after they have a fever and works better in adults. Make the lemon balm into a hot tea. It'll help induce a temperature in the little girl which starts to break the cold. Conversely, the baby will relax."

"Couldn't I give catnip for that?"

"You could, but my guess is they probably also have some seasonal allergies too. The lemon balm is a far superior all-around remedy," Basilia offered.

Carlton shook his head as he stepped off of the porch and entered the structure.

"Where did you guys ever learn this stuff?"

"I read a book," Alysin answered awkwardly. "But then they gave me a lab."

"Medicinal herbs are a way of life in South America. It's not that difficult. You just need to know what grows in your area. If it doesn't, find a suitable replacement and keep moving forward," Basilia added.

"How about you, Lily. Where'd you pick this stuff up?"

"I spent a lot of time trying to cross pollinate different plant species naturally. Not like those abominations Sam's father and the rest of the GMO's created."

"Lily! Control the crazy!" Alysin stated excitedly. "Ha! I always wanted to say that. I never get to say that, but I finally got to say that!"

"It only means something when one of us is about to go on a tangent, Alysin. I simply stated a fact. No emotion. No digression. See? Cool as a cucumber," she replied.

"Yeah well, I'll be watching you, little miss missy miss," the oddest of the Tin Hatters retorted.

Her friend came back at her with, "Whatever," then turned back to address the former corpsman. "Here are the big five in my book, ya ready?"

"Yes, ma'am. Fire away."

"Okay, number one is Echinacea. Not only is it used as an antibiotic to treat scarlet fever, syphilis, malaria, blood poisoning, and diphtheria, but it can also enhance the activity of the immune system, relieve pain, and reduce inflammation. It has hormonal, antiviral, and antioxidant effects too."

"She's right," Basilia offered. "Professional herbalists recommend Echinacea to treat UTI's, vaginal and ear infections, athlete's foot, sinusitis, hay fever, as well as slow-healing wounds."

Carlton reached in his back pocket for his notepad. "Hold up a bit," he implored them. "Let me take some notes."

After scribbling a few remarks, he said, "Okay, number two?"

"I'd say that would be the pleurisy root you were asking about a minute ago. Native Americans say it's good for lifting and running strength. That's why we've been giving it to the firewood brigade."

Alysin included, "It can also be used to handle poopy problems like diarrhea and dysentery."

The man didn't blink at the Tin Hatters comment. Shit happens, literally.

"Nice," Lily countered.

"You probably read somewhere that it serves as an expectorant. This makes it a valuable medicinal herb for chest complaints and in the treatment of many lung diseases. Which is why you most likely wanted to give it to the little girl," Basilia stated.

"You gettin' all this?" Lily asked

"Every word. Number three?"

"What do you think, Basilia, nettle or lemon balm?"

"Probably the balm. It treats a wider variety of issues."

"Like what?"

"Oh, let's see. We already told you about the fever and the colic. There's also the treatment of mumps, cold sores, and other viruses."

"It was the anti-viral agent that had me doing some lab experiments on its usefulness for Chronic Fatigue Syndrome and Shingles," Alysin interjected.

"So how is it going to help the little boy with colic?"

"One of lemon balm's key medicinal attributes is as a tranquilizer."

"I'm sorry? A what?"

"Its effects are similar to a mild sedative and it calms a nervous stomach, colic, or heart spasms. Some people think that the leaves aid in lowering blood pressure. It is very gentle, but effective. That's why it's used for children and babies."

"Oh, and it has anti-histamine properties so it's useful to treat eczema and headaches, as well as insect bites and wounds. More recently though, they discovered that it impacts the limbic system of the brain so it was added to the ADHD formula."

"So why is it only number three?"

"Because silly," Alysin said. "Without the antibiotic nature of Echinacea, all of your patients would be dead."

Without skipping a beat, Carlton asked, "And nettle?"

"I call that the 'woman's herb'," Basilia answered.

"Seriously? What's it treat?"

"Cramps, my child. Cramps."

"Oooh," he replied and circled the word several times in his notepad. "Anything else?"

"Yeah," Lily stated. "If you figure out a way to extract the juice, it's a natural bug spray."

"Juice equals bug spray, got it. Number five?"

"If there are no objections, I'm gonna go with hyssop… or maybe the catnip. Both are used for cold and flu, but hyssop can also address sore throats, bruises, and burns."

"Yeah, but catnip handles headaches and fever," Alysin added.

"That's why, ladies, you give the patient both at different intervals like we did with Tylenol and ibuprofen."

"Excellent stuff," Carlton muttered under his breathe. "This is what I needed."

"You're welcome," Alysin announced awkwardly.

Not realizing he was speaking out loud, Carlton said, "Huh?"

\* \* \*

In preparation for a resistance effort, Hoplite had several bundles of lumber from the stalled train trucked to Fox Lake. Under the cover of night, Gregg loaded three teams of recruits into a deuce and delivered them at dawn. Scott wasn't a fan of losing Katherine for weeks of training, but she was a born leader and everyone knew it. Her skills needed to be honed so Josh's youngest daughter was at the top of the list when it came to assigning squad leaders.

Many of her childhood friends eagerly petitioned to be placed with her, but familiarity was actively being avoided by James and the other trainers. To them, it was a bit of a double edged sword. Team members that knew each other could instinctively learn faster, but their goal was to make the parts interchangeable.

With no roads servicing the small body of water, hiding the fighters in the dense forests for their training would be a far easier task there than among the population of any town, or the Lake Hope cabins.

The entire Hocking Hills area had been surveyed by the Engineers in the late winter and early spring. There was a dearth of places to hide. Ash Cave, Old Man's Cave, and Conkle's Hollow were all deemed suitable rally points as well, but had distinct disadvantages that Fox Lake didn't. Chief among them was their lack of escape possibilities should they be discovered. They'd never serve their purposes long term.

Prior to the truck of recruits or the lumber delivery, James, Gregg, and Hoplite created a three-fold training regimen in an effort to bring militia troops online. Once they were chosen and moved to the remote location, the deuce's laden with construction materials would arrive. The recruits would need to construct their accommodations between exercises. It was very reminiscent of the movie, *The Dirty Dozen*.

The first phase dealt with weapons drills. Even the locals that had been hunting for decades were required to display marksmanship and maintenance efficiency with not only their rifles, but also with handguns and scopes. Phase II took the students into the 'classroom' to understand advanced ballistics, scouting, and to establish a consistent language among the group. This was essential given the desire to interchange team members when necessity, mission parameters, injury, or death called for it.

In preparation for the third phase, Gregg and Hoplite had taken several hundred two-by-four's and built structures for close quarters training purposes. They were crude in their design and the framing had been quick and dirty. Gregg particularly enjoyed the fact that they didn't have any ceilings or a roof. He took great pleasure in directing and instructing the militia units from above as he observed from his makeshift catwalk.

It wasn't uncommon to hear the refrain, 'No, no, and hell no!' barked at the trainees. 'How many times have I got to tell you people! The second guy through checks behind the door! None of you looked! Congrats! Everyone's been fragged! You're all dead!'

When he and Hoplite weren't around, the students would take part in the age old act of disparaging their trainers. Katherine pointed out Gregg's proclivity to vigorously rub his head and sigh before proclaiming, 'Reset and do it again'. The group was convinced that he'd be bald in fairly short order. The other trainees delighted in her ability to be one of them when it was apparent she was being groomed for something more.

Hoplites favorite past time was firing live ammunition over their heads to see how each unit would react. Some didn't handle it well at first, but they learned to channel the fear into completing the various tasks and missions.

By mid-May, as the first class of students was about to 'graduate' from the three phased course of instruction, James implemented a shooting contest. This would be his pre-qual for entry into his adhoc sniper school. With Gregg onboard, it was the pair's intent to tap the top six shooters from each of their classes for the invitation only sniping education.

* * *

On what would have been Memorial Day, Dallas found himself manning one of the more remote OP's around the park. Through his high power scope he watched a mother and her two children noisily make their way down the road. The son, who was eight to ten years old by his estimation, was pulling a plastic wagon. It wasn't the metal Red Rider type he remembered hurtling down hillsides in during his youth like *Calvin and Hobbes*. Someone, the father perhaps, had wrapped each wheel in cloth and then duct taped it in place. He was thoroughly impressed with the noise reducing ingenuity.

The man watched and observed the three as the mother and daughter continued their argument about a cell phone, of all things. Dallas decided that it might be fun to put the disrespectful teenager in her place. Technically, at least according to the SOP, he was supposed to radio it in and have someone pick them up a few miles down the road. If he had a weakness, it was his propensity to fuck with people.

As they neared, he didn't want to give away the position of the earthen structure so he quietly exited the OP and worked his way down to the roadway. He left the intimidating AR-10 and the .308 hunting rifle in place, but grabbed his Mossberg 12 gauge just for effect. His sidearm was always with him, securely fastened in its thigh holster.

When they were only twenty yards away, he casually came out of the roadside brush.

"Halt!" he decreed in a commanding voice. "Identify yourself, this is a restricted area."

The sight of a fully camouflaged man with face paint barking orders had the desired effect. The mother immediately grabbed her two children and began to shield them. Dallas was impressed with her maternal reaction.

"State your business," he demanded.

"We heard there was a park near here. It's supposed to be safe. We don't want any trouble," she quickly answered.

"It's gotta be safer than that whack job you made us shack up with for weeks," the daughter mumbled under her breath.

"Shut up!" the woman said in a hushed tone toward her.

"Whatever. If we had a working phone, we could at least call someone to come and run over this asshole," the teenage girl replied indignantly.

"Watch your language young lady," her mom cautioned.

The family was disintegrating right in front of Dallas. The father was obviously missing, dead, or split before the EMP. Had he been around or recently deceased, surely one of them would have at least invoked his name, wishing he was there. The son seemed oblivious to the bickering, or at a minimum was used to it. He kept poking his head out from behind his mother and observing the strange man in the street.

Catching the youngster a third time, the sentry smiled at him. In an effort to ease the youngsters fears, he stated, "The park's a few 'klicks' down this road." As he gestured toward the young boy, he asked, "You hungry?"

The little one slowly nodded in return and then ducked back behind his mother. He swung his pack off and retrieved a meal replacement bar and held it out as he approached the three. "It's okay. I won't hurt you," he said as he slung the shotgun.

The son wouldn't budge.

Playfully, he offered, "How about a trade? This snack for your sister's cell phone. Deal?"

"Absolutely!" the mother emphatically replied as she snatched it out of her daughter's hand.

"Hey! That's mine! I bought that with my own money! Give it –,"

"Silence!" Dallas barked and interrupted her petulant tirade. "Learn some manners and some respect and you might see it again. If I ever spoke to either of my parents like that, I wouldn't have gotten the third word out of my mouth before being punished."

"Screw you, mister," she retorted indignantly and started to approach. Before she finished her first step, he placed his hand on top of his sidearm. She quickly stopped.

"What's your son's name?" he asked more toward the mother than the little boy.

"Nick," he replied confidently as he came out of his shell.

"Nick! I'm Dallas. It's a pleasure to meet you," he responded and offered a handshake to the youngster. As they shook, their interrogator remarked, "Hey, that's a pretty strong grip. I'm bettin' you play baseball?" he asked.

"Yeah!" the boy answered excitedly. "I got to pitch last year!"

"That's great! Where are you guys from?"

"Where from up near Massillon," the mother stated. "It was hit pretty hard by the inner city gangs out of Canton in February."

"Dare I ask where the father is?"

"He left us for his pregnant heiress girlfriend in New York! What's with the twenty questions?" the daughter rudely interrupted.

As calmly as he could, Dallas answered, "Either provide me with the answers I seek or you won't be invited into the park. Speak that way to me again and I'll whoop your butt right here in the middle of this street in front of your mother. Am I clear?"

She grunted in reply.

"So it's going to be baby steps in the manners and respect department I see. Tell me about the 'whack job', as your daughter so eloquently put it."

"I have a name you know," she spat.

"Eve! Knock it off or I swear I might even help him!"

"That's a very pretty name. Too bad your mouth keeps getting in the way. You can call me Mr. McKutcheon or sir. Are we clear on that?"

Eve crossed her arms over her pre-teen chest and nodded slightly.

"Good girl. And you are?" he asked the mother.

"Josselyn Dell," she answered. "Everyone just calls me Joss."

"Pleasure to meet you, Joss. Now, about the 'whack job', if you please," he requested as he discreetly handed the bar of food to Nick.

"When we started hearing that looters and gangs from Canton were raiding Massillon, we didn't feel a need to relocate because we thought we were out of the way."

"What did you consider to be 'far enough'?" Dallas asked.

"Brookside Country Club," Joss answered.

The man just shook his head. Targets that were perceived to be high value were always hit first. *When will people ever learn.*

"I know, I know. In our defense, we stayed because no one knew what had happened. We've heard plenty of theories though."

"It was an EMP," Dallas said flatly.

"What's that?" Nick asked.

"That's when a nuclear weapon is set off high up in the sky. It stops the electricity from being used in fancy cars, power lines, computers, and," he began and glared at Eve. "And cell phones."

"TV's too?"

"Yup, those too."

Nick pondered the explanation and then surprised himself when an idea popped into his mind. "So I get to play outside all the time?"

"Exactly like that," Dallas answered with a smile. "Sorry, please continue."

"We were pretty much left alone for the first weeks. We swapped food and what not with neighbors. A couple of empty nesters doubled up to conserve firewood and stuff. Then the gangs in Canton and Akron started a turf war of some kind. The group out of Canton attempted to claim the area as being within their borders. Some 'representative' came to the front gate for the club and tried to strong-arm the community into paying them for protection," Joss explained.

"Let me guess. You guy's said 'no' and then they tore down the gates and burned it all to the ground," Dallas offered.

"Pretty much, yeah, that's how it played out. We managed to get out before they made it to our end of the club. All we had with us was this wagon, a case of water, a container of rice, a dozen or so cans of soup, and a box of macaroni. Fortunately, we used to be an outdoorsy family so we also had a single burner propane stove with some extra cylinders, a tent, and some sleeping bags,"

"So let me get this straight. You walked here from Massillon without any weapons? No gun? No knife?" Dallas asked surprised at their lack of planning.

"My ex was a surgeon. He said he saw enough of the damage in the ER so we never bought one. Plus we lived in a gated community so we didn't have much crime to speak of."

"So what route did you take to arrive here on this fine day?"

"We stuck to the back roads and made it to Dundee after a couple of days. Some parishioners spotted our campsite behind their church and let us stay in the chapel for a week or so. There was a break in the weather and we got as far as Baltic. I used to be a geriatric nurse so I bartered my skills for a roof over our head."

"Good thinking," he stated clearly impressed. "What did they have you doing?"

"They needed help out at the Oak Point Nursing Center."

"How was that?" Dallas interrupted.

"They had it bad. When the power went out, everyone on life support or dialysis was gone within a few hours or days. By the time we got there, most of the meds had been dispensed. It wasn't pretty. After another few weeks there wasn't much else to do besides bury the dead, so we headed out again."

"Where were you going?"

"I have a sister in Coshocton, or had, I should say. She was a diabetic. Her neighbors told me she made it about six weeks."

"I'm sorry to hear that," he said offering her his condolences. He glanced down at the children and saw that they were eagerly devouring the power bar. Without the kids noticing, he slid another snack from his pocket and handed it to Joss. When they did manage to look up, Dallas' canteen was being offered to the trio. They greedily drank in the liquid nourishment.

"While we were there, we stopped at a place called Woodbury Outfitters. They'd pretty much set up a trading post of sorts. Unfortunately, we didn't have anything we were willing to part with, but one of the locals mentioned an elderly man on the outskirts of town. They suggested we offer to trade my nursing skills for food and shelter from the son."

"I'm guessing this is where the 'whack job' comes in," Dallas stated matter-of-factly.

"Yeah, mom had to sleep with him just to keep him away from Nick. Creepy jerk," Eve blurted.

Joss flushed and resisted the urge to smack her daughter in front of the stranger.

In as calm a tone as she could muster, Joss stated, "I did what I had to do to protect *both* of my children from that…" she began as her voice trailed off.

"Pedophile," Dallas inserted.

"Yeah. Anyway, when the dad died sometime later there definitely wasn't anything keeping us there."

"How'd you get away from the son?"

"He was always lurking and watching to make sure we didn't leave, so we poisoned his stew," the daughter said bluntly. "Which sucked because we had been saving that can. Bastard deserved it though."

"Eve!" Joss shot back at her. "That's enough with the language!"

"What? What else would you call him? You should have seen the way he looked at me and Nick when you were checking on his dad. Sleazy whack job. It was like he was savoring his next meal!"

"Okay, I think I get the picture little miss potty mouth. So how did you find out about us out here in the boonies?" Dallas asked.

"Carl, that was the son's name, he had some radio stuff. Maybe it was a HAM radio or military grade, I don't know. He'd been listening to Radio Free America and the BBC on it. Are UN troops really on American soil?"

Instead of offering an explanation, Dallas just nodded.

"Yeah well, he was trying to tune something in and found a bunch of Army guys talking on the radio. They mentioned a refuge in Lake Hope and…" she started to say as her voice trailed off again.

Dallas cocked a weary eyebrow at her. "And?"

"Carl said he heard them mention buried treasure, a lot of it. Like they emptied Fort Knox or something and made it disappear."

The man truly couldn't think to do anything other than laugh. *Josh is gonna be so pissed when he hears about this*, he thought.

In an effort to redirect them he asked, "Seriously?" through his feigned laughter.

"That's what he told me."

"Well the only thing in these hills is iron, lumber, and rock." Then he redirected the conversation to Nick. "Hey, do you like magic?"

"Yeah!" he answered excitedly.

"Great! Before I call the truck to have you guys taken to the park, I'll show you my favorite trick. Here's what I want you to do. When I count to three, take this phone and throw it as high as possible. I bet you I can make it disappear and then reappear right here in the palm of your hand."

"Hey!" Eve protested.

"Oh, knock it off, young lady. That thing hasn't worked in months. Seriously, I don't know why you're even carrying it around anymore," the mother warned.

While her daughter silently fumed, Nick appeared to be trying to figure out how the trick would work.

"Really? Are you sure?" he asked.

"Absolutely," Dallas replied. "Ready?"

The young boy nodded that he was.

"Okay, here we go. One, two," he began and dragged out the pronunciation of the words to make him wait for it. "Three!"

The aspiring pitcher heaved the device as high and as hard as he could. The phone flipped and spun as it arced down the street. Without warning, Dallas swung his Mossberg up and quickly fired at the target blowing it into dozens of shards across the road.

Without saying a word, he slid the weapon back and went down the roadway toward the debris. He picked up a handful of pieces and casually returned to the family.

"Look," he said to Nick as he placed the tiny fragments he had collected in his hands. "Magic!"

The little boy and his mother smiled.

"I've wanted to do that since the day she bought it," Joss explained as she gave Nick a squeeze.

"You jerk!" Eve decried. "That was a brand new smartphone with a hundred dollar LifeProof case!"

"Well maybe you should have spent the extra fifty bucks for the *bulletproof* case," Dallas quipped and squawked his radio.

"This is OP4 requesting a pick up. Three friendlies inbound."

"Copy that. Any Committee Chairs requested?"

"Roger that, Medical. Send my relief and contact El Jefe. Request he meet on arrival," he stated.

"Copy. Transpo ETA ten minutes." came the reply.

"OP4 out," the sentry answered.

"This is bullshit! You owe me six hundred dollars!" Eve wailed.

Dallas abruptly removed his Glock from its holster. This time he depressed the magazine release. Without looking, he ejected six rounds and into to his hand and then offered them to young girl.

"There. That should about cover it."

# Chapter 15

*Summer*

Carlos and Heather finished their load out and departed shortly after dawn. Josh had finally relented and allowed his oldest daughter the opportunity to serve. She was excited for her first taste of duty and the horses provided almost a full hour of uninterrupted time together for the budding couple. Horseback was now the preferred transportation method for sentry rotation. Granted, they were slower, but they didn't require any of the fuel from the farm's tanks. Being extremely quiet was a plus. As an added bonus, most of the regulars that were manning the huts were afforded the opportunity to pick up some extra grub in the form of fruits and berries growing along the side of the road.

Once the pair was situated on their mounts, Carlos began to explain to Heather, "Coastwatcher relief is probably the most exciting part of the program. When we get there, we have five minutes to swap out sentries."

"Why so little time? Don't we need to debrief or something?"

"Everything is recorded in the logbooks that stay on station. The rider returning turns in a copy for review. Just remember, if you find yourself in trouble, each of these desolate OP's have the ability to communicate to the farm and the park. None of it would have been possible given the terrain if Josh hadn't collected his friend from Columbus."

"That's what Dad says. Oh, that reminds me," she quickly added. "What does it mean that they couldn't cut new crystals for the hand held devices?"

Carlos spent the next few minutes explaining the comment.

When he was finished, he turned the conversation. "So you used to be an actress, huh," he asked as they ducked under a limb in unison.

"How have you never seen any of my movies?" she replied.

The man smiled as he answered, "These last four months represent the longest, most consecutive, amount of time I've spent in-country, in one place, in nearly a decade. I did see a number of your mom's flicks though."

"You and Greg saw the world I heard. Were the two of you always together when you went out?" Heather wondered.

"Longbow's practically an old timer by comparison. I'd only been there a handful of years. For the most part though, yeah, I was always his team leader once I arrived. When his transport got shot down, I was waiting on the tarmac. Saw the whole thing and there was nothing I could do. It took us a couple of hours to reach the wreckage. Once we were there though –," he started to say as his voice trailed off.

After taking a few seconds to compose himself, he concluded with, "We lost a lot of good men that day," he answered solemnly.

"Do you miss it?" she asked.

"Before all of this, it was the only family I had. My dad left when I was a baby and mom passed away some years ago. I missed that familial aspect of it until I got to know all of you. I can say without hesitation though, I definitely don't miss being shot at on a semi-regular basis."

"Five months of training for five minutes of sheer terror, right?"

"Exactly. What's the transition been like for you? One minute you're an A-list starlet living the dream in Hollywood and the next you're the farmer's daughter butchering cattle with a sister you didn't know you had. That can't have been easy."

"Oh, that?" she answered sarcastically. "We had a rocky start, but everything dad and Papaw told me has come to fruition. Being with mom and becoming a singer and an actress was great, but something was always missing. I've got that now. I just wish my mother was here to see it. I never could quite have both at the same time. Having sisters has been a blast though. Katherine is running around the country side with her squad and Layla is helping treat and heal people. In some ways, around here anyway, it's more difficult living up to the expectations by being the daughter of Josh Simmons than casting calls, auditions, press tours, and all of that other Hollywood BS."

"How do you think your friends in California are faring? I bet you're glad you weren't there when it hit the fan. The reports they are hearing on the network aren't pleasant."

"Honestly, I've tried not to dwell on it. I've read what Uncle Dallas posts downtown. Compton and Watts exploded and took over Beverly Hills, Inglewood, and Santa Monica. The UN forces just let 'em have those places. Those blighted areas were already so overrun with drugs and weapons that I'm sure the English lackeys didn't want anything to do with a true gangland."

"That and they were too busy looking for gold in San Francisco," Carlos added.

"Yeah, that too."

"How's your friend, Anna? She making do over at the camp?" he asked trying to continue the conversation.

Heather glanced at him and smiled. "What's happening here?"

He arched his eyebrows in reply, "What?"

"Either you're doing a horrible job of flirting with me or you're attempting to distract me and handle my emotions before I go off and become one of dad's Coastwatcher's," she answered.

Hoplite returned half a smile and sighed.

"Would I be out of line if I said a little of both?" he offered in response.

Heather laughed, "I appreciate the concern, but I'm fine. I know what's comin'." Then she leaned over and punched him in the arm. "Took you long enough to make a move."

"Hey!" he stammered in defense. "It's not my fault. Your dad's been keeping me busy," then paused before saying anything more.

When no more words came, she glanced over at him expectantly.

"And?" she asked.

"Huh?"

"You were gonna say something else, what was it?"

"It's nothing, I was just remembering the night we showed up with our hair on fire."

"Yeah, that was crazy for sure… what about it?"

Carlos sighed and responded, "I remember thinking you looked like an angel."

Surprised, Heather smiled, but didn't react to the comment. Now it was her turn to question the man and his intentions.

"How come you're not married? I'm guessing the 'job' didn't allow a lot of free time for that."

"Oh, I had lots of first dates," he said as he chuckled. "Unfortunately, the minute they heard I was in ROTC, or that I was active duty… The thought of being a young widow wasn't something they could overcome."

"Those bitches," Heather answered flatly.

Carlos laughed hard at the comment and replied, "That's what I figured, but whatever. Military wives are cut from a different cloth I guess."

"So is that what this is? You looking for a wife?" she asked.

"Oh, no! That's not it at all!" he declared quickly in defense.

"Relax, I'm just messing with you," she proclaimed. Then she flashed a warm smile and added, "Any girl would be lucky to have you. I think you've made it over the first hurdle though."

"How's that?"

"You're already in the good graces of my father and grandfather."

"Ah, well. Being viewed through that lens as a peer is far different than that of a daughter's boyfriend. Rules and expectations change."

"I'd say spending over four months resisting your natural urges coupled with your skillset might get you some leeway. Unless you're chicken," she retorted and started making clucking sounds.

The two continued their conversation and joked with each other for the entire ride to the first Coastwatcher outpost. Throughout the journey, he caught himself admiring everything about her. The way she talked and giggled at comments. How she kept brushing her shoulder length dirty blonde hair back behind her ear. Every single thing she did or said had him hooked and entranced. The man was falling one hundred percent, head over heels, in love.

After unloading her horse at the OP, he confided, "If it's not too forward of me, I have to admit something."

Heather cocked a weary eyebrow at him.

"Even though this wasn't like an official date or anything, by comparison, this is the best first date I've ever been on."

"If you try and kiss me, I *will* deck you," she stated sternly.

"No ma'am," he stammered as he quickly stepped back. "I wouldn't. I –," he began before her laughter interrupted him.

"Dude! You've got to relax!"

Hoplite turned red with embarrassment as she stepped toward him and gently kissed him on the cheek. He'd been able to communicate with women just fine before today. *What is the matter with me*, he thought.

Not really sure what to do at this point, he slowly backed away and retrieved something from his pack. As he clumsily thrust his hand out, he said, "Here."

"What's this?" she asked.

"It's an old walkie, but it's got a built in solar charger. I saw some security lights on a house during one of my patrols. The bulbs used the charge to draw power. The place was empty so I grabbed a pair. I had Bryan rig the chargers to the radio special for me. I have its mate in my pack. This way, if you want to talk to someone, and not broadcast across the net, you can call me."

"Look at you. What a resourceful little MacGyver you are."

\* \* \*

"You're sure that's what she said? Buried treasure?" Josh asked his friend as he watered his horse at the stream. "And some guy near Canton heard this?"

Dallas just nodded his reply as he placed the reigns atop the saddle, grabbed the bridle, and walked over as well. Gregg was fuming at the breach in protocol as he dismounted his ride. The man looked as if he was seriously contemplating some form of medieval discipline.

"If he could hear it, there's no telling how far that signal bounced. Do you think it's worth my talking to her?" Josh wondered aloud as the three men walked up the bank while the horses watered.

"Not unless you want to lend any credence to her story with the people here. She said it right in front of her children and Lord knows who they've told in the camp. I played it cool though," Dallas answered. "Aside from the folks involved in its burial, no one on the Board of Governors at the park knows a thing about it."

Josh thought about the statement for a few long moments in silence as he began aimlessly placing kindling for a fire.

Before he could formulate his thoughts into words, Gregg interceded. "I've heard one, maybe two, of them use the term 'buried treasure'. At a minimum, we should have the entire platoon muster at your hay barn at 18:00 for a conversation."

Dallas snorted at the response.

"What?"

"You've come a long way is all... despite the look of pure aggression on your face," he replied.

Gregg shrugged and went to his horse to retrieve their meal. With a hunk of fresh corn bread wrapped in a cloth napkin in one hand, he searched his bags for the can of cans. Lost in contemplative thought, Josh quietly lit the fire. When he returned, Gregg produced his P-51 opener and dumped the contents into a small soot coated pot.

"That the kind with the bacon in it?" Dallas finally asked.

"Yeah, you want some? There's another in my satchel."

Before heading over to retrieve the extra food, he added, "I've been meaning to ask, are we going by civilian law or military? Gregg said you were non-committal when Sam brought it up. It might be time to set up some kind of a court system. We've got lawyers coming out of our ears and the nasty crap is starting to pile up."

His friend walked away and Josh sighed loudly.

"Damn it," he groaned. "I was hoping we wouldn't be saddled with these types of issues."

"What did you think would happen? As far as I'm concerned, this is regular everyday societal law enforcement, but he's got a point," Gregg stated to the pair. "We need to hammer this stuff out because four months without law and order is long enough. I mean, Jim's been doing a good job in town, but the dregs we're encountering out there... that's some shit I never thought I'd ever see in this country."

"What do you suggest?" Josh asked inquisitively.

Before he could answer, Dallas offered, "Since we're throwing compliments around, he's right too. Hell, you heard what they did in Athens. We need some folks to have a 'sit down' and come to some sort of localized legal agreement for all manner of lawlessness."

"Okay, say I'm open to the idea. Who would you suggest?"

"For starters, you couldn't keep Sarkes and the General away from that meeting," Dallas answered.

"The Sheriff either. They need to decide what we are going to do for everything from looters and thieves, to rapists, cannibals, and murderers," Gregg interjected.

"And all the crap in between," his friend added. "Lord knows our OPs have seen just about all there is to offer in society anymore."

"Speaking of the junk being seen by our patrols, how's Katherine faring out there?" her concerned father asked.

"Let me put it this way," Gregg answered. "If circumstances hadn't dictated that she and her sister be hidden away for a decade...," he started to say them paused. "Ya know what, scratch that. I'm not even going to preface it. She's is, without doubt, one of the best damn leaders I've ever seen."

Filling with pride, Josh sat a little straighter on the log he was currently perched on.

"So she's doing well then?"

"Better than well," Dallas interrupted as he dumped the contents of his can into another pot.

"She doesn't tell you how her patrols go?" Gregg asked.

Josh sighed, then offered, "I'm trying to not be a helicopter parent. I *do* know that her chief concern is always to bring everyone home unscathed, but she needed to be taught by someone other than me. Not that I couldn't do it, mind you, it's just that having a variety of instructors that can teach from different perspectives matters on occasion. Does any of that even make sense."

"It does," Gregg stated. "I can tell you this much," he continued. "Whatever you did teach her over the years, definitely took root."

"Have you seen how she and the other squad leaders interact?" Dallas wondered.

"Yeah, it's uncanny."

"How so?" her father asked.

"We set the teams up to function independently with each receiving mission orders from Hoplite, Brent, or myself. But, we're at a disadvantage because we don't know the area as well. Katherine recognized this and began secretly giving the briefings to us to give to the other squads."

Josh started laughing.

"Not only that, but the individual squad leaders picked up on it and just cut leadership out of it entirely. They go directly to her, have been for weeks."

"Seriously?" her father asked through his chuckles.

"Yeah," Gregg replied, chuckling himself. "We've got four teams that we've trained plus two in reserve coming out of the combat engineering unit and she rotates them around. Three of the active units are in the field at a time, while one is on R&R. Then she inserts the engineers in once a month."

Beaming with pride, Josh simply added, "That's my girl."

\* \* \*

"I think that does it. I've checked and rechecked everything three times over. It should work this time," Scott said confidently.

"Should we try it before we bring in Dad and the rest of them?" Katherine asked. "Maybe take it for a test drive?"

"He does hate it when I show 'em stuff and it fails."

"That's only happened twice. You fixed both right away and now the park has more bow hunters than they know what to do with… and I've never seen a windmill get built so fast. You're over thinking this. If he's mad or annoyed, trust me, he'll tell you. My biggest concern is the welding for the sidecar," she replied as she changed the subject.

"Abelardo triple welded the arms and used some scrap quarter inch steel plate for the floor. It'll hold, but you're probably right about your dad. He scares me, but not in an 'I fear for my life kind of way'… at least not anymore."

"Then what is it?"

"I don't know. It's more of a, 'So your dating my youngest daughter, what are your intentions?' thing."

Katherine gave a little laugh. "You're weird."

"You just figuring that out, *Rodin*?"

"Whatever, *Tink*!"

The two laughed at the use of their monikers for a few seconds before Scott added, "Help me load some kindling?"

"Absolutely!"

During a routine patrol of the area, Dallas and his team were notified that an elderly man had recently passed. After the home had been inventoried by the family, they were unsure what to do with the man's possessions. The team suggested they take part in the upcoming 'McArthur Swap and Barter Sale'. However, as he reviewed the list of items, one item stood out, a 1973 Honda CB125 motorcycle. He knew as soon as he read the line on the inventory list that Scott could make something out of it.

Three days later, the young couple pushed the old modified bike out of the barn and slowly built a fire in the drum residing in the sidecar. Once it was lit, Katherine retrieved an arm full of peat.

"Are you sure this stuff is gonna work?"

Scott smiled at her and replied, "Awe, you're kinda cute when you doubt me."

As he kissed her on the forehead, he tore off a hand full, and threw it into the burning drum. It immediately caught.

When he turned back toward her, she dropped the load she was carrying on the ground and tackled him. Katherine landed on top of him and began showering him with kisses.

"You think you're so smart," she said in between pecks.

"Let's see you," more followed.

"Get out of this," she proclaimed as she stopped her affections, flipped him over, and put him in a choke hold.

"Not again!" he wailed. "Uncle! Uncle!" he bemoaned.

"I win… again," she declared as she released him and stood up.

"You know, one of these days," he began as he brushed himself off, "I'm gonna beat you!" he declared and tackled her back.

Standing off in the distance, her father, Sam, and Dallas just watched the interaction.

"What do you suppose that's all about?" Josh asked.

The other two slowly turned their heads toward him in disbelief.

His friend starting a hissing laugh through his teeth and answered, "Dude, that's flirting… or foreplay. Or what passes for both with this generation."

"Like hell!" he declared and started walking over.

Sam quickly grabbed his hand and slowed his walk in an effort to let the kids have their fun.

"You know, our wedding is in two weeks. Have you decided what you're going to wear?"

"I was planning on going as myself, but a little bird tells me you've outlawed flannel. Given that, I was thinking a black suit or my dress uniform."

"I'm coming in my hip waders and a fishing vest!" Dallas interjected. "I'm going for Colonel Blake… complete with a hat full of lures!"

"That'll be fine," she remarked not really paying attention. "I'm not marrying you."

"Sweet! Thanks Sam!" he replied and then clapped his friend on the shoulder. "Tough luck, bro."

"Let's just do this the easy way. Honey, what am I wearing?"

"Oh! Oh! Do I get a vote? I wanna vote!"

Exacerbated, Samantha reacted, "Fine. What's your vote, Dallas?"

"I say he wears the uniform. He did look rather dashing," he declared and then made a clicking sound like he was calling a horse while he smacked Josh on the butt.

His friend just kept on walking as if nothing had happened.

"You two have known each other how long?"

"Since we were seven or eight. So what's that, fifty plus years?"

"Is this what I'm marrying into?"

"'Fraid so, sweetie. Every family has a crazy uncle, right?"

Dallas took this as his cue to start singing, "Zip-A-Dee-Doo-Dah, Zip-A-Dee-A…"

"Oh, Lord. He can't stay in the cabin."

The three approached and found a fire burning in the drum and Scott on top of Katherine. The two love birds were gently making out on the ground.

Josh cleared his throat and declared, "You guys lose something down there?"

His daughter screamed at being startled and quickly thrust her boyfriend off of her. The young man, ever fearful of her father, immediately rose to his feet and ran into the barn.

Dallas just started raucously laughing. "Look at 'em go!"

It took a few minutes of cajoling from Katherine, coupled with a promise from Josh not to kill him, but Scott eventually came out of hiding.

As he exited, Sam said, "Scott, I'm no engineer, but I think you need to hook this up to the manifold."

"Correct," he replied as walked past her father with his eyes on the dirt. "I haven't hooked it up yet because I wanted the moisture to burn off. Once that step is done, I'll shut it down, let it cool just enough, and then connect it to the engine. We can test it and see where we are though."

Josh couldn't resist. He wasn't above messing with fearful suitors. "Interesting way to spend your down time, son."

"Yes, sir. I'm sorry about that. When we finish up here, I would like to speak with you regarding a private matter."

Katherine and Sam shared a knowing smile while he simply nodded his acceptance.

"So how are you going to test it," Dallas asked.

"With this," he replied and picked up a propane torch.

In an attempt to extend an olive branch, Scott held it out toward Josh and said, "Mr. Simmons, would you care to do the honors?"

"It's your rig. You light it," he answered as he took several pronounced steps backwards.

The young man pressed the igniter button and positioned it in front of the pipe. After a few seconds the white cloud dissipated so Scott removed the flame. The plume was replaced with waves of heat.

Katherine leapt on him and squealed, "It's works!"

The two twirled around while the other three ran their hands over the heat vapor.

"Well I'll be," Dallas declared. "Kid's pretty good."

Josh walked over and held out his hand to the man.

"Very nicely done, Scott. You've successfully built a functioning gasifier." As they shook, the father asked, "Now, what did you want to talk to me about?"

"Yes, sir. If you'll follow me to my workshop... Dallas, Sam, you're welcome to come as well."

Knowing what was coming, Sam turned to Katherine and said, "Sweetie, can you go in and start making lunch. We'll be along in a few minutes."

"Sure," she replied.

"Oh, and send James out here too."

"Will do."

Scott busied himself by looking for chairs and placing the ones he found around a table he had fabricated from an old door and a sheet of plywood.

As James entered, he asked, "What's up?"

"Good, you're here. Please have a seat."

Across the table sat the three men most responsible for the raising of Katherine and her sister. Seated with them was the woman that was to become her step mother. Scott couldn't decide if he would stand or sit so he alternated between both. Unfortunately, he was having trouble finding his words.

James leaned over and whispered to his friend, "What's he so antsy about."

Josh shrugged. "Beats me."

Just as he was about to speak, Brent walked in the barn.

"Is it true?" he barked.

"Is what true," Josh replied. "He hasn't said anything yet."

"Are you seriously going to ask for his blessing and not include me? Who do you think made the man sitting in front of you? I'm every bit as responsible for their rearing as these two!"

"Blessing?" Dallas asked. "Ah man, you're so screwed, Tink. I'm outta here," he declared and started to stand.

"Stop!" Scott declared forcefully. "Sit back down… please."

He then turned to Brent and said, "General, it was an incorrect assumption on my part. I apologize." He then grabbed the chair he had been using intermittently and concluded, "Please, have a seat."

Sam just sat there quietly with a smirk on her face. The young man noticed it and it put him at peace.

"Yes, I've asked to meet with you to tell you that Katherine and I have fallen in love. She and I have many shared and complementary interests and skills. Given the times we live in, we feel it is important to profess our love and devote ourselves to one another in front of God and family. So yes, I would very much like to ask her to marry me. However, I am unwilling to do so without the blessing of the people who shaped every fiber of her being."

Silence permeated the barn. Samantha was quietly trying to hold back her tears. She wanted to jump up and hug him. Those were some of the most beautiful and articulate words professing someone's love as she had ever heard.

After a few tense moments, Brent offered, "Josh, if I may, I'd like to administer the test and continue the tradition."

Remembering Brent administering the test to him all those years ago back in Bosnia, Josh nodded his agreement.

Brent reached over to James' belt and unsnapped the survival knife. He quickly withdrew it and thrust the blade into the table. When he removed his hand, the implement swayed back and forth tauntingly.

The General cleared his throat and the memory of the fear he felt as a young man in Scott's place and said, "Using only your wits, and what is within reach, solve the equation."

Scott looked at the assembled in a state of bewilderment. After a few moments, he flashed a crooked little smile and picked up three lose pieces of drawing paper. One by one, he used the razor sharp blade of the knife, which was still embedded in the makeshift tabletop, to trim each piece down. Over the course of the next ten minutes, the young man folded, cut, and constructed.

When he was done, he placed an elaborate origami swan on the table. Josh actually chuckled as he rose and said,

"You have my blessing."

# Chapter 16

Heather stole quick glances at the little solar powered device Hoplite had given her while she boiled water for tea over a small fire. *When's he gonna call and check up on me*, she thought as she waited to steep the bag.

When she originally volunteered to be a forward observer (FO), Josh immediately forbade it. It wasn't until she had been exhaustively trained by Hoplite, and could demonstrate those skills, did he relent. Unseen by her father and grandfather's watchful eye, the pair were growing close. The relationship was being built on respect, words of encouragement, and the occasional caressing hand.

Before anyone was allowed to become a Coastwatcher though, they were trained extensively in the art of concealment. This training wasn't limited to just camouflage. It also included a solid knowledge base on minimizing ones visual footprint. Things like smoke from a fire could get you killed. The smell was easily masked due to the abundance of wood burning fires littering the area, and the nation.

She knew her father's unmistakable hand was at work though. When the assignments came out, Heather was placed in one of the better camouflaged structures near the military crest of a wooded hill within sight of Logan. From her position, she could see movement throughout the intersection of routes 33 and 93. A moving car was a rare sight and an immediate target, but foot, bike, and horse traffic was increasing in the area.

Originally, the structure she currently inhabited was intended to watch over the town and the crossroads. However, when gangs out of Columbus burned the town to the ground, her father had the engineers reposition it further from the charred ruins so the observer could watch the quarter mile stretch of road where the roads ran parallel. Her closest back-up was Hoplite, almost six miles away.

The tiny hut only measured eight by eight and had a slightly sloped roof to shed water and snowmelt. Its dirt floor was covered with large chunks of slate that was abundant in the foothills of the Appalachians. The inch thick tiling aided in the retention of any heat put off by the small fires that were permitted. A raised platform was erected by the FO training graduates and allowed the occupant to sleep off of the hard ground. Any gaps in the structure had been plugged with mud during the harsh winter months. Heather was glad to see that previous Coastwatcher's had left some books and magazines behind for her to read in an effort to ward off the boredom.

The morning sun had finally crested the ridgeline to the east and was burning off the last of the fog and dew when her radio crackled to life.

"You up, 'Sunshine'?"

Giddy at her first communication with Carlos, so greedily snatched the device off of the rack. *Play it cool. Calm down.*

"Yeah, I'm up. Been up for a couple hours. You sleep in or something?" she said nonchalantly.

"Yeah, right. I've been getting up at 5:00 AM since I don't know when. My body's so accustomed to it that I don't even need an alarm anymore. You see anything up there so far?" he asked.

"Plenty of wildlife, but not much else. Being a Coastwatcher is – ," she started to say when she heard something that sounded like a gunshot. "Hold on. I think I just heard a rifle go off."

"Probably some locals out looking for breakfast," Hoplite responded. "I wouldn't worry about it."

Off to the west, the long forgotten distinctive sound of tire noise began to grow. Then she saw it. A small mud brown economy sized vehicle crested the hilltop and was headed toward the remnants of the town. As it decelerated, the engine backfired again.

"Crap. It wasn't a gunshot. It was a backfire. I've got a car."

"Details," the man ordered.

She gave him the description as she observed the driver pull off the side of the road. The man exited and relieved himself in the middle of the highway.

"Great, he's taking a leak."

A few tense moments passed in silence while Heather continued to perform her sentry duty.

"No other passengers that I –," she added to her intel. "Wait… Damn it! He just pulled a radio out of the car. He's callin' in. I think he's a scout! Shoot! Shoot! Shoot! What do I do, Carlos?" she said hurriedly.

"Calm down, hun. Continue to watch and observe. He can't see you, okay? If you have a fire going, go ahead and put it out."

In a panic, Heather wheeled around and grabbed her cup of tea and threw it on the flames. The small hut immediately started filling with the billowing smoke. *Oh no! What have I done!*

She communicated her mistake to Hoplite who calmly told her to continue to observe. When the driver caught sight of the telltale sign in his peripheral vision, he retrieved a pair of binoculars from the passenger seat and scanned the hillside.

"He's looking right at me!" she decreed in a panicked whisper.

Off in the distance two more cars cleared the crest of the hill. "Crap!" she declared. "His friends are coming down into the town."

"Damn it!" Hoplite barked into the radio. Thinking quickly he said, "Is there anything left of the fire?" he asked hurriedly.

Heather stole a glance at what was in the small pit and saw a few embers still burning.

"I've got enough to relight it, why?" she questioned.

"Stoke it and then torch it all! While that's building, I want you to take a few shots at the guy and the other cars when they arrive. In between, while they are ducking for cover, stuff your go-bag with as much food and water as you can carry! Start heading east toward me! Stay on the south side of the river! Make them traverse it to get to you!"

"Carlos, I'm scared. What have I done!"

"It's gonna be okay, Heather. Do exactly what I say and get out of there! Meet me at the second off ramp southwest of your position! I'm on my way!"

"How will I find you?"

\* \* \*

Captain Carlos 'Hoplite' Rayna may have been the CO of a Special Operations unit, but if he was anything, he was in shape. All of the men that formerly occupied these unique ranks were, for better or worse, chiseled specimens. Endless training and meager food supplies while on deployment prevented excess body weight. The constant PT, mission rehearsal, and deployments allowed the units to perform almost herculean tasks by comparison.

Given his years of field experience, less than sixty seconds had transpired before he, his weapon, and his barely unpacked gear were out the door. As he began his plodding march, he managed to change the channel on his Baofang two-way handheld HAM to the designated emergency frequency.

"Briar Patch, this is 'Charlie Whiskey Three'. Come in over," Hoplite said over the radio as he settled into his rhythmic pace.

"Channel clear," Brent stated in return so no one broke into the conversation. "What have you got Charlie Whiskey Three?"

*Damn it*, Carlos thought. *Why did it have to be her grandfather manning the comm room? Of all the days.*

"Charlie Whiskey Two was spotted," he replied breathing heavily under the weight of his pack. "I am en route to rendezvous and will be in possession of precious cargo within sixty minutes… mark," he concluded and then set the timer on his wristwatch.

Brent grabbed the stop watch lying next to the radio and pressed the start button. As he placed it back on the table, he glanced at the duty log for the Coastwatcher's. The Charlie Whisky Two hut was currently being manned by… Heather.

With broken voice, the retired General replied solemnly, "Sixty minutes mark, copy." Before he sat the mic down, Brent added, "Bring my granddaughter home, son."

"Roger that, sir," Hoplite answered and changed channels back to try and reach the woman that had enchanted his dreams since the day he'd met her.

There was no reply.

\* \* \*

"I gotta tell ya, Josh. I don't know where you managed to scrounge up these solar panels, but I'm sure glad you did. They take their time, but they do the job," Mayor Cranston proclaimed as he sat down behind the large desk.

"You'd be surprised how many of these things were put up by the DOT and railroads. We just collected and repurposed them," Josh replied.

On the table lay one of the five devices that Bryan managed to piece together from cannibalized parts of formerly innocuous electronics gear. The other four had been distributed to the mayors of Nelsonville to the north, Wellston toward the south, Athens to the east, and South Bloomingville to the west.

"Okay, so when we delivered these, we also provided them with instructions on what channels to monitor. So turn that dial to the frequency labeled 'ALL' and we can communicate to each of the other four town halls," Josh instructed as he directed the Mayor's attention to the tuning knob and accompanying cheat sheet.

"If you only need to reach one town, use the individual frequencies we listed."

"Well that seems easy enough," the Mayor proclaimed.

"Now, when you want to speak, just depress this button. To listen, simply let go."

"Press to talk, got it. What's this other number?"

Before he could answer, Cranston interrupted and said, "My word, what is that?"

Josh looked out the window to a group of locals looking over the gasifier motorcycle on Main Street.

"That is my future son-in-law and daughter showing off their latest invention."

"Really? Well congratulations! He sure is a creative one."

"That he is. Katherine seems to be very happy," he replied and then lost himself in a moment of reflection.

He stopped himself from dwelling on his mistakes as a father and continued. "As I was saying, this extra frequency, that's the Coastwatcher channel. You can listen to it if you want, but we have strict rules on its use. Ninety-nine percent of the time you aren't going to hear a thing. It's only used to call in a report or an emergency. Only the OP can initiate a call on that channel. So no idle chit-chat, understand?"

"Got it," he said as he turned the dial to see if there was anything happening on the channel.

As the static dissipated, the pair heard, *'Go ahead Charlie Whiskey Three'.*

"Hey, what's this?" Cranston asked.

"Shhh," Josh answered tersely in reply.

*'Need to amend ETA. Charlie Whiskey Two is headed toward me through rough country. Reduce by twenty. Over.'*

*'Roger that. ETA is now in twelve minutes. Channel open.'*

Josh abruptly took control of the radio and immediately changed the frequency so he could speak only with the comm room.

"Briar Patch, come in Briar Patch!"

The scanner quickly grabbed on to the transmission and locked in the signal.

"This is Briar Patch. Identify."

"El Jefe!"

"We've been looking all over for you! Where are you?" Brent asked in a rush tone.

"Mayor's office. Explain the chatter I just heard on the Coastwatcher frequency," he replied in clipped response.

"Charlie Whiskey Two was spotted and is on the run, hostiles in pursuit. Charlie Whiskey Three is en route to intercede."

Josh glanced up. His mind was moving at a hundred miles per hour. Then it hit him. "I'm on my way."

In less than thirty seconds he was breaching the front doors of the Town Hall.

"Katherine!" he bellowed as he exited.

His daughter wheeled around not knowing what was going on. She hadn't heard that intense of a sound from her father in, well, in a really long time.

As he approached, he hastily asked, "Do you have your sidearm!"

"Yeah, I always do. Why?"

"Get on!"

"Wait!" she bemoaned and grabbed a backpack from Scott while he kick started the small bike.

"Hey!" her fiancé cried out.

"Gotta run! I'll find you later!" she decreed as she leapt onto the back of the seat. Their combined weight fully compressed the aging shocks with a thud.

Her father quickly worked his way through the downtown streets until he was headed north on Route 93.

When they were finally on open road he opened the throttle. He glanced down at the speedometer. The needle wouldn't budge beyond thirty miles per hour, even when on the downhill.

"Where are we going?" she half yelled in his ear.

He turned his head slightly and responded in kind, "Charlie Whiskey Two was spotted and she's running. Charlie Whiskey Three is on his way to help her."

"Who's she?"

"Heather!"

Before Katherine could process the information, her father wailed, "Can't this thing go any faster?"

"It's a glorified moped without liquid fuel. Sorry. Maybe if I add more peat," she concluded as she slid the backpack in front of her.

"A little at a time. You don't want to smother the fire."

She did as instructed, but it only helped slightly.

It took a full twenty minutes to reach the crossroads near Logan. As they approached, Josh slowed the motorcycle. He was surprised at how quiet the machine was. Once he pulled the bike onto the shoulder, he crept up to the intersection from behind the dense cover. He stopped it several dozen yards short of the old stop sign and shifted into Neutral.

"Wait here," he whispered as he dismounted and un-holstered his weapon. Katherine did the same.

Josh slowly placed one foot down before moving the other, ever careful to avoid a noisy footfall that might give away his position. He kept his head on a swivel looking for the men and their vehicles. The protective father carefully pulled a heavy flower laden limb down a little further for a better sight line while still remaining concealed.

In front of him, approximately seventy-five yards ahead were three cars and a lone sentry. He quietly observed for a minute from his vantage point and saw no other movement.

He cautiously released the branch and started to turn to give Katherine a message via hand signals. He was startled to see her standing five feet behind him.

"I told you to wait!" he whispered harshly.

She shrugged and replied, "Just the one?"

Her father answered, "Hm hmm."

Over his daughters head, Josh noticed the last of the smoky whispers from the burning OP. He nodded in its direction.

"I saw," Katherine responded. "Which way did she go?"

"South. Brent said Hoplite was headed north toward her. I'm guessing that they figured out a means to communicate while they were out here on station."

His daughter flashed a knowing smirk at him. Josh just shook his head.

"We have to get around this guy first," she remarked.

After a few moments, almost in unison, they both decreed, "I have an idea."

His youngest deferred with a hand gesture.

"I'll go over there acting like I looking for my dog. You cut the corner through the woods behind him. We can't afford to have a gunshot so just crack him in the back of the head with your pistol."

"Seriously? That's the best you've got?" she remarked, turned, and started walking to the motorcycle.

Her father followed suit.

When they reached the bike, she quickly unbuttoned her top shirt, threw it on the seat, and grabbed her pack.

"What do you have in mind?"

"Boobs," she answered flatly.

"I'm sorry?"

"You heard me," Katherine retorted.

Josh had never looked upon his daughters as a sexual object. His only concern had been that they were healthy and well adjusted. Sure, they were pretty, but he hadn't ever noticed just how physically attractive and toned they were. All three were athletically built and modestly developed.

"Hell no!" he decreed. "Absolutely not!"

"How about you not argue with me. You and I both know that if a man walks around the corner, that guy is gonna shoot first and ask questions later. However, if a young buxom woman asks for help, he's less likely to do so, don't you think? Besides, I've seen Heather do this to Hoplite dozens of times."

Josh thought about it briefly. *She does have a point.*

"You might be – ... wait, what did you say?"

"Oh, Daddy. Sometimes you are so blind. Here," she declared. "Take this," and yanked a crossbow pistol from her pack.

"Where did you get that?"

"Evan confiscated it from some looters about two months ago. What do you think I've been using for all of the small game I provided?"

Her father just shook his head.

"You and I need to have a nice long talk young lady."

"Yeah, yeah. Help me push the bike back to that thicket."

The pair quickly stashed the motorcycle out of sight then Josh began his methodical movement through the woods. When he was in position, he made his distinctive bird call.

On cue, Katherine started hollering for her imaginary dog.

"Dusty! Come here boy!"

The sentry immediately arose to slowly head in the direction of her voice.

"Dumb dog, where are you?" she called out as she came up to the intersection.

Once she saw him, she took a few steps toward him and stopped. His weapon remained lowered, but he appeared ready to fire in an instant.

"Hey, Mister! Have you seen a scruffy brown dog come through here?"

Taken aback, he replied, "No can do on the pooch," as he glanced left and right. "What's a pretty thing like you doing out here all by your lonesome?"

"I'm just looking for my dog. You sure you haven't seen him?"

The man started toward Katherine, looking her up and down and licking his lips. Then he made a sound like he was purring.

"You have some car trouble? I don't think I've seen one of those things moving through here in about a month."

"Oh, my buddies are off trying to catch some lunch."

*Liar*, she thought. Then in a move that baffled her father, she changed tactics and started walking toward him as well.

"So they left you out here all by your lonesome, sweetie?" she asked innocently.

"Sure did," he replied in a pouty playful voice.

"How about I give you something they won't find in those woods," Katherine suggested as she awkwardly struck as seductive a pose as she could muster.

"What did you have in mind," the sentry answered as he continued toward her.

"Put that weapon away and I'll show you. Guns make me nervous. Besides, we wouldn't want it to go off… unexpectedly," she concluded with a wink as she pulled her tank top taught over her chest and accentuated her assets.

"Sure thing, honey," he replied as he leaned the rifle against the rear quarter panel of the car.

Josh let him get a little closer before he loosed his bolt from the contraption. At one hundred sixty feet per second, the tiny six inch dart hit its target in no time.

The man hollered in pain as he looked down to see his thigh pierced by the small impaling object just above the knee. Before he had time to think straight, Katherine pulled her Glock from her back and drew down on him.

"Men are so obscenely predictable," she declared as her father exited the woods.

He quickly took the man's weapon, cleared the loaded round, and withdrew the magazine.

"Don't move," he growled. "On your knees."

"I can't! You shot me!" the sentry bemoaned.

Josh was in no mood to waste any more time. He swung the rifle like a bat and struck him in the back of the legs sending him to the pavement in a lump.

"Your stomach works just as well," he declared as he started looking for something to tie him up. "Cover him," he commanded as he went to the car. Lying on the floor of the vehicle was a mostly used roll of duct tape. *This'll work.*

"Where are your friends? The ones who came in the other vehicles?" he asked as he securely fastened the man's wrists and ankles together.

"I'm not telling you jack!" he declared.

"Is that right," Josh responded as he searched the wounded man's pockets. He forcefully rolled him over. Before the prone man could adjust himself to a comfortable position, he was cracked in the face with a quick right jab. His head bounced off of the pavement.

"Now, shall we try that again?" the father asked as he continued searching the man's remaining pockets.

In all, he removed a dime bag of weed, three silver coins, and a small Swiss Army knife.

"He's clean. Go check the cars," he ordered as he grabbed him under the shoulders and sat him up against the rear tire of the vehicle.

Dazed, the sentry mumbled, "Do you what you want with me. I'm a dead man anyway."

"Is that so," the protective father replied as he unbuckled the man's belt and wrapped it around the bleeding thigh. Without warning, he yanked the bolt from his leg.

Katherine was unprepared for the blood curdling screams of agony emanating from the wounded sentry. Josh quickly covered the man's mouth.

"Glad to see you're still awake. Now, where are your friends and why are you a dead man?"

"They're off chasing some bitch through the woods. Just having a little fun is all."

"That 'bitch' is my daughter and fun is not what they have in mind," he declared and cracked him again. His head ricocheted off of the car from the blow.

"All right, man! All right!"

"That's better. Now, how long have they been gone?"

"I don't know. Maybe half an hour. She took off through the woods after she wasted our vehicles."

Josh leaned back and glanced at the disposition of the three cars in the road. Two were leaking radiator fluid and all had at least one flat tire. *Damn it. Hoplite trained her too well!*

"You stay here! We'll continue this discussion later," he declared and then pistol whipped the man into unconsciousness.

As he stood he called out to Katherine, "Anything in the cars?"

"Porn mags, beer, and bullets. Just what every redneck needs!"

"Grab the bullets! Let's go!"

Before exiting, she thought she should at least try to start it. The alternator spun a few times, but it eventually caught, and started the engine.

Her father quickly turned toward the now running car.

She immediately popped out of the driver seat, "I have an idea!" she declared. "Help me swap out this flat!"

During the five minutes it took to change the tire, Josh and his daughter quickly formulated a plan.

Katherine would give him a several minute head start before following suit. This gave him an opportunity to make it the mile or so down the road and stash the motorcycle. They both agreed that this was Heather's approximate range on foot through the woods in the time allotted.

Once her timer reached zero, she would crank the car back up. The tire noise would almost certainly be heard. The only real question mark was Heather. Would she bother to look through the scope at the driver or would she just open fire?

# Chapter 17

Hoplite looked off in the distance and identified the Rocky Boot warehouse as his landmark. His exit was only a quarter mile away. The twenty pounds on his back hadn't slowed him as much as he'd thought. He covered the last stretch as fast as he could and then took the old quarry access road off into the woods.

As he used the shadows of the hedgerow to break up his silhouette, he quickly made it to the edge of the Hocking River in a just a few minutes.

From where he sat, he could see up the waterway a fair distance. He quietly observed for movement across the impediment. There wasn't a sound to be heard outside his breathing and the wildlife. Diagonally across from him, the tributary to the Ohio River gradually bent and meandered its way around the forests edge. In its wake, with every subtle change in direction, the flowing water left a small sandy area.

Hoplite lifted his weapon and used the scope to examine the shore. There were tracks in the dirty silty sand, but he couldn't tell if they were human or animal given the angle. Following the impressions back into the woods, it became clear that a game trail exited at the location. As he examined the area, suddenly, something flashed through his optics.

*Heather!*

He quickly started searching behind her for a target. Trailing by several hundred yards, two men were giving chase. It looked like one had a handgun while the other had a hunting rifle. Both were sweating profusely. *Good girl, give 'em a run for their money!*

Hoplite waited for them to get a little closer before taking a shot at either. Abruptly, the pistol wielding pursuer stopped and called out to his buddy, "Just shoot her! I'm done chasing this bitch!"

With their appetite for carnal pleasure exhausted, the only thing the two wanted now was blood.

The second man took his stance and hefted his weapon in Heather's direction. Before he could pull the trigger, Hoplite put a round in his chest. The round hit him below his outstretched stabilizing arm. The bullet ricocheted off of bone and pierced his heart, dropping him instantly.

His partner didn't wait for the body to hit the ground. He took off like a jack rabbit toward Heather.

Carlos reversed course and sprinted the length of the unplowed field down the east side of the river trying to catch up to her. When the waterway abruptly turned and formed a peninsula, he launched himself down the riverbank and into the muddy water. Not worrying about noise, he quickly waded through the knee deep coolness and made it onto the far western bank.

As he sat and quietly observed, his heavy breathing became an annoyance unto himself. Suddenly, gun shots echoed through the full green canopy. He swiftly moved forward and repositioned himself behind the uprooted trunk of a tree. The four feet tall root ball made the perfect cover. Hoplite peered around the edge of the earthen mass in time to see Heather hurdle a fallen limb only thirty yards in front of him.

Without warning, he popped out with his weapon leveled and barked, "Get down!"

She threw herself face first toward the ground as he pulled the trigger and hit her pursuer in the abdomen. He quickly reacquired his target, but not before he squeezed off a round of his own. The slug hit Carlos in his chest plate.

Heather looked up in time to see her savior wince and take a step back from the hit. She watched as he fought through the pain and fired again. The man, on his knees now, took Hoplite's unsteady kill shot in the throat. The shot severed the spine from the brain stem as it passed through.

"Got 'em both," he declared as he lowered his weapon and fell to a knee. He immediately started to inspect his body armor and assess any damage to his chest.

"Carlos!" she gushed as she leapt up and rushed to him.

She took just a few steps before two shots rang out, dropping Hoplite onto his back with a grunt.

Heather cried out in horror and screamed, "Stop! Stop! Stop!" as she lifted her hands in surrender.

"You sure are a runner," the third unseen assassin declared as he removed himself from the safety of cover.

With her arms raised, she stated, "I'm not armed, let me check on my friend, okay?"

After a few contemplative seconds, without lowering his pistol, he motioned with his weapon and waved her over to the prone Carlos.

As she placed herself between the fallen Hoplite and the last of her pursuers, she began checking him for wounds. Heather breathed a sigh of relief when she felt that he was wearing his body armor.

"Took one in the ass," he stated as he labored through the pain. "I think the other one went through my bicep and entered above my side panel. I can barely breathe. Damn it!" he bemoaned. "It's probably in my chest."

She quickly checked the specified injury sites.

"Two flesh wounds there," she declared methodically.

As she probed his upper body, Hoplite hollered out in pain.

Heather gently rolled him away from their pursuer to examine the wound. He groaned loudly at being moved. While he was up on his side, hidden from view, she unholstered his Sig from his thigh holster and slid it down his belly.

She slowly turned toward her attacker and asked, "Can I at least treat him before you have your way with me?"

The man walked over and snatched Hoplite's bag and backed off. With his weapon still trained on Heather, he unsnapped the quick release and up ended the bag, dumping its contents on the ground. Once the first aid kit tumbled out, he put his foot on it.

"You know, it didn't have to be like this. We were just passing through til you started shootin' at us. All we wanted was to have a little fun as payment for our shot up vehicles. What's the harm in that?"

"Harm? What's the harm? It's called rape you jackass!"

"To you maybe. To me, it's a trade. One car for one piece of ass."

"Don't you have a soul?" she asked.

"A while ago I might have. It's survival of the fittest now, darlin'."

Heather exhaled loudly. There was no point in debating.

"Please," she implored him. "He's bleeding pretty bad. Can I just treat my friend?" she begged. "Gimme five minutes then you can show me how much of a man you are," she concluded with tinge of aggression.

"What's he to me? Let him bleed out. He killed my friends."

"She was going to be my wife," Hoplite decreed in a dazed whisper as he rolled on to his back, concealing the handgun at his side.

The assailant laughed raucously.

"The hell you say, Mister. She's way out of your league."

Heather had had enough. She quickly stood to confronted him.

"Look you redneck moron. I'm not out of his league," she stated as tears began streaming. "If anything, he's out of mine. He represents everything that is kind, and good, and decent, and loyal in this God awful shitty mess... and you're about to rob me of that. Isn't that enough? Aren't you satisfied?"

"Oh, I will be in just a few minutes. Don't you worry about that, Sweet Pea," he replied coolly as he grabbed his junk.

She quickly wiped her eyes.

"Let me at least help him before you press your dirty sweaty flesh all over me!" With his view of Hoplite partially blocked, and his eyes trained on Heather and her pleas, the man didn't notice Carlos slowly training his weapon. "Please!" she implored once more.

Without warning, the .45 caliber Sig snarled to life from between her legs. The sudden gust of warm air from the shockwave startled her to the point that she physically jumped.

When the echoes stopped, Hoplite declared, "Get his gun. Make sure he's dead."

Heather quickly ran over and removed the man's pistol from his hand as he gurgled through his last remaining breaths. Without thinking, and full of fear, anger, and adrenaline, she hit him twice in the chest and once in the head.

Satisfied, she greedily grabbed the med supplies and sprinted back to Hoplite. She hastily went to her knees, opened the kit, and searched for the compresses and wraps.

She quickly applied a compress of gauze to his bicep and wrapped it with an ace bandage to keep it in place.

"This might hurt a little," she declared as she rolled him up on to his side once again.

The torrent of hissed and muted expletives he let fly surprised her, but wasn't all that unexpected. Moving just as methodically as she had been taught by Carlton and Basilia, she didn't waste time trying to retract the bullet with the forceps. Heather tore his shirt open and applied a thick wad of gauze to the 9mm diameter hole.

"Hold this she declared," and tucked his right hand under the left bicep to keep the absorbent material in place.

She didn't want to have to move him again and decided to address the million dollar ass shot at the same time. Not bothering to find the scissors or a knife, she tore away the material of his pants. Heather efficiently packed the third injury site and prepared the elastic ace bandages. Then she turned her attention to the chest wound.

As she assessed the entry point, she paused. "I'm so sorry, Carlos. This was entirely my fault."

"No it wasn't," Hoplite replied. "I didn't scan the rest of my surroundings like an idiot and got hit."

Turning her away from pity, Carlos removed the bandage. "Can you see the bullet? It might not have penetrated that deeply since it went through my arm and the side of my vest."

"Your breathing is labored. It's deep enough for me not to mess with."

"Damn it!" he declared angrily. Thinking quickly, he asked, "Did Carlton put a chest seal in the kit?"

Heather searched through the contents rapidly.

"Should say something like Halo or Bolin on the package," he instructed.

"Bolin chest seal kit, got it!" she decreed.

"Good girl. Now open that up and apply it to the wound. Place the three one way valves directly over the entry point. Then we're gonna pray we can get back to the farm."

Heather haphazardly tore open the packaging, removed the seal, and peeled away the plastic protecting the sticky surface.

"Ready?" she asked.

"Do it," Carlos answered as he flung the bloody remnants he had been holding in place.

Through his gritted teeth, she pressed the adhesive into place, making sure it was secure, and then rolled him onto his back. After he was flat again, she quickly tied the ace bandage to secure the gauze on his butt.

He groaned in response as she jostled his body trying to get the wrap from underneath him, but managed to contain the vulgarity.

Heather knew nothing about human anatomy, but she knew enough to realize that the round was most likely in his left lung. After several minutes of terror induced treatment, she had successfully field dressed all three wounds and covered him with an emergency Mylar blanket to ward off hypothermia.

Her body didn't know what to do with all of the emotions. Fear, panic, and relief all coursed through her veins. She'd been shot at, the man she loved was bleeding, she'd just killed a guy, and they were stranded in the middle of nowhere. She couldn't decide if she was going to puke or cry. Thankfully, the rumbling in her gut subsided, but the tears started flowing.

Through the wetness of her eyes she asked, "Do you have anything in your kit for the pain?"

"Carlton issued all of us a fentanyl lollipop," he winced.

She quickly went through the contents and found the sucker. When she turned back toward him, she saw Carlos staring at her longingly.

He half chuckled as the sun broke through the clouds above.

"What?" she asked in reply.

"Look at that. You brought me sunshine and gunpowder. Best birthday ever."

"I'll give you a birthday present," she declared as she leaned over and passionately kissed him on the lips.

When she withdrew, he decreed with a devilish smile, "Got the girl too." Then he promptly passed out.

Heather traced her fingers across the side of his face, memorizing every line and scar. When they were resting on his rising chest she quietly wept. Not sure if he would ever see the light of day again, she leaned into his ear. "I love you," she whispered gently.

"Tape the lollipop to the back of his hand," her father stated from behind her. "He's going to wake up as soon as we move him and we've got a twenty plus minute ride to the farm."

His daughter started balling with relief.

* * *

"Clear the room!" Carlton declared as he, Josh, and Heather carried Hoplite into the farmhouse.

When the call came in from the checkpoint, he and the Martinez family, along with Joss all worked quickly to clean and sterilize the kitchen as best they could. The table had been scrubbed, dried, and draped in fresh linens. Any devices running or charging on the marine batteries were removed from Bryan and Chester's 'mini-grid'. Tools, instruments, tubing, and bandages were laid out neatly. Every light, regardless of wattage, was relocated to aid in the pending emergency surgery. All that had been missing was the patient.

No sooner had the limp body turned the corner as Basilia grabbed Heather and Josh and whisked them to the living room recliner and couch.

"Hey!" she extolled the doctor. "I need to be with him!"

Calmly, the matriarch replied, "You want to save his life?"

"Yes!" she decreed emphatically.

"Good, then sit here while I draw some blood. We might need it and we might not. Either way, it takes time… and that's something we don't have."

"How do you know we even match?" she stated confused.

"What do you think we've been doing out here for the last six months? Just sitting around dolling out lemon balm?"

Heather shrugged.

"Young lady, we've typed and cross matched every single person living on this farm, most of the residents in town, and about a third at the lake. As soon as they said it was Carlos we knew who would match and who wouldn't. Now sit there and let us work," she concluded forcefully. Then Basilia sighed at her lack of compassion and bedside manner. "You'll be standing by his side in about twenty minutes, okay?"

"This is what we have to work with, Carlton," Joss declared as she waved her hand over the piles set neatly on the kitchen counter.

There were separate stacks of pre-packaged sterile instruments, bandages, tubing, various gauge needles, bottles of betadine and Chlorhexidine solution, as well as small vials of numbing lidocaine and antibiotic creams.

"Got a chest tube in any of that crap?" Carlton asked as he walked over and began inspecting Basilia's stash.

Joss reached into the mostly unpacked tub labeled 'Medical Supplies' and produced four.

"Okay, let's get to it."

As Josh's arm was being prepped, he called out to the corpsman, "You guys seen Lt. Stokes or Gregg?"

"Eustace is at the park and Gregg and James are training recruits at Fox. Why?" Carlton asked.

"Get him fixed up quick, then grab some shut eye," Josh declared. "I have a feeling it's going to be a long couple of days."

The two looked at him quizzically through the cased opening. Josh motioned to the pair. "Don't stare at me. Do your job!"

Shaking it off, Carlton looked over at Heather and said, "We've got this." Then he looked back at Joss. "Ready?"

She nodded.

"Do exactly what I tell you. We don't have time for twenty questions during the procedure, so save 'em for later. Go to the sink and scrub everything up to your elbows like you've never scrubbed them before. Then I want you to remove his body armor. Here," he declared, "Take these scissors and cut off his shirt after the vest is removed."

Then Carlton paused and began mentally ticking off the tools he'd need. *Alright, time to show them my smash and grab routine. One scalpel with an 11 blade, one chest tube, a bucket, a four foot length of rubber tubing, three pairs of Kelly clamps, 1.0 or greater silk sutures, gauze, and a pump of some kind if I can find one.*

The former corpsman confidently grabbed each of the items and began setting them off to the side. As he prepped everything they'd need for all Hoplites wounds, he solved his own issue by flipping the medical supplies bin over, emptying its contents, and placing it under the table as a bucket. She watched in amazement as his hands quickly located the spot for the chest tube.

"I'm gonna go quick so pay attention."

Joss nodded.

"Beginning at the collar bone, start counting ribs on your way down to the mid-axillary line... one, two, three, four ribs. This area right here," he declared as he gestured, "This is the triangle of safety. There's nothing major in here. Typically we insert the tube between the third and fourth intercostal space. However, he's already got a hole near there so I'm going between the fourth and fifth. Pick a spot on the mid-axillary line that relatively aligns with the nipple and mark your spot."

Carlton grabbed the unconscious man's left hand and moved it up to place it under his head.

"And don't forget arm placement," the former corpsman concluded.

"First things first, sterilization. We need gloves, some gauze, and the Chlorhexidine solution."

Joss ripped two pairs from the box and handed him one. The duo quickly inserted their hands and seated their fingers. She then removed the pads and grabbed the bottle of Chlorhexidine solution. He took the items as she produced them and set everything on the sterile table.

"Okay, slowly remove the Bolin chest seal," he ordered as he busied himself with removing items from their packaging.

"Shit!" she declared and quickly stuck her finger in the hole that was now seeping bloody fluid. "He's leaking!"

"Mother –!" Hoplite hollered as her finger was jammed in.

"Carlos!" Heather shrieked. "You're awake!"

"Yeah I'm awake!" he retorted as he started to move his arm out from behind his head.

"Leave that up there, Captain," Carlton commanded. "We're gonna insert a chest tube and drain that excess fluid out."

"The bandage was holding all of that in, Joss," Basilia said compassionately from the other room.

"Go ahead and remove your finger," the corpsman whispered as he reassured her.

Hoplite hollered in protest.

No sooner had she removed the plug as Carlton inserted his own into Carlos' frame.

"What the hell, doc!" the patient screamed.

"Just feeling around a bit," the former medic replied and then paused. "Well I'll be a monkey's uncle. I can feel the bullet, gimme some forceps."

Joss grabbed the instrument and slapped it in his palm efficiently.

"Could I get you to wipe away some of this blood," he asked as he prepared to remove his digit.

Hoplite whimpered in reply.

She did as instructed, threw the now soaked pads in the tub, and then adjusted a flexible lamp down toward his hand. Carlton slowly removed his finger and let the wound drain on to the table. Eventually it found its way to the improvised bucket.

"Let's have some of this come out on its own for a few seconds and then I'll go in after the bullet."

"Do you mind?" she asked as she motioned at the prone Hoplite.

"Not at all," he replied and stepped back.

Joss moved in closer and picked up the gauze she had handed him previously. She carefully wiped away some additional blood from around the wound. Before she inserted her own finger to feel for the bullet, she inspected the site.

"I think the entry point is too ragged for re-use. We'll have to go ahead and do the blunt dissection at a different spot," Carlton offered. "Sometimes we got lucky, but I already marked the spot I want between the fourth and fifth rib mid-axillary."

"I agree. Where's the bullet?" she asked as she looked up at him.

"Run you finger along the third rib posteriorly," he replied. "Looks like it hit the bone on the way in and went down toward the bottom of the cavity."

"This might hurt a little, try to stay still, Carlos."

"Sure thing. Whatever you say, Nurse Ratched," he answered.

Carlos gritted his teeth as she entered his chest again.

Joss followed Carlton's instructions and declared, "Got it," she decreed and slowly removed her finger.

"We should probably remove it before we drain him while the lung is still collapsed and out of the way."

"What the hell?" Hoplite moaned. Then declared, "This sucks!"

"That's why you had a hard time breathing, honey," Heather clarified from afar. "I didn't want to scare you."

Carlton and Joss changed places. Carefully and deliberately, the corpsman slowly retraced his fingers path with the forceps through the parietal pleura. Once he was into the chest cavity, he opened the tool's jaws.

"This would probably be a lot easier with some x-rays to look at," she stated.

Carlos' legs started twitching as he tried to keep from screaming in agony.

"Yeah well, you do what you can with what you've got," he answered in reply. Then he called out, "Basilia, find a belt or something to strap him to the table."

"Oh, oh," he declared as he closed the tool and captured the foreign brass.

"Remind me not to play 'Operation' with you," Joss deadpanned.

Carlton slowly withdrew the forceps with the bullet locked in his grip. As the bulk of the offending object exited his body through the entry wound, Carlos began slamming his boots on the table. Before she knew what she was doing, Joss dove on top of them.

"Okay. Alright," the corpsman said calmly. "The worst is over," he concluded and then dropped it in his hand to inspect it.

"Looks like it's intact, very little mushrooming. Your boyfriend is one lucky guy," he declared as he directed the comment at Heather.

"He's my fiancé," she corrected as she smiled at Carlos.

Tears were streaming down Carlos' cheeks from the pain, but he managed to smile back.

"Sorry, Dad," she offered to her father sheepishly. "It just kind of happened."

"I know. I was there… remember."

"But don't worry, he'll still totally take Papaw's test," she clarified.

Josh smirked.

The Martinez matriarch stood up and decreed, "Alright, you two are good to go. Sit here til the bag is full, about twenty-five minutes. I'm going to observe the procedure."

Carlton adjusted the light over his open hand to review the object further, then he placed it in Joss' open palm.

"Okay, time to numb it, make the incision, and insert the tube," he said as she stared at the blood coated mass.

"Here's your belt," Basilia declared as she strapped Hoplites legs together.

"Can you check his pulse and BP?" Carlton asked then turned to his nurse assistant. "Here we go. I'm gonna numb the site. That's the skin, sub cutaneous tissues, deeper tissue layers, parietal pleura, and periosteal surface of the rib below the insertion point. Before I do that, I need you to wipe the area down with the Chlorhexidine solution."

Carlton then handed her a clamp with gauze captured in its grip and the solution bottle. Without asking for direction, she dumped a healthy portion on the sterile fabric and coated half his pectoral muscle and most of his side. The medic busied himself by loading a syringe with lidocaine.

When he turned around and saw what she had done he exclaimed, "Whoa! I think we're good!" Then he shifted his attention to the patient. "Sorry buddy, but this might hurt a bit."

Carlton injected the site in a wheel pattern while Carlos fought through the pain and held on for dear life. In less than sixty seconds it was all over. He checked his watch, then began preparing the chest tube, scalpel, and sutures.

After two minutes passed, the corpsman pinched Hoplite. "Feel that?"

"Only pressure," he replied.

"Excellent," he declared. "I'm gonna make a two centimeter incision between the fourth and fifty ribs along the mid-axillary line. Then I'll take a curved Kelly clamp and began dissecting the subcutaneous tissue and intercostal muscles. I'm basically clearing a path for the tube."

Joss watched on in amazement as Hoplite remained still and unaffected.

After efficiently working his way through the outer layers, he reached the chest wall. "Now, I gently pushed the clamp on the parietal pleura until it gives and I enter the pleural cavity."

Setting the instrument down, he inserted his finger. "I do this as a double check to ensure that the lung isn't stuck against the side."

Satisfied that it wasn't, he removed it. More fluid flowed out. Carlton quickly picked up the 24 French sized tube that he had clamped at both ends.

"Now, for a hemothorax condition, which is when there's blood between the chest wall and the lung, you want to guide the hose basally, or down," he instructed as he slid one end in and detached the leading clamp. "If it were a pneumothorax, that's air, aim it up. Always make a mental note of the measurement on the side once it's inserted. That's the fasted method to tell if the tube is moving."

"Can you hold this while I suture it in place?" he asked her calmly.

Joss quickly grabbed it.

"Easy now," he cautioned.

"Sorry."

"It's okay. I know you're scared and more than a little nervous. Everything's gonna be fine, alright?"

She nodded.

"That was fast. BP's one hundred over seventy. Pulse is sixty-five. You're doing good, Carlos," she stated reassuringly as she smoothed his hair back off of his sweat soaked forehead.

As if he were running on auto pilot, Carlton wheeled around for the 1.0 silk to suture the tube to his body.

"You're not gonna purse string suture that, are you?" Basilia asked.

"Hell no!" he answered incredulously. "I don't want him to get skin necrosis. Mattress sutures work best for holding chest tubes in place."

"What?!" Hoplite stated just as emphatically.

"You shush," she replied as she rebuked the wounded man on her kitchen table. "He said he *didn't* want you to get necrosis."

After a minute or so, the stitching was done.

"You can let go, Joss. It's not going anywhere."

She gingerly released it, fearful that it would slide out. When she realized it didn't move, she finally breathed.

"Now that that's in place, I'll quickly check the entry wound. It needs to be cleaned and debrided of any dead tissue. From there, we'll apply an occlusive dressing and seal the chest cavity. As soon as that dressing is on, we'll pack the tube site and get ready to drain."

Joss stepped back and let the two doctor's work. It felt like an eternity as she observed. To distract herself, she turned her attention to the blood donors and checked their bags.

Basilia worked on cleaning the flesh wound in Carlos' bicep while Carlton handled the chest. When their aid returned to the room, she was tasked as their triage nurse. She spent the next several minutes handing each syringes of saline, dressings, and various implements as they called for them. They pair worked quickly and Hoplite's anterior wounds were cleaned and bandaged in no time.

Carlton affixed the rubber tubing to the chest tube, cut it to length over the bucket, and let it dangle.

"Ever syphon gas from a car?" he asked Joss earnestly.

She shook her head slightly.

"We don't have a pump so this is the next best thing," he stated as he removed the remaining clamp from drain. He then proceeded to kneel. "If the fluid doesn't exit on it's on, sometimes you have to coax it out," he said as the pair observed.

As predicted, the cavity began disgorging the watery liquid, but stopped midway. The former corpsman casually leaned over and began sucking ever so slightly on the end.

"There it goes," Basilia declared and he quickly withdrew it from his mouth and let it drain into the makeshift container.

"Now we're cooking!" Carlton stated. "Grab that empty water pitcher. We need to be able to measure how much comes out. Any more than a liter or so in thirty minutes and we've got bigger issues."

Joss lunged across the counter, quickly grabbed the plastic container, then spun down to her knees and placed the tubing in the opening.

"Relax," Basilia offered. "Is this your first surgery?"

The mother of two swallowed hard and nodded. "I unfortunately discovered during nursing school that I didn't like blood. That's why I chose geriatrics."

"Well, look at it this way. You haven't passed out from any of this," Carlton offered reassuringly. "With time you'll learn to relax. Just remember, the presence of blood doesn't always mean that they are dying."

"How long til we know it worked? When can we take that thing out? What about his other wound?" Heather asked from her recliner.

"We'll leave him be for the next half an hour at a minimum," he began to answer reassuringly. "If he doesn't drain more than a liter or so, we should be good to go to remove the tube in about twenty four hours. That's assuming the lung re-expands and we don't collect more than 200 cc's of serous fluid. As for his other wound, we'll see what we can get to without turning him. It might have to wait awhile."

Basilia chimed in and provided the remainder of the answer Heather was looking for. "Once the tube is out, we'll pack that site with another occlusive dressing. His bandages have to be changed once or twice a day, maybe more depending on a variety of factors. After that, we'll assess the need for sutures."

"I'm sorry, Sweetie. Hoplite is out of commission for the next several weeks, probably a month," Carlton added.

# Chapter 18

"Rise and shine, dipshit!" Josh declared as he dumped the bucket of water.

The captive awoke with a start, but for all his flailing, he didn't exit the chair he was bound to. Before him stood five of the angriest looking men he had ever seen.

"That was a stroke of genius to bolt it to the floor with those 'L' brackets," Josh stated to the group. "That last one toppled over."

"Thanks. I try," Dallas replied.

"Look man," James began. "I don't know why we's wastin' time on this peckerwood. I've got my chainsaw right out in the truck. Why don't we just cut 'em up and cook 'em? I don't mind me some white meat."

"You'll have your chance," Brent declared. "If he isn't forthright with his answers, you can break 'em down and chuck 'em in the pot."

"Whatever. Ya'll ain't gonna do that," the prisoner pronounced.

"Alright," Lt. Stokes replied. "It's your funeral. Go get the chainsaw."

"Sweet!" the big guy replied giddily as he exited Old Man Wrigley's derelict farmhouse. Within seconds the sound of a chainsaw firing up could be heard outside.

All color drained from the bound man's face.

When he re-entered the side door, James was carrying the now running chainsaw in one hand and had Heather's meat cutting face shield in the other. Draped over his forearm was Katherine's black leather butcher's apron.

Playing on the man's fear, he excitedly set the machine down. The thumping two-cycle engine started bouncing on the floor causing the joists to absorb the vibration. The rhythmic dancing of the saw could be felt throughout the house.

James quickly donned his borrowed meat cutting clothing and wheeled around to pick up the little tree trimmer.

"Ya'll want legs or wings!" he joked from behind the face mask.

The others began uproariously laughing with him, and then he stopped to lift the shield.

"Oh, I almost forgot. Can some of you go get the bins? I promised Mimi I wouldn't spill any more blood in the truck."

Stokes and Dallas quickly exited. When they returned, they were noisily carrying stainless steel commercial size soup pots. The pair nonchalantly placed them in front of James with a clang.

"Thanks guys, how do you want 'em?" he asked as he lowered the face shield.

"Just make sure he fits," Josh answered. "Last time you had arms and legs sticking out and they took forever to cook!"

"Wait! Wait! Wait!" the man screamed. "You said I had to answer some questions!"

Dallas chucked Josh in the shoulder. "Damn it!"

"Sorry guys," James declared as he shut off the engine and flipped his visor up. "That was my fault. I got excited about cuttin' up another one. I guess I jumped the gun."

"I asked them when we caught you at the crossroads," their leader began. "Would you like to revise your statement? Or…" he stated as his voice trailed off and he gestured to James and his saw.

"If I answer, you'll let me go?! Right?!"

"Not only that, but we'll give you your car back with a full tank of gas. How'd that be?" Brent offered.

The prisoner quickly nodded his agreement.

"Alright," Josh replied with a sigh. "What's your name?"

"Tyler. Tyler Chaffee," he stammered as he answered.

"Okay, Tyler… you said you were a dead man earlier, why?"

"Because I keep messin' up. I don't know this stuff… guns, hunting. It's just as foreign to me as Latin."

The men stood there waiting for a more thorough explanation. No one offered any further commentary. The visual cues were lost on the prisoner until Lt. Stokes made a gesture then added, "And?"

"And TK's getting tired of it. I heard him tell the other guys that if I screwed up again they were to leave me in a ditch."

"Why were you and those men down in Logan?" Brent asked to start gathering intel.

"Food's running low. We were scouting for a good place to setup a deer camp."

"Along a main road, near a town your little gang in Columbus burned to the ground not two months ago? I find that hard to believe. You, sir, are either lying, or you're one of the worst hunters I've ever seen," Dallas rebutted.

"I'm not a hunter!" he declared. "I'm only a driver for the wolf pack. I was a freaking accountant! Okay?!"

"What's that?" Brent asked.

"That's just what TK calls them."

"And who, pray tell, is that? He the leader of your little gang?" Dallas interjected.

Tyler scoffed.

"So how many are there?"

"I don't know. A hundred if you count the whores and addicts," he replied nonchalantly with a shrug.

"If you don't include the working girls and addicted wastes of space?" Josh asked wanting clarification.

The man shrugged again and answered, "Twenty or thirty or so I guess."

"Where are you guys based? Locations? Buildings? Downtown or suburbs?"

"Before I answer, what happened to the others?"

The inquisitor smiled, "What's the line… 'He sends one of yours to the hospital, you send one of his to the morgue'."

"That's the Chicago way!" Stokes added for emphasis.

Chuckling, Josh clarified, "Well, in this case, three went toes up."

"Good," Tyler responded. "Sickest bastards I've met."

"You seemed pretty lock step with them out there."

"No I wasn't. They were chasing after that girl so they could rape her. I could never do that. Not six months ago, not now, not ever!"

"That wasn't what it looked like when I shot you," the protective father intoned.

"She was coming on to me. I wasn't forcing her to do anything. I thought I was gettin' me a freebie til you skewered me in the leg."

Josh realized the man was right. "Let's put a pin in that for the time being. Now, where are TK and his merry band of miscreants?"

"They took over all of the luxury high rent condo buildings down by the old Huntington ballpark. Turned the entire outfield into a marijuana crop."

"Weapons?"

"Big guns, little guns, some as big as your head! How the hell should I know!" Tyler volleyed back forcefully. "I'd never even held a gun, much less shot one, until all of this started."

"Tell me about the area. Is it derelict? Are the buildings intact, in disrepair, or are they burned down?

"TK took over and united all of the gangs by spring. Then he appointed himself their defacto leader. He's been directing traffic ever since. Most of the high rises are still there. They tried burning the Nationwide and AEP towers down, said they blocked his view. When that didn't work they shot most of the windows out. Drunken idiots," he stated adding a bit of commentary. "Whole place looks like a tornado went through there. Friggin' glass and debris everywhere you go."

"Any guards or sentries? Observation posts? Road blocks?" Brent asked.

"Isn't much need. Anyone not in the organization either left or is rotting somewhere," Tyler replied coldly.

"How'd you guys survive winter?"

"That guy is a master organizer. He had groups cleaning out cars, delivery trucks, and eighteen wheelers looking for anything that could be eaten. Teams of people were going restaurant by restaurant looking through each cabinet, cooler, and freezer for scraps of food. When that was done, they went floor by floor in the office buildings. They cleaned out every vending machine and desk drawer stash they could find."

"Pretty resourceful," Stokes interjected.

"You the guys that hit Chillicothe, burned Logan to the ground, and made a run on Athens?" Dallas asked.

"Yeah well, when everything in the city was consumed, TK expanded our territory. He called them his locust brigades. I think he's actually trying to link up with gangs from Cincy and Cleveland for some trade."

Silence permeated the room. The five men stood stoically as they contemplated Tyler's responses.

"One last question before you go. This TK, he got a name?" I mean, a full name?"

"I don't know if it's true or not, but I heard some of the guys in his inner circle refer to him as 'Tim'."

"Tim?" Josh asked through his arched brow.

"Knight something or other. That's it, I swear."

Josh's eyes became as big and white as saucers.

"Knightsbridge?"

"Yeah, yeah, that's it! How'd you know that?"

"Okay, I've heard enough. You can cut him up now," Josh responded as he turned and left Old Man Wrigley's former living room. As he exited, he heard his friend pull the cord on the saw and fire it up.

"Hey! Wait!" Tyler begged. "You said if I answered your questions you'd let me go!"

At Dallas' encouragement, the men remaining in the room started chanting 'white meat… white meat' in a taunting gesture. As James approached, he revved the engine several times to wind up the small two-stroke. Plumes of white smoke billowed out as it burned off the moisture in the fuel. Just as he laid the bar across Tyler's thigh, the man emitted a shrill like scream and passed out.

The four men began raucously laughing as he shut the machine off. There was no chain.

* * *

The young Lieutenant from the UN detachment in Charleston, South Carolina couldn't believe his eyes when he finished decoding the latest message. Just to be sure it was correct he decoded it a second time.

There was no mistake.

With paper in hand, he grabbed his notebook containing the peace keeping troop capabilities, bolted from his make shift communications room, and sprinted towards Brigadier Smythe's office. His CO would definitely want to see this straight away.

Nigel entered the outer room in an almost full sprint. He didn't bother waiting to be announced by the Brigadier's staff officer.

As he bullied his way through the closed door, he proclaimed, "Sir! An urgent message from Whitehall!"

"Bloody hell, Lieutenant!" the Brigadier exclaimed as the papers were thrust at him.

"Read it, sir! You can reprimand me later!"

The General took a cursory glance at the hand written document and looked up with a start. He didn't have to utter a single word.

"Decoded it twice," the young Lt. offered.

"Excuse me, gentlemen," he stated to the two officers seated before him. "Something's come up."

The men quickly excused themselves and closed the door behind them as they departed the room.

"Nigel," the Brigadier began.

"Yes, sir," he declared as he brought himself to attention and reprimanded himself. "I should have showed more restraint. I have no excuse. I'll do better next time."

"That's a good lad. How much petrol do the dragoons have?"

The Lieutenant opened his notebook and began flipping pages. In just a few seconds he found what he was looking for.

"They have thirty six hundred liter's, sir."

"And what do they have in the form of APC's (armored personnel carriers)?" his CO asked as a follow up.

Nigel flipped back and forth as he counted up the unit's available equipment list.

"If we are going for fuel economy, they have ten Husky's which carry five men each and five Cobra's carrying eleven. Call it eighty five with their gear."

"Send the message," the Brigadier stated flatly.

"Orders, sir?"

"Kill every single one of those French bastards and anyone else who gets in the way. Find the damn gold so we can get out of this God forsaken country."

"Very good," Nigel replied as he snapped a salute.

As the comms man was about to open the door, his CO stopped him.

"Any word from Omaha?"

The Lieutenant retracted his hand and turned to face him. "Only that she is a few days away from assuming control. No further details were offered, sir. I'm sorry."

The officer nodded. "That woman will stop at nothing to be President… even if it's a barren wasteland," he stated more to the empty room than to anyone in particular. "Thank you, Lieutenant. That'll be all."

Once the Lieutenant had shut the door, the Brigadier reread the handwritten message and muttered, "Bloody French!"

* * *

"Whatever we decide, we need to get him back before Tim gets suspicious," Katherine stated to her father and the rest of the group. "How long were you expected to be gone?" she asked as she directed the question to Tyler.

"A day or two is normal," he replied. "Oh, and for the record, that crap with the chainsaw wasn't funny."

"Hell yeah it was!" James declared as the five men started giggling again.

"Alright, alright... focus," Samantha scolded. "Here's how I see it. Josh, Bryan, Dallas, and you, James, cannot be part of the equation... and neither can I for that matter. All of us are known, or were seen, by Tim when the plane crashed in Columbus. That goes for Agent Monahan too. Let's not forget that someone is getting married tomorrow," she continued with a wink in Josh's direction. "Hoplite would have been the best candidate, but he's out for the next month. Gregg's out too, Emily's not letting him out of her sight for the foreseeable future. That leaves Eustace, an engineer, or one of the recruits from the patrols."

"Just so we're clear, you are *absolutely* sure Tim isn't going to bat an eye at this story? Four guys leave and a single man returns... with a new prospective member to boot? That would make me suspicious from the get-go," Katherine stated looking for clarification.

"He's is as vain as they come. A fact that your dad, I think, knows all too well," Tyler responded and then paused. "If I can aid in the removal of that psychopath and his inner circle, then there might actually be some hope for something to survive in Columbus. Even if we're not successful, I return with you to the park, right?"

Josh nodded his agreement.

"No more chainsaw tricks?"

James extended his hand with a little smirk, "No BS this time. You have our word."

The two shook on it and Tyler asked, "So who's it gonna be?"

"Looks like I'm the odd man out," Lt. Stokes stated as he extricated himself from the tailgate. "What's the plan?"

Katherine produced the map page she had torn from the Tin Foil Hat Club's road atlas and placed it on the seat Eustace vacated.

"It's summer now, so sundown isn't until almost 9:00 so, if what Tyler says is true, you should be able to take his Yugo to here by dusk," she declared as she pointed to a spot on the chart. "The Martinez brothers are working on it now to remove that backfire and get it tuned up for quick escape. Find the highest ground possible and observe for the rest of the evening and overnight. Tomorrow morning, you two stroll into town as if nothing is out of the ordinary."

The pair of men nodded.

"Call out patterns and strays. We want counts and routines... that means everything from the washhouses and latrines to guard towers and road blocks. The Farmer's Almanac says we should have good weather for the next few days, so that's working in our favor. Your signal should be able to make it to Circleville without any issue. They'll relay the message on to us and the rest of the towns on a need to know basis."

"Seriously? An almanac? You've got to be joking," Tyler inferred mockingly.

"Last I checked, the Weather Channel was off the air and Atlanta burned to the ground... again," Katherine responded, shutting down his sarcasm immediately.

"What do we do from there?" Stokes asked.

"Tim has either purposefully left us alone or he's forgotten we are here. We have that working in our favor and I'd like to keep it that way. We need to know the best avenues for entry. Where will we find the least resistance and the most? Where are people being housed aside from the high rent condo structures?" she replied candidly.

"And then?"

"Radio in your daily's at 02:00 and use the all clear signal 'Carolina', but we'll be listening the entire time you're in there," she responded assuredly and then looked at the pair. "Any other useful questions or comments?" Katherine asked, clearly drawing the line at Tyler's sarcasm.

When neither responded, she declared, "Alright, Tyler, you stay here with James and Dallas while they assess your weapon skills. Eustace, walk with me to get the car from the boys along with some gear, food, and water."

The pair proceeded to walk toward the end of the drive, but didn't make it very far before they were joined by her father and Sam.

"Don't take your eyes off of him for a minute," she declared in a whisper as they entered the abandoned roadway.

"Huh? I thought he was good to go," he responded.

"Not a chance in hell," Josh interjected. "This is a trap set by Tim. Can't you smell the desperation? I don't trust him as a far as I can throw him."

"Did you see the old track marks on his arm?" Sam asked as the four continued walking to the cabin. "Someone went through a lot of trouble to clean this guy up," she concluded with a hint of compassion.

Lt. Stokes sighed. "What do you want me to do? Maybe some of what he said is on the level."

The father and daughter half grinned at one another as ideas swirled through their collective minds.

"I think the less you know at this point, the better," Katherine stated keeping her cards close.

"Great," he declared reluctantly. "Welcome to the Army."

Josh clapped his meaty hand on the shoulder of the young Lieutenant. As the continued to walk away from Old Man Wrigley's farmhouse, the former field commander within him came to the surface.

"Look son, this is a tricky detail, but I have faith in you and your abilities. Rest assured that you won't be alone, someone will be watching you. We are asking you to infiltrate and assimilate all while growing eyes in the back of your head to keep an eye on that squirrely SOB. Oh, and do yourself a favor and don't ever let Tyler, if that's even his name, and Tim have a conversation in private. Where he goes, you go."

Eustace nodded his reply.

"Give us a few days to get all of the other pieces in place. You know what ordnance we have at our disposal. If 'TK' turns this into a shooting match, which I'm sure he's bound to do, when the avalanche of lead starts, find somewhere safe to hole up until we give the 'all clear', got it?"

"Roger that, sir."

# Chapter 19

When Gregg entered the Martinez farmhouse, he was greeted by stern and furious looks plastered on the faces of the 'Board of Governors'. Circumstance dictated that they were finally informed about the platoon of combat engineers living among them, and they were visibly angry.

Before any of them could start their collective thundering, he held up his hand to silence them.

"Ben, Jerry," Gregg said in a serious, but light hearted tone. "You're upset. I can see that."

"You're damn right we are… and stop calling us that! Our names are Benjamin and Jerod. And that's Susan, not Sue, Suzy Q, or 'Sweetie'," Ben stated coolly.

"Fine. You called this little meeting. So what's got the Board of Governors in a twist?"

"We should have been told who was living among us. We should have been told what was under that stage. There are children in there," Susan quantified in a manner that bordered on hysterics.

"So you're afraid for the children, is that it?"

"That doesn't account for the arsenal of guns they hauled out of there!" she continued.

"And now that you know about the men, the stash under stage, and the weaponry in their cabins… you're afraid for the children? I'm sorry, I don't understand the issue."

"How can you not –," she started to retort.

"Look folks, whether you like it or not, those guns and the Second Amendment 'gun nuts', as I've heard you so eloquently refer to them, are all that's standing between you and a gang rape," he thundered tersely and continued. "How about you show a little more respect and gratitude for the people willing to protect you and your beliefs, because right now it's the only thing keeping the wolves at bay, sweetheart."

"How dare you say –," she began to reply before Gregg interrupted her.

"And I let you in on another certainty, these people we're up against, they only understand the bullet. So you can save the holier than thou attitude for the land of rainbows and unicorns. The world as you knew it doesn't exist. All that remains is this cold hard life you are currently enjoying in the park *we* provided."

As his breathing began to slow, he struck a calmer tone and concluded, "Maybe in time, once the country is rid of the gangs, death squads, and serial rapists, then you can raise your hand and preach peace and love."

"I didn't say I was unsupportive, Gregg," Susan replied more calmly as well. "It was just a shock is all. We should have been told."

"If it were me, I'd trust active duty combat veterans to safely handle the ordnance over most, if not all, of the civilians taking refuge. The men and women we personally trained notwithstanding.

"My question for the three of you is why? Why are you *really* pissed? What would it have changed had you known? The firewood, water, and food still needed to be collected. We simply added two dozen extra bodies to aid in those endeavors."

"But we –," Jerod began.

"Not finished," Gregg stated as he cut him off. "Now, correct me if I'm wrong, but in addition to the assistance in the completion of chores, they also taught you how to survive… how to hunt, snare, skin, and shoot didn't they? More importantly, they taught you how to protect yourselves. All of which are skillsets you didn't have when you got here. By my accounting, every single person living in those cabins, yourselves included, should be dead, but you aren't.

"Josh and his infinite flippin' wisdom saw fit to save your travelling horde from the winter storm you foolishly walked straight into the face of. Then on top of that, he provided what basically amounts to life skills teachers to assist you. And, just so we're clear, when these guys weren't covering for the lazy, weak, and infirmed on chore duty, they were volunteering for OP duty, watching over their flock as it were. Yes, these men lived among you and you didn't know. Yes, they have skill sets that might possibly have allowed you to accomplish some additional tasks. However, their chief and overriding mission has been the protection of the residents taking refuge in the park. So I ask again, why are you so pissed?"

With all of their bluster successfully sucked out of the room, and a healthy dose of reality thrown in for good measure, the Board struck a more conciliatory tone.

"It would have been nice to know is all," Jerod decried.

"Fair enough. Now, is there is anything else I can help you with?" Gregg replied.

"When will they be back? I only ask because it's not just the engineers that are missing. I did an informal head count and we are lacking over fifty men and women as of this morning."

"All of those residents have gone 'operational'."

"What does that even mean? Speak English!" Benjamin stated.

"Okay," Gregg replied with a smirk. "Ya see, there are some really bad people with guns. They want what we've got and they're willing to kill you for it. We are going to stop them. How's that?"

"You're patronizing sarcasm isn't needed," Susan rebutted.

He shrugged in response.

"What are we supposed to do to fill the void in the meantime?" Jerod asked.

"What's up, Sarg?" the soldiers asked as they entered the house out of breathe.

"Stand fast, gentlemen," he reflexively stated. "I'll be with you in a minute," he concluded before turning his attention back to the park representatives.

"Jerod, I walked through there just this morning too. I counted at least fifteen to twenty people that I'm pretty sure were laying out due to minor issues. That's just about half of your shortfall right there.

"Listen folks, let's get one thing straight, because this is important. That park wasn't setup and prepped to be section eight government housing. Whether you and that enclave survive is entirely up to you. They aren't military and, therefore, will not respond well to my flavor of motivation. That being said, those socialist programs that our country became so enamored with and reliant on, *they... do...not... exist*," he added with emphasis.

"You were all told when you arrived that everyone pulls their own weight. That was a non-negotiable condition of your residency. If I were you, I'd remind them of that little nugget and start finding a way to motivate those people.

"Now, if you'll excuse me, I have more pressing matters to attend to. You're dismissed."

"You can't dismiss us!" Benjamin shot back.

Gregg smiled. "You're right. You're *civilians*. I forgot. My sincerest apologies," he quipped sarcastically as he bowed.

Ben stormed out of the house in response followed shortly thereafter by Jerod. Susan lingered a bit.

When he saw her waiting patiently, he said with a sigh, "Yes, what can I do for you?"

The spritely mother of three stepped forward and abruptly slapped him in the face. Gregg just stood there and took it, more from shock than anything else.

"There, now that that's out of the way, let me say that, we all appreciate everything that was done for us, and we are all well aware of the score. We'll figure out a way to get those people better assimilated. However, you don't need to treat the residents like second class citizens. Every time you say 'civilians' it drips with hostility and disdain."

Gregg was taken aback by her candor, and the slap. He knew what she was saying was true.

"You're absolutely right," he responded with another sigh. "Please tell Benjamin and Jerod that I apologize for my conduct as of late. My only defense is that I was raised this way. I was taught to do everything with maximum effort to the best of my ability at all times. No handouts. No free rides. It's very frustrating for me to see people given a better than average shot at surviving this mess just hanging out, laying around, pissing away the opportunity to do something for themselves all the while waiting for someone else to do it for them."

"I agree. The work ethic has slipped a bit."

Gregg nodded his response.

"I'm not saying we should go all draconian rule with corporal punishments and what not," she began with a wink. "However, that being said, we should probably start with a friendly reminder," she explained.

"After that I'd humbly suggest some form of written code of conduct and expectation, complete with repercussions," Gregg offered.

"Now *that's* something to think about. I'll talk to the boys and see what we can come up with," Susan answered cheerfully.

"A word of caution though."

"Oh?"

"I would avoid any kind of inclination to have the community vote on every article being presented. They already voted when they put you three in charge."

"Sound advice. Thank you," she responded.

"It's just a suggestion," he concluded as he turned to afford her enough room to exit the house.

The men watched as she stepped off of the porch and climbed aboard the waiting horse. Once the Board of Governors were safely out of ear shot, Gregg said, "Have a seat, gentlemen. Wasn't the first time I've been slapped, and it won't be the last."

"So what's the story?" one asked as they took their respective seats on the couch.

"El Jefe and Rodin have cooked up a game plan," he began as he referred to Josh and Katherine by their call signs. "We need two volunteers, so I chose you. After this, you'll be all square after that little slip up with the radios." As if they had forgotten, he reminded them of their error in judgment. "You know, where you discussed the gold stash on the net."

"But we mucked stalls for three weeks and took extra OP duty," one of the men whined.

"That was Josh's punishment, this is mine."

The pair hung their heads.

"On the plus side, you both work well together *and* you both scored above average in James's amateur sniper school."

A smattering of pride was re-installed.

"What's the mission?"

"BB and that gang member, Tyler, returned to Columbus last night. He's going to be embedded for a few days gathering intel. You two are to take Tink's gasifier to a spot designated by Rodin and provide overwatch. The remainder of our force arrives some time later. Questions?"

"Ordnance, provisions?" one man asked.

"We good with her running this Op?" the other inquired.

"I had my hesitations too, but that girl is smart as a whip. Good decision making, good mission planning skills, knows what we have at our disposal. War God and I reviewed it with El Jefe after she left the room, we didn't change a thing… it's that squared away. Now, as for gear, you'll both need full combat loads along with a weeks' worth of food and provisions. Tink customized an aluminum pull behind bike stroller for your gear. As an added bonus, and at the request of Rodin, Agent Monahan has kindly donated the Secret Service's McMillan TAC-338, complete with their Nightforce scope. I've shot it, it's nice."

The pair whistled at the hardware.

"I thought you guys would like that. Any other questions?"

Neither man spoke up.

"Alright, collect your gear and be at the cabin in thirty minutes to load out and get your final instructions."

"This sucks," one of the men stated flatly. "I saw what James, Mama Mimi, and Jacques were cooking for the wedding reception. Any way we can get a plate to go?"

\* \* \*

As the sun continued its slow arc toward the horizon, the residents of McArthur began to fill the pews of the church. Aside from a few moments of harrowing panic associated with helping Chillicothe and Athens repel the travelling hordes, Josh and Sam's wedding was the biggest thing to happen in the town since Christmas.

Josh stood stoically and watched as his groomsmen escorted the last of the guests to the few remaining seats. He quickly checked his watch. On cue, the small band of orchestra members that Gregg and Hoplite referred to as the 'travelling renaissance festival' started playing Vivaldi.

Greg, Juan, and their wives were the first two couples down the aisle and took their places. They were followed by Dallas and Heather. Behind them stood Katherine and her fiancé Scott. The final pair to enter were James and Layla. Once the last of the wedding party hit their designated mark, the ensemble changed to the 'Wedding March'.

The two front doors of the church opened slowly to reveal Samantha and Brent. The white strapless body hugging dress shimmered with the last rays of the sunlight as she entered the shaded church. The retired General donned the Marine Corp Dress Blues that he had safely stowed away upon his arrival at the farm. The mere sight of her in the wedding gown took Josh's breathe way. Sam, for her part, was greatly relieved when Dallas arrived in a clean pair of Josh's old business clothes instead of the hip waders and fishing hat he had threatened to wear.

Josh adjusted the sleeves of his suit as he shifted in place and looked around the church. Everyone was smiling and happy. The joy being exhibited was a stark contrast to the grim and worrisome faces he had seen for the last several months.

In the front two pews sat a healthy collection of close friends. On one side were Mama Mimi and her new French lover, Jacques, President Sarkes and his ever present shadow, Agent Monahan, along with the Sheriff and his wife and daughter. On the other, were the three remaining Tin Foil Hat Club members, Bryan, and Josh's former sister-in-law, Kristin. Behind them were the mayors and associates from the neighboring towns. The townsfolk and numerous residents from Lake Hope filled the rest. As Samantha and Dallas took their places, before a single word was uttered, Alysin began weeping.

"Please be seated," the Reverend stated. "We are gathered –,"

Before he could finish, the Sheriff's walkie crackled to life.

"Come in! Come in! Anyone there? Damn piece of junk!" echoed throughout the church amid the static of the transmission.

Jim hastily grabbed at the device on his belt as he headed for the front doors and better reception. The entire congregation watched on in anticipation.

"This is Sheriff Watson, identify."

"It's fucking Hoplite," came the haggard response.

Heather reflexively held her breathe at the resonating broadcast.

* * *

A four man team of French Foreign Legion soldiers trudged their way down the steep hillside. The men half stumbled and tripped in the dense underbrush as they did so. By the time they made it back to the column head and their commanding officer, a Sergeant was finishing up his assessment of what remained in the town.

"Oui, Mon Capitaine. There don't appear to be any residents. I'd say it burned to the ground in the spring."

"Very well. And you?" Capitaine Philip Marceau asked as he turned his attention to the returning men. "What did you find up there?"

"By all appearances, it seems there was an OP sitting just below the crest of the hill."

"They probably torched it with the town," he replied dismissively. "Je crois que non, (I think not,)" the man answered in French. "Il y avait des braises. Ce était récente… au cours des deux derniers jours. (There were embers. It was recent… in the last two days.)"

"Qu'est-ce que vous avez dit? (What did you say?)"

"I found shell casings all over the place," his mother, Colonel Sophie Desjardins, announced as she inspected the few in her hand. "Those cars are full of holes from large caliber weapons fire and all of the road signs are missing too."

"Merde!" her son exclaimed from atop his horse drawn wagon.

"Mon Capitaine!" a Private called out as he too approached. "Il y a une traînée de sang ici. (There's a blood trail over here.)"

"Where!?" Philip proclaimed.

"In between the two cars," the man replied in heavily accented English.

Slowly, the Captain surveyed his surroundings trying to make sense of the information being presented. He quickly stood so he could turn and retrieve his map from the communication officer's satchel. As the he flipped it open, the pages snapped taught.

*Why would an outpost be burned months after the town was ransacked*, he thought to himself. *What the hell is going on? All of the road signs and landmarks are missing or destroyed. Two disabled vehicles block the road and they're riddled with weapons fire.*

Making the best decision he could with the information at hand, he declared, "We turn south, Mon Colonel. This is Route 93. McArthur is twenty miles in that direction," he concluded as he pointed.

The men started loading back up when Sophie abruptly shushed them. "Everyone quiet!" she stated harshly, immediately drawing everyone's attention. "Do you hear that? What is that?"

The one hundred strong force representing three platoons of the Foreign Legions 2$^{nd}$ Foreign Infantry Regiment became instantly silent, ceasing all movement at the Colonel's terse command.

"Sont-ils cloches de l'église? (Are they church bells?)" her son asked quietly.

The soldiers looked around, expecting their eyes to aid them in pinpointing what they were hearing.

"Non, mon cher fils. Cela ressemble cloches de marriage, (No, my dear son. That sounds like wedding bells,)" his mother replied with a smile.

# Chapter 20

The mid summer's heat continued to beat down on the slow moving convoy as it made its turn off of Route 93 onto McArthur's tiny Main Street. In front of them stood a solitary figure.

"Qui est-ce? (Who is that?)," the Second Class Legionnaire (Private) said as he brought the horse drawn wagon to a halt fifty yards short of the man.

"Looks like the Prefect of Police," his CO replied in his native tongue. "Wait here. I'll go see what this is about."

As the Foreign Legion Captain approached, Sheriff Watson slowly, deliberately moved his hand to the butt of his side arm. It wasn't unnoticed.

"What's the phrase from your movies? We come in peace? I am Capitaine Philip Marceau. Are you the Prefect?"

"Foreign troops on American soil doesn't scream 'peace', bub, and I have no idea what a 'Prefect' is, so how about you translate for me," Jim replied.

"Uh, Prefect… it's like the chief of police," Philip answered as he continued his approach.

"I am the Sheriff of this town. That's close enough *el Capitaine*."

"Monsieur, I'm French, not Spanish."

"But you ain't American, and that's a big problem. You say you come in peace?"

"Oui."

"We?"

"Means 'yes'."

"Okay, prove it. Tell your men to lay down their weapons."

"Not all French soldiers surrender at the first sign of trouble. You have been watching too many films."

"Is that right?"

"Oui, I mean, yes," Capitaine Marceau stated as he slowly began moving his hand to his own sidearm.

"Have it your way," Jim replied and made a quick circling motion with his arm as he whistled loudly.

The roar of engines could be heard all around them as vehicles were cranked up and quickly moved into position, blocking every direction. Large yellow school busses blocked the road in front and behind. Deuce's and Humvee's with their top mounted Browning's wheeled to their places, taking the north and south. Windows were flung open with abandon. The glass replaced with the barrels of long guns and shotguns poking through the opening. Foreign Legion troops instinctively began reaching for their weapons in defense.

Above them, on the roof tops, men and women peered over the edge of buildings, weapons trained on the stopped convoy. The clicking of safeties and the clacking of rounds and shells being chambered filled the narrow death box of a street.

As the last of the residents fell into position, Sheriff Watson said, "You were saying?"

Capitaine Marceau removed his hand from the sidearm and made a slow turn, taking in his new surroundings.

"Did you really think we weren't watching every road?"

"Very impressive display of force. You've effectively blocked all means of escape and taken the high ground," Philip responded impressed. "I thought this town might have had eyes."

The Sheriff smiled broadly.

"Les positions défensives!" the Capitaine barked abruptly.

Without warning, two columns of soldiers wearing green and brown T41 camouflage, body armor, and bush hats quickly exited a narrow alley and began dispersing up and down Main Street. Their FAMAS assault rifles securely abutted to their shoulders, up, and at the ready.

"And what do we have here?" Capitaine Philip Marceau announced in accented English

It was the Sheriff's turn to observe his new surroundings.

"Looks like we got ourselves a Mexican standoff to me," he stated in a nonchalant manner.

"I told you, we're French, not Spanish," Philip growled.

"Uh oh," Jim proclaimed as he nodded for the man to look behind him.

"Philip," his mother whispered hoarsely from behind him. "I think you should reconsider your position."

He quickly turned to see her in a headlock with a Glock pointed at her head. Calmly, he glanced around and beyond her assailant. The remainder of his force was standing in the street with their weapons on the ground and hands in the air. Had he had the time to count, he would have been astounded. Philip's ninety odd men were outnumbered almost three to one.

"Like he said, did you really think we weren't watching every road in an out of this town," Hoplite growled.

President Sarkes and the wedding party slowly emerged from the church doors. Tom glanced at the nearest soldier and observed the French flag patch and 'Foreign Legion' identification badge that were staring him in the face.

"Ne tirez pas, (Don't shoot,)" he stated calmly to the soldier. "Permettez- moi de vous expliquer que vous êtes amis. (Let me explain that you are friends.)"

"Oui," the Sergeant grunted.

The former President began making his way onto the street, toward Hoplite. "Captain Rayna," he called out. "These men are Foreign Legion. Look at their insignia. They are allies."

Philip turned ever so slightly to afford Carlos the view he was seeking. He was weak, but was able to discern the vertical red, white, and blue striping of the French national flag. With a grunt he let her loose and said, "Here, you can have your Colonel back."

The ordeal from the previous day, coupled with activity far too soon after surgery, taxed the man and he half collapsed. To keep himself from falling over, Hoplite quickly recovered and was able to take a knee to steady himself.

"Carlos!" Heather exclaimed as she shot from the front of the church and started to rush toward him. Before she was halfway down the street, Philip reached out to help him. He didn't have to see the man's wounds to know he was wounded, he could smell it.

"Monsieur, you should be in hospital."

"I'll live," he groaned as Heather rushed over.

"Looks like I made it to Josh's wedding after all," he said jokingly as the pair began helping him across the street.

"Josh?" Sophie asked herself quietly. She trained her eyes on the front of the church. "Il ne peut pas être, (It can't be,)" she declared as she followed the three toward the bride and groom.

The former POTUS made his way toward her, stopping her progression. With an extended hand, he introduced himself to the French Officer. "I'm President Thomas Sarkes, and you are?"

"Colonel Sophie Desjardins," she stated as she accepted the handshake. "And this is my son, Capitaine Philip Marcaeu."

Now it was Josh's turn to be shocked.

"Sophie? What are you doing here?"

"Hello, Josiah," she replied with a warm smile.

"Do you know her, Josh?" Sam inquired from behind him.

"I should say so, Madame. I'm the one that shot him."

"No freakin' way!" His daughters exclaimed almost in unison as they exited from behind their father.

"Philip? Look at you!" one continued. "You're all grown up!"

"Layla and Katherine, right?" he replied just as astonished and quickly approached, leaving Heather to get Carlos into the church by herself.

Sheriff Watson grabbed his walkie and announced, "Stand down, folks. They're friendlies."

Weapons immediately withdrew from the open windows as quickly and efficiently as they had filled the void.

"Enchanté," Philip said as he took each young woman's hand and kissed it in turn.

Josh's daughters giggled in response.

"How did you find your way here?" Josh asked Sophie.

"That is a matter best held in private, Monsieur Simmons," her son replied candidly.

She gave Philip a disapproving look, but added, "He is correct. We should discuss this privately after," she declared. "It looks like we've interrupted." Then it dawned on her. "This… this your wedding? Josiah has finally found love again?"

"Oui," Samantha said as she exited from behind him in her shimmering white gown carrying an AR-10. She handed the incongruous weapon to Hoplite as he and Heather made their way into the church.

Sophie was taken aback at the image of a bride with a weapon.

"Is this what it is has come to, then?"

"Sadly, yes. I'm Samantha," she stated as she extended her hand.

The Colonel stepped through the handshake and kissed her on each cheek. "Pleasure to meet you. I'm Sophie Desjardins." She repeated the gesture on Josh. "It is so good to see you again, my old friend."

"Come," Sam said. "Join us. We were about to get started when the warning bells went off."

"No, we couldn't impose like that."

"Oh, don't be silly. The more the merrier, I insist."

* * *

"Please be seated," the Reverend began. "We are gathered here today, in front of friends and family, in the sight of God, to join Josiah and Samantha in holy matrimony. Over the last several months, I've had an opportunity to speak and work with both. Typically, when a couple plans to marry, we talk, and listen, and I watch them interact. Once I have a fair sense of their relationship, I then provide guidance on any issues that might befall the union.

"In all my years as shepherd of this church, and others, the majority of the couples that I worked with needed to address many things, but chief among them is communication…" the reverend continued as his assembled flock listened. Josh and Sam heard nothing except the other's breathing.

As the two stood before God, they were equally overcome with the joy, hope, and optimism that, together, they would navigate their way through the seemingly never ending array of chaos around them.

When the preacher's words came back in to focus, they heard, "Now, the world as we knew it was irrevocably altered, but, in many ways, it has been both a blessing and a curse. We've lost friends and loved ones as a result, yes. However, what I've witnessed recently pales in comparison. This small town in America's heartland got its identity back. The old adage about neighbor helping neighbor is no longer reserved for Norman Rockwell and his calendars. For God said, 'love thy neighbor', and that my dear friends is what I see before me each and every day. The lack of electricity forced husbands and wives to talk, children to hear, and friends and neighbors to show genuine compassion."

Then the preacher directed his comments at Sam, "Samantha," he began. "Prior to your arrival, the man standing here, he didn't exist. Aspects of him were there, but the entirety was broken, metaphorically speaking. His spirit crushed, his fire dampened, his thoughts dark and wrought with anger and despair. Piece by piece, through your kindness, encouragement, drive, and antagonism, he is once again whole. The transformation we have witnessed in him is entirely of your doing. Well, maybe not *all* your doing, per se. He might have helped a little," the man said as stole a quick glance upward.

The congregation chuckled.

"In fact, the etymology of his very name, Josiah, in ancient Hebrew, means 'healed by God'." He turned his head slightly toward Josh and continued. "However, while Samantha was aiding you in your healing process, you my friend, have had a similar, and profound, effect on those around you as well," the preacher stated as he took Sam's hand.

Josh looked at the two confused.

"Samantha, with the help of some friends, has expressed her desire to recite a few words. My guess is you have no idea just how much you mean to this community and the people you've encountered throughout the winding journey of your life." Then the man leaned in real close and whispered, "I've heard most of them, I dare you not to cry."

Brent stepped around Josh and handed Sam a folded piece of paper.

She cleared her throat and began, "You and I have been through so very much that it's hard to imagine it's only been a year and half. It actually feels like an entire lifetime has already been spent by your side. It hasn't always been smooth sailing either, but we persevered. In talking with the assortment of friends and family that have graced the cabin, one thing kept repeating. No matter what memory or story was shared, there was the same recurring theme… 'and there was Josh'. So with their help, I asked some of those friends and family members to jot down their thoughts. The poem is titled, 'And There You Were'."

Sam unfolded the paper and began reading the words she had written for the occasion.

"My life was a shambles. My father had been taken from me. I was wounded and cold. And there you were. Holding my hand and telling me everything would be alright."

She quietly folded the note as James stepped out of the line of groomsmen and glanced at his palm as he read.

In a shaky voice, he continued the poem.

"Our friend had fallen, and so had I. I was broken, unable to see through the fog. And there you were. Standing on my doorstep, dragging me to other side of grief."

"I, too, was broken in every way possible," Gregg started with a lump in his throat. "My child was gone, my wife incapable of being found. And there you were. Staring me in the eye, proving that is was possible to survive the depravity of man."

Heather then stepped forward.

"As I prepared myself for the worst day of my life, I didn't think anyone could possibly understand my pain. And there you were. Whispering hints and clues from shadows, showing me that it's never too late to re-build and discover my family."

"After hours of surgery, and days of recovery, I finally awoke. And there you were. You had driven cross country to collect my parents and bring them to the hospital, displaying the true meaning of friends," Dallas added.

Sheriff Dobson stood and assisted Hoplite to his feet.

"You'll have to forgive me, I've had to re-write this as of an hour ago," he deadpanned to some laughter. "Here, sir," he stated to the former President. "You take this one."

With Jim's hand on his back to steady him he read, "I was barely hanging on. I had professed my devotion. And there you were. Scooping me up like an Angel of Mercy, providing one more day with the love of my life."

Heather started tearing up and blew him a kiss.

"The Tin Hatters ride again," Chester proclaimed as he stood. "That was what you said as you entered our collective lives. We were adrift in an endless sea destined to never reach port. And there you were. Sharing just enough of yourself to help each of us eventually make landfall… that and a big damn cake!"

Before he finished, Alysin rushed at him and gave him the biggest hug she could. "Thank you," she whispered as she released him and returned to her seat.

Josh flashed the three a wide grin and a wink acknowledging his role in the last Tin Hatters escape.

Bryan and Kristin stood in unison, alternately reading their prepared words.

"The lights were out," he started.

"And the winter weather was on its way in," she continued.

"And there you were," they decreed simultaneously.

"Backing a massive truck in my driveway," Bryan stated.

"Get your gear loaded, you've got five minutes," Kristin declared while trying to do an impression of her former brother-in-law.

"Proving that even through the passage of time, you were still unable to ever leave a friend behind," he concluded with a nod to his old neighbor.

After Hoplite's handoff, Josh wasn't surprised when President Sarkes stood next.

"We were on the run, hellhounds on our trail. And there you were. Opening your home to the weak and weary, declaring to a world gone mad that there wasn't a chance that it was going to claim everything in its path."

Mayor Cranston and the other assembled town leaders rose up. "This is from all of us," he stated before he began. "Your desire to protect cost you ninety days. While you were quietly planning, we were loudly panicking. And there you were. Fresh from a jail cell, full of ideas and the inspiration needed to feed the hungry masses."

Next up were the Board of Governors.

"We were cold and hungry and the lights had been out only since morning. We hadn't planned for a thing. And there you were. Standing on that bumper, providing clear voice and direction. Willing us to survive."

"We were dazed and confused. Not knowing day from night," Katherine began.

"Nothing we saw or heard made any sense. And there you were," Layla stammered tearfully.

"Rescuing us from an uncertain future, you provided a life as only a devoted protective father can," her sister concluded.

"That is a debt that can never be repaid," Layla ad libbed as she rushed forward toward her father's embrace.

Katherine quickly joined her.

Those present in the church could no longer hold back the tears. Neither could Josh.

Once the two eventually returned to the line of bridesmaids, Brent attempted to speak but was interrupted by Sophie.

"If I may," she directed at Samantha.

"Please do," she replied casually.

"Josiah," she began in accented English. "We were cursed to share an unbearable burden. I was prepared to be sullied as only a woman can. And there you were. Protecting my honor by separating yourself from yours. Your selfless act spared all of our lives, but also provided a life for the son I would eventually carry. Merci."

Sam rubbed Josh's back gently. The pride she felt for him and the kind words each of the readers were providing was almost too much to take. She never imagined when she asked each to write four or five sentences that it would turn out the way it had.

As Sophie sat back down, Brent began. "My daughter was searching. Direction and meaning alluded her. And there you were. Showing her what men of character looked like. You were able to lift the veil and show her what real purpose is through the eyes of the child you created." The retired General placed the paper back in his pocket and shifted his gaze toward him.

"She is the greatest gift I could have ever possibly received. I am so very sorry. Each of my decisions led to the incredibly hard path your life has travelled."

"All is forgiven," his friend replied weakly.

Josh then turned toward his bride.

"You guys suck," he declared to laughter as he wiped away the tears.

The pair faced the official who quickly stuffed his handkerchief back into his pants pocket.

"Do you have the rings?" he asked as he glanced over at Brent. He promptly reached in his pocket and dropped them in his outstretched palm.

"Please face each other," the Reverend directed as he placed Samantha's wedding ring in Josh's hand.

"Do you, Josiah Grant Simmons, take this woman, Samantha Marie Jameson, to be your wedded wife, to have and to hold from this day forward, for better for worse, for richer for poorer, in sickness and in health, to love and to cherish, till death do you part, according to God's holy ordinance?"

"I do."

"Do you, Samantha Marie Jameson, take this man, Josiah Grant Simmons, to be your wedded husband, to have and to hold from this day forward, for better for worse, for richer for poorer, in sickness and in health, to love, cherish, and to obey, till death do you part, according to God's holy ordinance?"

"I do," she replied as she smiled at Josh.

"Josiah, repeat after me please," he began as he nodded in Josh's direction.

Unfortunately, the man was already distracted. No sooner had Sam said 'I do' as she started making him laugh by displaying funny faces and grins at him.

"With this ring I thee wed," the preacher started. When he saw that Josh wasn't paying attention, he exclaimed, "Josiah, didn't you hear my message about communication and listening?"

"Huh?" he replied, finally hearing the Reverend's words.

The assembled collection of residents, friends, and family began laughing.

"She's making faces at me!" he protested.

The laughter only escalated at his protestations.

The Reverend sighed, "Let's start again... With this ring I thee wed."

Josh, fully aware and paying attention, was able to repeat the sentence and the remainder of the exchange of rings as directed. Sam didn't wait for the official to begin and recited the words without direction as she slid Josh's ring on.

"By the authority vested in me, and in the name of the Holy Spirit, I now pronounce you husband and wife. What God hath joined together, let no man put asunder. You may kiss the Bride!"

# Chapter 21

"Oui, Monsieur," the Foreign Legion Officer answered into his mic. "We've only reached McArthur this afternoon."

"Any news or progress on locating the person, or persons, referencing 'buried treasure', Capitaine Marceau?"

"Negative, Brigadier Smythe. As I've mentioned, we've only just arrived. If they are still alive, it shouldn't take that long to locate them. We still have our triangulation equipment."

"What do you mean? What is the status of the town?"

"Feeble, weak, and malnourished... like the rest of them. Some gangs from one of the larger cities have been razing towns looking for resources. I'm afraid that there isn't much left."

"Understood. Find the men, find the tunnel, then report back in a week's time."

"Affirmative, Monsieur. Capitaine Marceau out."

Josh and the others stared bug eyed at the man as he placed the mic on the table.

"Thank you for that," Josh offered.

"Josiah," Sophie began. "That is why we have come to McArthur."

"If those guy's survive the next few days, I'm gonna kill them myself," Gregg groused under his breathe.

"Well damn," President Sarkes proclaimed. "We are now, officially, between a rock and hard place."

"Exactement," Philip replied in French before switching to English. "Not to make matters worse, but if we don't appease his curiosity, the dragoons that sacked Cleveland will leave West Point and make their way here as reinforcements."

"This is turning into a freakin' Greek tragedy," Hoplite proclaimed.

"I'm not saying the missing gold shipment from Denver is here, but if it is, can it be moved?" Sophie asked delicately.

Sideways glances and awkward stares ensnared the room until they all eventually landed on their leader.

Clearing his throat, Josh provided as non-committal an answer as he could. "Impossible," he answered in French.

"What he is trying not to tell you, Sophie," Sam interjected. "Is that it is currently buried under a couple hundred tons of rock and dirt."

"Merci," she replied. "Josiah, please don't be coy with me. I am your friend. Now, can it be found easily? What I mean is, are there landmarks, signs, or anything that could lead the British directly to its location?"

"If the Brits do show up," Sheriff Watson offered. "The locals didn't trust outsiders before all of this. Plus there's the added benefit that no locals were present when it was stashed. They'll keep their mouths shut regardless. The residents from Lake Hope are a collection from all over though. Some may have heard of the location because they've done some hiking or camping in the area previously, but they don't know it's there. I don't think any of them could get there today without a GPS."

"We could check in with the men tasked with its observation. See if they've witnessed anything or anyone around that location," Brent added. "I haven't seen any reports stating otherwise so I don't believe anyone has ventured out that way."

Sophie looked around the room skeptically and observed each of the faces in the room.

"I'm curious," she began.

"And what's that?" Josh asked casually.

"Did everyone in this room take a page from your interrogation playbook?"

"Is that what this is then?" he replied.

Exacerbated, Sophie abruptly exited her chair and stood behind it.

"No," she stated forcefully. "This is not! Did you not hear each of the pieces of information being offered? Samantha says it's under tons of rock and dirt. The Prefect indicated that the locals won't talk and the outsiders are unaware. The General indicated that men are on constant watch observing its location, but not one of you actually said where this location is!"

"I did notice," he rebutted as he smiled broadly. "Perhaps the less you know the better."

"Inacceptable, (Unacceptable,)" she replied candidly. "I can't help protect you or this town if the details are being hidden from me!" she concluded exacerbated.

Josh crossed his arms in defiance.

"Ach," Sophie declared. "You're just a stubborn now as you were twenty years ago! I've come five hundred miles in a horse drawn cart to see you so the British wouldn't send their dragoons and slaughter everyone! I don't think a request for a little candor is out of line!" she thundered.

Josh nodded his agreement at her assertion. After a few tense moments of silence, he placed his hands on the edge of the table and declared, "Why don't you and your son make yourselves comfortable at the McArthur Hotel for the night. We'll discuss it and give you an answer in the morning. Fair?"

"Vous exaspérante home! (You infuriating man!)" she decried.

"And I see you still haven't lost any of your fire, Sophie. Always loved that about the French. Such passion," Josh stated calmly.

"Venez mère, nous allons les laisser à leurs deliberations, (Come mother, we'll leave them to their deliberations,)" Philip said as he attempted to guide her toward the door.

Sophie stood fully upright, straightened her uniform blouse, and attempted to regain her composure.

"How about I walk you across the street and introduce you to Jacques and Mimi. Perhaps he can take a request and fix you something to make you feel more at home in the morning for breakfast," Sam offered as an olive branch.

"I doubt that," Sophie declared as she stormed toward the door.

"I'll join you," Layla stated more than asked, taking the young man arm in arm.

"Who is this, Jacques? Is he a Frenchman?" Philip wondered as the pair started walking.

"Oui," she answered emphatically.

No sooner had the four exited the Sheriff's office as Josh decreed, "Relax, relax. It's all part of the game. The French are masters of it. They want information, but need to feel like they've worked for it. Sophie has forgotten that I know how it's played."

"So you're going to tell them?" Brent asked.

Josh turned his head toward President Sarkes.

"You swear on the memory of your late wife and a stack of King James bibles that they are allies?"

"Brokered the deal myself, you can trust them. Hell, we all heard the Capitaine's transmission. He didn't have to do that. We damn sure didn't ask him for that kindness."

"Agreed," Josh replied. "Does anybody have any objections to showing them tomorrow?"

"Whatever you think is best, Dad," Heather decreed as she checked Hoplites bandages.

Katherine nodded her agreement, as did the others.

"Gregg, you're awfully silent."

"Oh," Dallas answered. "He's just conjuring up ways to dismember those two."

Chuckles permeated the room.

"Then it's settled," he declared. Now, if you don't mind, I'm going to join my wife, get the French situated into their new digs, and then I'll be taking my new bride home."

\* \* \*

Lt. Eustace Stokes quietly crept toward Tyler's bunk, ever mindful of the ancient, creaky wooden floor. The old buggy factory in downtown Columbus had been dormant for nearly a century until some developer bought the aging structure and revitalized it. Tim had evicted any tenants that remained and repurposed it as a barracks shortly after consolidating the gangs and his power. The site had been chosen personally by the man for its location. It lay only a hundred yards from Huntington Park and his cash crop of marijuana in the outfield.

Through the heavy breathing and intermittent snoring, Lt. Stokes glanced around the room. The only movement he noticed was a couple quietly having sex in a corner rack.

As he moved in closer to awaken the sleeping man, Tyler abruptly opened his eyes and startled him, taking his breathe away momentarily.

Without saying a word, the two men snuck out through a broken bathroom window. Keeping to the shadows, the pair worked their way toward, and into, a shot up five story condominium complex that fronted the Scioto River. The structure stood only a block from the barracks, but provided a clear southerly exposure for their transmission to Circleville twenty miles away. From the rooftop, his communication should be able to travel unencumbered as no high rises blocked his line of sight. Only the curvature of the earth would inhibit their radio check.

The duo made short work of the stairwell access and exited onto the roof in no time. Tucked in among the HVAC components, Eustace retrieved the small radio they had stashed previously.

As he turned to make his way toward the southern face, an arrow nicked the outside of his shoulder and embedded itself into the side of the mechanicals.

"Hello," he heard a voice announce from the shadows.

Stokes quickly looked over at Tyler. The man was being held tightly by one of Tim's goons, a gun directed at his head.

Tim, making a grand entrance, slowly exited from cover. As he came into view, the smoke he exhaled from the joint he had lit formed a wafting cloud around him. Continuing to progress toward the two only served to make the exhaled white vapor swirl.

"I'll take that," TK decreed as he attempted to retrieve the device from the Lieutenant's hand.

Eustace quickly withdrew the radio from his reach, then, in act of supreme defiance, Lt. Stokes abruptly threw it off the building. The men assembled on the roof followed its arc over the ledge. Several seconds passed before they heard it crash onto the sidewalk below.

"Huh, well would ya look at that... it musta slipped," the combat engineer offered casually.

"I really hate it when that happens," Tim concurred. "Kinda like this," he rebutted and tried to abruptly remove his weapon from his shoulder holster in a show of force. The man was only able to withdraw it halfway before it got caught and discharged, blowing a hole in the rig and his shirt, startling him.

Eustace started laughing uncontrollably at the man's folly.

Tim's men remained silent. When their inebriated leader smiled broadly and joined him in the laughter, only then did they join in.

"Now," the Lieutenant declared in a serious tone. "Which one of you bastards shot that arrow at me?"

"Uh, that'd be me," a young 'soldier' offered reluctantly.

In a lighting fast motion, Eustace withdrew his side arm and shot him in the forehead, dropping him immediately. Before anyone knew what happened, the weapon was back in his holster.

"Whoa! Whoa! Whoa!" Tim proclaimed. "We're just having a conversation!"

"Conversations don't start with bolts from a cross bow. How about you tell me what you want?"

"I've got people everywhere. They saw you two slip out of the wash house," the man answered with a wide grin as he waved his hands around.

The moon light betrayed Tim's state. Eustace could clearly see the man's swollen bloodshot eyes. As he neared, he could smell the bourbon.

*This guy's hammered out of his gourd*, Lt. Stokes thought. *Josh and Bryan were right. He's still a screaming alcoholic.*

Pausing momentarily to look over his dead soldier, Tim continued. "When we talked this morning, you didn't say anything about a radio. What was that for?" Tim said somewhat slurred.

Thinking quickly, Eustace replied, "I wasn't completely honest earlier. I've got some friends that are camped just outside town. I agreed to come back with Tyler and scout it out. See if what he was telling us was on the level."

"And are we?"

"So far."

"What did you do before… you know, before all of this loveliness?" Tim asked as he gestured wildly.

"Engineer," he answered truthfully. "And you?"

"Hey, buddy," Tim's capo Todd said as he kept a strong hold on Tyler. "We're askin' the questions."

"Be nice, I'm conducting an interview," the gang leader stated as he put Todd back in line. "What kind of engineer?"

Eustace smirked. "Chemical."

"How do I know you're not here to kill me?" Tim asked. "Sneakin' around in the middle of the night to make clandestine radio calls appears a little unseemly, doesn't it?" he continued.

In a building several hundred yards away, the back-up team observed from the safety of their nest. Tucked behind some over turned office furniture, the pair watched the exchange.

"Can we shoot this clown?" the man asked as he adjusted the focus on the scope slightly.

"Negative. We are to observe only. You know that."

"Well, it looks like our Lieutenant has found himself cornered. At the very least we should radio this in."

"Agreed. You keep watch… no shooting," he concluded forcefully. "I'll head up to the roof to try and get a clearer signal."

The man on the McMillan TAC-338 rifle continued to watch as Tim and Stokes conversed. If he didn't know better, it seemed as if his CO was casually repositioning himself to make an escape.

"So what kind of skills do your men have? I've already seen your pistol skills. What else can you bring to the table? How much ammo do you guys have?"

"Well, since we seem to be courting now, let's just say we're a helluva lot more skilled than those lame ass hunters you sent to Logan. Hell, one guy took three of 'em down and was about to plant Tyler six feet under before we arrived."

Tim wobbled as he half smirked and half laughed at the comment. "Pussies. Never liked them anyway, always trying to get free pokes at the honeys just for doin' their jobs and bagging some game." In a moment of clarity, he declared, "Hey! We've got some openings now that this young lad has met his end. You guys wanna join up with us?"

"Boss, you think that's a good idea?" Todd asked. "We don't know anything about this guy, or his friends. I'm telling you man, we shoulda just rolled into McArthur and that park and taken them all out."

Flipping a switch, Tim lashed out and struck him with a back hand. "I told you, Todd! *HE* was there… in Chillicothe… som-bitch had a bazooka dude! The only thing missing was the Ride of the freakin' Valkyries theme music blaring from speakers!"

*Oh, crap. Play it cool, Eustace.*

"Who?" the engineer asked casually.

"A guy from my former life in the 'burbs. Mister goody two-shoes."

Silence permeated the rooftop as Tim hung his head. The Lieutenant thought TK was going to pass out on his feet until he abruptly moved.

"I got it!" he proclaimed. "Are you and your friends up for a test? Ya know, to see if you're worthy of joining our gang?"

Smiling, Lt. Stokes said, "I thought you'd never ask."

"Excellent! Come find me in the morning, we'll talk it over."

"Sounds good," Eustace declared then added, "Boss."

"Oh, one more thing, how are you going to contact your people now that you've thrown the radio off the roof?"

Eustace feigned mock confusion. "Umm, I guess I didn't think that all the way through. You guys have a means to communicate or something, right?"

"Sure," TK slurred reassuringly. "Just give Todd here the channel number and any safe words we might need and he'll get them the message."

Eustace actually started laughing at the man. "Look, Tim. Those are my men, not yours. Any calls go out to them, they'll be sent by me."

"Uh oh," the gang leader declared.

"What?"

"I introduced myself to you as TK. Who told you my name?"

Lt. Stokes swallowed hard and quickly tried to recover. "Beats me. I must have heard it somewhere. I think he might have told me. What does it matter?"

"Shoot Tyler in the leg please," Tim ordered nonchalantly.

Without warning, Todd took a step back and shot him in the calf, dropping him on to the roof in wailing heap.

"Whoa! I thought we were just having a conversation!" Stokes barked. "That's what you said, remember?"

"Oh, I do. I also gave an order forbidding anyone from speaking that name. Tyler knows this. My name is TK, not Tim. Now, what's the channel? Are there any safe words? I'm not going to ask again."

When nobody answered, he added, "How about this, first one to answer gets to live."

The Lieutenant stood still and said nothing. He wanted to withdraw his sidearm and blow the pair away, but couldn't. There was already a gun being pointed at him.

From the ground, Tyler weakly offered, "Channel 12, call signs are 'Viper' and 'Pumpkin Patch'."

"Shut up!" Eustace barked at the injured man.

"Woo! There we go!" their leader exclaimed loudly. "Don't stop now! Is there anything else?" Tim asked as he squatted down toward him. "A safe word?"

There was no other alternative. While TK and his goon had their collective attention on the bleeding heap, Stokes quickly went to withdraw his sidearm. Tyler saw it.

Just as he was about to pull the trigger, he said, "Briar."

The Lt. couldn't believe his ears. The man had given them the wrong intel.

Eustace paused as Tyler nodded ever so slightly. Eustace inferred it as a signal that it was okay to put him out of his misery.

He quickly fired before the gang member's collective attention returned to him. The round entered just above his forehead, blew out the back of the fallen man's head, and then lodged itself in Todd's shin.

Reflexively, the pair jumped. Once Tim's goon realized he was hit, he threw himself onto the roof and began writhing in agony.

With his gun up and aimed at TK, Lt. Stokes said, "I think I've seen just about all I care to see of this little gang of yours." Then added, "*Tim*," for emphasis.

Moving quickly, Eustace went around Tyler's corpse and retrieved Todd's weapon. "You want me to end your suffering to?" he asked the wailing man as he circled toward the roof top door.

"Go to hell, you son-of-a-bitch!" the man shot back.

"Have it your way," Stokes declared as he yanked open the door.

He was met with a blinding flash and an ear splitting 'boom'. The Lt. was lifted off of his feet as he fell backward. It felt like he had just been punched in the chest by three heavyweight champions at the same time. All of the air immediately left his lungs.

"Watch that first step! It's a doozy!" Tim declared tauntingly as he cackled and took the two weapons away from Eustace. "Rock salt's a bitch, ain't it!"

TK turned his attention to the two men exiting the stairwell. "Pick this piece of shit up," then continued his taunting.

"Hurts like a mother, but it's non-lethal," his interrogator stated as they threw him against the wall.

Stokes dug at his chest in an attempt to brush off the burning sensation. Nothing helped.

The man on the Secret Service's McMillan rifle bolted from his nest and sprinted up the emergency stairwell toward his teammate. By the time he reached the roof, his partner was already on the line with someone, calling in the play by play and begging for permission to shoot.

As he approached, he heard, "Listen little girl! That's our friend over there!"

The airwaves burst alive with Katherine's contempt, "You call me that again, I swear I will stomp a mud hole in your ass! I said stand down and you better damn well do it!"

The man wanted to scream in protest when the crack of a round discharged, stealing his attention. "Someone's shootin'. Hold one!"

Eustace screamed out as the bullet tore through his inner thigh. Instinctively, he glanced down, willing himself to clamp his hand on the hole in his leg.

"Awe, that looks like it hurt. Here," Tim said as he squatted down and offered the roach from his joint. "It'll help with the pain."

Stokes waved him off as he attempted to stand.

"Boys, give the Lieutenant hand."

"How did you –," he started to say.

"Did Josh honestly think after his sidekick bulldogged me that I'd just let it go?"

"You don't know anything!" Stokes said defiantly as his body began growing weak. As he leaned against the sidewall of the roof, he knew he didn't have long. The leg was pouring blood quickly.

With all of the bravado Tim could muster, he loudly proclaimed from the rooftop, "You idiot! I know everything! I have a mole in your camp!" He declared as he laughed mightily at the pronouncement. "He's one of the governors!"

The man holding the radio nearly dropped it onto the gravelly rooftop surface. Catching himself, he clicked in on the hand set, "Be advised, one of the camp leaders is a mole for TK."

Disbelieving what she just heard, Katherine stated, "Say again. A Governor is a mole?"

"Roger that," the man said as he continued to watch. "It's either Benjamin or Jerod," he clarified in a demoralized tone.

"Copy that," she replied.

"Now, what I want to know is," Tim began. "What does Josh have over there? Weapons, men, vehicles… I need a full accounting of all of it... since he's done such a masterful job of hiding things from the people in the camp."

"Go to hell," Stokes replied.

"Oh, you'll be there long before me… but I'll be sending Josh there to keep you company real soon."

The Lieutenant smirked at TK.

"Something funny, soldier?"

Eustace chuckled. "Yeah, you hit my femoral artery. I'll be dead in about a minute and half so I ain't tellin' you shit… roll that up and smoke it, mother –,"

The Lieutenant never had the chance to finish his last defiant statement as Tim lunged forward and shoved him over the ledge.

As they watched, their friend and commanding officer tumbled down the side of the building to his death. The overwatch team filled with rage. They wanted nothing more than to flip the bipod legs down, take a position, and send every last one of those men to an early grave, but orders were orders and they had them… stand down.

"Be advised…" the man began as he choked back his emotions. "I say again, be advised… BB is down," then added in cracked voice, "He's gone, ma'am." After a long pause, he concluded, "Resuming overwatch."

What they couldn't see on the other end were the slow salty tears working their way down Katherine's cheeks. She took a few silent moments to compose herself. "Copy that," she finally replied and threw the mic on the table in disgust.

While she held her face in her hands and silently wept for Eustace, she heard Hoplite say from across the room, "The first one's always the toughest. I'm sorry."

Katherine didn't ask for his pity. She was angry.

"You stow that shit, Carlos," she spat. "Brent, Dallas, James… on me. We're going to go and have a little chat with the Governors. If either one of them jack rabbits, make sure you shoot 'em in the ass! I want 'em *alive!*"

# Chapter 22

The moonlit night was muggy, the air heavy. Everything on their bodies was sticky from the humidity, but Katherine was on a mission. She had been handed operational control of the entire attacking force by Brent and her father and the burden was weighing on her. A man, a friend, was dead. Her gamble hadn't paid off. The three men with her were content to let her ride several yards ahead. She needed to clear her head.

Breaking the silence in a barely audible whisper, James asked, "Are you still confident in your decision to give her this much responsibility?"

The retired General thought for a moment before he replied, but Dallas answered first. "She knows what's at stake. She knew enough to not take a vehicle when there were two parked right out front of Juan's. No, Katherine's working this through, you'll see."

"You and I have faith in her," James inserted. "I'm asking about her ability to handle the rigors and stress as a field commander."

"She has all of the requisite qualities," Brent offered. "Josh may not have realized what he was doing, but both those girls have been in OCS for the last decade."

"You know I can hear you, right?" Katherine said into the darkness of the night.

The trio snapped their heads in her direction.

"Good," the four star replied. "Now explain to me why you barked at an enlisted man."

"He was questioning my authority and decision making abilities even when he knew I was in command. Next question," she stated unemotionally.

The three men glanced at the others, then gave each a half shrug, as if to say, 'why not'.

"Why not take a car or truck? We could have been there by now," Dallas asked.

"Needed to cool off. I want answers, not another corpse. Next question."

"What's in your head?" James questioned metaphorically.

"A brain," she replied in the literal. "Next question."

"You know what I mean," he corrected.

"I know," she said with a sigh as she brought her horse to a stop. A few seconds later, the three men caught up and she prodded hers to fall in line.

"Questions are what are in my head."

"Go on," Brent offered encouragingly.

"I want to know *why* one of them betrayed us, more for my own edification than anything else. I want to know *what* was shared. I want to know *when*, and I want to know *how* they were communicating. I can't adjust without the variables."

"The 'why' is immaterial. Focus on the 'what', 'when', and 'how'. Explain those to me."

"I think, in terms of order of priority, 'when' is the most important. If he hasn't communicated in a few days, then Tim isn't aware of what we removed from the park in plain sight of the Governors. Gregg said they were pretty upset that they weren't in the loop." Katherine paused briefly. "Hey, Dallas, you and Brent handle the OP logs regularly. How many times did either of the male camp leaders take Coastwatcher duty?"

The two men looked at each other.

"Every couple weeks, no more than anyone else," Dallas offered.

"That sounds about right," Brent confirmed.

"Which outpost were they stationed at? Did they request a specific structure?"

"Why do you ask? Where are you going with this?" the General stated earnestly wanting to know where she might be headed.

"I'm thinking that Tyler and those guys weren't there looking to set up a deer camp at all. Maybe they were there to meet Benjamin or Jerod, or both. According to Heather, one vehicle approached, radioed, then the others followed."

"That little –," Dallas muttered. "I know who it is."

* * *

Josh and Sam approached the cabin, but with no lights or candles lit, the entire structure was completely hidden from view. The yellowish headlights from the deuce bounced and danced on the glass like the glow of a firefly. Once the truck was stopped, Josh went around to help her out of the workhorse vehicle.

"Welcome home, Mrs. Simmons," Josh proclaimed as her feet touched the ground.

"Why thank you, Mr. Simmons," she responded in a mock Scarlett O'Hara style accent.

Her husband bowed in a grandiose manner then stood upright.

With a smirk on his face he declared, "Me man! You woman! Me take!"

Samantha hiked her dress up to the knees and started running for the door. She was quickly and playfully caught then scooped up into his arms.

With their faces so close, Josh whispered, "Welcome home, Sam."

"You too, hun," she replied before leaning forward to kiss. "Now, carry me across the threshold so I can take off this dress."

"Wow! Alright!"

Realizing what she had just said, his bride playfully smacked him on the shoulder. "Very funny. Not for that, I have to pee."

"Ouch, buzz kill," he answered woefully.

"Oh, stop your pouting. We'll get to that. I'm sticky from this heat and humidity. I was thinking of taking a shower."

Josh immediately picked his head up and smiled broadly.

"Want someone to wash you back?"

"Sure," she answered with a return smile.

He quickly responded like an eager teenager, "Want someone to wash your front?"

"Maybe," she replied coyly.

\* \* \*

James and Dallas sat in the darkened cabin waiting for its occupants to return. As with all park inhabitants, Benjamin and Jerod were forced to share accommodations. The rumor mill, being what it was, indicated that both had lost wives and family escaping from the suburban hell they had once enjoyed. However, given their former occupations as managers with large staffs, the residents had voted the pair, plus Susan, as the camp's first Board of Governors.

Most of the occupants had already returned from the festivities in downtown McArthur and were preparing for the much needed rest. Since the power had been knocked out six months before, everyone's daily routine and schedules had to be recalibrated. There was no need to stay up until the wee hours burning the midnight oil for an ungrateful boss or that report that *had* to be ready by 8:00 AM. Distractions like TV, video games, email, and cell phones were replaced by the exhaustive tasks necessary to survive. There was food to collect, crops to tend, firewood to be split, and water to be hauled. As a result, sleep came easy and early. By now, everyone was unaccustomed to being up so late.

When the last of the trucks pulled up, Katherine emitted her distinctive bird call to alert the pair in the cabin that she had a visual. She and Brent slowly slid back into the shadows and waited. They watched Ben and Jerry, as Gregg liked to refer to them, exchange goodbyes with other residents as they made their way to the cabin.

"I can't wait to crawl into my bed. I could probably sleep for days if someone let me," they heard Jerod say.

"Me too," Benjamin answered. "I'll be there in a sec. I gotta use the latrine."

"Okay, I'll see you in there then," came the nonchalant response as the pair separated.

"I can't catch a friggin' break tonight," Katherine observed.

"Easy," Brent quietly instructed.

The first of the two male Governors stepped onto the wooden decking of the porch and used someone's idea of a homemade boot scrapper and shoe horn to clean and remove his boots before entering the cabin. Once down to thin socks, the man opened the door and entered as if he didn't have a care in the world.

In a series of movements he'd made a thousand times before, he walked through the darkness to the fireplace mantle. His hand immediately found the small battery operated lantern that resided there. He quickly turned it on. Next to him, only a few feet away, stood James and Dallas.

"Oh my –," he proclaimed as he jumped.

"Easy, Jerod," the big man said slowly and deliberately. "We just need to talk."

"You guys scared me half to death," he answered as he clutched his hand to his chest. "Damn near gave me a heart attack!"

Once he finally took the two men in visually, he noticed both had slung large caliber weapons across their body armor.

"Uh, don't shoot," Jerod said disarmingly.

"Have a seat please. We'll be outta here in a minute," Dallas offered as he motioned toward the kitchen table.

"What's going on?" he asked confused as he sat.

"We've got a problem and need you and Ben to help us sort it all out," James replied reassuringly. "Where did your roommate go?"

"He said he was headed to the, well… the head actually."

"When you two were on OP duty, which post did you get assigned most often?" Dallas inquired.

"Charlie Whiskey Three, why?"

"And Benjamin?"

"He was usually in Two. We'd ride out there together. What's this all about? You guys are kinda freakin' me out."

"Oh, it's probably nothing. Just following up on some news we received this evening."

As if on cue, the second man came strolling through the door.

"Hello, Ben, we need to talk," James stated.

The man turned three shades of pale, ducked out the way he came, and started running. The pair could hear his boots on the porch as he attempted his escape. They had barely begun to give chase themselves when they heard a thud.

By the time the men exited the cabin, Benjamin was lying flat on his back. Katherine stood menacingly over him. Both watched as he slowly rolled on to his side to make it up on to all fours. He spat a mouthful of blood onto the deck boards then reached into his mouth and removed a tooth.

"You have no idea what you've done," he moaned. "You've killed her!"

In a hushed tone, Katherine gave her instructions.

"Get him up. Drag his ass back in the cabin."

* * *

"Are you sure no one is out here?" Sam asked disbelieving what she was about to do.

From the water some feet below, her husband called back.

"Yes, besides, Brent and Dallas are staying elsewhere for the next forty-eight hours and the girls have their own house. So come on already. Just grab on, swing on out, and let go. Gravity will do the rest… that is, unless you're chicken."

"I'm not afraid of a little rope swing, *darling*. I'm more concerned about passers-by seeing me swing butt naked into the creek! This is *not* what I had mind when I said I wanted to take a shower."

"It's refreshing, now stop being such a baby," he answered and antagonized her further. "What do you care? You're a married woman skinny dipping with her husband."

Samantha groaned and replied, "Fine! Move out of the way."

She then proceeded to back up to get a running start.

"This is crazy, this is crazy, this is crazy," she muttered to herself as she worked up the nerve.

"Any time, sweetheart!" he declared in his best drill instructor voice, further goading her into action.

With courage mustered, she took off and started running toward the bank with the rope in her hands. As she neared the edge she leapt like a child full of reckless abandon. Josh watched as she squealed her way out over the water and let go, plunging into the brisk water below.

When she re-emerged, she proclaimed, "Holy crap, why didn't you tell me it was so cold!"

Her husband just started laughing and reached out to grab her. "Come here, honey. I'll warm you up," he said compassionately as he pulled her toward him.

Josh bent slightly to pick Samantha up and place her in his embrace. With their flesh pressed together, she gently wrapped her legs around him.

As they were about to kiss, Sam drew her head back, "You are *never* to mention that I swung butt naked from that contraption, got it?"

"Mum's the word, Mrs. Simmons."

* * *

"Now, if I take that tape off of your mouth, you think you can speak in a normal tone of voice?" Katherine asked as she stood in front of the visibly shaken Benjamin.

The man resumed his thrashing and struggling.

"Not ready yet then. Brent, can you do me a favor and go get Susan please?"

"I suppose. What do you want her for?"

"Because, I'm trying to prove to him that he isn't going to be hurt or abused. Send Jerod and Dallas back in on your way out."

The General smirked.

"What?" she asked.

"Oh, I was remembering something," he answered nonchalantly.

"What's that?"

"Just that I haven't taken this many orders from a woman in a long time. I've kind of forgotten how unpredictable it can be," he remarked as he exited the cabin.

James let out a snicker, but quickly straightened up when his adoptive niece glared at him. "Ma'am," he corrected.

Through the darkness in the doorway, she heard, "Dallas, Jerod, front and center."

Several minutes later, Brent returned with a somewhat comatose Susan in tow. She was yawning as she entered.

"Why can't this wait 'til morning. I'd just fallen asleep."

"Because I need all of you here to prove to Benny here that no harm is going to come to him, regardless of what answers he might provide."

When her eyes finally focused on the man in front of her she was shocked. "Why is he restrained in a chair? Did Gregg put you up to this 'cause this isn't funny!"

"I can assure you that he most certainly did not," Dallas replied without hesitation.

"Gregg doesn't know we are here, Susan," Katherine offered. "But I promise you this, you'll be glad that I am here instead because the next thing they'd be fitting him for is a pine box." Then she plastered a demure smile on her face and requested, "Please join us. Have a seat."

As she took the last seat at the table, she asked, "So this isn't a test?"

"Oh, it is, but not the kind you're thinking of. No, it seems that Benjamin has been planted here by the same lunatics that tried to rape my sister and almost killed Hoplite."

Incredulously, Susan replied forcefully, "He's nothing of the sort! He's been helpful since the day we arrived! Benjamin's organized everything from the shower schedule to the firewood detail."

"All true, but let me ask you this. Before my dad showed up in Bryan's driveway, how long had Benjamin been living on the street?"

"Oh, I don't know. A few weeks maybe. It was winter with Christmas and New Year's parties… the weather kept most people inside. You remember that from your childhood. There isn't much socializing with neighbors when it's zero degrees outside."

"Did you ever see his wife?" Katherine asked continuing to lead her down her carefully thought out path.

"Once or twice. She was getting out of her car or taking the recycling to the curb or something. A very attractive brunette I believe, why?"

"How did she die?"

"I was told that after your father scared the hell out of everyone in Bryan's driveway, they went home and she became hysterical. He finally got her calmed down and into bed. When he woke up the next morning, she had taken her own life. I was very saddened to hear that news, Benjamin," she concluded as she comfortingly patted his restrained arm.

"Jerod, have you ever seen this?" the youngest Simmons daughter asked as James handed her a military style radio. Katherine placed it on the table with a thud for effect.

"Well I be damned," Brent said astonished. "That's a Vietnam era AN/PRC-77 field radio... No wonder we never picked up any transmissions with the channel scanner!"

Jerod had a look of complete confusion on his face.

"I'll take that as a 'no' then. So," she proclaimed. "That answers the question of 'how'. I believe the answer of 'when' will reside with the OP duty logs back at the comm center. That leaves only the 'what' and 'why', doesn't it, Benjamin."

The man looked utterly demoralized. The only thing he could do is give a little nod.

"Brent believes that the why doesn't matter. I disagree. Ya see, in my experience, while not as vast as the others, is that the world isn't entirely black and white, but for the General, not so much. In my estimation, there's quite a bit of grey, and again, for the General, not so much. Here's what I'll tell you though, the breadth of your answers to these questions will determine just how much latitude you are afforded at your sentencing."

Benjamin's eyes grew large and he began shaking his head vigorously.

"Oh, there's no way around this, Benjamin. Your actions just cost Lt. Stokes his life. The monsters we've been protecting you from just killed him!"

Susan gasped and placed her hand over her mouth. Katherine was undeterred.

In a more subdued tone, she continued. "That's right, Benjamin. Lieutenant Eustace Stokes was the commanding officer of the combat engineering platoon we embedded at the camp. Two of his subordinates just watched TK execute him not an hour ago. Now, the only way he could have possibly been identified by that lunatic was through your direct action. Oh, and as a side note, you're little confabs almost cost us two more lives in Heather and Carlos. In my opinion, these clandestine conversations with that gang are nothing short of treason."

Katherine paused to let the word sink in.

"At the very least you're an accessory to murder, two counts of attempted murder, and one count of attempted rape. Now, I'm going to take that tape off and you *will* provide me with the answers I require so nobody else gets hurt, is that understood?"

The man sighed as he nodded, signaling his cooperation.

"Good," she declared as she quickly yanked the tape from across his mouth and face.

Benjamin groaned at the pain that was inflicted and then proceeded to flex his jaw.

"Okay, let's start with what information you have provided the enemy. What does he know?"

"Everything I knew up until my last rotation in Charlie Whiskey Two," he offered immediately.

"Such as," Brent interjected.

The prisoner stammered in the beginning, but then quickly picked up speed. By the time he was finished he was going a hundred miles an hour, but managed to provide a full accounting of his treachery.

When he was done, Dallas stated, "So basically, you told him what you had seen or heard while in your capacity as a Board member. The stuff around the Lake… anything else?"

He shook his head in reply.

"On me," Katherine declared as she headed toward the back of the cabin.

Once the four were assembled, she asked the men, "So what've we got?" without taking her eyes off of Benjamin and the others.

"TK doesn't know much other than the number of residents in the camp and the equipment Josh provided," Dallas offered. "I mean, yeah, he told 'em about the crops and the greenhouses and some goings on in McArthur."

"He knows about the men being trained by me and Gregg, but not how many. He didn't know a thing about the combat engineers or their gear until today. He'd never been to the farm until this morning," James added.

"He thought Eustace was trading on a former military career, but that was enough to get him killed," Brent concluded with a tinge of anger in his voice. "What would you like to do now?"

"I told you," Katherine explained. "I want to know why. I think it matters, whether you do or not. As for the original plan, with some minor adjustments, we are still a go. I'll get back to you and Dad with a new Op order in the morning," she concluded.

As she approached the bound man, the young commander proclaimed, "Okay, Benjamin, time for the million dollar question… why do all of this?"

The rest of the group hadn't even reassembled before he blurted out, "He kidnapped my wife and threw her into his damn brothel!"

"Whoa!" Katherine declared. "Slow down. Start from the beginning."

"When Josh finished giving us the information in Bryan's driveway, we went home and started packing. We were new to the neighborhood; we weren't going to defend it. We couldn't. Traci and I were IT engineers that had just transferred in from Seattle to handle the new data center coming online. She and I were hardcore northwest liberals. You know… protest capitalism, espouse socialistic principles, stick it Wall Street, and grab all of the guns types."

"How'd that work out?" Brent muttered.

Katherine briefly glance his direction.

"Okay, go on," Brent said in a non-threatening manner.

"We had all of our stuff packed, our mountain bikes loaded, the cold weather ski gear… all of it. Then went to bed. Traci and I actually commented to one another that there was no need to try and set the alarm on the house since there wasn't any power."

Katherine sighed, "And Tim knew that too I'm guessing."

Benjamin nodded.

"Had he made any passes at her before this? Come on to her in any way?"

"Not that I'm aware of. Traci did say that he seemed kind of creepy. We were asleep and the next thing we know there's four guys hauling us out of bed! He told me that she wouldn't be harmed if I went to the state park with the group. I was to supply him with information, so I did. I've been trying to get her back ever since."

"Why not tell us this? We could have helped," James said compassionately.

"I was the outsider. Nobody from the neighborhood knew me. No one was going to believe me here."

"But they elected you to the Board of Governors," Susan interjected.

"No they didn't," Ben replied somewhat forcefully. "I rigged the balloting. Some guy named Ashe was the actual selection, but he died when his insulin ran out so I figured it was no big deal."

"How'd you get the radio?" Dallas asked as he tinkered with it on the table.

"I was late one night, out collecting something or another, and needed to clean off. When I walked in to the shower hut, Tim was just standing there… with Traci. He had it with him," Benjamin replied solemnly.

"I'm sorry, what?" Katherine said shocked.

"When I told him about the Coastwatcher program he changed our communication method. I hardly recognized my wife. She was skin and bones." Demoralized, he concluded, "Traci was barely clothed and she looked strung out, like they'd been drugging her."

"Tyler had needle marks. He's got to be getting drugs from somewhere. Now I really want this guy dead," Katherine proclaimed.

Benjamin just kept talking, continuing to lift the weight that had been drowning him since the lights went out.

"He was touching her, groping her, sticking his hand in her shorts, right in front of me. Said he was a 'mergers and acquisitions man' now that he had united the gangs. He actually bragged that she was doing a

330

fair amount of business in his little whore house up in Columbus. Pushin' ass, as he called it."

With everything out in the open, Ben began weeping and crying uncontrollably.

Through the emotion, Benjamin meekly added, "He had these old polaroid style pictures of her." Then he paused as the anger set in. "She was doing unspeakable things with whole groups of men!" he hollered. "I'm sorry!" he protested. "I didn't know what else to do! What would you have done?!"

Stunned silence permeated the room. Katherine's only thought was that the man in front of her was feeling what her own father must have felt all those years ago. Except, her father did something about it.

Redirecting him, Katherine asked, "So now you've got the radio. What then?"

He sniff heavily and sucked all of the snot and drool back into his head before he answered. "I just started volunteering for Coastwatcher duty... specifically asking for Charlie Whiskey Two every Wednesday."

His interrogator looked over at Brent and Dallas. They nodded their collective confirmation.

"Thank you, Benjamin. You've been incredibly helpful," she stated. "Dallas, go outside and see if the keys are in that deuce. We're going to deposit him with Sheriff Watson."

"What? But I told you everything?" the man stammered.

"You did, and I'm grateful, but that doesn't excuse your behavior. You will stand trial for your actions and a jury of your peers must decide your fate. If you're lucky, we'll bring Traci back."

# Chapter 23

Out of breathe from their latest endeavor; Josh laid his head on Samantha's bare, sweat laden chest.

"You okay?" she asked.

"Yeah," he replied, breathing heavily. "Whose idea was it to christen *every* room?"

"I read about it somewhere," she paused and added, "I think it was meant for twenty-something's though," she lamented.

"I woulda never guessed," he answered sarcastically.

"Awe, is my poor wittle baby tired?"

Josh picked his head up and gently kissed her flesh. "You could say that." Through his labored breathing, he quoted a movie he'd seen decades ago, "This mortal form has grown weak. I need sustenance!" Then he abruptly stood and backed away.

As Samantha sat up, she looked around the cabin and surveyed the damage. Clothing was strewn about, cushions were askew or missing from the couch, and picture frames which hadn't moved in years were haphazardly shoved out of the way. She giggled when she saw a piece of art hanging crooked on the wall.

"Oops," she declared as her husband helped her off the table. The gymnastic like escapades they had been engaged in for most of the night was felt quickly when she stood. "Oh my," she decreed. "I'm a little sore."

Josh thrust his hands in the air and boomed, "Victory!"

"Whatever makes you feel better, sweetie."

"She giveth, and she taketh away!"

"I need a shower," his wife lamented.

"Want me to wash your front?" he asked suddenly rejuvenated.

"Thanks, but I'm good for the time being. That's how all this started, remember? Get breakfast going, then we'll trade," she said as she quickly pecked him on the lips.

"Roger that, Mrs. Simmons. Starting breakfast."

His oldest friends and Brent stood just off the porch contemplating entry into the cabin. Nobody wanted to be the first to speak, let alone tell them that they should have closed the blinds.

James nudged Dallas' shoulder as if to say, 'you first'.

"Did you know she had a body like that," Dallas said into the summer air.

"Lucky bastard," his friend replied.

"Forget this," Brent declared. "I'm not knocking on that door."

"Give 'em an hour?" James asked.

"Sounds good to me," Brent responded and walked away.

"I'm with him," James decreed and followed suit.

"I guess I could check the comms from Three Sisters," Dallas offered as he went to catch up.

\* \* \*

Bryan and Kristin had been handling the early morning shift in the basement of the girls' farmhouse for so long, that the duty log started reading 'B&K' when they had a shift. Similar pairings were becoming more commonplace at the farm and in town. Two of Josh's daughters were now engaged, an 'exclusive' relationships had developed between Mimi and Jacques as well as a number of others. Spring had definitely been in the air around McArthur as many of the couples had continued their dalliance on into summer.

When Dallas entered the basement and relayed what he and the others had witnessed outside of Josh's cabin, Bryan decided to have a little fun and raise his friend on the walkie. The three listened as their friend informed his new bride. The threats and vulgarity emanating from the previous demure Samantha caused the room to erupt in laughter.

The trio was jolted back to reality when the channel scanner stopped and picked up an incoming call. "This message is for 'Carolina D', this is 'Pennsylvania Dutch', do you copy? Penn Dutch calling Carolina, over."

"That's your handle, Dallas. Ever heard of this guy," Bryan asked.

"It's not familiar, but that accent is a little off-putting. Especially with UN forces running around," he answered.

As he cautiously picked up the mic, Dallas replied, "This is Carolina, go ahead Dutch, over."

"I don't know where you are or who you can connect with, but I was told to contact you with information, over."

"That's fine. What do you have for me, Dutch, over."

"Fifty Brit Peace Keepers just rolled through Everett, headed west toward Somerset, PA, over."

That got everyone's attention.

"Copy that. Anything else, over."

"They stopped to syphon gas, grabbed some food and medical supplies too, over."

"Med supplies? Did they have wounded, over."

"I'd say a dozen and half, over."

"How many vehicles, over."

"We counted eight. Some of our residents over heard them talking about Harrisburg. My guess is they had more when they entered than when they left, over."

"Hold one," Dallas said as he laid the mic on the table and went over to the makeshift map.

"Now where did those boys originate from, I wonder," he muttered to himself as the others followed suit.

The maps standing before them showed the history of the last six months. Latent dry erase markings depicted the various UN troop movements throughout the eastern seaboard over time. The largest concentration, at present, was represented in the New England and Mid-Atlantic states.

"I think they are most likely coming out of New York, maybe some of the troops from West Point," Bryan offered. "Harrisburg is too far for it to be any of these," he concluded as he directed Dallas's attention to Charleston and Richmond.

"You're probably right," Kristin offered. "Dutch said they were headin' west, but where are they going?"

"Let's ask 'em and see if he can give us anything more to go on," Dallas replied.

Bryan abruptly picked up the ruler and drew lines on the board connecting West Point with Harrisburg and Everett and stood back. His mind was in overdrive trying to figure out the latest riddle presented by the UN troops. 'Where are they going?' was always the first question to try and answer. On a whim, he put the straight edge back up and carried the line out.

"Hey guys, you might want to see this," he declared.

The group spun around and glanced back at him. "Whatcha got?"

"I don't think you're gonna like it."

The three stood motionless, staring at what Bryan had drawn.

Dallas crossed his arms and slowly shook his head.

After few silent moments, he acknowledged, "Well, crap. Seems that McArthur just entered the war."

"How much time do we have?" Kristin asked.

"They could stay on I-70 and skirt the south side of Pittsburgh. That'll take them into Wheeling, Cambridge, and Zanesville," Dallas replied.

"Or they could duck into West Virginia and get on I-68 and head to I-79," Bryan offered.

Dallas approached the board and followed the interstate markings on the map. "That leads them down into Morgantown. If they hit Route 50, that'll take 'em through Clarksburg and Parkersburg, straight to us. Either way, it's about three hundred miles through the mountains and they're low on fuel. We've got a few days depending on who or what they encounter along the way. Maybe more if they run out of gas."

"Honeymoon's over," Kristin declared.

"I'll stay on with Dutch and try to figure out which way they went and gather as much intel as I can. If I'm lucky, we'll reach some folks that'll be in their path and slow 'em down. At a minimum, reduce their numbers. You two go get the exhibitionists and the others and bring them back here."

\* \* \*

Downtown McArthur was a flurry of activity. Colonel Sophie Desjardins and her son Philip spent the morning trying to verify Dallas' intel. By all accounts the remains of a British Dragoon unit were headed straight for them. It was a necessary task and one they gladly accepted. If the French, Dutch, and Indian government's involvement in complicity was known to the King, they needed to know.

Josh could be seen stomping around the Sheriff's office seething. Not only had a friend been murdered, but they had managed to extract information. The extent of which was unknown. However, he took some solace in the fact that the Columbus gang made an attempt at some form of miscommunication by initiating contact with an incorrect safe word. Dallas was content to let him continue with the charade for a few days, completely ignoring everything the man offered.

"Okay, Daddy, here's what I've got," Katherine stated as she entered the office with Brent.

"Gimme some good news, sweetie. I don't know how much more crap I can take today."

She and Brent shared a glance that was missed by him.

"Okay," she began. "First things first, you're not going."

"I'm sorry, what did you say? Because it sounded an awful lot like my daughter is trying to handle me."

"I didn't stutter and it's not open for debate. I'm in charge, granted with a great deal of guidance from you, General Howard, James, and Gregg, but my decision is final."

Josh had never been so conflicted in his life. His emotions were all over the board. He hadn't slept much and was physically exhausted. So much had happened while he and Sam had enjoyed their wedding night.

However, he was extremely proud of the leader his daughter had become. He'd had no small part in that progression. She and her sister, Layla, had both taken to their independence with trepidation, but quickly found their footing. On the flip side of that though, the man's generosity had been exploited by TK and Benjamin from the start. The anger and hatred he felt for Tim's ilk was all consuming.

When she received no rebuttal, she offered, "I'm taking Brent, Dallas, James, and Grappler as my principle squad leaders. You're staying here with Sam, Gregg, and the French to help prepare for the British… should they arrive."

The man was crestfallen and it showed in his body language.

Katherine walked over and wrapped him in a hug. "I love you, Daddy, but I need you here. This town, the camp, and Colonel Desjardins, they all know and respect you. They will follow your lead."

As she withdrew, she kissed him on the cheek. "You wanna see my modifications? It involves tunnel rats and Sheriff Watson using the 'big' gun."

A smile formed on his face.

"I can't wait to hear it, honey."

* * *

Jim Watson had been the Sheriff of McArthur for over twenty years. He'd arrested all manner of criminal and seen just about everything there was to offer given the depravity of man. However, in all that time, no one had ever asked him to trade on his Army experience, let alone help level a city.

"I gotta tell ya, Josh, I'm not sure you and Katherine are fully grasping what those shells do. I'm talking four feet deep, fifteen foot wide craters. Hell, anyone inside fifty yards is either dead or wounded."

"I understand completely, Sheriff," his daughter replied. "All I need to know is if you are capable of giving me five rounds in quick succession."

"Depends on how many men we have. Six is the minimum. Are we using the auto loader or loading and ramming manually?"

"You'll find out when you get there. I've got six in you, Juan and his sons, the owner from Motts Military Museum, and his grandson. From what Dad found out on his way out of Columbus, the machine has been restored and maintained meticulously."

"Okay, but what are you looking to achieve?"

"I need your best traffic cop routine. I want you to hit in and around this intersection… force the sheeple to go north to this open field," she explained as she gestured toward the heavily creased document on the table.

Jim leaned forward and reviewed the map sprawled out before him. His immediate thoughts forced him to challenge her plan. "What's stopping them from turning south?"

"The AEP building," she replied casually.

He stole his attention away from the downtown Columbus map and glanced up at her, confused.

"According to our inventory, we have two dozen forty pound cratering charges remaining after sealing the tunnel. Plus Dad and Hoplite procured six crates of C4, miles of Det cord, timed fuses, and blasting caps. Now I don't know what half that stuff is, or whether it'll be enough, but I've tasked the Sappers with the demo of the Plaza One building off to the east and the AEP building down here in the south. They'll be dropping those in the street as a very large impediment. Our tunnel rats will use the underground storm water pipes to infiltrate the city and start herding them south and west towards the crossroads. Your shelling then diverts them into this open area as they approach the river front."

"What happens when they reach the field?"

"Checkmate," Josh replied. "With no cover, anyone with a weapon has a choice to lay it down or…"

\* \* \*

Secretary of Defense Lawrence 'Larry' Fielding entered the POTUS' office without knocking or preamble.

"We got his ass, sir!" he proclaimed without hesitation.

"Where did you find him?" President Culpepper asked in an excited response as he stood.

"We had people scanning the fence line with thermal imager's all night. He was hiding under some brush in a shallow hole with a clear sightline to his wife's office."

The new Commander in Chief sensed there was more.

"And?"

"He had a high powered rifle with him, sir," Fielding added.

"Where is he?"

"MP's are bringing him in right now," the SecDef answered.

"Good," the POTUS replied almost exhausted from the weight of the effort.

After President Rayburn had been found dead in his office, the Secretary of Defense had been doggedly pursuing his murderer. He read and re-read every personnel file for every service member, staff member, and civilian on the base. For months he had made little to no progress until the remarkable happened. It wasn't much. To the less paranoid, it would have seemed like a simple comforting gesture between two co-workers.

Unfortunately for the man now in military custody, when Larry Fielding saw it, his mind immediately warped into overdrive.

"Do you want to have a few words with him before we confront the wife?" the SecDef asked with a smile.

An equally devilish grin flashed across the President's face.

Thirty minutes later, it was the POTUS that entered the Secretary of State's office without knocking or preamble.

"Mr. President," she said as the man crossed the threshold. "I didn't think you were going to be able to attend," she stammered as she stood.

"Gentlemen, and ladies, let us have this room."

The assembled staff looked around the conference table quickly, confused.

The POTUS sighed.

"It means get out," he proclaimed.

Like rats scurrying off a sinking ship, people began gathering notebooks and papers.

"Leave everything as it is. You may collect your personal belongings later," he barked.

The staff froze, but eventually began moving toward the doors, empty handed, and exited hurriedly.

As the last of the attendees departed, President Culpepper walked to the head of his Secret Service detail and whispered, "I want every single document, flash drive, electronic file, email, and bag searched and I want each and every person detained and questioned… vigorously." He then turned his attention to Secretary Hixton. "Please, have a seat."

Secretary of State Chloe Hixton hesitantly did as she was instructed. "Is there something wrong?"

Culpepper chortled and replied, "Not anymore. Bring him in."

At six feet three inches, his two hundred and fifteen pound frame struck an imposing figure. The President used that to his advantage as he lorded over the diminutive woman.

"It seems your husband isn't quite the man we thought he was," Culpepper began.

The look of shock and horror on her face told him everything he needed to know.

"Bus-ted," he stated tauntingly as her husband, bloodied and bruised, was unceremoniously shoved into a chair at the far end of the conference table.

"I'll admit, it took some doing, but we got it figured out. Ol' Chuckie here was quite adept at hiding the whole kit and caboodle, but unfortunately for him, he let an emotional attachment to you seal his fate. And you... the Harvard educated attorney, have managed to cause a controversy at every position you've held. I swear... I really don't know how you finagled this post in Rayburn's cabinet. You must've had some serious dirt on someone. At a minimum, you had everyone fooled with regard to your true ambitions, didn't you?" he asked rhetorically.

Then the POTUS abruptly stood and began heading toward the other side of the room.

"Mr. Charles Emerson Rothchild III, born May 5th, 1975 to Donald and Ester Rothchild in Greater Manchester County, Manchester, England. He is an only child, attended Eaton and then went on to Sandhurst. Commissioned upon graduation and assigned to the 16 Air Assault Brigade in Colchester. After that it gets a little murky. It is believed that either sometime during his career at the military college or shortly after joining the 16, he was recruited into MI6." President Culpepper then paused and turned to his SecDef. "Have the French left anything out, Fielding?"

"The part where these two married and she brought him to the U.S. under an assumed name, perhaps."

"Oh, that's right. You can understand our confusion. I mean, she claimed that he's been dead for how many years?" the POTUS asked rhetorically as he began heading back toward Ms. Hixton. "The proverbial George Glass as it were."

"At least five," Fielding replied as he crossed his arms.

"So if he's been dead for half a decade or more, I'm curious, just how long has the King been planning this little coup of his?"

"Sir, if you'll permit me, I –," the chief diplomat stammered.

President Culpepper, now standing in front of the guilt ridden Secretary, abruptly hit her with a brutal backhand. As she cried out in pain, her husband attempted to lunge from his seat, but was immediately stopped by the MP's.

"No you may not!" he hissed at her. "I've seen enough of your 'press conferences' to know that whatever comes out of your mouth is a damned lie carefully crafted to cover your own ass!"

The POTUS reached down, grabbed a handful of hair, and yanked her head up. "Pay attention!" he commanded as he thrust her back into the seat.

Once he had released the Secretary, he steadfastly walked across the room toward the prisoner.

"Sergeant, your sidearm please," the President extolled the MP standing next to the restrained man.

Unflinchingly, the soldier unholstered his weapon and handed it to the Commander in Chief.

"Charles Emerson Rothchild III, given the current state of war that exists between our two countries, you have been captured as an enemy spy. You have successfully killed a sitting President of the United States and have attempt to kill his replacement. For these crimes, you have been sentenced to death. How do you plead?"

"You ever touch my wife again, I'll —," he began to threaten before Culpepper struck him with a vicious jab to the face.

"How do you plead?"

The prisoner half chuckled then turned to look at him. "I'm guilty as bloody sin, what do you think?"

"Do you have any last words before your sentence is carried out?" the POTUS asked unemotionally.

The man swallowed hard and glanced over at his wife. "I'm truly sorry, Chloe. I never thought it would come to this... that's all," he stated compassionately as he started to turn his head back toward Culpepper.

Before he was even able to get his eyes back around to his accuser, the POTUS pulled the trigger, shooting him in the head.

As casually as he had performed the deed, the President handed the still smoking pistol to the Sergeant.

"Gentlemen, I want the following, in order. This room searched, their individual quarters searched, her and her staff questioned. You have twenty-four hours."

Shocked at what he just witnessed, Secretary of Defense Fielding was barely able to get the words out. "What's at the end of that timeline?"

344

"A firing squad will perform their duty."

The POTUS paused as he looked around at the faces of those present. Each conveyed a wide range of emotions. He wasn't interested in a debate.

"Get it done, gentlemen," he proclaimed, then exited the room with his Secret Service detail and the handcuffed former Secretary of State in tow.

# Chapter 24

Planning, packing, and preparing had consumed the small town of McArthur for a little over a week. Katherine wanted to check and recheck that all of her pieces were in place before she moved on the city. She was content to let TK sweat it out. Resupplying the forward observers (FO's) was a chore, but they managed to get the pair what they needed.

Before departing for the rally point on the outskirts of Columbus, Katherine found herself in an alley behind Mama Reni's. The rumbling in her gut was too much to ignore. Without warning, her nerves got the better of her and she started puking. After a minute or two, a shadow filled the narrow passageway.

"You 'bout done with that," Brent asked as he approached.

She slowly stood in response as she used the back of her hand to wipe off her mouth.

"Yeah," she replied sheepishly. "I'm guessing this is why dad told me to eat a light lunch."

The man stood and casually observed her as she attempted to collect herself. When he didn't offer any advice or speak in general, she asked, "What?"

"It's nothing."

"Spill it," she ordered irritated, but still managed a playful tone.

"I was just thinking how you reminded me of your mother, Amanda."

"Yeah well, aside from physical appearance, there isn't much to compare," she stated somewhat exhausted from her nerve induced endeavor in the alley.

"That's not entirely true, Katherine. Granted, she went off the deep end, but her drive and commitment to seeing things through, there's a shade of that in you. You didn't get all of it from your father."

"You didn't even know her, Brent. What makes you an expert on her all of a sudden?"

"Who do you think she spoke with during those weeks Josh was in his coma? I didn't just zip in, read his chart, and zip out. I was there, by his side, by hers, until he woke up. The compassion that woman felt for her patients, for your father, was something to behold. I know a great deal about her. One of my regrets in life, of which there are many, is that I wasn't there for you and your family when she lost it."

She looked at him quizzically. The man never ceased to amaze her with the things he knew.

"Tell you what, we come out of this alive," he continued. "I'll let you and Layla in on the conversations I had with your mother. Maybe then, in some small measure, it'll help you to better understand yourself as a whole. Deal?"

She was skeptical, but agreed.

As the pair began to exit the alley she stopped him.

"You're not gonna tell anyone I was hurling my guts out, right?"

"Oh, Katherine," he answered somewhat condescendingly, but just as playfully as she had been earlier. "We've been waiting for it. Frankly, we were concerned that you hadn't done it sooner."

As they exited onto the sidewalk, her father, Dallas, James, Gregg, and the Sheriff were lying in wait for them.

"Good news!" Brent proclaimed. "She's in the club!"

The men mockingly thrust their hands in the air and cheered.

"Yeah, yeah… bunch of wisenheimers. Get in the truck," she deadpanned in response.

Josh pulled her to him and wrapped her in his fatherly embrace. As he held her, he whispered, "You be careful, got it? These aren't pieces on a board anymore."

"I will," she replied as she nuzzled deeper into his chest. "Your shirt smells like Samantha. Been married less than a month and she's wearing your stuff?"

"What's mine is hers," he answered.

The two stood in the middle of the street sharing what could be their last moments together. Neither of them wanted to be the first to break the embrace.

"If it gets to be too much, and I'm not saying it will, but if it does, you need to be strong enough to turn the Op over to Brent. Understand?"

"Oh, Daddy, we all know I'm commanding in name only."

A wave of panic washed over him and Josh abruptly detached.

"That is one hundred percent not true! If that's how you're approaching this, I'm replacing you right now!"

"Relax, I was just kidding. Geez."

Her father grabbed her and pulled Katherine back into him as he sighed loudly. "Little brat."

Across the street, the pair heard, "Before you guys load up, can you come over here for a few minutes?"

When they turned to look, Heather was standing outside the doors to the church, wearing Samantha's wedding dress.

"It won't take long I promise."

Josh whistled to get the groups attention.

Heads popped out from behind and within the deuces.

"To the church, double-time."

As the group approached, Brent caught a glimpse of his granddaughter and proclaimed, "What the –!"

"Papaw, you're walking me down the aisle," Heather said calmly. "Sorry, Dad."

"Not a problem," he replied.

"What? The hell I am!"

"Can you guarantee that everything is going to go according to plan? Can you guarantee that you are coming home? The answer is 'no' to both, so don't bother. I'm getting married, right here, right now... whether you like it or not."

"I think I'll just head up front and find my seat," Josh discreetly stated as he tried to sneak away.

"Oh," she stated half remembering something. "Take this," Heather said as she handed him her grandmother's wedding band. "You're the best man, you'll need this."

Her father looked over at his former commanding officer who was visibly shaken by the display. An idea popped in his head and he smiled.

"Carlos Rayna!" he barked into the church. "Front and center!"

It seemed as if he was half way down the aisle before Josh even finished his command.

"That's our cue to leave, Dallas," James declared.

"Ah, not so fast, James. Gimme your knife," he commanded.

When he started to reach into his pants, Josh clarified.

"The big one... if you please."

James un-sheathed it and handed it to him butt first.

As Carlos approached, Josh thrust it into the wooden bannister.

"Yes, sir?" he said as he painfully, but reflexively came to attention.

Josh looked at Brent and his future son-in-law then stated, "Solve the equation," and promptly walked away.

Before he entered the church though, he leaned into Brent's ear and whispered, "One of these days you'll have to explain this."

Out of the corner of his eye, he caught Hoplite smirking.

Carlos took two steps forward, unholstered his side arm, and then used the barrel of the pistol to dislodge the blade knocking it into the bushes below.

As he re-holstered his weapon, he turned toward the General and asked, "Who's the idiot that brought a knife to a gun fight?"

Brent Howard half chuckled when he replied, "That'll do."

* * *

At dusk, the Sheriff, Juan, and his sons pulled the loaded deuce into Motts Military Museum grounds. Jesus discreetly exited the cargo hold and began working his way toward a non-descript out building through the woods and brush. The gravel being crushed by the deuce, combined with the diesel engine, told everyone within earshot that someone was approaching and where they were. The steel warehouse located at the back end of the property was so far removed from the main structures that it looked like it didn't even belong to the museum.

Their cargo, not including the men, included an assortment of supplies. The dozen high explosive shells Josh procured from the DSCC had been packed tightly and strapped numerous times to prevent shifting. The accompanying fuses were still locked in the original wooden crate. The remainder of the gear consisted of ten jerry cans of diesel and the necessary goods to get back to McArthur, should things go awry. As a precaution, the fuel and ordnance were stowed as far away from each other as possible. It would have been better to ship them separately, but the group only had so many operable vehicles.

When Katherine first started planning the Op, her chief overriding concern had been the most precious of commodities, fuel. Everything about her planning came down to it. The disabled train behind the farm hadn't been the gold mine Josh had hoped for. Aside from the few cars full of hogs, cattle, and lumber, the fuel containers were nearly empty as they had been offloaded before stalling on the tracks the morning of the HANE.

Her original concept for the taking of Columbus from Tim, or at least when she first included the M110A2 self-propelled howitzer into her planning, was that they would fire a full twelve round volley at the crossroads and at Tim's cash crop in Huntington Park. However, once they learned that the British were on their way, the plan needed more fluidity.

Katherine's amended Op plans called for a maximum barrage of six shells into Columbus in two three round sets. The second set would only be called in if necessary. They would have to make do with the burning of the marijuana crops. She hated to lose the fuel to the movement of one chess piece, but the fifty gallons of fuel, plus whatever diesel was available at Motts, would be needed to reposition the artillery piece and cover McArthur. Ever the planner though, she managed to barter another thirty gallons of diesel from Chillicothe in gratitude for the assistance Josh and the engineers had provided months earlier with their defense and perimeter construction. In truth, the self-propelled piece of weaponry could be repositioned just under half way to their weigh point and still be within range of the crossroads with its massive barrel.

As it stood, from their southern Columbus location, Sheriff Watson and the museum was, as the crow flies, only twelve miles from their target. Chillicothe lay only fifty the other direction.

The Sheriff brought the lumbering deuce to a stop near a set of massive closed over-head doors and killed the engine. Abelardo leapt from the back as Juan and Jim exited the cab of the truck.

Before their feet even hit the gravel, two men sprung up from a pair of shallow spider holes and leveled what appeared to be some heavy duty firepower in their direction.

"Halt!" a man barked. "Stand fast or be cut down!"

The three immediately froze.

"Turn around, lace your hands behinds behind your head, get down on your knees, and cross your ankles," one of them ordered. "You in the back, get up here with the other two!"

Abelardo and the others did as instructed without complaint. All three wanted to reach for their fully exposed side arms, but thought better of it.

Once they complied, one of the men approached cautiously, and removed each of the pistols. He wasn't cavalier about their removal though as he didn't toss them away at distance. He did, however, quickly stuff each into a satchel strapped across his chest.

"Check the back of the truck."

He did as instructed. "All clear," was shouted as he exited the vehicle.

"Very good. Turn and face me," the man directed from his hole in the ground.

Again, the three men did as instructed.

Just as they were nearly facing the pair, Jesus burst from the brush from behind. Within seconds, he had a K-bar at the man's throat and his pistol leveled at the other.

"Play time's over, Señor. Lower your weapon or the spray from my blade will cover your friend before I put him down," Juan's son snarled.

The man swallowed hard and turned his head slightly to look at his executioner.

"You must be Jesus. Josh said you were a crafty SOB. I'm Dick Brashier, that's my grandson, Holland."

"Qué? How do you know – ,", Jesus started to ask.

"Josh said you'd probably be one of the ones coming to use our little baby."

"You're lying. He never contacted you... I was right next to my CO when she made the call. She didn't mention his name, or mine! Time to die!"

"Wait! Wait!" Holland exclaimed as he abruptly raised his hands. Jesus stole a quick glance in the man's direction.

"I'm going to put my gun on the ground... nice and easy, see" he said calmly. "Let's not do anything rash, okay?"

"Your man, Josh, he stopped by here, last winter, with President Sarkes and a Secret Service Agent, I swear. They were driving this exact truck," he explained as he gestured toward the deuce next to him. "The truck had more gear in it at the time, but he had twelve, two-hundred pound high explosive rounds and a wooden crate of fuses."

Jesus wasn't fully on board with the man's explanation. He'd seen and done too much in the last few months to take anything anyone said at face value.

"I'm going to reach into my pocket for a piece of paper. It has the serial numbers to the truck and all twelve shells. He told us that, if someone ever did come by, you might need some convincing."

Jesus nodded in his brother's direction. He promptly got up, took the note from Holland, and verified the information in the back of the truck.

As he hopped out of the cargo hold, he proclaimed, "He's telling the truth."

"Why not just come out and meet us?" Jesus asked.

"We were expecting four. Only three exited the truck."

Juan's oldest son slowly removed the knife from the man's throat and helped the older gentlemen to his feet.

"I'm Jesus Martinez," he began. "The one in uniform is Sheriff Jim Watson. The one in the cowboy hat is my father, Juan. The scrawny one about to piss himself, that's my little brother, Abelardo."

The man turned and extended his hand in friendship. "Pleasure to meet you," he said as they shook hands.

The Sheriff and Juan swallowed hard, but eventually began walking toward Dick.

"Josh stopped here?" Jim asked as they approached.

"Yes, sir, same day the lights went out. Said he hoped he was wrong, but there might come a time when our services could be called on."

The farm manager half chortled through his nose and slowly began shaking his head. "Patron knew it would come to this long before that."

"How'd you manage to keep your museum intact?" the Sheriff wondered aloud.

"Honestly, we didn't. The main building was ransacked a few months in. Holland and I watched as they tinkered with the Huey and the M110."

"You have a chopper?" Jim asked excitedly.

"Ha! You wish," Dick replied. "That damn light show fried all of the circuits. Can't get replacement parts. That and there's only enough fuel for about a fifteen minute flight."

"That's too bad," Juan stated.

"We disabled the howitzer before they arrived though," he added. "A few days later we moved her over here, hidden away as best we could. Now that the introductions are over, your boss lady said you boys wanna bring the rain down on a city block, eh?"

Jesus looked at him confused.

"Something like that," the Sheriff interjected.

Dick just smiled at him. "Good! Those scavenging bastards have put the hurt on a lot of people." Then he turned toward his grandson and said, "Holland, why don't you get ol' Daisy on out here, give her a little vitamin D. Jim was it? You mind backing that deuce up a bit?"

Being a veteran of the Army, and having been trained on the piece of equipment, the Sheriff knew exactly what was about to come out of the garage. He grinned back. A minute or two later, the truck was relocated and he was on his way over to stand with the others again.

Beyond the door, the group heard several locks being removed, then the grinding of a bar being repositioned. Holland began pulling the chain and the door lifted, receding into the wall above. The cavernous opening was icky black behind the man as darkness began to fall outside. Then the man's grandson disappeared. Seconds later, the whine of the eight cylinder turbocharged Detroit diesel came to life.

Juan and his sons stood in amazement as nothing seemed to exit the structure except the massive barrel of the beast. After what felt like an eternity, the tank like frame emerged from the darkness.

Holland expertly maneuvered the behemoth, rotated the tracks until he was aimed north, and then shut down the hulking power plant.

Jim whistled at the presentation. It was immaculate and looked like it had just rolled off of the assembly line.

"Okay, who's ready for the nickel tour?" Dick asked excitedly.

# Chapter 25

About the time the Sheriff, Dick, and his grandson, Holland, were giving Juan and his sons a crash course on artillery fire, Katherine, Brent, Dallas, and the rest of the contingent arrived at their rendezvous point. Her FO's were dirty and exhausted, but on their game. The engines to their vehicles had barely been shut down before the pair emerged from the brush, produced a makeshift table, and their marked up map.

In the weeks they had been observing, the men had stealthily circumnavigated the downtown area numerous times, witnessed all manner of movement, and documented each of Tim's defenses. Included in their sitrep were the best and worst possible ingress and egress points as well. For almost an hour, the FO's presented their observations and answered questions from their CO's. Most of the intel had already been relayed during their communication sessions, but the exercise was worthwhile nonetheless given the introduction of their detailed renderings and maps.

Katherine and the others listened intently. As new details emerged, they'd review their own map looking for incompatibilities in the initial planning. As the meeting was breaking up and darkness began to fall, Josh's youngest daughter requested a moment alone with the General.

Before the two were able to separate, the FOs approached. "Ma'am, may we have a word?" one of the men asked.

"Certainly," she replied. "What's on your mind?"

With a former four-star at her side the pair stood resolute and swallowed their pride. "I don't know if this is a standing army or a militia or what, but it is clear to us now that you know what you're doing."

"Oh, I wouldn't go that far. I've been receiving a great deal of counsel lately," she replied casually and nodded toward Brent to try and put them at ease.

The man half smiled.

"Yes ma'am, but I –," he began before Katherine cut him off.

"All is forgiven. You're won't refer to me in derogatory terms and I'm not going to threaten to stomp you into oblivion. Deal?"

The two men looked up surprised and beamed wide smiles.

"Deal!"

"Come here you two," she stated and hugged them both. As she released them, she added, "Now, I'm very proud of the work you've done thus far, but I need the two of you to use those night vision goggles one more time. For the time being though, find some place quiet and get some shut eye. We head out in a few hours."

"Yes ma'am. Thank you."

As they departed, Katherine glanced over at Brent who was beside himself.

"What?"

"Hugs instead of an ass ripping? What kind of touchy feely outfit is this?" he said somewhat jokingly.

"You have your command philosophy, I have mine. Besides, they were already punishing themselves pretty good," she declared as she checked her watch. "Let's get the Team Leaders on the same page then we'll get everyone fed and bedded down for a few hours. We're outta here at 01:00."

* * *

Sophie and Philip sat and listened as Josh outlined their various defenses. There were several points where the astonishment couldn't be hidden behind the veneer of their stoic poker faces.

"The only weakness that I saw exposed by your arrival was in this area here," he stated as he directed their attention to the Chamber of Commerce map of McArthur. "You were able to dismount some of your force and enter Main Street through this alley." Then he paused while grimacing. "I'm curious though."

The mother and soon raised their eyebrows in anticipation.

"What made you give that command to your squad?"

"I've entered hundreds of small towns, just like this one," Philip began, "From New Orleans to Cape Girardeau to McArthur. Became the SOP after we were shot at in Sardis, Mississippi."

Josh nodded knowingly.

"How many OPs do you have?" Sophie interjected. "You didn't mention those."

He wheeled around and pulled a different map out of the top drawer of the Sheriff's desk.

"When you made that right on Route 93 in Logan," Josh replied as he pointed to map. "You saw what was left of OP2. You passed OP1 a few miles north. That was the one that alerted us to your arrival. Had you stayed on 33, you would have been spotted by OP3. After that, we have one each to the east, west, and south at these locations," he continued as he directed their attention.

"In addition to those, we have relays set up in the various towns around McArthur. It's basically a communication ring around us.

Doesn't much matter which way they enter from, we'll see them. That or we'll be notified."

"Can't they hear your communications?"

Josh sighed at the question.

"Unfortunately, yes. That's why we've been using the radios sparingly. We didn't grab any comm gear from DSCC when we got our truck of goodies. To make matters worse, all of the available walkies went to Columbus to support that Op. Bryan, Chester, and Scott have been working around the clock to come up with some form of an alternate. We've only made it as far as the twenty-first century equivalent of the Pony Express."

The pair stepped closer to the desk, seemingly in unison, and silently continued their review of the town.

Philip pointed and Sophie nodded, neither spoke.

"Monsieur Simmons, have you thought about disabling their vehicles before they can enter? I see no reason to allow them a free pass into the town square."

"We talked about trenching something, or installing barricades, or a half-ass tank trap of sorts, but diesel is running low. We need as much as we can salvage for the harvest in a few months. We'll be lucky if we have enough fuel to get half the spring crop planted. After that though, everyone around here will be farming the old fashioned way."

"Maybe your 'tinkerers' can conjure up some road spikes like we used to see in your movies," Sophie stated. "They seemed very effective."

"You mean the Tin Hatters?"

"Oui, your Tin Hatters."

A devilish grin appeared.

"Merde," she exclaimed as she caught the smirk.

Josh knew why she said it. He cleared his throat and said, "I don't know if we've shared this piece of information with you, but we captured one of the portable EMP suitcases."

Now it was Sophie's turn to smile.

\* \* \*

"Ok, Grappler, Evan… Dallas. The Sappers and snipers left an hour ago. You and your team's depart in five. James and his squad are dispersing throughout the city to provide overwatch while the engineers prep the buildings for demo. You guys ready to roll out?" Katherine asked sincerely.

"Yes ma'am," the trio said in unison. Grappler then added, "I just wish we had a map of the storm water system."

"Me too, but Tim and his band of idiots torched all of the government buildings. Sorry."

Katherine's eagerness and nervousness were getting the better of her. She continually asked and re-hashed the numerous questions and scenarios multiple times.

"Everybody is clear on the rally point if this thing goes sideways?"

The men and their assembled teams nodded.

"According to Sheriff Watson, we all need to be south of the crossroads if I call in a barrage in retreat. So if you hear that, move your asses! Stay at least a block north if we're not, clear?"

Grunts and nods permeated the group.

"Expect a minute to a minute and a half to reload and fire between shells. That means you can move around between shots, but I would keep even that to a minimum. Brent will function as the FO for the Sheriff.

"Now, based on our rough estimates, you and your tunnel rats will traverse a half 'click' up the main sewer line, hang the nearest right to that distance, go another hundred yards, and you should come out pretty close to the barracks."

"Yup, that's the plan."

"All hell is going to break loose at 05:00 so don't be out there lollygagging. This Op is all about the timing. The buildings come down in unison. So link up with your Sapper and his demo team as quickly as you can. Dallas, Brent, and I will be coming over the rubble of the AEP building with our teams at 05:05. Start herding everyone south while we send 'em west. I want as little collateral damage as possible.

"Most of these people are not armed. Many are doing the best they can just to survive with the hand they've been dealt. If you're engaged, then by all means defend yourself. Let James and his shooters clear a path from distance though. That's what they're there for. We aren't giving out medals today, gentlemen. So no hero shit, got it?"

The collected group smiled and half chuckled.

"Yes, ma'am, understood," Grappler replied.

"Okay. Get going," she said as she started to turn and head to the command vehicle.

"Uh, ma'am?" the squat heavy wrestler said hesitantly.

She turned toward the group of men who were smiling and looking at her expectantly. Katherine glanced around and quickly figured out what was giving them the giggles.

"I only give hugs to those that make it back," she stated flatly. "Except for Evan and Dallas, they get 'em anytime," she concluded with a smile.

"Totally not fair!" the men groaned in response.

"Suckers!" Dallas proclaimed as he went over for his hug.

\* \* \*

With the radios compromised, a team of runners on horseback ferried messages and information from the farm and Lake Hope to Josh downtown and back again. In the days since Eustace's death, he had been quietly planning the defense of McArthur. The horseback riders were a delay to the positioning of his primary force and reserve measures, but it would have to do. Much of what he was placing had already been somewhat concocted as he had an inkling that they'd be defending the town at some point.

On top of that, as much as he hated to admit it, his place was in McArthur. Katherine and Brent heading up the Columbus Op hadn't been his intention, but holding her back any longer would have been futile. If he had anyone to blame for that, it would be Brent and Dallas.

The pair, not through any direct vote or spoken directive, had taken to assigning her to head up at least one patrol a week for the last several months. She'd gotten her team through some scraps here and there, but she'd figured it out and always brought the entire team home.

As part of Josh's McArthur defense planning, he had instructed Chester to reassemble the portable EMP suitcase device. It took the man about three hours since he had built a prototype of the weapon some twenty years earlier for the DoD. The leader of the Tin Hatters shook his head in disbelief the entire time.

He had warned them that a device like this was the future and might be our military's undoing. Unfortunately, his warnings went unheeded. The repeated admonitions merely served as one of his many 'Chicken Little' predictions and only earned him a one way ticket to the Appalachian Behavioral Healthcare Hospital. Regardless, he was reluctantly ready to deploy at a moment's notice, per Josh's request. His protective detail consisted of a recently trained patrol team and a few French Foreign Legion soldiers used to fill out the complement.

Carlton and Basilia were stationed downtown, presumably where the fighting was most likely to occur. The matriarch of the Martinez family would handle the makeshift triage center while the former Navy Corpsman would scurry around assisting the fallen where they lay. Or, at least, that was the plan.

The rest of their assembled medical staff would be safely hunkered down and sheltered in the camp with the refugees and the lone remaining patrol team. Katherine had cherry picked the four best, most experienced teams for the taking of Columbus. All that remained were trained well enough, but the two groups had only taken part in a hand full of reconnaissance missions in the area. None had fired their weapon. However, given the success of the welcoming committee that greeted the French upon their arrival, Josh was confident with what he had.

In the pre-dawn hours, Samantha and Sophie reviewed the overnight messages. Once finished, they decided to head toward Mama Reni's for one of Jacques and Mimi's one pot breakfasts. As they exited the Sheriff's office the two hardly spoke. The pair was nervously awaiting word that the assault on Columbus had begun. As a result, their conversations were reduced to small talk about insignificant things like the weather. The awkward conversation was halted when Sam spotted a message carrier entering the town at speed.

"Hold on a sec, Soph. There's a message inbound," Samantha declared as she grabbed the woman's arm.

The women walked to the curb as the messenger slowed his mount. Sophie casually held out her hand to receive the hand written note. The rider slapped it into her palm as he trotted by and went straight toward the repurposed store front that now served as a livery stable to begin swapping out horses. The exchange of beasts for runners wasn't an uncommon occurrence and was barely noticed by the early risers milling about in downtown McArthur.

The two women opened the note and read:

*Good news, all teams are in position. Op on schedule. British forces went south to Parkersburg, WV. Lost all vehicles. Twenty five KIA. Bad news, remaining force strength, condition, and whereabouts unknown. Believed to be on foot and continuing with mission. Intel is three days old.*

"Well, this maybe became a much easier defensive situation," Sam declared after reading the message.

"Britannique puantes ne savent jamais quand abandoner, (Stinking British never know when to give up,)" Sophie spat in French. "Where's your darling husband? I think his plan might need to be downsized."

The two women looked at each other; half smiled at one another, and then started laughing at the thought of Josh downsizing anything.

# Chapter 26

"… Seven, six, arm the shot, three, two, one, detonate," Jake, the Senior Sapper, said calmly as he steadily counted down into his comm device.

The teams watched from a thousand yards away as the rumble of the detonations tore through the support structures for each of the buildings. It took a few seconds before the sway turned into a pronounced lean. Then eventually, all four hundred and eighty five feet of the Nationwide Plaza One building groaned as it began crashing down onto the streets below like a wave on the beach.

The sound of the twisting steel and shattering windows was all encompassing as it smacked into streets. The debris wafted effortlessly down on the wind of the destruction while the dust billowed out for blocks. Any exit to the east was now blocked.

The thirty one floors of the former AEP headquarters came down more quickly. It didn't take long before the structure eventually pancaked a railroad trestle and crumbled to rest on Spring and Long Streets, effectively sealing the southern egress.

No sooner had the plume of dust started to settle, restoring some degree of visibility, as the teams scurried over the debris and began heading toward Huntington Park and TK.

The Sheriff and his team stationed twelve miles away at Motts Military Museum watched what they could in the low light of the early morning dawn as the downtown Columbus skyline changed forever. It took a little over a minute for the rumble of the explosions and the vibrations of the destruction to reach the secluded knoll.

"Well, there's no turning back now," the Sheriff proclaimed. "Alright, guys. Just like we practiced. Dick, you've got command along with horizontal traverse and vertical elevation adjustments. I'll work the auto-loader."

Then he addressed the others directly. "You three stay in the deuce out of the way until I need to reload. As soon as the mechanism picks it up, you guys begin moving the next shell into place. Questions?"

Juan, Abelardo, and Holland looked at each other and the two men manning the M110A2. They shook their heads 'no'.

"Watch for my hand signals," Dick added. "You'll want to cover your ears. This thing's gonna make a hell of a racket when it goes off. Jesus is covering from above, should anyone come calling. So just focus on your job."

Abelardo gave an impromptu thumbs up sign.

"Okay, let's fire this thing up and get 'er loaded," Jim proclaimed as he took his station at the levers. "With any luck, the gun laying calcs will put this first one pretty close to the target."

* * *

Katherine had never been so thankful as she was for Jake's advice regarding the demo. The issuing of standing respirators (dust masks) and goggles were proving to be absolute life savers as they climbed over and through the rubble and windblown debris. The thought actually went through her head as she worked her way over, if she had to do it over again, that she'd have positioned the teams on the other side of the obstacle *before* they were felled. As it stood, only Grappler's team was being spared the arduous climb. Unfortunately, cover beyond the towers was sparse. After Eustace's death however, she was *not* in a gambling mood.

No sooner did Grappler see the first of the Sappers clear the rubble as he gave the hand signal to enter the barracks.

"Slow and steady people," he whispered to each of the paired teams as they went past him in to the void.

The structure was only two stories, but it was long. The original occupant had been an assembly line buggy works at the dawn of the twentieth century. In theory, it was a giant warehouse with few walls. However, the redevelopment effort in downtown Columbus one hundred years later meant that much of the interior had been redesigned and repurposed. A central corridor ran down the middle with eight studio apartments on each side, sixteen per floor. Every one of them would need to be searched. Any inhabitants were to be flushed from their digs and corralled toward the exit.

Jake and his team approached as the last of Grappler's men entered the building.

"I've got my guys upstairs, plus another four outside waiting for jumpers. We are corralling them north," Grappler declared. "You guys have the downstairs. Send two pairs of yours to link up with mine at the other end. My teams are playing leap frog the length of the corridor going room by room. The field is due west of our position."

"Roger that," Jake replied then turned toward his team. "You four," he declared as he pointed. "Outside on riot duty; move to the north end of the structure and herd the mob west to the open field." As they dispersed, he motioned for the other men to draw closer. "The rest of you, on me in pairs." As they approached to hear their squad leader, the Sapper gave his directions, "We've got the first floor. Sweep and clear each room and get these people headed toward the exit at the far end. Move out."

Sleepy 'residents' began their exodus only to find the streets still darkened by the night. Many wandered from the various complexes aimlessly. The thunderous crashing of buildings, coupled with the rumbling of the earth from the destruction, woke nearly everyone. The warmth and glow of the sun had not started to crest the horizon. The only sure thought the masses could muster was that the air was choking them and they didn't know why.

Katherine broke her two dozen strong force into four six-man teams and began advancing west on Spring Street before each turned north and headed toward Nationwide Blvd.

As she and her complement were about to turn up Neil Avenue she noticed that the others were lingering beneath a condo complex. Katherine gave the hand signal for her team to hold their position while she went over to investigate. As she approached, the smell of death was pungent. Two of the men peeled off from the group and vomited.

"What the hell are you guys doing?" she asked emphatically, but in a hushed tone. "We need to clear the Neil and Nationwide intersection before the Sheriff starts shelling."

Dallas turned toward her with his head bowed.

"You don't want to see that, Katherine," he said gently.

"What? Why? What is it?" she demanded in earnest as she started an attempt to go around him.

He grabbed her and wrapped her in his arms before whispering, "It's Eustace, hun. The bastards just left him there."

She quickly jerked her head up with wide eyes, shocked at what he had said. She'd have given anything to allow herself to weep for her

369

friend in that moment, but she couldn't. Dallas held her helplessly as the sadness washed over her.

"I'll take care of it," he declared as he released her.

Choking back the emotion, she whispered, "Thank you."

As she began a slow progression toward her team, Katherine heard him say, "Jackson, gimme your poncho, I need to cover him up. We'll grab him on the way out. We've got a job to do people, so let's get to it."

Everyone's pace was quickened when the sound of sporadic gunfire broke out north of their position.

Brent and his squad were handling the McConnell Blvd ingress and were unaware of Dallas and Katherine's discovery. His team used cover and concealment to efficiently work their way toward the shooter. It didn't take long to find the sentry perched in a broken window of the Arena District Athletic Club. As they approached the Columbus Union Station Arch, one bullet was a little too close for comfort. Brent started to reflexively reach for a grenade on the man next to him so he could chuck it through the window when a distant shot rang out.

"McConnell is clear," crackled over the radio in James' unmistakable baritone.

"Well, that problem's been solved," Brent stated. "Let's go. Stay against the buildings."

The General's team only went a few dozen more yards before he gave the signal to halt and assemble on him.

"Okay, boys," he began. "This is where I get off. 'Jugg', you're in command while I deviate and call in the artillery. Move your asses up the block, then turn west. You've got fifteen minutes to clear any stragglers off of the street. Do yourselves a favor and don't be anywhere near that intersection. I'm not all that sure where the first shot's gonna go."

"Copy that, General. Give 'em hell, sir."

* * *

The three remaining squads comprising Katherine's platoon redirected a couple dozen dazed and unarmed foot-draggers that had exited random alleys and buildings north toward the open field for the round up. Very few shots were being fired. The mere show of force was having the effect that Katherine had desired all along.

According to her FOs, TK was holed up in a building across the street from Huntington Park. Presumably, it was to keep an eye on his cash crop. They had until 5:45 to find him and clear the area. If they were successful, the planned barrage from the Sheriff wouldn't be needed.

As they worked their way north, Dallas' team met zero resistance for the first block and half. Then all hell broke loose. A wall of lead began raining down on them from above.

"Cozzins Street is taking heavy fire!" he practically yelled in to his walkie as they dashed toward the nearest cover. Fortunately, the road was still littered with abandoned cars from the HANE months earlier. Dallas and his men quickly dove under or behind the closest hulk they could find.

"East side high rise! Maybe third or fourth floor!" he barked giving James' team of shooters some place to begin their scan of the area.

After a few of the longest seconds of his life, he heard the worst thing he could possibly hear.

"Damn it! No joy! I don't have a shot! I say again, no shot!"

Katherine, Brent, and Dallas all knew what was in that building. According to her FO's, this was TK's headquarters. Based on their observation, the exterior wasn't heavily fortified. Unfortunately, they'd never been able to lay eyes inside the structure except for what could be seen through the windows.

"Help's on its way," came across the airwaves like the soft whisper of a baby's breath as the bullets continued to fall.

"What are we supposed to do now, Dallas!" one of his men asked. "We're pinned down here!" he concluded as he attempted to be heard over the gunfire.

"Keep your ass under this car until the 'all clear' is given is what you're going to do!" their leader retorted.

Dallas then began scanning the area to see where everyone was positioned. Most of his squad were under cover on the east side of the street, same as the shooters. This was both a blessing and a curse as neither force could get a clean line of sight. Spray and pray seemed to be prevalent tactic from TK's men. Two of his men sat behind what used to be a small truck until someone torched it.

Dallas quickly got their attention and flashed numerous hand signals at them. In response, they slowly raised their weapons. One peered over the hood of the vehicle while the other leaned ever so slightly around it.

A fresh round of fire in their general direction met their movement. Their team leader could only shake his head as the bullets sparked on the ricochet off of the street and truck.

"Damn it!" he muttered under his breath cursing his initiative. "Come with me," he said to the man next to him as he started backing his way out from under the car.

The two men shimmied on their bellies for a few seconds until they were both clear of the under carriage and kneeling behind the vehicle. Without saying a word, Dallas handed him his AR-15 and took the man's hunting rifle.

"On the count of three, give me some covering fire and spray those corner windows. I'll scoot across and see if I can't end this little stand off a little sooner."

"Roger that," the squad member replied.

He then turned toward the two men and relayed the message. They nodded their understanding.

Before starting his countdown, he took a few deep breathes in an attempt to muster the courage for the insane idea he was about to execute.

"No time like the present," he said as his began. "Three, two, one… covering fire!" he bellowed as he began his run.

The man next to him popped up and barely aimed as he pulled the trigger repeatedly and started spraying holy hell out of the building. The men across the street did likewise. What followed was the most harrowing handful of seconds of Dallas' entire life.

* * *

"Rodin! Rodin! Come in Rodin!" Grappler radioed in excitedly.

"Slow down, Grap. What have you got?" she asked slowly and deliberately.

"We found her!"

"Traci! Where?!" Katherine replied ecstatically.

"The last apartment on the first floor was a romper room of sorts. She was strapped to a bed with a half dozen other women."

"How does she look!" she replied enthusiastically.

"She's in pretty bad shape," he said more somberly. "All of them are. It's going to take months for them to recover physically. I don't know if they ever will emotionally. They've pretty much been through hell and back."

"Copy that. Anything else?"

"You could say that… believe it or not, but the madam is TK's wife and boy is she a wealth of intel!"

*What a disgusting pig*, Katherine thought.

"I'll radio in once Sapper 1 (Jake) and his squads are done checking the rooms for ordnance and contraband. I don't have a full picture yet," Grappler added.

"Copy that. Keep her talking and radio in any new intel."

"Roger."

\* \* \*

Brent exited the small lane connecting McConnell Street to Neil Avenue and ran almost headlong into Katherine's team. He was nearly shot by accident for his trouble.

"It's War God! Don't shoot me for crying out loud!" he exclaimed in raised voice.

"Brent! I've got an idea!" Katherine said as he approached. "What were the gun laying calcs targeting? Dead center of the intersection, right?"

"Yeah," he answered hesitantly. "Why?"

"Because I'm not in a dying mood and I don't want to lose anyone, not one single soul. Grappler found Traci so there's no need to storm TK's headquarters. I'm thinking we just level the damn thing and be done with it!"

"Whoa!" Brent said clearly taken aback by the suggestion. "You sure you can live with that? You don't know who or what's in there."

"Hold that thought," she declared as she pulled her handset close to her mouth. "Grappler, Sapper 1, do you copy?"

"This is Sapper 1. Go ahead, Rodin," came an immediate reply.

"Find Grappler and the madam and ask her to answer one question: what's in TK's building."

"Copy that. Hold one," Jake replied.

"If he comes back and says it's just TK and his cronies, I'm leveling the place. Any human shields we have to go in. Agreed?"

Brent nodded. What could he really say? Tim and this gang were a blight that required extermination.

Barely a minute passed before Jake was on the line.

"Good news," he began. "He's turned it into a hoarder's wet dream. Place is pretty much an ammo dump, supermarket, and marijuana dispensary rolled into one. According to her, it's just him and his cronies."

Katherine looked at her mic confused.

"Next time... do yourself a favor, let go of the button first," he added. "How long have we got to get clear?"

She half smiled, shook her head in disbelief, and then glanced at her watch.

"Five minutes."

* * *

Dallas deliberately moved his finger off of the trigger guard and was about to take a second shot when his radio squawked.

"Clear the area! Incoming ETA five minutes! Clear the area!"

He exhaled slowly, taking in the broadcast message, wrapped his index finger around the trigger and squeezed ever so slightly.

The echo from the blast of the .308 bounced and ricocheted off of the downtown buildings. Once it dissipated, he queued his handset, "Two down. Three left. How are you doing upstairs?"

"Almost there," was the labored reply. "Twenty seconds."

The fire team from Hanover Street had finished their sweep and was currently en route to Dallas's position. They hadn't encountered a single person. The FO's had been correct about the distribution of people in the downtown area, but everything still needed to be swept. The squad had spent last several minutes hoofing it up a half dozen flights of stairs to reach a position parallel to the shooters.

"Taking positions now."

"Fire when ready," he reported.

"Copy that. We're gonna break the rest of this glass window out with some office furniture and then we'll send a hand grenade over there for good measure."

Dallas waited what seemed like an interminable amount of time before hearing, "Three, two, one… watch yourself," being announced over the radio frequency for all to hear.

He looked up in time to see a desk being shoved through a window. The heavy object went right through the glass and crashed onto the street. The disintegration of the wood coupled with the falling glass sent the men below into 'duck and cover' mode. Bullets began flying in an attempt to keep the opposing force's heads down. As several members opened fire, one of the half dozen 'Willie Pete' (white phosphorous) grenades Josh had procured from the DSCC was thrown into the shooters lair.

Screams and death throes emanated from the opening as it exploded.

Immediately following the original grenade was a frag. Anyone rolling around writhing in pain was quickly put out of their misery.

"Hold the artillery barrage, Rodin. We believe we have the site neutralized. Let us clear the building to be sure," Dallas said into his mic.

"Copy that. You have an additional five minutes. Move it or lose it!"

# Chapter 27

Given the new force information, Josh changed his tactics, to a degree. He was planning on continuing his observation of the surrounding area and keeping the downtown response that had welcomed the French in place. However, he had spent the evening and early morning hours painting signs. Once a set was complete, he sent riders out to erect them along several of the more probable road entry points.

His concentration was broken when Sophie, who had been standing behind him observing, loudly exited the Sheriff's office.

"Sam! I can't take it anymore! The man's lost his mind!" she declared as she called out for his wife.

Josh just smirked at her pronouncement.

Several minutes later, Samantha entered the building calling his name. When he finally answered, she found him in his old cell. He'd turned the bedframe into a table of sorts. In the corner, standing on end, was what remained of the two foot by two foot square pieces of plywood. Between his feet sat an old can of black paint.

"Sweetie, what are doing?" she asked compassionately.

"Just sending the Red Coats a little message that we know they are en route is all," he replied proudly.

"You sure that's a very good idea?"

"Absolutely!" he answered incredulously as he stopped painting, stood, and turned toward her.

"Put yourself in their shoes," he began. "I'm serious, if you were them, and someone left messages while you were on your way to your mission objective, *and* the messages were able to accurately detail your entire hellish journey, what would be your thought process?"

"A sane person would turn around," she started to reply then sighed. "But a soldier would attempt to complete the mission, no matter what."

"Exactly!"

"So what's the point of the signs then?"

"Think of it as psychological warfare," he answered as he turned back toward his latest message. "I'm actively changing their mindset before they even enter the town."

"Mr. Simmons," a child said from the hallway. "Are you down there?"

The pair straightened up, and looked at each other confused by the innocent sounding voice. Sam leaned back through the cell door to see who it was. Her husband just started walking toward the sound. He quickly turned the corner in front of her and began heading up the forty feet of cell block hallway.

As he drew closer to the figure, he was able to discern the face of a little girl in the knee length nightgown.

"Rachael," Josh said softly in a comforting tone. "Is that you?"

The young girl nodded her head.

"Sweetie, what are you doing out of bed?" his wife asked directly behind him.

"Hi, Sam!" she stated excitedly as she began waving.

"Are you okay? Are you hurt?" Josh wondered aloud, concerned. "Is everything alright at home? Where are your parents?"

She crinkled her nose and made a funny face at him as he started to kneel in front of her.

"He sounds like my mom," little Rachael directed over his shoulder to Sam. She smiled a knowing smile in return.

"Okay, Rach," Sam said as if it were an old friend. "Give it to me straight. What's going on?"

Josh turned to look at her bewildered.

His wife whispered, "It's a thing we do. Just go with it."

"I've got a *big* problem," she declared as she placed her hands on her tiny waist.

"Oh, I see," came Sam's pre-planned response. "Is it big like your stuffed koala or big like your bike?"

"Bigger," the girl declared continuing her emphasis. "Big as a man!" she concluded with her arms outstretched in despair.

"You don't say!" his wife replied. "Why don't you pull up a chair and tell me about it."

"Okay," Rachael replied cheerfully.

As Sam and the girl walked toward the Sheriff's office hand in hand, Josh whispered in a hushed tone, "What is this?"

"She was tired of being treated like a baby because she's five, so we came up with this game."

"Is this something important or can I go back to painting signs?" he wondered.

"Oh, give the girl three minutes of your time. She's here looking for you," she declared and then turned her attention to Rachael. "So, are you gonna sit in the big chair behind the desk or one of these in front of it?" Samantha asked the Kindergartner.

"Mr. Simmons should sit in the big chair. That way he can't get away," Rachael stated in more serious tone.

Sam smiled down at her. "You're probably right. He does tend to wander off, doesn't he?"

The child nodded and then pulled Sam to the two seats in front of the desk. Once they were all situated, Rachael ordered, "Raise your right hand."

Josh half chuckled at the request, but did as asked.

"Now repeat after me. I, Mr. Simmons."

He looked over at his wife who was smiling from ear to ear, shook his head, and said, "I, Mr. Simmons, promise to tell the whole truth and nothing but the truth, so help me God."

"Those aren't the words!" she whined as she scolded him. "You have to repeat after me. Do it right! I, Mr. Simmons."

"Okay," Josh replied in an exacerbated but in a playful tone. Then he proceeded to repeat Rachael's words.

"Promise not to freak out like my dad did when my stupid big brother left the chicken coop door open."

Josh's smile disappeared. Something was up and the little girl was putting him through the ringer before she'd say anything about it. He had no other choice but to quickly comply to find out what it was. He stated her pledged words verbatim without playing this time.

"Okay, good," she concluded. "You can put your hand down."

"So what's going on Rach," Sam asked concerned now herself.

"A few days after those weird talking visitors got here," she started to say.

Josh interrupted her with, "You mean the French soldiers?"

"Yeah, those people. They talk funny," she answered with a giggle. "A few days later my chickens started waking me up when I'm supposed to be sleeping. They've been doin' it every morning. So one night, I decided to sneak out there and find out what they were clucking about. And that's when I saw him!" she stated emphatically.

Josh visibly stiffened and looked like he was going to stand up.

"Hey!" Rachael declared. "You promised! No freaking out."

Trying to put the little girl at ease, he sat more fully in the Sheriff's chair.

"You're right," he replied and started shaking his head. "You're right. I promised. No freaking out. Where is the man now?"

"In my treehouse, silly. He's my friend."

"I see," Josh stated as he leaned back casually and crossed his arms imitating Sam's initial response. "Does he have a name?"

"Vic!" Rachael answered. "He's a police occifer, just like Mr. Watson is."

"Well that's good."

"Yeah, we have a deal. I bring him my leftovers and he watches over me and my family. Now he wants to meet you."

"He does," Josh declared, taken aback.

"Uh huh. He says he sees everything and everybody. He knows you're in charge. He said he followed those weird talking soldiers from some place near the Missi… Missip…"

"Mississippi?" Sam offered.

"Yup, that's the one!"

"When would he like to meet me?" Josh asked as casually as he could.

"He said you can come now, but then he said something funny."

"What was that, sweetie?" Samantha asked reassuringly.

"He said you could bring your sidearm if you want, but that you wouldn't need it."

"Why's that weird?" Josh questioned.

"Cause your arms are already at your side!" she declared to her own laughter. "He's always saying funny stuff like that!"

The over protective father could barely contain himself as they escorted the little girl back to her house on the north end of town. As they approached, shadows and silhouettes started moving around in the treehouse.

The three stood and stared at the structure for a few moments before Josh said, "Officer Victor Henry from Portland, Oregon?"

His head abruptly popped up into the child sized window.

"They made it?" he asked excitedly.

"Yes," Josh answered. "Chester, Alysin, and Lily arrived here safe and sound several months ago thanks to you. I've already radioed the farm. They're on their way here now."

As Vic started to hurriedly come down the ladder backwards, her husband whispered, "Back away and keep your hand on your pistol. Something's off about this guy."

* * *

"Be careful, Shades (Evan)," Dallas declared. "We don't know if there's anyone still in there."

"Copy that," he replied and stowed his handset and turned toward his team.

"Okay, guys, let's do this by the numbers. You three," Evan declared. "You're up first. Just remember your training and you'll be fine."

The men he had chosen to breach the door looked stoic, committed. They didn't need a pep talk. Each of them was intently focused on the mission. The leading team member would kick open the door. The second man would enter first, followed closely by the third.

"Ready?" he asked.

The trio nodded.

"On my mark," he stated as he stepped aside and stood with the follow-on team that would breach a few seconds later.

He quickly glanced around at his assault team. All of them were staring at the closed door.

With a slight movement of his hand, he gave the 'Go' command. The first man in line kicked it open and moved to his right just as they had trained. The second and third men immediately began squirting passed him.

A handful of seconds passed before a delayed fuse triggered an explosion that rocked the entry way. The lead man was thrown back into the others and was killed instantly. The blast threw all manner of dust and debris out of the cased opening inundating the trailing men with shrapnel.

Evan watched helplessly as time seemed to be suspended. The three were tossed around as if they were in slow motion. The concussive blast ruptured his ear drum.

Only a few seconds went by before the doorway started spewing bullets from whoever was still alive inside. The prone and wounded assault team members were quickly bullet ridden and killed.

Dallas watched from his perch across the street and radioed it in. "The building's booby trapped, Rodin. Gimme a couple minutes to clear the team and the bodies, then call in the arty."

*Damn it*, she thought before replying.

In as an unemotional tone as was humanly possible, she answered. "Roger that, commencing fire in three minutes."

Katherine slowly turned to Brent, "Give 'Opie' the adjusted targeting corrections and time table," she ordered dejectedly.

The General queued his handset and began relaying the new information.

"Opie, this is War God, we have a fire mission. Correction from original target, come left 30, drop 200. Target is hostile HQ. Hold fire for three minutes, over."

"Copy that," came the two word reply from the Sheriff. Jim glanced at his watch and then turned in his seat. "Ok, Dick, we need to adjust before the first shot."

"I heard, I'm on it," he declared as he fired up the M110A2's massive engine. Once the machine's Detroit diesel settled down into idle, he added, "Adjusting range and deviation now."

The seconds ticked down as Dallas hauled ass from his elevated position. In less than a minute, he and his team were assisting Evan with the removal of the dead. Two of the three men were dragged, and then eventually carried, from the area as quickly as possible.

"Get them as far down the block as you can in the next ninety seconds!" Dallas barked as he and Evan worked to place the last of the deceased into a fireman's carry on Dallas's back.

Twelve miles apart, Katherine and the Sheriff stared at their watches as the few remaining moments wound down.

With the barrel near its max elevation, the round would arc up and then begin its almost vertical descent. Given the distance, the massive two hundred pound shell would impact its target in less than fifteen seconds after being fired.

Nearly in unison, the Commander and her artillery team counted down. "Three, two, one…"

\* \* \*

"Bloody hell, sir! There's another one!" the British Army Sergeant stated as the remains of their eighty man strong force staggered down the deserted road.

"Go see what it says!" the Lieutenant ordered.

The Sgt. sprinted forward the few hundred yards, read the sign, and came jogging back.

"Well?"

"This sixth sign reads, 'Medical attention, food, and shelter will be provided to gentlemen'."

"You must be joking!"

"No, sir. That's what it says."

"Bugger me," the CO said under his breath. "Read off the messages we've received thus far, please."

"Right! We have," the Sergeant started to summarize as he removed a notepad from his trousers pockets. "Let's see, the first one was, 'You left West Point eight days ago'. Then we received, 'You lost half your force in Harrisburg, PA'. After that we found, 'You took gas, food, and med supplies in Everett, PA', 'Dropped another quarter and the last of your vehicles in Morgantown, WV', and 'Ten KIA's followed in Parkersburg'." Then he paused and reflected for a moment before adding, "Sir, do you think it's possible we've stumbled upon some friendly chaps?"

The commanding officer glanced over at his limping exhausted men then pinched the bridge of his nose.

"Friendlies? No, they are nothing of the sort. All I do know at this point is that his forest has eyes and whoever is painting these signs has thrown every conceivable roadblock at us for nearly five hundred kilometers."

"Sir, if I may. It would appear that there is no element of surprise. Our force of five, three of which are wounded, is not going to be taking any towns alone. Our radio is full of holes; we are low on provisions and ammo. If you're open to suggestion, sir, we might want to see what they are offering."

The Lieutenant wasn't surprised by the man's words. In fact, he'd been thinking them himself. He couldn't say it in front of them of course, but now that it was out there, he could make a show of reluctantly agreeing.

"What say you men?" he asked as he turned toward the remaining three. "Are you in agreement with the Sergeant? Shall we go and see what this chap with the paint brush is carrying on about?"

The trio looked each other over before one spoke.

"If it's all the same to you, sir, we need the medical attention. Simpkins' leg wounds need treatment. I don't want to have to cut it off for gangrene."

"Bloody hell! For the last time… you're not cutting it off! Damn witch doctor!" the man replied indignantly.

"What about you?" the Lt. questioned the third.

"We've got enough food and water for another day before we have to start settings traps and snares. At a minimum, we might want to consider behaving like gentlemen if for nothing more than to be resupplied."

The weary Lieutenant half smiled then asked, "And our mission to eradicate the French force in town and find the bounty?"

Simpkins staggered forward to address his CO.

"Sir, I believe this little dust-up with the colonies is over for us. They've been watching our every move since the Royal Marines took Cleveland."

"So surrender then? Is that what the men of the British Army are asking of their Commander?"

"Not in a million years!" the Sergeant stated forcefully. Then he cleared his throat and struck a more conciliatory tone and added, "However, given our current state, we could negotiate a cessation of hostilities on humanitarian grounds."

"Mr. Coker, I believe you've missed your calling. You should be at the UN… not in the Army!"

* * *

The freight train in the sky screamed toward its target unabated at a mile per second. The forces on the ground had only a handful of precious moments to find shelter before the shell made impact.

Those residents of the downtown area suddenly became scared out of their minds. The mere sound of the two hundred pound juggernaut thundering through the early morning sky had those present nervously clutching spouses, siblings, and children. Screams of 'Take cover!' were being barked at them from the dozen or so men that had been standing and guarding over the flock. As soon as one took to their belly, the rest followed suit.

Brent and Katherine watched from a structure well short of TK's headquarters so they could call in corrections until the building was hit.

The shot had barely exited the M110A2 before the barrel and auto-loader were being lowered into position to pick up and load the next shot.

The retired General and his protégé watched with baited breath as the sound grew in intensity. On impact, the round seemed to punch a massive hole in the pavement covering the street below. Asphalt, concrete, dirt, and debris were launched into the air with the concussive blast. The explosion knocked out windows and could be felt by anyone within a quarter mile.

The Sheriff handed his handset to Dick as he directed Juan, Holland, and Abelardo. Dick, in turn, sat eagerly at the controls and listened intently for targeting corrections. Over the whine of the auto loading mechanism, he heard what he was waiting for.

"Spotting: Over, line. Correction: Drop 50. Fire when ready."

Brent's corrections told him that the shot was on target, but fifty yards over. As soon as the Sheriff had the next round loaded, and the breach closed, he would adjust his range and immediately launch the second shot.

Katherine observed the impact sight through her binoculars. *The Sheriff wasn't kidding*, she thought. Then she turned to Brent and said, "Jim was right. There's a four or five foot deep, fifteen foot wide crater in the street."

Ninety seconds later the freight train sounded the alarm over their heads again as the incoming projectile began it's descent into downtown Columbus.

With a whoosh it screamed over them and slammed into TK's headquarters. It didn't hit as perfectly she would have liked as it only caught a corner of the building. The impact and the detonation's concussive blast set off a series of booby traps that had been placed within the structure.

"Bingo!" Brent proclaimed giddily to Katherine. Then he grabbed the radio the group had seized from Benjamin and excitedly called in the remaining shots. "Fire for effect! Fire for effect! Send two more down using those settings," he hollered into his mouthpiece.

At intervals of approximately ninety seconds, the remaining artillery rounds impacted the site and demolished the building. Whoever was in there was now buried under a couple tons of steel and concrete.

The retired General took great joy in announcing the success of the bombardment over the network.

"End of mission! Target destroyed!"

# Chapter 28

"Vic!" Alysin squealed as she leapt from the back of the cart. "You found us!" she declared as she raced toward their reunion.

Officer Victor Henry, even with weeks of observation, hadn't laid eyes on any of the three remaining members of the Tin Foil Hat Club. Upon seeing the joy exhibited by the oddest of the Hatters, he dropped his fork onto his breakfast plate of rabbit stew and biscuits. It didn't take Vic long to extricate himself from the picnic table outside Mama Reni's and begin lightly jogging toward his long lost friends.

The embrace broke through his aloof veneer as he began to openly weep in her arms.

As Alysin held him tight, Chester asked, "And how are you my friend? When did you get here?"

His new caregiver, Alysin, admonished the old scientist, "Let him have a good cry first before you start peppering him with questions!"

The other Tin Hatters glanced at one another confused before he started to reply, "But I –."

Lily grabbed his arm and gently shook her head. "Just let 'em be," she whispered.

Chester shrugged as he walked past and went to Josh. The pair shook hands as he handed him a hand written piece of paper.

"What's this?" Josh asked before upending the document and starting to read.

"Possibly our worst nightmare."

"Really?" he said as he chuckled. "How can this get any worse?"

"That transmission came over the EBS system at 6:00 AM Eastern Standard Time."

With his curiosity fully peaked, Josh raised his eyebrows in anticipation.

"Same deal as before," Chester added. "The message played in its entirety a few times and then static. I recorded it if you want to hear it later with the Columbus contingent when they get back."

"Any news from downtown?" the worried father asked "I re-tasked the riders so we haven't heard anything down here. I know I heard the howitzer fire four rounds about half an hour ago."

"They cleared the barracks and brothel without much fanfare. TK booby trapped the HQ and we lost a few trying to take it. Katherine opted to cut her losses so she authorized the shelling," Chester explained before adding, "Dallas sniped a few before Opie leveled the place with a handful of remaining hostiles inside."

"What *were* their losses?" Josh asked with great concern.

"Tough to tell. The reports are coming through Chillicothe, then to us. She lost three in an explosion at the HQ and almost a dozen wounded or injured throughout the morning. Nothing major by the sound of it." Then as an afterthought he continued by stating, "We've already passed along your message that the big gun doesn't need to be repositioned."

Josh nodded then asked, "Did they manage to find Traci?"

"Yeah, found her and some others chained to beds in a whorehouse of sorts. They're bringing her back."

"Anything else?"

"I don't think so. That's about all we've heard."

"Good," was his only reply as he returned his attention to the sheet of paper in his hand.

*The following message comes directly from President Alan Culpepper.*

*My Fellow Americans,*

*This is President Culpepper. I don't know how many of you can hear my voice, but it is my most fervent hope that my message finds you in good spirits and good health.*

*Since my last broadcast, our nation has taken the fight to the enemy on all fronts. We have proven ourselves to be the resourceful, courageous nation I always knew we were. Our foreign enemies are in retreat and our domestic traitors have met their end.*

*Unfortunately, I do not have a lot of time to explain everything in detail due to the state of the communication and electrical systems, so I'll be brief.*

*First, I would like to announce that we have not been alone in our fight. Through the tireless efforts of Presidents Sarkes, Rayburn, and myself prior to the blackout, we have been receiving assistance from the French, Dutch, Spanish, and for a time, the Indian armies and navies. Any and all hostilities towards these coalition forces must stop immediately. Embrace these fighting men and women as your brothers and sisters for they have come to our aid during the most critical time of need.*

*Second, in the Rockies, numerous bands of patriots have fought tirelessly to push the Pacific Rim nations back to their ships. These militias have suffered mightily for their resistance, but they have persevered and won the day. In the east, I am happy to report that similar groups of fighters have retaken West Point. The home of the Black Knights is once again safely in American hands. New Orleans is under the protection of the French Navy while the Dutch finalize the clean-up of hostile forces in Charleston.*

*Third, it is with deep regret that I disclose that a coup attempt was made against what remained of our government by the Secretary of State. She has been executed by firing squad along with three of her staff. Her husband was executed by me personally as it was he who was responsible for the death of President Rayburn.*

*And lastly, it is incumbent upon us all to work together and rebuild our once great country. As a result, Martial Law is being declared throughout the nation. I am calling on all local law enforcement and military personnel to make a full accounting of all resources within your area. Food, fuel, ammunitions, weapons, and medicines should be counted for possible collection and redistribution as needed.*

*Please do not resist these efforts as we attempt to put our nation back together.*

*This is President Alan Culpepper signing off.*

Josh sighed while refolding the piece of paper. As he stuffed it in his pocket, Chester asked, "Thoughts?"

"Depending on how it all goes, he may have just lost the backing of the people."

"Yup," his old friend replied.

* * *

At 8:00 AM, two hours after the shelling had ceased, the deuce carrying Sheriff Watson and the Martinez family contingent rolled into downtown McArthur. Behind them, in a dilapidated Nissan pick-up, were Dick Brashier and his grandson Holland.

Josh, Heather, and his new son-in-law, Carlos, exited Mama Reni's when they heard the massive diesel approaching. The three were waiting out front as the two vehicles turned onto Main Street. Jim rolled it to a stop along the curb and killed the motor.

"Jim!" Josh proclaimed as he approached the driver side door with arms outstretched. "How'd it go? Daisy didn't give you guys any trouble, did she?"

"Hell no!" Dick exclaimed from behind him. "I told you when you stopped in there that she was mechanically flawless."

"That she was, Dick. That she was. To be honest, I kept waiting for the auto re-loader to crap out on us, but it worked like a charm," Jim added.

"Any news from downtown?" the father asked eagerly.

"Last we heard, Katherine and her teams were conducting interviews and separating the residents into groups."

"Smart kid," he replied. "Is she assessing the viability of leaving people there?"

"Yeah, but one thing's for certain, as soon she and the rest of them pack up and head home, that mob is gonna execute about a dozen or so sympathizers."

"I didn't get the impression," Juan added as he approached, "That Katherine was in the mood for any bullshit."

Josh chuckled at the comment as the pair shook hands.

"You guys hungry?"

"Starving!" Holland proclaimed.

"Well alright then, go grab some grub from Mama Reni's!" Josh answered in kind.

"You heard the man," his grandfather stated. "Food first, re-supply is gonna wait. We're not in a hurry, so chew your food for a change."

As the group began making their way toward the restaurant and a well-deserved meal, Jim quietly asked, "Why aren't you at the farm? I figured you'd be monitoring communications."

"It was too tempting to try and lead from afar. Don't worry though, I kept myself busy."

The Sheriff glanced over at his friend with a cocked brow.

"The British are comin'. The British are comin'," Josh half whispered.

Both of the Jim's eyebrows arched up.

"Relax… relax. I've got scouts two miles out on every road. We've received confirmation that they number less than ten and they are on foot. Everything is well in hand."

\* \* \*

"She's a lying whore!" the man screamed as Katherine continued to ask TK's wife questions.

"Whoa!" she shot back. "Any more outbursts from you and I'll have you gagged. Am I clear?"

"But she –," he stammered. "All I –,"

"NOT another word!" she demanded forcefully then turned demurely to address the madam. "Mrs. Knightsbridge," she began.

"Don't call me that," she growled. "My husband was a philandering sadist and a pig. Please, call me Emma."

"Emma the lying freakin' whore," the man mumbled under his breath.

"Dallas, please gag him."

A smile broadened across his face. "With pleasure," he replied as he withdrew a bandana from his pocket.

"Hey now wait a minute," he sputtered as he tried to turn and get away.

Evan grabbed him by the back of his collar and threw him to the ground. The cloth was quickly placed in his mouth and tied behind his head by Dallas.

When he finished, he stood up and proclaimed, "Done!" like he was roping a calf.

"Emma," Katherine began again. "If possible, please give me the truncated version of the events."

"Okay," she answered meekly.

"What happened the first night the lights went out? Benjamin stated that TK and a few others broke into their house and kidnapped his wife. Is this true?"

"Yes, but I was unaware of this until after the fact."

"When did you become aware?"

"It wasn't until he had united the gangs and setup that room of horrors. One day he says to his men, 'My bitch can run the whorehouse. She likes putting out just as much as a hooker'."

"Sounds like a real charmer," Katherine muttered.

"Oh, he was at first," she quickly clarified. "But then he changed."

"How so?"

"He was so sweet and kind and then he started working for that pig of a lawyer downtown. Shortly thereafter, he's not spending as much time with me. He starts gambling, comes home hammered out of his gourd…" then her voice trailed off and she started crying.

"And working for this lawyer changed him that much? Where's this lawyer now?" Katherine asked.

Emma took a few seconds to collect herself and added, "He never gambled and barely drank before he started working for that prick, Kelyn Kershaw. Then one night he takes me to a party at a 'friends' house and I had too much to drink… or at least I thought I did," she continued as the sobbing became more pronounced. Then, at a hundred miles an hour, she confessed her darkest sins.

"The wives were being auctioned off like cattle! That bastard drugged me… all of the wives were drugged and forced into open marriages! He took pictures of the whole thing so I couldn't leave him. He said he'd splash them all over the internet for all of our friends and family to see!"

Emma's face flashed red hot as she told the story. Eventually, she added, "We heard Kelyn was murdered and his wife raped by some gang banging former clients. His big house on the hill was burned down for added measure."

Katherine stared at her blankly with wide eyes. After a few silent moments, she cleared her throat.

"Can anyone corroborate this?"

She nodded slightly. "The brunette your men pulled out of there, she can."

"I'll be sure to ask her once the drugs are out of her system. Speaking of which, how was TK getting supplied?"

"One of the gangs he took over received a shipment from Central America shortly before the lights blinked out of existence. He confiscated their entire stash after he executed their leader. Started doling it out what they had left from the delivery like tic-tac's."

"And the weed growing in the ballpark?"

"He had a thing for it, said it mellowed him out... needed it for 'medicinal purposes'."

"How did Lieutenant Stokes get killed?"

Emma shrugged. "I didn't know him. I only saw him once or twice."

"I can answer that," a scrawny dirt covered man said as he stepped forward. "I was there."

Four weapons were immediately drawn and pointed at him.

"Wait! It ain't like that! I didn't have shit to do with it! I's just up there tryin' to get me some sleep!"

"Let him talk, guys," Katherine stated. "If we don't appreciate what he has to say... well... So what's your name?"

"Eddie, but I didn't have nuthin' to do with it, I swear!"

"So you've said. Go on," she said leading him down the path she wanted to hear.

"The housing units was pretty full and all 'em boys snore loud, like a bunch of truckers. I went to the roof to get some shut eye in peace and quiet, that's all."

"Go on," she cajoled.

"Next thing I know, TK and his gestapo friends are questioning your man and that accountant dude... Tyler something 'er other."

Katherine motioned with her hand to continue.

"Yeah well, they shot Tyler and he started to talk, but then he gave Stokes a weird look. Your guy put one in 'em an another guy too. Then he circled 'round and went for them stairs, but ol' TK had guys waitin' behind the doh. Blasted his ass with rock salt or some shit."

"Any of this check out?" Katherine asked without taking her eyes off of Eddie.

"So far so good," one of her FO's replied from behind her.

"Do you recognize him?"

"We've seen him around over the last few weeks. He didn't take part in Eustace's death, he's clean."

"Very well. Please continue," she said.

"TK shot your man in the leg, but that dude was defiant to the end. Told him to pound sand so TK pushed him off the roof."

"And where were you during all of this?"

"Me? I was keepin' my ass in the shadows behind all 'em A/C units. Bullets and shit be flying all over the place… I ain't comin' out during all that!"

Katherine thought for a moment. When none of her men said anything to counter his story, she gave him what he was looking for, "Okay, thank you Eddie. You can head back to your group."

"Ya'll ain't gonna shoot me?"

"Not today, no," she said with half a smile as she tried to picture Eustace's defiant last stand.

She then turned to Dallas and Evan and gestured to the gagged man on the ground. "Pick him up, please."

Once the loud mouth was vertical and the gag was removed, she asked, "So what's your malfunction? What's she lying about?"

The man stared at the ground and didn't answer.

"Well? I'm waiting," she demanded.

Emma spoke up and answered for him. "He's just afraid that I'm gonna start pointin' fingers and naming names cause I was the 'madam.'

He doesn't want his darling wife to know that he was one of the better, more frequent customers is all."

"You bitch!" he muttered as he lunged toward her.

Evan and Dallas quickly grabbed his arms and stopped his forward progression before he made his first full step.

"Gerald! You promised!" his wife angrily spat at him from yards away. "That's it! I want a divorce!"

"Oh, Lord," Katherine silently said to herself and she placed a hand on her forehead.

"Ma'am? Miss?" the wife asked.

"That's Captain Simmons," Brent corrected.

Josh's youngest daughter glanced at him quizzically.

"We voted. Just go with it," he whispered as he leaned in.

"Capt. Simmons. I'd like a divorce, can you grant that?"

"Fine," she decreed as she sighed loudly. "Gerald, on the grounds on infidelity, you have violated God's covenant. You are hereby divorced. Pick up your stuff and move to a different structure by sundown."

His now ex-wife was beaming ear to ear.

As she looked around, she saw several dozen smudged and gaunt faces staring back at her expectantly. These people needed guidance and direction. Then she laughed to herself at the thought of her father's words. *They need a purpose.*

"Everyone come in close so you can hear me," she began.

Many of the surviving inhabitants looked up at her, optimism in their eyes. Groups of individuals started slowly coming forward to be within ear shot.

Once Katherine was satisfied, she asked them all to have a seat on the ground.

"How many of you have any idea how we lost power?"

Emma offered, "Your dad stopped in the neighborhood that first night. Picked up Bryan and your aunt."

Katherine glanced down at her confused.

"Yes, I know who you are."

"Good," Josh's youngest daughter retorted. "Then you know I'm not here screwing around. What did he say?"

"He told us a terrorist detonated some nuclear weapons in the atmosphere and knocked out our power grid," TK's wife replied.

"Okay, thank you," she stated more gracefully then turned her attention back to the assembled. "Now, I'm sorry I have to put it this way, but I see no alternative. You people, through specific intent or willful ignorance, have failed every single test of human survivability. Instead of trying to maintain any semblance of society, your leaders chose booze, drugs, and prostitution as a means to subdue and mollify the masses. And you went along with it."

Heads began hanging. There was no rebuttal that could be made that justified their continued existence. Many fully expected to be lined up and shot. Several men began glancing casually, prairie dogging, looking for an exit.

"However, we are a nation founded on second chances. I'm not going to tell you what to do, but there is a town not far from here that your horde of locusts burned to the ground. It's more rural and the food in the form of wildlife is more attainable. I'm offering you a chance at redemption by rebuilding it. Once that task is done, you will be asked to establish some form of commerce and trade with other communities in the area. Those of you that would like to take this opportunity, you are welcome to do so. There is food in the hills if you know where and how to look. There is shelter if you are willing to work for it. If you decide to stay and rebuild here, that's up to you. My guess is that we will have a little of both."

Clusters of families and groups of people began looking around at one another.

"But make no mistake, what happened here today was necessary. It was necessary for the survivability of the surrounding towns and communities. It was necessary for the survival of the women that inhabited your whorehouse. It was necessary if for no other reason than to free you from your bonds of servitude instilled by TK and his ilk.

"We are not here to hand down punishments for the actions of those within your city walls. However, I would imagine that a fair amount of retribution might be at hand specifically regarding the repeated drugging, rape, and torture of some of your citizens. You people can solve your own problems after we've left."

Katherine paused to let the full weight of her words sink in. Some of the residents actually looked… happy. However, there were more than a few that carried the shame and worry on their sleeves.

"Are there any questions?"

"What's the name of the town?" came from a distant group.

"Logan," she replied.

Then it was like a dam burst open and the questions began flooding at her.

'It's already mid-summer. How are we supposed to grow enough food for winter? You've taken all the weapons we had. How are we supposed to shoot anything? Where will we get the plants, the seeds, everything needed to start a garden? Are there any buildings still standing? Is anything salvageable down there? How will we get there? Is it safe to travel the roads?'

Katherine and her leadership team stood patiently and answered all of the worrisome questions. After a nearly twenty minute long Q&A session, the McArthur contingent had a brief conversation. In the span of five minutes, they knew what they had to do. In the end, Evan summed it up best.

"Look people, what you've earned and what you deserve, in either case, doesn't amount to much. We'd be well and good to just roll outta here and let you folks figure it out, like the rest of us did, but I'm a 'teach people to fish' kinda guy. Once upon a time this was a Christian nation and it wouldn't be very Christian to prolong your suffering when we are in a position to assist you.

"Those of you heading to Logan, you have three hours to gather your possessions. My team and I will escort you and get you acclimated to your new surroundings. Any one staying in Columbus, assemble under the shade tree over there," he concluded as he pointed off to his right. "You have fifteen minutes to decide."

# Chapter 29

"HALT!" came the booming order from the woods.

The British Army Lieutenant and his men quickly stopped their methodical plodding.

"Do not move or you will be fired upon! Nod if you understand my instructions."

The CO looked over at his contingent. All were frozen in their tracks. Sergeant Coker swallowed hard. The Lt. turned his head slightly in the direction of the command and gave a polite, but curt, nod.

Suddenly the woods came alive. Six men, three from each side of the road, displaced and silently exited from their hides. Weapons were up and trained, safeties off.

"Gentlemen, unload and sling your weapons. Sir," the team leader said as he addressed the Lieutenant. "Please unload and holster your sidearm. Leave it snapped in place."

"What, we aren't going to do name and rank?"

"Sir, I don't give a shit what your name is and I can see that your collection is made up of one Lieutenant, a Sergeant, two Corporals, and a Private."

Their commander glanced over and gave the order through a quick nod of agreement again. In as non-threatening a manner as possible, he and the rest un-chambered their rounds, removed magazines, and slung their weapons as directed.

"There are only the five of us," the Lt. offered.

"We know. We've been tracking you for the last three miles."

The totality of the message immediately sunk in with the surrounded British troops.

"So are you the bloke that's been leaving all of the signs?"

"No, sir. That'd be Colonel Simmons. He's tasked me with escorting you into town. We are to treat you as pleasantly as you treat us. As a sign of good faith, you are being permitted to hold onto your weapons, albeit unloaded. If it were up to me though, I strip every last one of you UN bastards down to you Fruit of the Looms and march you the rest of the way wearing a damn diaper."

The Lieutenant cleared his throat at the pronouncement of Josh's rank and with the candor being spoken.

"Did the chap give himself that rank when the jihadist's turned out your lights?" Sergeant Coker asked under his breath as a dig at the men before him.

"Ah, no. That would be Colonel Josiah Simmons, United States Marine Corp. I believe he's more than earned it."

"Bloody hell!" the Lieutenant exclaimed.

"Exactly right," the camouflaged team leader stated.

"They told us stories about that guy like he was the boogie man!"

"Then I guess you better mind your P's and Q's." As an afterthought, he added, "If you're still around come supper, that'd be a few hours past your afternoon tea, General Howard should be back from shelling downtown Columbus. You might remember him as the former Chairman of the Joint Chiefs."

"Blimey! Anyone else?"

The leader thought for a second and remembered, "Only President Sarkes."

The five British Army soldiers stood in the middle of the abandoned country road stock still and bug eyed.

"Now, if you men will fall in line, we'll make the last half mile together. Does your man require a litter? We can whip one up in a few minutes."

The Lieutenant glanced over at Corporal Simpkins, who shook his head in reply.

"That won't be necessary, but we could do with some water if you have it. This bloody heat is soul crushing."

"Certainly, sir," the team lead responded with a smirk and motioned in the direction of his men.

The two teams from opposing forces stood alone in the road quenching their collective thirst for the briefest of moments. Silence permeated the group. When a few minutes had passed, the Lieutenant asked, "How come it doesn't have that purified tablet taste."

"We have a number of natural springs in these hills that we are able to utilize. Most everything is boiled. We save the tablets for excursions and patrols."

"Good idea," the CO replied then motioned to the team leader's uniform. "I see you've removed your patches, as well as your insignia."

"Yes, sir. We also took down every road sign and landmark within a couple of dozen miles."

"We noticed. Might I ask with whom I have the pleasure of dealing with?"

"Staff Sergeant Isiah Barnes, 37th Engineers, 82nd Airborne."

"Interesting."

"How's that Lieutenant?"

"It's curious that we stagger into a town that happens to be the new primary residence of a former President, Joint Chief, and an engineering platoon. You blokes might want to cut and run because we know about the gold. This could come as a bit of shock to you chaps, but there *will* be a follow on force. Just because our unit was unsuccessful doesn't mean Whitehall won't keep trying."

"Awe, he doesn't know, Sarge," one of the Staff Sergeant's men proclaimed playfully.

"Know what? What are we not being told?"

"That's an excellent question, Lieutenant. You be sure to ask Colonel Simmons when you see him."

Barnes turned toward town and gestured, "After you, *sir.*"

\* \* \*

Shortly after 4:00 PM, Philip and his mother, Sophie, were sitting outside Mama Reni's enjoying a small meal and a glass of homemade wine. At Philip's request, Layla was asked to join them. Try as he might, she wasn't interested in any relationship that was anything more than platonic. She was warming to the idea though.

The trio made small talk, discussed the President's latest communication and its possible ramifications, as well as the goings-on in the park. Seated next to them sat the newlyweds, Heather and Carlos, and President Sarkes. On the other side was a picnic table that held the three Tin Hatters and Officer Vic.

As the meal was winding down, Layla noticed the flare in the sky.

Josh's daughter casually leaned back in her chair and yelled for her father, "Dad, they're here!"

"Roger that," he replied as he and the Sheriff exited their seats in the shade.

With no electricity, came no air conditioning. Try as they might, the stagnant July humidity was all encompassing and damn near suffocating. Scott was actively tinkering with the concept of a no-ice evap air conditioner, but was having difficulty resourcing some parts. Until he was successful, Basilia and her roving medical team had taken to stopping in regularly to check on the elderly and make them as comfortable as possible. Water was being boiled, cooled, and consumed as quickly as it was being collected.

Under a large tree casting a healthy shadow over Main Street, Josh had placed a spare desk from City Hall and positioned a number of chairs around it. The Sheriff bypassed the configuration and went to the center of the road. His friend was only a few steps behind.

The two stood in silence as they looked west. The rural two lane street turned downhill after passing through downtown so neither man could see the approaching group until they began to crest the horizon.

"Five men plus Sergeant Barnes' team," a sentry from atop the McArthur Hotel called down.

Josh turned and gave him a nod acknowledging the message and replied, "Call back the other patrols."

The shooters stepping into positions from above readied their weapons. He wasn't going to be taking any chances. It didn't matter how many or how few there were. Everyone not in a defensive firing position watched with baited breath as they approached, but none moved from their current positions. Josh wanted the town square to look as normal as possible, so it was a calculated risk. Had the UN troops materialized with a larger more significant force, he would have given a different order. Regardless of how languid and docile the scene looked to the casual observer, every single person was armed.

As the eleven men approached, Sergeant Coker remarked under his breath to his CO, "It's like an old western on the tele."

"Gentlemen, welcome to McArthur. Sgt. Barnes?"

"Yes, sir?"

"Did they behave themselves?"

"Yes, sir."

"And what are they aware of?"

"Only what I was permitted to inform them of, sir."

"Very good. You squad is dismissed. Grab some grub and some shade. Well done."

As the six man patrol disappeared into the periphery of Mama Reni's, Josh looked over the men standing before him. It didn't take long for him to notice the leg wound on Corporal Simpkins.

"Corpsman!" he called out and Carlton seemed to appear from nowhere.

"With your permission, Lieutenant, our medical team is prepared to treat your man."

He replied, "You have it, Colonel." Without looking, he ordered, "Simpkins, go with the medic." As the pair began heading off, the Lt. added as an afterthought, "But stay where I can see you."

Josh inserted, "Before you get treated, give your weapon to one of the other men."

Simpkins looked at his CO for confirmation which he received.

"Do you have need for any other medical attention?"

"Not at this time," the weary British officer stated.

"You can drop your packs and hand your weapons to Sheriff Watson. You *will* see them returned when your group is fit enough for travel, you have my word."

410

The four remaining soldiers thought long and hard about this decision. Too long for Josh's liking.

"Gentlemen, either you drop your gear and hand over the weapons in good faith or I will have no other choice but to have you shot down in the street," he declared and gave a wave to the overwatch.

A dozen and half watchers quickly revealed themselves and acquired targets from the assembled group below.

"We have food, water, showers, cots, and a laundry at your disposal, but you will not take another step in this town with those weapons slung on your backs. Do I make myself clear?"

The oppressive heat and their collective exhaustion levels seemed to be the ultimate deciding factors.

Reluctantly, their CO gave the command, "Do as he says."

Jim collected the five rifles and disheveled packs. When he began to reach for the CO's sidearm, Josh stated, "He can keep that."

The man nodded and replaced it back in its holster.

The town leader then turned his attention to the Lieutenant. "If you and your men will follow me, there are more than a few things you need to be brought up to speed on."

Josh led the procession over to the desk he had prepared and gestured toward the chairs.

"Please, have a seat."

As the remaining British soldiers took their seats, he introduced himself, "My name is Colonel Josiah Simmons, United States Marine Corps. Up until about three months ago, I was retired. Now, I'm not active duty military per se, but the uniform still fit and these people needed guidance. I can see your ranks so I'll simply ask your names."

The four men straightened up in their seats as their CO made the introductions.

"In order of rank, we are, Lt. Fitzpatrick, Sergeant Coker, Corporal Watson, our Corporal Simpkins is currently being treated by your medical staff, and the one on the end is Private Waite."

"Pleasure to meet you," Josh replied earnestly. "Now, do you have any questions or statements of record for me?"

"Only that we have received your messages and request your assistance on humanitarian grounds."

"You have it. Anything else?"

"We only offer our word that we shall conduct ourselves in accordance with your provisions and that we will depart and return to our unit when all of my men are fit enough to travel."

"That might be more of a problem than you think."

"Right," Lt. Fitzpatrick stated. "Your Sgt. Barnes mentioned that I should ask you about that."

Josh opened the top drawer and removed a manila folder. He then stood and reached under the desk. One by one, he retrieved his HAM radio, microphone, and a deep cycle battery with a converter. He then walked to the trunk of the tree and grabbed a dangling wire. Josh spent about thirty seconds connecting everything.

"Lieutenant," he began as he picked up the folder. "The war is over. You are no longer an invading force or enemy combatants. You and your men are now refugees."

On cue, he handed the folder and its contents to Fitzpatrick and explained, "Everything we have heard or intercepted since 06:00 is in that folder. The first two pages are a transcription of a broadcast this morning from President Culpepper. The remaining documents are messages we received confirming the voracity of the message."

"And the radio?"

"I am providing this so that you may attempt to confirm the claims being made. We have nothing to hide."

"So that's it?" Sgt. Coker asked. "We're done? We can go home?"

"That's exactly right, Sergeant. However, you might be hard pressed to make it to the coast before the last of your ships leave port. That being said, you and your UN allies took just about all of the resources you were looking for. However, we managed to use what was left of our naval subs and sever your supply lines. On land… well, you saw what we were capable of. In short, no food and no fuel always equates to a losing campaign. Just like Napoleon and Hitler.

"Now, as for the radio, we have the ability to hear civilian chatter and limited unencrypted military comms. From what we've been able to discern, on our side at least, is that all of the President's statements are true. The English contingent at West Point was defeated shortly after your departure and Charleston was back in U.S. hands as well. Same thing's happened on the west coast.

"One of our men will stay with you for our own insurance as you attempt to confirm our reports."

The Lieutenant handed the folder to his sergeant and approached Josh. The three British soldiers, for their part, started eagerly leafing through the folder.

"Colonel, might I have a word?"

"Walk with me, Fitz" he replied.

As the two separated from the remainder from the group, the Lt. asked, "Just how long can we expect your hospitality? I'd hate to wake up one morning and find my men missing parts of their genitalia and hanging from a tree."

"Ah," his host declared immediately understanding the reference. "So am I required course study now at Sandhurst?"

"How did you –,"

"Educated guess. A lot of the British officer corps goes through there." Josh paused and then asked something that had been gnawing at him for years. "You know, that's not the first time someone has referenced that. I'm curious, what exactly are they trying to teach using that event?"

"It's used primarily as a deterrent for the enlisted men. *Better keep your trousers on or Colonel Simmons will turn you into a eunuch*," he concluded as he imitated one of his instructors. "For the officers though, it was more of a warning to keep an eye on our men and recognize when someone is too close to the edge."

Josh closed his eyes and turned his face to the blazing afternoon sun as he took in the deepest of breathes.

"I see," he replied and he brought his head back down to look at the Lieutenant. "Your contingent is welcome here until your man is fit for travel. However, should you forget the provision which has gained you entry, you'll be sent on your way sooner."

The British officer thought for a few moments before continuing the conversation. "I believe you're right. We've been abandoned here. That being said, how do you imagine that we make it to the coast? And, once there, how are we to return home?"

"First thing I'd tell you is that you will need to ditch the uniforms and UN insignia. Those'll get you shot, especially crossing the Appalachians. Baltimore harbor is about three hundred and seventy five miles due west of our position. Averaging twenty 'clicks' a day, you and your men should be there in about two and half weeks. If you've got anything to trade you might be able to procure a horse and wagon and cut your time in half. But that's not you biggest problem."

"Excusing my candor, sir, but that seems like a bloody large obstacle. What am I missing?"

"Your accents and funding to book passage. You want to get back to the other side of the Atlantic, it's gonna cost you."

Dumbstruck, Fitzpatrick muttered, "Bloody hell," under his breath. "What's considered a tradable item?"

"Food and provisions are always tops on everyone's list, but your team has none. After that comes security in the form of bullets and weapons or services rendered. Labor is pretty high up there too."

"Services rendered? Define that please."

"The small towns that were able to survive are starting to set up trade routes. Unfortunately, trading isn't exactly the safest occupation just yet. Some merchants need help getting things to and from the Ohio River in Pomeroy so they can be floated from Pittsburgh to Cincinnati and all the places in between. Your men could sign on as a security detail. Or there are people looking to hire on folks for protection. We may have kicked the UN forces out, but most of our prisons were emptied. Again, not one of the safest places on the planet to be right now."

"Tell me about labor, something local," the Lt. wondered.

"Harvest will be here before we know it and most of the diesel needs to be used sparingly. If you can stretch some farmer's fuel savings by helping in the fields, you could earn something that might get you on a boat."

"I believe all of the men are bachelors. Should they decide to stay, would they be welcome?"

"No loved ones back home?

Before the Lieutenant could answer, a rider made the turn onto Main Street behind them. The clacking of the horses gallop on the pavement stopped the conversation immediately. The pair turned as the rider steered the horse directly toward them.

The man on horseback slowed the beast as he retrieved a folded message from his shirt pocket. He slapped it into Josh's outstretched hand as he trotted by and headed toward the livery.

He quickly unfolded the paper and began reading. Within seconds his face flushed. His entire being filled with a rage he hadn't felt in more than decade.

Without warning he abruptly turned and barked, "Philip, Hoplite! Grab your gear! You got two minutes!"

The two bolted from their seats at Mama Reni's and the town immediately became a flurry of activity. Many onlookers wondered aloud what in the world was going on. No one had ever seen Josh's demeanor change on a dime. No one had ever heard him issue a command with the volume and tone being exhibit in the street. For those within earshot, there was no misunderstanding that something had gone horribly wrong.

Jim immediately stopped his inspection of the British packs and rushed from of the Sheriff's office. When his friend saw him exit, he began quickly walking toward him. Without saying a word, Josh handed him the note and headed toward the deuce parked up the street.

Samantha heard the commotion and exited the restaurant as purposefully as the Sheriff had flown out of the station.

"What's going on?" she asked Heather and Layla who were still standing out front with Sophie.

"No idea," her step-daughter replied. "A rider just came through town and handed him a message. One second Dad's talking to the Lieutenant and then he starts giving commands."

"Stay here," Sam said as she side-stepped the girls.

"Josh? What's going on? Talk to me," she implored him as she approached.

Without thinking, he blurted, "That little bastard survived the shelling. He's got Katherine… and I'm gonna kill him!"

Thank you for reading *Foreign & Domestic, Part III – By the Dawn's Early Light*. I hope you will consider visiting the Amazon website to leave a review so others may know what you thought of the book and/or the series and to purchase the remaining installments in the series.

Other books by David J. Kershner:

*Foreign & Domestic, Part I – When Rome Stumbles*

*Foreign & Domestic, Part II – Hannibal is at the Gates*

*Foreign & Domestic, Part IV – Colder Weather*

*Foreign & Domestic, Part V – A Time for Reckoning*

*Just a Small Gathering*

Coming Soon:

*Home Remedies, Poultices, Salves, & Tinctures*

*Preparing to Prepare: A General Guide to Self-Sufficiency & Preparedness*